"Cowboy is no Rambo; he is a thoughtful, intelligent hero. He and Sarah are two of the many good things about HARDWIRED. Another is the world they inhabit—an incredibly detailed future of personality transfers, bizarre drugs, cybernetic implants, and complex political and economic power maneuvers. Williams tells their story with a propulsive yet almost elegant prose. HARDWIRED is always on the move. Yet its greatest strengths are the mythic overtones of Cowboy's story and the intricate power plays that pervade the novel. For at its cold, brutal heart HARDWIRED is about power—and about what happens to enduring American myths when events conspire to render them obsolete. It is one of the best SF novels I have read in years; I heartily recommend it."

— *Fantasy Review*

"The story moves with the speed of a hovercraft, the climax has all the action and excitement of *Star Wars* and the ending has a delightful twist."

— *The Providence Sunday Journal*

"Williams' use of language is as explosive and as techno-tinged as the world he describes. Reading the book is like taking a jet ride across a futuristic America, with acceleration forcing you back in your seat all the way."

— *The Rockland Courier-Gazette*

"Williams has created a three-dimensional world, characters who develop believably, and a fast-moving story. Any writer who has done all this shows enough respect for his readers to deserve theirs in turn."

— *Chicago Sun-Times*

Look for these Tor books by Walter Jon Williams

AMBASSADOR OF PROGRESS
HARDWIRED
KNIGHT MOVES
VOICE OF THE WHIRLWIND (Hardcover)

HARDWIRED

WALTER JON WILLIAMS

A TOM DOHERTY ASSOCIATES BOOK

HARDWIRED

Copyright © 1986 by Walter Jon Williams

First printing: June 1986
First mass market printing: April 1987

A TOR Book

Published by Tom Doherty Associates, Inc.
49 West 24 Street
New York, N.Y. 10010

Cover art by Royo
Cover design by Carol Russo

ISBN: 0-812-55796-4
CAN. ED.: 0-812-55797-2

Library of Congress Catalog Card Number: 85-52255

Printed in the United States of America

0 9 8 7 6 5 4 3 2 1

Thanks and a tip of the ten-gallon hat to Terry Boren and Laura Mixon, aka the Barkonspirators.

And special thanks to Roger Zelazny, who let me play in his Alley.

Chapter One

By midnight he knows his discontent will not let him sleep. The panzerboy drives north from Santa Fe, over the Sangre de Cristos on the high road through Truchas, heading for Colorado, wanting to get as close as possible to the night sky. He drives without the use of hands or feet, his mind living in the cool neural interface that exists somewhere between the swift images that pass before his windscreen and the electric awareness that is the alloy body and liquid crystal heart of the Maserati. His artificial eyes, plastic and steel, stare unblinking at the road, at twisting dirt ruts corrugated by the spring runoff, tall stands of pine and aspen, high meadows spotted with the frozen black shapes of cattle, all outlined in the rushing, almost liquid light of his high beams as he pushes the Maserati upward. The shapes that blaze in the headlights stand boldly against the darkness of their own shadows, and Cowboy can almost see himself in a monochrome world like a black-and-white celluloid image projected before his windscreen, flickering with the speed of his passage. It's almost like flying.

He'd thought, when he got his new Kikuyu eyes, that he'd ask for a monochrome option, amused by the idea of flicking some mental switch in his head and being plunged into the action of some black-and-white fantasy, an old moving picture starring the likes of Gary Cooper or Duke Wayne, but there hadn't been much demand for monochrome and the option had been discontinued. He'd also wanted irises of chrome steel, but the Dodger, his manager, had talked him out of that, saying they were too conspicuous for a man in Cowboy's line of business. Cowboy agreed reluctantly, as he always did when the Dodger came up with a new restriction on his fantasy. Instead he'd taken pupils of a storm-cloud gray.

But here in these mountains named after the Blood of Christ are fantasies older than any on celluloid. They pass in montage before his steel and plastic eyes: an old whitewashed church, the area around its doors painted like a turquoise heaven, clashing with the reds and yellows that form a pyramid and all-seeing eye at the rounded cap of the arch; some massive white castle in the Moroccan style, the playhouse of a long-vanished Arab, its crumbling minarets streaked with brown, its rococo iron grillwork scored with advancing rust. Suddenly around a curve a pair of pale ghosts appear like figures of supernatural warning, Indian pilgrims dressed in white, from the cloth binding their foreheads and braiding their long hair to the white doeskin moccasins that wink with silver buttons. Walking patiently by moonlight, a penance, to the sanctuary at Chimayo, there to give thanks to the carved *santos* or ask the Virgin for a favor. Visions like outposts of another time, preserved here on the high rim of Earth, shimmering in the sudden brightness of Cowboy's eyes.

Cowboy pushes the machine to the max, redlining the scales on the dashboard. Flying at night is the thing he does best. The engine whine echoes from the trees, the hills. Wind gusts through the open windows, bringing the sharp smell of pine. Cowboy pictures the celluloid speeding through the projector, moving faster, images blurring. Neurons pulse their messages to the crystal in his head, transmitting his will to the throttle, the gears, the jouncing wheels. Now the Maserati is moving downhill, gaining speed as it races through the switchbacks, finally tearing across the surface of the ford in front of Peñasco, throwing up a wall of mist that, for a short moment, reflects the headlights in rainbows, a hallucinatory shimmer on the edge of vision, a foreshadowing of color here in the monochrome world.

It's dawn when the Maserati blurs across the Colorado line, and early morning by the time the bronze machine enters Custer County. The mountains are brown and green now, alive with pine and the mountain wind, the monochrome fantasy gone. Cowboy has friends here. He turns into a private dirt road, knowing there are electronics suddenly taking an interest in him.

The road twists upward and ends at a high mountain meadow landscaped flat and crisscrossed by the alpha of a private airstrip. Where the black deltas once flew on their occult midnight errands, grasses and flowers now grow in the cracks of the paving. Still visible is a gouge in the bright green aspens, where one jock overshot the strip with his wounded delta and splashed himself and his cargo over a half mile of mountainside, but the furrow is green again with saplings. The airfield is turning dreamlike now, a little fuzzy around the edges; but Cowboy does not intend that the memory should ever die. There are memories that live for him as his present reality does not, and he shines them daily, like the finish of a fine new car, to keep them bright.

For eleven generations Cowboy's ancestors farmed an area of southeastern New Mexico, living as dots on a featureless red plain as different from the world of the Sangre de Cristos as is the Ukraine from Peru. Every so often one of Cowboy's family would shoulder a rifle and march off to fight for the United States, but they concentrated most of their energies on fighting the state of Texas. The Texans were water-hungry, consuming more than they could ever replenish, building at the finish vast pumps just a few inches over the Texas side of the border, sucking the alkaline New Mexico water across the line, stealing what others had so carefully preserved. Cowboy's people fought them, holding on to what they could until the last pump rattled dry and the dusty red earth rose on the wind and turned the world into a sandblasting hurricane.

Cowboy remembers his days in the dust bowl, living at his uncle's ranch after his father broke himself trying to hang on.

Existing inside a gray assortment of bleached planks on the edge of the desert the Texans had made, a place where red earth drifted inches deep behind the door whenever the wind blew, and days passed without seeing the sun as anything brighter than a ruddy warm vagueness behind the scouring sand. Farming was impossible, and the family ran cattle instead, an occupation only slightly less precarious. The nearest town bragged about the number of churches it had and Cowboy was raised in one of them, watching the congregation grow bleaker week by week, their skin turning gray, their eyes ever more desperate as they asked the Lord to forgive whatever sin had led them to this cleansing. Texans, once the enemy, wandered through on their way to somewhere else, living in cardboard boxes, in old automobiles that sat on blocks and had long ago lost their paint to the sand. The Rock War came and went, and things got harder. Hymns continued to be sung, liquor and cards foresworn, and notices of farm auctions continued to be posted at the courthouse.

The Dodger was an older man who had moved to Colorado. When he came home he drove a shiny automobile, and he didn't go to church. He chewed tobacco because chewing didn't interfere with his picking when, in his free time, he played left-handed mandolin with a jug band. The gray people in the church didn't like to talk about how he'd made his money. And one day the Dodger saw Cowboy riding in a rodeo.

The Dodger visited Uncle's ranch and arranged to borrow Cowboy for a while, even paid for his time. He got Cowboy some practice time on a flight simulator and then made a call to a thirdman he knew. The rest, as the Dodger would say, is history.

Cowboy was sixteen when he took up flying. In his cracked old leather boots he already stood three inches over six feet, and soon he stood miles taller, an atmosphere jock who spread his contrails from one coast to the other, delivering the mail, mail being whatever it was that came his way. The Orbitals and the customs people in the Midwest were just another kind of Texan—someone who wants to rape away the things that keep you alive, replacing nothing, leaving only desert. When the air defenses across the Line got too strong, the jocks switched to panzer—and the mail still got through. The new system had its challenges, but had it been up to Cowboy he would never have left the skies.

Now Cowboy is twenty-five, getting a little old for this job, approaching the time when even hardwired neural reflexes begin to slacken. He disdains the use of headsets; his skull bears five sockets for plugging the peripherals directly into his brain, saving milliseconds when it counts. Most people wear their hair long to cover the sockets, afraid of being called buttonheads or worse, but Cowboy disdains that practice, too; his fair hair is cropped close to the skull and his black ceramic sockets are decorated with silver wire and turquoise chips. Here in the West, where people have an idea of what these things mean, he is regarded with a kind of awe.

He has his nerves hardwired to the max, and Kikuyu Optics eyes with all the available options. He has a house in Santa Fe and a ranch in Montana that his uncle runs for him, and he owns the family property in New Mexico and pays taxes on it like it was worth something. He has the Maserati and a personal aircraft—a "business jet"—and a stock portfolio and caches of gold.

He's also got this place, this little meadow in the Colorado mountains; another cache, this one for memories that won't go away. And a discontent, formless but growing, that has led him here.

He parks by the big camouflaged concrete hangar and unfaces the Maserati before the engine gives its final whimper. In the silence he can hear the sound of a steel guitar from somewhere in the hangar and a stirring in the grass that is the first directionless movements of the afternoon's thermals. He walks to the hangar, unreels a jack from the lock, studs it into his head, and gives it the code.

Past the heavy metal door there is a Wurlitzer, shiny chrome and bright fluorescent plastic, venting some old Woody Guthrie song into the huge cathedral space. Looming above are the matte black shapes of three deltas, their rounded forms obscure in the dim light but giving an impression of massive power and appalling speed. Obsolete now, Cowboy bought them for little more than the price of their engines when the face riders started using panzers.

Warren stands at his workbench in a pool of light, tinkering with a piece of a fuel pump. His lined face flickers blue with the video pictures Cowboy's arrival has prompted—he's got security cameras all over the place and cares for them with the same methodical diligence with which he keeps the deltas ready to fly.

He was a crew chief at Vandenberg on the day of the Rock War, and he did his duty knowing that he could expect nothing for his diligence but to feel on the back of his neck, for a fragment of a second, the overpressure of a nickel-iron missile coming down through the atmosphere, followed by termination . . . but he did what he was trained to do and got his cutterjocks up to fight for Earth against the Orbitals, wishing them well with all his heart, hoping that a few, maybe, would say "Here's one for Warren" when they burned an enemy. But the scenario turned out different from what he'd expected: looking up into the night sky for the meteor that had his name on it, he saw the falling, blazing arcs all right, but it wasn't descending rocks that lit the night sky—it was his boys and their craft, the young, bright men with their azure silk neck scarves and their bright needle cutters, coming down in pieces, failing systems giving their last electronic cries, blood streaking the insides of broken faceplates, ruptured oxidant tanks gushing white crystal plumes into the near-vacuum. . . . The last hope of Earth blown apart in the post-boost phase by the Orbital knights.

For hours he waited at Vandenberg, hoping one of them might bring a cripple in. None came. Next thing Warren knew, Earth had surrendered. The Orbitals occupied Vandenberg, along with Orlando, Houston, and Cuba, and Warren survived because he was stationed at a place that was too valuable to destroy.

There was a lot of talk about the Resistance afterward, and Warren did his share of talking . . . probably more than talking, if the story about a sabotaged shuttle, carrying a cargo of executives from Tupolev I.G. to an impact on the Mojave, could be given any credence. Warren's history after that grew a little more obscure, until he appeared working for the thirdmen in Colorado and met Cowboy. The rest, as the Dodger would say, being history.

"Hi, C'boy," Warren says. He doesn't turn from his work.

"Hi." Cowboy opens the front of the Wurlitzer the lock hasn't worked in decades and collects some quarters. He tells the machine to play some scratchy old country swing and then walks across the darkened hangar.

"Low-pressure fuel turbopump," Warren says. Disassembled, the pump looks like a plastic model kit for a Galápagos turtle. "Running red lights on my tests. See where the metal's bright, here, where the blade is rubbing? I think I may have to machine a new part."

"Need a hand?"

"I just might."

Warren's face is craggier than usual in the bright overhead light, his eyes and forehead shadowed by the brim of his cap so that his beaky nose seems bigger than it is. He's erect and intense, and though he's flabby in places, these are places where flab doesn't matter much. Behind him the soft colored lights of the Wurlitzer shine on the matte-black nose of a delta. He's the actual owner of the airfield, with Cowboy as secret partner. Cowboy doesn't like data trails that point in his direction.

Warren fiddles with the part a while more, then takes measurements. He moves over to the lathe and puts on his goggles. Cowboy readies himself to hand him the tools when necessary. Spare parts are hard to find for military-surplus jet engines, and the parts that are available often have too many questions attached.

The lathe whines. Sparks spill like tiny meteors against the concrete floor. "I'm making a run Wednesday night," Cowboy says. "In five days."

"I can come down Monday and start my checks on the panzer. Is that too late?"

"Not for where I'm going." There is resentment in Cowboy's voice.

"Iowa again?"

"Hell, yes." Anger flares in Cowboy's soul. "Arkady and the others . . . they keep looking at their damn analyses. Saying that the privateers are undercapitalized, all we have to do is wait and keep them from taking any cargoes."

"And?"

"And it's *wrong*. You can't beat the heat by playing their own game. We should be running into Missouri every night. Making them eat fuel, ammo. Rock them if that's what it takes." He snorts. "*Undercapitalized*. See what the loss of a dozen aircraft will do for their cash flow."

Warren looks up from the spinning lathe. "You running for Arkady on Wednesday night?"

Cowboy nods.

"I don't like the man. I wonder about him." Warren, in a studied way, is working the lathe again. His white hair, sticking out from under his cap, flashes in the light of sparks.

Cowboy waits, knowing Warren will make his point in his own time. Warren turns off the lathe and pushes his goggles up above the brim of his cap. "He came from nowhere in particular. And now he's the biggest thirdman in the Rockies. He's got sources of supply that the others can't match. Dresses in all those cryo max fashions from the Florida Free Zone."

"So? He's got organization. And I don't like his clothes either."

Warren holds up his gleaming alloy creation to the light. Narrowing his eyes. "He's supposed to be getting it through cutouts. Hijackings, corrupt Orbital executives. That sort of thing. The usual. But in this kind of quantity? You can't get that much in the way of goods without the Orbitals knowing."

A protesting whisper runs through Cowboy's mind. *In it for the ride, not for the cargo*. He's said it often enough. An ethic, this, a kind of purity. Half the time he hasn't even known what he's been carrying.

"I don't know if I want to hear this," he says.

"Don't hear it, then." Warren turns away and goes back to the pump. He puts on a headset and runs through some checks.

Cowboy thinks for a moment about Arkady, the burly man who runs half the traffic across the Line these days, who exists in a strange swirl of assistants, bodyguards, helpers, techs, hangers-on of no apparent function who imitate his fashionable dress and his mannerisms. Women always present, but never a part of business. An existence cognate with what Cowboy can understand of Arkady's mind: convoluted, filled with violent prejudices and hatreds, sudden anger juxtaposed with sudden sentimentality, suspicious in a strange, offhand Russian way, as if paranoia were a way of life, not merely a set of reasonable precautions but a religion.

Cowboy doesn't like Arkady, but hasn't so far bothered to dislike him. Arkady considers himself an insider, a manipulator, but he's outside what really counts; outside the life of the panzerboy, the mutant creature with turbine lungs and high-pressure turbopump heart, crystal implanted in his skull, eyes like lasers, fingers that point missiles, alcohol throbbing through his veins. . . . Arkady thinks he's running things but he's really just an instrument, an excuse for the panzerboys to make their runs across the Line and into legend. And if Arkady doesn't understand that, his thoughts don't count for much in the scheme of things.

Warren is reassembling parts of the pump, ready to run his tests, and will be busy for a while. Cowboy leaves the pool of light and walks into the blackness of the hangar. The deltas loom above him, poised and ready, lacking only a pilot to make them living things. His hands reach up to touch a smooth underbelly, an epoxide canard, the fairing of a downward-gazing radar. Like stroking a matte-black animal, a half-wild thing too dangerous to be called a pet. It lacks only a pilot, and a purpose.

He moves a ladder from an engine access panel to a

cockpit and climbs into the seat that was, years ago, molded to his body. The familiar metal and rubber smells warm up to him. He closes his eyes and remembers the night splattered with brightness, the sudden flare of erupting fuel, the mad chase as, supersonic, he bobbed and weaved among the hills and valleys of the Ozarks, the laws on his tail, burning for home. . . .

His first delta was called *Midnight Sun*, but he changed the name after he'd figured out what was really going on. He and the other deltajocks were not an abstract response to market conditions but a continuation of some kind of mythology. Delivering the mail across the high dome of night, despite all the oppressors' efforts to the contrary. Keeping a light burning in the darkness, hope in the shape of an afterburner flame. The last free Americans, on the last high road. . . .

So he'd begun to live what he suddenly knew. Accepting the half-scornful, condescending nickname they'd given him, living it, becoming Cowboy, the airjock. Answering to nothing else. Becoming the best, living in realms higher than any of the competition. He called his next delta *Pony Express*. And in it he delivered the mail as long as they'd let him.

Till times changed, and modes of delivery changed. Till he had to become a *boy* instead of a *jock*. The eyes that could focus into the night blackness, straining to spot the infrared signature of the laws riding combat air patrol over the prairie, were now shut in a small armored cabin, all the visuals coming in through remotes. He is still the best, still delivering the mail.

He shifts in his seat. The country swing fades and all Cowboy can hear in the echoing silence is the whirr of Warren's lathe. And sense the restlessness in himself, wanting only a name. . . .

Chapter Two

TODAY/YES

Bodies and parts of bodies flare and die in laserlight, here the translucent sheen of eyes rimmed in kohl or turned up to a heaven masked by the starry-glitter ceiling, here electric hair flaring with fashionable static discharges, here a blue-white glow of teeth rimmed in darkglow fire and pierced by mute extended tongue. It is zonedance. Though the band is loud and sweat-hot, many of the zoned are tuned to their own music through crystal wired delicately to the auditory nerves, or dancing to the headsets through which they can pick up any of the bar's twelve channels. . . . They seethe in arrhythmic patterns, heedless of one another. Perfect control is sought, but there are accidents—impacts, a flurry of fists and elbows—and someone crawls out of the zone, whimpering through a bloodstreaked hand, unnoticed by the pack.

To Sarah the dancers at the Aujourd'Oui seem a twitching mass of dying flesh, bloody, insensate, mortal. Bound by the mud of earth. They are meat. She is hunting, and Weasel is the name of her friend.

MODERNBODYMODERNBODYMODERNBODYMODERN

Need a Modern Body?
All Electric—Replaceable—In the Mode!
Get One Now!

NBODYMODERNBODYMODERNBODYMODERNBODY

The body designer had eyes of glittering violet above cheekbones of sculptured ivory. Her hair was a streaky blond that swept to an architecturally perfect dorsal fin behind her nape. Her muscles were catlike and her mouth was a cruel flower.

"Hair shorter, yes," she said. "One doesn't wear it long in freefall." Her fingers lashed out and seized Sarah by the chin, tilting her head to the cold north light. Her fingernails were violet, to match her eyes, and sharp. Sarah glared at her, sullen. The body designer smiled. "A little pad in the chin, yes," she says. "You need a stronger chin. The tip of the nose can be altered; you're a bit *too* retroussé. The curve of the jawbone needs a little flattening—I'll bring my paring knife tomorrow. And, of course, we'll remove the scars. Those scars have *got* to go." Sarah curled her lip under the pressure of the violet-tipped fingers.

The designer dropped Sarah's chin and whirled. "Must we use this girl, Cunningham?" she asked. "She has no style at all. She can't walk gracefully. Her body's too big, too awkward. She's nothing. She's dirt. Common."

Cunningham sat silently in his brown suit, his neutral, unmemorable face giving away nothing. His voice was whispery, calm, yet still authoritative. Sarah thought it could be a computer voice, so devoid was it of highlights. "Our Sarah has style, Firebud," he said. "Style and discipline. You are to give it form, to fashion it. Her style must be a weapon, a shaped charge. You will make it, I will point it. And Sarah will punch a hole right where we intend she should." He looked at Sarah with his steady brown eyes. "Won't you, Sarah?" he asked.

Sarah did not reply. Instead, she looked up at the body designer, drawing back her lips, showing teeth. "Let me hunt you some night, Firebud," she said. "I'll show you style."

The designer rolled her eyes. "Dirtgirl stuff," she snorted, but she took a step back. Sarah grinned.

"And, Firebud," Cunningham said, "leave the scars alone. They will speak to our Princess. Of this cruel terrestrial reality that she helped create. That she dominates. With which she is already half in love.

"Yes," he said, "leave the scars alone." For the first time he smiled, a brief tightening of the cheek muscles, cold as liquid nitrogen. "Our Princess will love the scars," he said. "Love them till the very last."

WINNERS/YES   LOSERS/YES

The Aujourd'Oui is a jockey bar, and they are all here, moonjocks and rigjocks, holdjocks and powerjocks and rockjocks—the jocks condescending to share the floor with the mudboys and dirtgirls who surround them, those who hope to become them or love them or want simply to be near them, to touch them in the zonedance and absorb a piece of their radiance. The jocks wear their colors, vests, and jackets bearing the emblems of their blocs—TRW, Pfizer, Toshiba, Tupolev, ARAMCO—the blazons of the Rock War victors borne with careless pride by the jocks who had won them their place in the sky. Six feet three inches in height, Sarah stalks among them in a black satin jacket, blazoned on its back with a white crane that rises to the starry firmament amid a flock of chrome-bright Chinese characters. It is the badge of a small bloc that does most of its business out of Singapore, and is hardly ever seen here in the Florida Free Zone. Her face is unknown to the regulars, but it is hoped they won't think it odd, not as odd as it would seem if she wore the badge of Tupolev or Kikuyu Optics I.G.

Her sculpted face is pale, the Florida tan gone, her eyes black-rimmed. Her almost-black hair is short on the sides and brushy on top, her nape hair falling in two thin braids down her back. Chrome-steel earrings brush her shoulders. Firebud has broadened her already-broad shoulders and pared down the width of her pelvis; her face is sharp and pointed beneath

a widow's peak, looking like a succession of arrowheads, the
shaped charge that Cunningham demands. She wears black
dancing slippers laced over the ankles and dark purple stretch
overalls with suspenders that frame her breasts, stretching the
fabric over the nipples that Firebud has made more promi-
nent. Her shirt is gauze spangled with silver; her neck scarf,
black silk. There is a two-way spliced into her auditory nerve
and a receiver tagged to the optic centers of her forebrain, at
the moment monitoring police broadcasts, a constant Times
Square of an LED running amber, at will, above her expanded vision.

Gifts from Cunningham. Her hardwired nerves are her
own. So is Weasel.

I LOVE MY KIKUYU EYES, SEZ PRIMO PORNOSTAR
ROD MCLEISH, AND WITH THE INFRARED OP-
TION, I CAN TELL IF MY PARTNER'S REALLY
EXCITED OR IF I'M JUST ON A SILICON RIDE . . .
                    —Kikuyu Optics I.G.,
                    A Division Of Mikoyan-Gurevich

She first met Cunningham in another bar, the Blue Silk.
Sarah ran Weasel as per contract, but the snagboy, a runner
who had got more greedy than he had the smarts to handle,
had been altered himself—she was nursing bruises. She re-
covered the goods, fortunately, and since the contract was
with the thirdmen, she had been paid in endorphins, handy
since she needed a few of them herself.

There is a bone bruise on the back of her thigh and she
can't sit; instead, she leans back against the padded bar and
sips her rum and lime. The Blue Silk's audio system plays
island music and soothes her played-up nerves.

The Blue Silk is run by an ex-cutterjock named Maurice, a
West Indian with the old-model Zeiss eyes who was on the
losing side in the Rock War. He's got chip sockets on his
ankles and wrists, the way the military wore them then.
There are pictures of his friends and heroes on the walls, all

of them with the azure silk neck scarves of the elite space defense corps, most of them framed with black mourning ribbons turning purple with the long years.

Sarah wonders what he has seen with those eyes. Did it include the burst of X rays that preceded the 10,000-ton rocks, launched from the orbital mass drivers, that tore through the atmosphere to crash on Earth's cities? The artificial meteors, each with the force of a nuclear blast, had first fallen in the eastern hemisphere, over Mombasa and Calcutta, and by the time the planet had rotated and made the western hemisphere a target, the Earth had surrendered—but the Orbital blocs felt they hadn't made their point forcefully enough in the West, and so the rocks fell anyway. Communications foul-up, they said. Earth's billions knew better.

Sarah was ten. She was doing a tour in a Youth Reclamation Camp near Stone Mountain when three rocks obliterated Atlanta and killed her mother. Daud, who was eight, was trapped in the rubble, but the neighbors heard his screams and got him out. After that, Sarah and her brother bounced from one DP agency to another, then ended up in Tampa with her father, whom she hadn't seen or heard of since she was three. The social worker held her hand all the way up the decaying apartment stairs, and Sarah held Daud's. The halls stank of urine, and a dismembered doll lay strewn on the second-floor landing, broken apart like the nations of Earth, like the lives of the people here. When the apartment door opened she saw a man in a torn shirt with sweat stains in the armpits and watery alcoholic eyes. The eyes, uncomprehending, had moved from Sarah and Daud and then to the social worker as the papers were served, and the social worker said, "This is your father. He'll take care of you," before dropping Sarah's hand. It turned out to be only half a lie.

She looks at the fading photographs in their dusty frames, the dead men and women with their metallic Zeiss eyes. Maurice is looking at them, too. He is lost in his memories, and it looks as if he is trying to cry; but his eyes are lubricated with silicon and his tear ducts are gone, of course, along with his dreams, with the dreams of the five billion people who had hoped the Orbitals would improve their lives, who have no hope now but to get out somehow, out into the cold, perfect cobalt of the sky.

Sarah wishes she herself could cry, for the dead hope framed in black on the walls, for herself and Daud, for the broken thing that is all earthly aspiration, even for the snagboy who had seen his chance to escape but had not been smart enough to play his way out of the game his hopes had dealt him into. But the tears are long gone and in their place is hardened steel desire—the desire shared by all the dirtgirls and mudboys. To achieve it she has to want it more than the others, and she has to be willing to do what is necessary—or to have it done to her, if it comes to that. Involuntarily her hand rises to her throat as she thinks of Weasel. No, there is no time for tears.

"Looking for work, Sarah?" The voice comes from the quiet white man who has been sitting at the end of the bar. He has come closer, one hand on the back of the bar stool next to her. He is smiling as if he is unaccustomed to it.

She narrows her eyes as she looks at him sidelong, and takes a deliberately long drink. "Not the kind of work you have in mind, collarboy," she says.

"You come recommended," he says. His voice is sandpaper, the kind you never forget. Perhaps he'd never had to raise it in his life.

She drinks again and looks at him. "By whom?" she says.

The smile is gone now; the nondescript face looks at her warily. "The Hetman," he says.

"Michael?" she asks.

He nods. "My name is Cunningham," he says.

"Do you mind if I call Michael and ask him?" she says. The Hetman controls the Bay thirdmen and sometimes she runs the Weasel for him. She doesn't like the idea of his dropping her name to strangers.

"If you like," Cunningham says. "But I'd like to talk to you about work first."

"This isn't the bar I go to for work," she says. "See me in the Plastic Girl, at ten."

"This isn't the sort of offer that can wait."

Sarah turns her back to him and looks into Maurice's metal eyes. "This man," she says, "is bothering me."

Maurice's face does not change expression. "You best leave," he says to Cunningham.

Sarah, not looking at Cunningham, receives from the corner of her eye an impression of a spring uncoiling. Cunningham seems taller than he was a moment ago.

"Do I get to finish my drink first?" he asks.

Maurice, without looking down, reaches into the till and flicks bills onto the dark surface of the bar. "Drink's on the house. Outa my place."

Cunningham says nothing, just gazes for a calm moment into the unblinking metal eyes. "Townsend," Maurice says, a code word and the name of the general who had once led him up against the Orbitals and their burning defensive energies. The Blue Silk's hardware voiceprints him and the defensive systems appear from where they are hidden above the bar mirror, locking down into place. Sarah glances up. Military lasers, she thinks, scrounged on the black market, or maybe from Maurice's old cutter. She wonders if the bar has power enough to use them, or whether they are bluff.

Cunningham stands still for another half second, then turns and leaves the Blue Silk. Sarah does not watch him go.

"Thanks, Maurice," she says.

Maurice forces a sad smile. "Hell, lady," he says, "you a regular customer. And that fella's been Orbital."

Sarah contemplates her surprise. "He's from the blocs?" she asks. "You're sure?"

"Innes," Maurice says, another name from the past, and the lasers slot up into place. His hands flicker out to take the money from the bar. "I didn't say he's *from* the blocs, Sarah," he says, "but he's been there. Recently, too. You can tell from the way they walk, if you got the eyes." He raises a gnarled finger to his head. "His ear, you know? Gravity created by centrifugal force is just a little bit different. It takes a while to adjust."

Sarah frowns. What kind of job is the man offering?

Something important enough to bring him down through the atmosphere, to hire some dirtgirl and her Weasel? It doesn't seem likely.

Well. She'll see him in the Plastic Girl, or not. She isn't going to worry about it. She shifts her weight from one leg to the other, the muscles crackling with pain even through the endorphin haze. She holds out her glass. "Another, please, Maurice," she says.

With a slow grace that must have served him well in the high starry evernight, Maurice turns toward the mirror and reaches for the rum. Even in a gesture this simple, there is sadness.

¿VIVE EN LA CIUDAD DE DOLOR?
¡DÉJENOS MANDARLE A HAPPYVILLE!
—Pointsman Pharmaceuticals A.G.

She takes a taxi home from the Blue Silk, trying to ignore Cunningham's calm eyes on the back of her head as she gives the driver her address. He is across the street under an awning, pretending to read a magazine. How much is she throwing away, here? She doesn't turn to see if he registers dismay at her retreat, but somehow she doubts his expression has changed.

With Daud she shares a two-room apartment that hums. There is the hum of the coolers and recyclers, more humming from the little glowing robots that move about randomly, doing the dusting and polishing, devouring insects and arachnids, and cleaning the cobwebs out of corners.

She has a modest comp deck in the front room and Daud has a vast audio system hooked to it, with a six-foot screen to show the vid. It's on now, silently, showing computer-generated color patterns, broadcasting them with laser optics on the ceiling and walls. The computer is running the changes on red, and the walls burn with cold and silent fire.

Sarah turns off the vid and looks down at the cooling comp deck, the reds fading slowly from her retinas. She empties the dirty ashtrays Daud has left behind, thinking about the man in brown, Cunningham. The endorphins are wearing off and the bone bruise on her thigh is hammering her with every step. It's time for another dose.

She checks her hiding place on a shelf, in a can of sugar, and sees that two of her twelve vials of endorphin are gone. Daud, of course. There aren't enough places to hide even small amounts of stuff in an apartment this size. She sighs, then ties her tourniquet above the elbow. She slots a vial into her injector, dials the dose she wants, and presses the injector to her arm. The injector hums and she sees a bubble rise in the vial. Then there is a warning light on the injector and she feels a tug of flesh as the needle slides on its cool spray of anesthetic into her vein. She unties, watches the LED on the injector pulse ten times, and then she feels a veil slide between her and her pain. She takes a ragged breath, then stands. She leaves the injector on the sofa and walks back to the comp.

Michael the Hetman is in his office when she calls. She speaks to him in Spanglish and he laughs.

"I thought I'd hear from you today, mi hermana," he says.

"Yes?" she asks. "You know this orbiter Cunningham?"

"So-so. We've done business. He has the highest recommendations."

"Whose?"

"The highest," he says.

"So you recommend that I trust him?" Sarah asks.

His laugh seems a little jangled. She wonders if he is high. "I never make that kind of recommendation, mi hermana," he says.

"Yes, you would, Hetman," Sarah says. "If you are getting a piece of whatever it is Cunningham is doing. As it is, you're just doing him a favor."

"Do svidaniya, my sister," says Michael, sounding annoyed, and snaps off. Sarah looks into the humming receiver and frowns.

The door opens behind her and she spins and goes into her stance, balanced to jump forward or back. Daud walks carelessly in the door. Behind him, carrying a six-pack of beer, comes his manager, Jackstraw, a small young man with unquiet eyes.

Daud looks up at her, speaks through the cigarette held in his lips. "You expecting someone else?" he asks.

She relaxes. "No," she says. "Just nerves. It's been a nervous day."

Daud's eyes move restlessly over the small apartment. He has altered the irises from brown to a pale blue, just as he'd altered the color of his hair, eyebrows, and lashes to a white blond. He is tanned, and his hair is shoulder-length and shaggy. He wears tooled leather sandals and a tight white pair of slacks under a dark net shirt. He is taking hormone suppressants, and though he is twenty he looks fifteen and is beardless.

Sarah moves over to him and kisses him hello. "I'm working tonight," he says. "He wants to have dinner. I can't stay long."

"Is it someone you know?" she asks.

"Yes." He gives a shadowy grin, meant to be reassuring. His blue eyes flicker. "I've been with him before."

"Not a thatch?"

He shrugs out of her embrace and goes to sit on the sofa. "No," he mumbles. "An old guy. Lonely, I guess. Easy to please. Wants to talk more than anything." He sees the plastic pack of endorphins and picks it up, searching through it. Sarah sees two more vials vanish between his fingers.

"Daud," she says, her voice a warning. "That's our food and rent—I've got to get it on the street."

"Just one," Daud says. He drops the other back in the bag, holds up one to let her see it. Cigarette ash drifts to the floor.

"You've already had your share," Sarah says.

His pale eyes flicker in his dark face. "Okay," he says. But he doesn't put the vial down.

His need is too strong. She looks down and shakes her head. "One," she agrees. "Okay." He pockets it, then picks up the loaded injector and dials a dosage—a high dosage, she knows. She resists the urge to check the injector, knowing that someday if he goes on this way he'll put himself in a coma, but knowing how much he'd resent her concern. Sarah watches as the endorphin hits his head, as he lies back and sighs, his twitchy nervousness gone.

She takes the injector and frees the vial, then puts it in the plastic bag. There is a half smile on Daud's face as he looks up at her. "Thanks, Sarah," he says.

"I love you," she says.

He closes his eyes and straps his back on the sofa like a cat. His throat makes strange whimpering noises. She takes the bag and walks into her room and throws the bag on her bed. A wave of sadness whispers through her veins like a drug of melancholy. Daud will die before long, and she can't stop it.

Once it had been she who stood between him and life; now it is the endorphins that keep him insulated from the things that want to touch him. Their father had been crazy and violent, and half her scars were Daud's by right; she had suffered them on his behalf, shielding him with her body. The madman's beatings had taught her to fight back, had made her hard and quick, but she couldn't be there all the time. The old man had sensed weakness in Daud, and found it. When Sarah was fourteen she'd run with the first boy who'd promised her a place free from pain; two years later, when she'd bought her way out of her first contract and come back for him, Daud had been shattered beyond repair, the needle already in his arm. She'd led him to the new house where she worked—it was the only place she had—and there he'd learned to earn his living, as she had learned in her own time. He is broken still, and as long as they are in the streets, there is no way of healing him.

If she hadn't cracked, if she hadn't run away, she might have been able to protect him. She won't crack again.

She returns to the other room and sees Daud lying on the sofa, one sandal hanging with the straps tangled between his toes. Tobacco smoke drifts up from his nostrils. Jackstraw is sitting next to him on the sofa and drinking one of his beers. He glances up.

"You look like you're limping," Jackstraw says. "Would you like me to rub your legs?"

"No," Sarah says quickly, and then realizes she is being too sharp. "No," she says again, with a smile. "Thank you. But it's a bone bruise. If you touched me, I'd scream."

ARTIFICIAL DREAMS

The Plastic Girl is a hustler's idea of the good life. There is a room for zonedance, and there are headsets that plug you into euphoric states or pornography or whatever it is you need and are afraid to shoot into your veins. Orbital pharmaceutical companies provide the effects free, as advertising for their products. There are dancers on the mirrored bar in the back, a bar equipped with arcade games so that if you win, a connection snaps in one of the dancer's garments and it falls off. If you win big, all the clothes fall off all the dancers at once.

Sarah is in the big front room: brassy music, red leather booths, brass ornaments. She does not, and will probably never, rate the quiet room in the back, all brushed aluminum and a lot of dark wood that might have been the last mahogany tree in Southeast Asia—that room is for the big boys who run this fast and dangerous world, and though there isn't a sign that says NO WOMEN ALLOWED, there might as well be. Sarah is an independent contractor and rates a certain amount of respect, but in the end she is still meat for hire, though on a more elevated plane than she once was.

But still, the red room is nice. There are holograms, colors and helixes like modeled DNA, floating just above eye level, casting their variegated light through the crystal and sparkling liquor held in the patrons' hands, and there are sockets at every table for comp decks so that the patrons can keep up with their portfolios, and there are girls with reconstructed breasts and faces who come to each table in their tight plastic corsets, bring you your drink, and watch with identical and very white smiles as you put your credit needle into their tabulator and tap in a generous tip with your fingernail.

She is ready for the meet with Cunningham, wearing a navy blue jacket guaranteed to protect her against kinetic violence of up to 900 foot-pounds per square inch, and trousers good for 750. She has invested some of the endorphins and bought the time of a pair of her peers. They are walking loose about the bar, ready to keep Cunningham or his friends off her back if she needs it. She knows she needs a clear head and has kept the endorphin dose down. Pain is making her edgy, and she still can't sit. She stands at a small table and sips her rum and lime, waiting.

And then Cunningham is there. Bland face, brown eyes, brown hair, brown suit. A whispery voice that speaks of clean places she has never been, places bright and soft against the black and pure diamond.

"Okay, Cunningham," she says. "Business."

Cunningham's eyes flicker to the mirror behind her. "Friends?" he asks.

"I don't know you."

"You've called the Hetman?"

She nods. "He was complimentary," she says, "but you're not working for him; he's repaying you a favor, maybe. So I'm cautious."

"Understandable." He takes a comp deck out of an inner pocket and plugs it into the table. A pale amber screen in the depths of the dark tabletop lights up, displaying a row of figures.

"We're offering you this in dollars," he says.

Sarah feels a touch of metal on her nerves, on her tongue. The score, she thinks, the real thing. "Dollars?" she says. "Get serious."

"Gold?" Another set of figures appears.

She takes a sip of rum. "Too heavy."

"Stock. Or drugs. Take your pick."

"What kind of stock? What kind of drugs?"

"Your choice."

"Polymyxin-phenildorphin Nu. There's a shortage right now."

Cunningham frowns. "If you like. But there'll be a lot of it coming onto the market in another three weeks or so."

Her eyes challenge him. "Did you bring it down from orbit with you?" she asks.

His face fails so much as to twitch. "No," he says. "But if I were you, I'd try chloramphenildorphin. Pfizer is arranging an artificial scarcity that will last several months. Here are the figures. Pharmacological quality, fresh from orbit."

Sarah looks at the amber numbers and nods. "Satisfactory," she says. "Half in advance."

"Ten percent now," Cunningham says. "Thirty on completion of training. The rest on completion of the contract, whether you succeed or not."

She looks up at one of the bar's moving holograms, the colors clean and bright, as pure as if seen through a vacuum. A vacuum, she thinks. The stock isn't bad, but she can do more with the drugs. Cunningham is offering her the drugs at their orbital value, where they are made and where the cost is almost nothing. The street value is far more, and with it she can buy more stock than the amount they were offering. Ten percent of that figure is more than she'd made last night, when she'd gone after the snagboy.

To get into the Orbitals you have to have skills they need, skills she can never acquire. There is another way: they can't refuse someone who owns enough shares. They are sucking up all of Earth's remaining wealth, and if you help them and buy up enough stock, they might free you from the mud forever. This is almost enough, she calculates. Almost enough for a pair of tickets to the top of the gravity well.

She brings her drink to her lips. "Let's say a quarter now," she says. "And then I'll let you buy me a drink, and you can tell me just what you want me to do to earn it."

Cunningham turns and signals to one of the smiling corset girls. "It's very simple," he says, and he looks at her with his ice-cold eyes. "We want you to make someone fall in love with you. Just for a night."

IS YOUR LOVER LOOKING FOR SOMEONE YOUNGER? YOU CAN BE THAT SOMEONE!

"The Princess is about eighty years old," Cunningham says. The holo he gives Sarah shows a pale blond girl of about twenty, dressed in a kind of ruffled blouse that exposes her rounded shoulders, the hollows of her clavicles. She has Daud's watery blue eyes and freckles above her breasts. She projects an air of vulnerable innocence

"We think he was originally from Russia," Cunningham goes on, "but the Korolev Bureau has always been secretive and we don't have a complete list of their senior staff and designers. When he rated the new body, he asked to be a woman. He's important enough so that they gave it to him, but they gave him a demotion—they rotate out all their old people to make way for the new. She's doing courier duty now."

Not unusual, Sarah thinks. These days you can get pornography read straight into the brain, plenty of chances to sample whatever pleasures you like and then, if rich enough, get yourself a new body to suit your tastes. But the technology of personality transfer is imperfect—sometimes bits get left behind: memories, abilities, traits that might be useful. A succession of bodies can mean successive senility. If you get a new body and aren't so powerful you can't be moved, you are often demoted until you can prove yourself.

"What's her new name?" she asks.

"She'll tell you, I'm sure. Let's just call her Princess for now."

Sarah shrugs. There are half a dozen imbecilic security rules in this operation, and she guesses that most of them are simply to test her capacity for obedience.

"Her new body doesn't seem to have altered his sexual orientation, just his manner of expressing it," Cunningham says. "Princess has exhibited some characteristic behaviors since she's started her new job. When she's on the ground, she likes to go slumming. Find herself a working girl— sometimes a dirtgirl, most often a jock—and take her home for a night or two. She wants a pet, but a dangerous one. Not too clean. A little rough. Not too removed from the street. But civilized enough to know how to please. Not a thatch.''

"That's me?" Sarah asks, with no surprise. "Her new pet?"

"We've researched you. You were a licensed prostitute for five years. And rated highly by your employers."

"Five and a half," she says. "And not with girls."

"He's a man, really. An old man. Why should it be hard for you?"

Sarah looks at the blond freckled girl in the holo, trying to find the old Russian in those eyes. The look that was always the same, wanting her to be some piece of private fantasy, real but not too real, orgasms genuine but never with genuine passion. The plastic girl, an object for things that grew hidden in their minds, something they could get rid of quickly and never have to take home. They were upset, somehow, if you didn't understand their fantasy right away. After a while she had got so that she could.

No different from all the other old men, she thinks as she looks at the picture. Not really. They want power, over their own flesh and another's. Pay not so much for sex, but for power over sex, over the thing that threatens to control them. And so they take their passion and use it to control others. She understands control all right.

She looks up at Cunningham. "Did they give *you* a new body as well?" she asks. "Guaranteed inconspicuous? Or did you have Firebud make you over, so that you had no style at all?"

He gazes at her steadily, the same calm gaze. She can't seem to touch it, or him. "I can't say," he says.

"How long have you worked for them?" she asks. "You were a mudboy once—you don't have the look that *they* do. But you work for them now. Is that what they promised you? A new body when you get old? And if you die on one of these jobs here in the mud, a nice funeral with the corporate anthem sung over your body?"

"Something like that," he agrees.

"Got you heart and soul, have they?" she asks.

"That's how they want it." Dryly, accepting. He knows the price of his ticket.

"Control," she says. "You understand that. You are owned by people who worship control, and so you control yourself well. But you're a pressure cooker, and the steam is just under the surface. Do you go slumming in your off hours, like Princess? To the clubs, to the houses? Are you one of my old customers?" She gazes into his expressionless eyes. "You could be," she says. "I never remembered faces."

"As it happens, I'm not," he says. "I never saw you before I was given this assignment." He is beginning to look a little out of patience.

Sarah grins. "Don't worry," she says, and throws the holo of Princess on the table. "I'll do your owners proud."

"I'm sure you will," he says. "They won't have it any other way."

IN THE ZONE/YES

Like Times Square neon, the amber LED tracks across the upper limits of Sarah's vision, just where the shadow of her brows would be.

PRINCESS MOVING PRINCESS MOVING PRINCESS MOVING . . .

The Aujourd'Oui is Princess's favorite spot, but there are others. Sarah should be ready to move at need.

The washroom at the Aujourd'Oui is a conglomeration of mirrors and soft white lights, red flock on the gold wallpaper, bronze waterspouts above the sinks, chromed dispensers that offer tissue for the adjustment of makeup. Sarah shoulders through the door, and a pair of dirtgirls standing in front of the mirrors glance at her. There is envy in their glance, and a kind of desperate awe, and then the eyes turn self-consciously back to the mirrors. The satin jacket represents something they want and will most likely never have, the freedom of the white crane to climb into the sky amid the silver glitter of stars. Sarah is suddenly aware of the sound of sobbing, magnified by the low ceiling, the hard edges of the room. The dirtgirl's eyes stay fixed in their own reflections as she passes and steps into a stall.

It is the girl in the next stall who is weeping, pausing only to draw massive shuddering breaths before bringing the air out again through the tortured muscles of the throat. It hurts to cry that hard, Sarah knows. The ribs feel as if they are breaking. The stall shudders to the impact as the girl drives her head against its wall, and Sarah knows that it is pain the girl is seeking, perhaps to drive out pain of another kind.

Sarah tries not to get between people and what they need.

To the sound of the impacts Sarah takes her inhaler from her belt, puts it to her nose, and triggers it. There is a brief hiss of compressed gas. Sarah throws her head back, feeling the rush of hardfire racing along her nerve paths. The stall quakes. Sarah inhales again, using the other nostril, and she feels her body go warm and then cold, the hair on her forearms prickling. Her lips peel back from her teeth, and she feels at once abnormally sensitive and abnormally hard, as if her skin is made of razor blades that can feel every mote of dust. She needs the bite of the drug, needs it to give herself that extra piece of conviction. She hadn't mentioned it to Cunningham. The hell with him—she'll play it her own way. . . .

PRINCESS MOVING PRINCESS MOVING . . .

The other girl's weeping is a whining, grating sound, like a saw on bone, syncopated with the hysterical crashing as she smashes again and again into the divider. Sarah can see flecks of blood daubing the floor of the next stall. She opens her door and sweeps through the room, past the dirtgirls, whose eyes stand out pale amid their rimming of kohl as they gaze at each other and wonder what to do about the sobbing

casualty. PRINCESS AUJOURD'OUI REPEAT AUJOURD'OUI AM
SWITCHING POLICE TRANSMISSIONS GOOD HUNTING CUNNINGHAM.

Sarah blinks as she steps into the darkness of the club,
feeling the hardfire impelling her limbs to motion, and she
rides the drug like a jock on the flaming roman candle of a
booster, climbing for the edge of the sky and still in control.
The corners of the room, the dancers and fixtures, flare like
liquid-crystal kaleidoscopes.

And then Princess comes, and Sarah's motion freezes.
Princess is surrounded by dirtboy muscle, but she stands out
clearly in the dark—there is an aura about her, a glow. She
has the Look as none of them have, a soft radiance that
speaks of luxury, soft and carefree joys, freedom even from
gravity. A life even the jocks can't share. It seems as if
there is a pause in the music, as the room inhales in mutual
awe. Two hundred eyes can see the glow and a hundred
mouths, hungry for it, begin to salivate. Sarah feels her
body tingle, flares of nerve warmth at her fingertips. She
is ready.

Sarah gives a soft private laugh, as if her triumph were
already a fact, and walks long-legged across the darkened bar
as Firebud has taught her, swinging her broad shoulders in
counterpoint to her hips, insinuant animal style. She gives
a grin to the muscle and holds her hands palms out to show
them she carries no weapons, and then Princess stands before
her.

She is a good four inches shorter and Sarah looks down at
her, hands cocked on her hips, challenging. Princess's soft
blond hair is worn long, ringlets playing with her cheeks, her
ears. Her eyes are circled with vast blooms of purple and
yellow makeup, to look like bruises, making public the secret
wish of a translucent white face that has never known pain.
Her mouth is a deep violet, another laceration. Sarah cocks
her head back and laughs low, baring her teeth, and thinks of
the sounds hyenas make on the hunt.

"Dance with me, Princess," she says to the wide corn-
flower eyes. "I am your wildest dreams."

PRACTICE CREATES PERFECTION
PERFECTION CREATES POWER
POWER CONQUERS LAW
LAW CREATES HEAVEN

A helpful reminder from Toshiba

Nicole has a cigarette in the corner of her mouth and wears a jacket of cracked brown leather. She has dark blond hair that reaches down her back in tawny strands, and long deep gray eyes that look up at Sarah without a flicker.

Cunningham stands behind her with his two assistants. One is huge, a muscleman with no neck. The other is small, blond, and has even less to say than Cunningham. Sarah thinks the smaller is the more dangerous of the two.

"You can't hesitate for a second, Sarah," Cunningham says. "Not even the fragment of a second. Princess will know it and know there's something wrong. Nicole is here for that. You are to practice with her."

Sarah looks at Nicole for a moment of surprise and then barks a laugh. Anger bubbles in her, whitely, coolly, like flares on the night horizon. "I suppose you plan to watch, Cunningham," she says.

He nods. "Yes," he says. "I and Firebud. You seemed uncertain at first about making love to a woman." Nicole draws slowly on her cigarette and says nothing.

"Make a vid record, perhaps?" Sarah asks. "Give me post-game critique?" She curls her lip. "Is that your particular pleasure, Cunningham?" she demands. "Does watching this kind of vid keep your demons away?"

"We'll destroy the vids together, if you like, . . . afterward," Cunningham says. His no-neck assistant grins. The other watches her, expressionless as his chief.

Sarah has been two months in training, has had her body altered and surgical work done, and all along she has been their willing dirtgirl. But however many candidates had been in Cunningham's files, she is sure she's the only hope now, the only charge Cunningham will have shaped by the time

Princess next comes down from orbit, and she knows now she has power of her own. They will have to go with her or the project will fail, and it is time they knew it.

She shakes her head slowly. "I don't think so, Cunningham," she says. "I'll be ready on the night, but I'm not now and I'm not going to be. Not for you, not for your cameras."

Cunningham does not reply. He seems to squint a little, as if suddenly the light is stronger. Nicole watches Sarah with smoky eyes, then shakes her long hair and speaks, "Just dance with me, then." Her words come a little too abruptly, as if impelled by some form of desperation, and Sarah wonders what she has been promised, how she has been made vulnerable to *them*. When she speaks, her voice gives her away; it is so much younger than her pose. "Just dance a little," she says. "It'll be all right."

Sarah turns her gaze from Cunningham to Nicole and back, then nods. "Will a few dances satisfy you, Cunningham?" she asks. "Or do we end the program where we stand?"

His jaw muscles tighten, and for a moment Sarah thinks the business is done, that it's over. Then he nods, still facing her. "Yes," he says. "If it has to be that way."

"That's how it has to be," she says. There is a moment of silence, then Cunningham nods again, as if to himself, and turns away. Nicole gives a nervous smile, wanting to please, not knowing who is her ticket to whatever it is she needs. Cunningham walks to the sound deck and presses a switch. Music buffets the walls. He turns back and folds his arms, waiting.

Nicole closes her eyes and shrugs out of her jacket. Either they have gone out of their way to find a woman of Princess's build or they have been lucky. Sarah watches as Nicole sways her body to the music, the plastic girl, waiting blindly to take an impression.

She steps forward and takes the girl's hands in her own.

DELTA THREE EMERGENCY ATTEMPTED SUICIDE AUJOURD'OUI EMERGENCY

Deep in her zone, Sarah shakes her head to clear the sweat from her eyes and feels the hardfire biting her veins. Princess has been her partner all night. She leaps and spins, and Princess watches with gleaming eyes, admiring. She feels like the crane on her back, arms stretching out to fly on pinions of purest silver. Sarah changes zones and Princess follows, letting her give a name to their motion, their liquid pattern. She is bringing Princess in closer until, like a wave, she can fall upon her from her crest of foaming white.

There is an intrusion into the zone, an attempted alteration in the pattern. Sarah whirls, an elbow digging deep into ribs, the zoneboy doubling with the impact. She slices at his neck with a sword hand and the boy flies from the zone whimpering. Princess is watching, rapt with glowing admiration. Sarah steps to her and catches her about the waist, and they spin like skaters on the edge of sharpened blades.

"Am I the danger that you want?" she asks. The blue eyes give an answer. *I know you, old man,* Sarah thinks in triumph, and bends her head to devour the violet lips, feasting like a raptor on her prey. The eyes of Princess widen, held in Sarah's gaze. Her lips taste of salt, and blood.

MODERNBODYMODERNBODYMODERNBODYMODERN

You Can't Claim You're a CYBORG Till You Have a MODERNBODY SEXUAL IMPLANT
Undetectable . . .
Gives You the Power to Last All Night . . .
Orgasm Chips Optional . . .
Your Partner Will Thank You for It!

RNBODYMODERNBODYMODERNBODYMODERNBODY

Cunningham's car hisses through the night on speed-blurred wheels. Holograms slide past the windows in neon array. Sarah watches the back of the driver's neck as it swells from its collar. "It'll be best if you go alone to the club," Cunningham says. "Princess may send some of her people ahead, and you don't want to be seen with anyone."

Sarah nods. He's given these instructions before and she can recite them word for word, even do a fair imitation of the whispery monotone. She nods to show she's listening. Earlier this afternoon she'd collected the second payment of chloramphenildorphin, and her mind is occupied chiefly with ways of putting it on the street.

"Sarah," he says, and reaches into a pocket. "I want you to have this. Just in case." His hand comes up with a small aerosol bottle.

"Yes?" she asks. She sprays it on the back of her hand, touches it, sniffs.

"Silicon lubricant," he says. "The scent is right, and should last for hours. Use it in the washroom if you find that you aren't really . . . attracted to her."

Sarah caps the bottle and holds it out to him. "I don't plan for it to go that far," she says.

He shakes his head. "Just in case," he says. "We don't know what happens when you go behind her walls."

She holds it out, expectant, then when he doesn't respond, she shrugs and puts it in her belt pouch. She rests her reshaped jaw on her hand and stares out the window, the hologram adverts reflecting in her dark eyes, until the car slides to a stop at the door of her apartment.

She reaches for the latch and opens it, steps out. The heat of the outside covers her like a smothering blanket, and she can feel the sweat springing up on her forehead. Cunningham sits huddled in his seat, somehow smaller than he had been. Up until now, until the firing of his shaped charge, he'd been in control—but now he's committed her to action and all he is able to do is watch the result and hope he calculated the ballistics correctly. His jaw muscles twitch in a tight smile and he raises a hand.

"Thanks," she says, knowing he's wished her luck without actually risking a curse by saying it, and she turns away and breathes out and feels a lightness in her body and heart, as if the gravity were somehow lessened. All she has left is the job. No more pleasing Cunningham, no more rules or training, no more listening to Firebud criticizing the very way she walked, the way she held her head. All that is behind.

The apartment is splashed with video color and she knows Daud is home. He's cleared the coffee table from the center of the room and is doing his exercises, the weights in his hands, the burning holograms outlining his naked body, his hairless genitals. She kisses his cheek.

"Dinner?" she asks.

"I'm going with Jackstraw. He wants me to meet someone."

"Someone new?"

"Yes. It's a lot of money." He drops the weights and lowers himself to the floor, begins strapping another set of weights to his ankles. She stands over him with a frown.

"How much?" she asks.

He gives her a quick glance, green laserfire winking from his eye whites, then he looks down. His voice is directed to the floor. "Eight thousand," he says.

"That's a lot," she says.

He nods and stretches his back on the ground, raising his legs against the strain of the weights. He points his feet and she can see the muscles taut on the tops of his thighs. She slips out of her shoes and flexes her toes in the carpet.

"What does he want for it?" she asks. Daud shrugs. Sarah crouches and looks down at him. She feels a tightness in her throat.

She repeats her question.

"Jackstraw will be in the next room," he says. "If anything goes wrong, he'll know."

"He's a thatch, isn't he?"

She can see the Adam's apple bob as Daud swallows. He nods silently. She takes a breath and watches him strain against the weights. Then he sits up. His eyes are cold.

"You don't have to do this," she says.

"It's a lot of money," he repeats.

"Tomorrow my job will be over," she says. "It'll pay enough for a long time, almost enough for a pair of tickets out."

He shakes his head, then springs to his feet and turns his back. He walks toward the shower. "I don't want your money," he says: "Your tickets, either."

"Daud," she says. He whirls around and she can see his anger.

"Your job!" he spits. "You think I don't know what it is you do?"

She rises from her crouch, and for a moment she can see fear in his eyes. Fear of her? A wedge of doubt enters her mind.

"You know what I do, yes," she says. "You also know why."

"Because some man went thatch once," he says. "And because when you got loose you killed him and liked it. I know the stories on the street."

She feels a constriction in her chest. She shakes her head slowly. "No," she says. "It's for *us*, Daud. To get us out, into the Orbitals." She comes up to him to touch him, and he flinches. She drops her hand. "Where it's *clean*, Daud," she says. "Where we're not in the street, because there isn't a street."

Daud gives a contemptuous laugh. "There isn't a street there?" he asks. "So what will *we* do, Sarah? Punch code in some little office?" He shakes his head. "No, Sarah," he says. "We'd do what we've always done. But it will be for *them*, not for us."

"No," she says. "It'll be different. Something we haven't known. Something finer."

"You should see your eyes when you say that," Daud says. "Like you've just put a needle in your veins. Like that hope is your drug, and you're hooked on it." He looks at her soberly, all his anger gone. "No, Sarah," he says. "I know what I am, and what you are. I don't want your hope, or your tickets. Especially tickets with blood on them." He turns away again, and her answer comes quick and angry, striking for his weakness, for the heart. Like a weasel.

"You don't mind stealing my bloody endorphins, I've noticed," she says. His back stiffens for a moment, then he walks on. Heat stings Sarah's eyes. She blinks back tears. "Daud," she says. "Don't go with a thatch. Please."

He pauses at the door, hand on the jamb. "What's the difference?" he asks. "Going with a thatch, or living with you?"

The door closes and Sarah can only stand and fight a helpless war with her anger and tears. She spins and stalks into her room. Her hardwired nerves are crackling, the adrenaline triggering her reflexes, and she only stops herself from trying to drive a fist through the wall. She can taste death on her tongue, and wants to run the Weasel as fast as she can.

The holograph of Princess sits on her chest of drawers. She takes it and stares at it, seeing the creamy shoulders, the blue innocence in the eyes, an innocence as false as Daud's.

TOMORROW/NO

Sarah and Princess follow the ambulance men out of the Aujourd'Oui. They are carrying the girl from the washroom stall. She has clawed her cheeks and breasts with her fingernails. Her face is a swollen cloud of bruises, her nose blue pulp; her lips are split and bloody. She is still trying to weep, but lacks the strength.

Sarah can see Princess's excitement glittering in her eyes. This is the touch of the world she craves, warm and sweaty and real, flavored with the very soil of old Earth. Princess stands on the hot sidewalk, while her dirtboys circle and call for the cars. Sarah puts her arm around her and whispers in her ear, telling her what Sarah knows she wants. "I am your dream."

"My name is Danica," Princess says.

In the back of the car there is a smell of sweat and expensive scent. Sarah begins to devour Danica, licking and biting and breathing her in. She left the silicon spray at home but won't be needing it: Danica has Daud's eyes and hair and smooth flesh, and Sarah finds herself wanting to touch her, to make a feast of her.

The car passes smoothly through gates of hardened alloy,

and they are in the nest. None of Cunningham's people ever
got this far. Danica takes Sarah's hand and leads her in. A
security man insists on a check: Sarah looks down at him
with a contemptuous stare and spreads the wings of her
jacket, letting his electronic marvel scout her body. She
knows Weasel is undetectable by these means. The boy
confiscates her hardfire inhaler. Fine: it is made so as not to
acquire fingerprints. "What are these?" he asks, holding up
the hard black cubes of liquid crystal, ready for insertion into
a comp deck.

"Music," she says. He shrugs and gives them back. Princess takes her hand again and leads her up a long stair.

Her room is soft and azure. She laughs and lies back on
sheets that match her eyes, arms outstretched. Sarah bends
over and laps at her. Danica moans softly, approving. She is
an old man and a powerful one, and Sarah knows this game.
His job is to rape Earth, to be as strong as spaceborn alloy,
and it is weakness that is his forbidden thing, his pornography. To put his bright new body into the hands of a slave is a
weakness he wants more than life itself.

"My dream," Danica whispers. Her fingers trace the scars
on Sarah's cheek, her chin.

Sarah takes a deep breath. Her tongue retracts into Weasel's implastic housing, and the cybersnake's head closes
over it. She rolls Danica entirely under her, holding her
wrists, molding herself to the old man's new girl body. She
presses her mouth to Danica's, feeling the flutter of the girl's
tongue, and then Weasel strikes, telescoping from its hiding
place in Sarah's throat and chest. Sarah holds her breath as
her elastic artificial trachea constricts. Danica's eyes open
wide as she feels the touch of Weasel in her mouth, the
temperature of Sarah's body but somehow cold and brittle.
Sarah's fingers clamp on her wrists, and Princess gives a
birth-strangled cry as Weasel's head forces its way down her
throat. Her body bucks once, again, her breath warm in
Sarah's face. Weasel keeps uncoiling, following its program,
sliding down into the stomach, its sensors questing for life.
Daud's eyes make desperate promises. Princess moans in

fear, using his strength against Sarah's weight, trying to throw her off. Sarah holds him crucified. Weasel, turning back on itself as it enters Danica's stomach, tears its way out, seeks the cava inferior and shreds it. Danica makes bubbling sounds, and though Sarah knows it is impossible, although she knows her tongue is still retracted deep into Weasel's base, Sarah thinks she can taste blood. Weasel follows the vein to Danica's heart. Sarah holds her down, her own chest near bursting with lack of air, until the struggling stops and Daud's blue eyes grow cloudy and die.

Purple and black rim Sarah's vision. She heaves herself off the bed, partly retracting Weasel as she gasps for air through the constricted passage in her throat. She stumbles for the washroom, falls and crashes into the sink. The impact drives the air from her. Her hands turn the spigots. Her hands put Weasel in the sink and feel the water running chill. Her breath comes in rasps. Weasel is coated with a gel that supposedly prevents blood and matter from adhering, but she doesn't want even a chance of Danica's flesh in her mouth. The cybersnake is tearing at her breast. The water thunders until she can feel nothing but the speed with which she is falling into blackness, and then she falls back and sucks Weasel into her and can breathe again and taste the cool and healing air.

Her chest heaves up and down, and her eyes are still full of darkness. She knows Daud is dead and that she has a task. She whips her head back and forth and tries to clear it, tries to scrabble upward from the brink, but Weasel is eating her heart and she can scarcely think from the pain. Sarah can hear herself whimper. She can feel the prickle of the carpet against the back of her neck as she raises her arms above her head and tries to drag herself along, crawling away, crawling, while Weasel throbs like thunder in her chest and she thinks she can hear her heart crack.

Sarah comes to herself slowly, and the black circle fades from her sight. She is lying on her back and the water is still roaring in the sink. She sits up and clutches at her throat. Weasel, having fed, is at rest. She crawls back to the sink and turns the spigots off. Grasping them, she hauls herself to her feet. She still has work to do.

In her room, Princess is spread-eagled on the bed. Dead, it is easier to see the old man in her. Sarah's stomach turns over. She should drag Princess across the bed and tuck her under the covers, delaying the moment when they find her, but she can't bring herself to touch the cooling flesh; and instead she turns her eyes away and steps into the next room.

She pauses as her eyes adjust to the dim light, and listens to the house. Silence. She reads the amber lights above her vision, and can find only routine broadcasts. Sarah takes a pair of gloves from her belt pouch and walks to the room's comp deck. She flicks it on, then opens the trapdoor and takes from her pouch one of the liquid-crystal music cubes Cunningham has given her. She puts it in the trapdoor and waits for the deck to signal her.

The cube would, in fact, have played music had anyone else used it. Sarah has the code to convert it to something else. The READY signal appears.

She taps the keys in near-silence as she enters the codes. A pale light flashes in the corner of the screen: RUNNING. She leans back in her chair and sighs.

Princess was a courier, bringing from orbit a liquid-crystal cube filled with complex instructions, instructions her company dared not trust even to coded radio transmissions. Princess would not have known what she carried, though presumably it contained inventory data, strategies for manipulating the market, instructions to subordinates, buying and selling strategies. Information worth millions to any competitor. The crystal cube would have been altered to a new configuration once the information was removed to the company computer—a computer sealed against any outside tampering, but which could presumably be accessed through the terminals in the corporate suites.

Sarah also has no clear idea what is on the cube she is carrying. Some kind of powerful theft program, she presumes, to break its way through the barriers surrounding the information so that it can be copied. She does not know how good her program is, whether it's setting off every alarm in Florida or whether it's accomplishing its business stealthily. If it's very good, it will not only copy the information, but alter it as well, planting a flow of disinformation at the heart of the enemy code, perhaps even altering the instructions as well, sabotaging the enemy's marketing patterns.

While the RUNNING light blinks, Sarah stands and goes over every part of the suite she might have touched, stroking anything that could retain a print with her gloved fingertips. The house, and Princess, are silent.

It is eleven minutes before the computer signals READY. Sarah extracts the cube and returns it to her belt. She has been told to wait a few hours, but there is someone dead in the next room and every nerve screams at her to run. She sits before the comp deck and puts her head between her legs, gulping air. For some reason she finds herself trembling. She battles the adrenaline and her own nerves, and thinks of the tickets, the cool dark of space with the blue limb of Earth far below, forever out of reach.

In two hours she calls a cab and walks down the cold, echoing stair. The security man nods at her as she walks out: his job is to keep people from coming in, not to hinder their leaving. He even gives her the inhaler back.

She takes a dozen cabs to a dozen different places, leaving the satin jacket in one, cinching her waist in tighter and removing the suspenders in another, in a third reversing her T-shirt and her belt pouch, both now glowing yellow like a warning light. The jockey persona is gone, and she is dirt again. She finishes her journey at the Plastic Girl, the place still running flat-out at four in the morning. As she enters, the sounds of dirt life assault her, and she takes comfort. This is her world, and she knows all the warm places where she can hide.

She takes a room in the back and calls Cunningham. "Come and get your cube," she says, and then orders rum and lime.

By the time he arrives, she's rented an analyzer and some

muscle. He comes in alone, a package in his hand. He closes the door behind him.

"Princess?" he asks.

"Dead."

Cunningham nods. The cube is on the table before her. She holds out a hand. "Let's see what you've got," she says.

She checks three vials at random and the analyzer tells her it's chloramphenildorphin, purity 98 percent or better. She smiles. "Take your cube," she says, but he plugs it into the room's deck first, making sure it has what he wants. Then he puts it in his pocket and heads for the door.

"If you have another job," she says, "you know where to find me."

He pauses, a hand on the knob. His eyes flicker. She receives an impression of sadness from him, as if he were mourning something newly dead.

He is an earthly extension, Sarah knows, of an Orbital bloc. She doesn't even know which one. He is a willing tool and an obedient one, and she has fed him her scorn on that account, but that doesn't disguise what they both know—that she would give all the contents of the packet, and everything else besides, if she could have his ticket, and on the same terms.

"I'll be on the ramp in an hour," he says. "Going back to orbit."

She gives him a grin. "Maybe I'll be seeing you there," she says.

He nods, his eyes on hers. He starts to say something, then turns himself off again, as if he realizes it's pointless. "Be careful," he says, and leaves without another glance. One of her hired muscle looks in at her.

"It's clear," she says. The muscle nods.

She looks at the fortune in her hand and feels suddenly hollow. There is a vacuum in her chest where the joy should be. The drink she has ordered tastes as flat as barley water, and a headache throbs in time to the LED light burning in her forehead. She pays off her hired muscle and takes a cab to an all-night bank, where she deposits the endorphin in a rented box. Then she takes the cab home.

The apartment hums softly, emptily. She finds the control to her LED and turns it off, then throws her clothing in the trash. Naked, she steps into her room and sees the holo of Princess on her night table. Hesitantly, she reaches out to it, then turns it face down and falls into the welcoming blackness.

LOVELY AND WAITING FOR YOU TERRY'S TOUGH 'N' TENDER NOW

It is still night when she awakens to the sound of the door. "Daud?" she asks, and is answered by a groan.

He is wrapped in a sheet and covered with blood. Jackstraw holds him up, panting, his neck muscles straining. "Bastard," he says.

She picks Daud up like a child and carries him to her bed. His blood smears her arms, her breasts. "Bastard went thatch," Jackstraw says. "I was only gone a minute."

Sarah arranges Daud on the bed and unwraps the sheet. A whimpering sound forces its way up her throat. She puts her hand to her mouth. Daud is striped in blood—the thatch must have used some kind of weighted whip. Weakly, he tries to move, raises a hand as if to ward off a blow.

"Lie back," Sarah says. "You're at home."

Daud's face crinkles in pain. "Sarah," he says, and begins to cry.

Sarah feels tears stinging her own eyes and blinks them away. She looks up at Jackstraw. "Did you give him anything?" she asks.

"Yeah. Endorphin. First thing."

"How much?"

He looks at her blankly. "Lots. I don't know."

"You weren't supposed to leave the next room," she says.

His eyes slide away. "It was a busy night," he says. "I was only gone a minute."

She turns her eyes back to Daud. "It took more than a minute for this," she says. "Get the fuck out."

"It's not—"

There is a savage light in her eyes. She wants to tear him but she has other things to do. "Get the fuck out," she repeats. He hesitates for another instant, then turns away.

She cleans the cuts and disinfects them. Daud cries silently, his throat working. Sarah looks for his injector and finds it, loads it with endorphins from his cache, and guesses at a dosage. She puts it in his arm, and he says her name and goes to sleep. She watches for a while, making sure he hasn't taken too much, and then puts the covers over him and turns down the light. "Just lie back," she says. "I've got the price of your ticket." She leans down to kiss his beardless cheek. The bloody sheet goes in the trash.

Daud normally sleeps on the convertible sofa in the front room, and after making sure he is asleep, she moves to the other room and, without bothering to open the sofa, lies down on it. The room hums, and for a long while she listens.

TAMPA'S TOTALS OVERNITE, AS OF 8 THIS MORNING—TWELVE FOUND DEAD IN CITY LIMITS ... LUCKY WINNERS COLLECT AT ODDS OF 5 TO 3

The explosion has enough force to throw the sofa against the far wall. Sarah feels a hot rush of wind that tears the breath from her throat, the elevator sensation of the world falling away, and then a final impact as the wall comes up. Screams are ricocheting from every corner, all the screams that Princess never uttered. There are fires licking like red laserlight.

She heaves herself to her feet and runs for the other room. She can see by the light of the burning bed. Daud is sprawled in a corner of the room, and parts of his body are open and other parts are on the walls. She is screaming for help, but alone she manages to get the burning bedding through the hole in the wall. Outside, the hot tongues of morning are rising in the east. She thinks she can hear Daud call her name.

BODY NEEDING WORK?
WE DELIVER

The ambulance driver wants payment in advance, and she opens her portfolio by comp and transfers the stock without questioning the prices he gives her. Daud dies three times before the driver's two assistants can get him out of the apartment, and each time they bring him back the prices go up. "You got the money, lady, and he'll be fine," the driver tells her. He looks at her nakedness with appreciative eyes. "All kinds of arrangements can be made," he says.

Later, Sarah sits in the hospital room and watches the doctors work and is told their rates of payment. She will have to make plans to convert the endorphin quickly, within a few days. Machines attached to Daud hiss and thump. The police surround her and want to know why someone would fire a shaped charge at her apartment wall from the building across the street. She tells them she has no idea. They have a lot of questions, but that seems to be the most frequent. Eventually she puts her head in her hands and shakes her head; and they shuffle for a while and then leave.

She wishes she had the inhaler: she needs the bite of hardfire to keep herself alert, to keep her mind functioning. Thoughts hammer at her. If Cunningham's people had been in her apartment, they would have known that she had slept in the back room, Daud in the front. They waited till the lights went down and she had the time to get to sleep, then fired with a weapon that would smash through the wall and scatter burning steel through the inside. They hadn't trusted that she wouldn't tell someone or that she wouldn't try to use the pieces of knowledge she had gained as leverage for some shifty little dirtscheme of her own.

Who would I tell? she wonders.

She remembers Cunningham at that last moment in the Plastic Girl, the sadness in him. He had known. Tried, in his way, to warn her. Perhaps the decision had not been his; perhaps it had been made over his objection. What did the Orbitals care for one more dirtgirl when they had already killed millions, and kept the rest alive only so long as they were useful currency?

The Hetman glides into the room on catlike feet. He wears a gold earring, and his wise, liquid eyes are surrounded by the spiderwebs of the old hustler's dirtbound life. "I am sorry, mi hermana," he says. "I had no indication it would come to this. I want you to understand."

Sarah nods numbly. "I know, Michael."

"I know people on the West Coast," the Hetman says. "They will give you work there, until Cunningham and his people forget you exist."

Sarah looks up at him for a moment, then looks at the bed and the humming, hissing machines. She shakes her head. "I can't go, Michael," she says.

"A bad mistake, Sarah." Gently. "They will try again."

Sarah makes no reply, feeling only the emptiness inside her, knowing the emptiness would never leave if she deserted Daud again. The Hetman stands for an uncomfortable moment, then is gone.

"I had the ticket," Sarah whispers.

Outside she can see the mud boiling under the lunatic sun. All Earth's soil, looking for their tickets, plugging into whatever can give them a fragment of their dream. All playing by someone else's rules. Sarah has her ticket, but the rules have turned on her like a weasel, and she must shred the ticket and spread it on the street, spread it so she can watch the machines hum and hiss and keep what she loves alive. Because there is no choice, and the girls have no option but to follow the instructions and play as best they can.

Chapter Three

As he stands in the hot summer of eastern Colorado, a steel guitar is playing a lonesome song somewhere in the back of Cowboy's mind.

"For the laws I have a certain respect," he says. "For mercenaries I have none."

Arkady Mikhailovich Dragunov stares at him for a half second. His eyes are slitted against the brightness of the sun. The whites seem yellowed Fabergé ivory, and the irises, old steel darkened like a sword. Then he nods. It's the answer he wants.

Discontent rises in Cowboy like a drifting wave of red sand. He doesn't like this man or share his strange, suspicious, involuted hatreds. Excitement is tingling in his arms, his mind, the crystal inside his skull. Missouri. At last. But Arkady is oblivious to the grandeur of what is going to take place, wants only to fit Cowboy into place with his own self-image, to remind Cowboy again that Arkady is not just a boss but the big boss, that Cowboy owes him not simply loyalty but servitude. A game that Cowboy will not play.

"Goddamn right," Arkady says. "We know they're offering their services to Iowa and Arkansas. We don't want that."

"If they find me, I'll do what I can," Cowboy says, knowing that in this business, talk is necessarily elliptical. "But first they've got to find me. And my op plan should give me a good chance of staying in the clear."

Arkady wears an open-necked silk shirt of pale violet, with leg-of-mutton sleeves so wide they seem to drag in the dust; an embroidered Georgian sash wound twice around his waist; and tight, polished cossack boots over tighter black trousers that have embroidery on the outer seams. His hair, at intervals, stands abruptly on end and flares with static discharges, a different color each time. The latest thing from the Havana boutiques of the Florida Free Zone. Cryo max, he says proudly. Cowboy knows Arkady couldn't be cryo max if he spent his life trying, it isn't in him. In fashion he is a follower, not a leader. Here he's just impressing the hicks and his toadies.

Arkady is a big, brusque man, fond of hugging and touching the people he's talking to; but he's got a heart like superconducting hardware and eyes to match, and it would be foolish to consider him a friend. Thirdmen do not have cargo space for friends.

Arkady crimps the cardboard tube of a Russian cigarette and strikes a match. His hair stands on end, suddenly bright orange. Imitating the match, Cowboy thinks, the steel guitar still bending notes in his mind. . . .

The Dodger, Cowboy's manager, strolls from where the panzer is being loaded for the run. "Best make sure your craft is trimmed," the Dodger says.

Cowboy nods. "See you later, Arkady." Arkady's hair turns green.

"I could see you were getting impatient," the Dodger says as soon as they're out of earshot. "Try not to be so fucking superior, will you?"

"It's hard not to be when Arkady's around."

The Dodger flashes him a disapproving look.

"He must have to butter his ass," Cowboy says, "to get into those pants." He can see the lines around the Dodger's eyes grow crinkly as he tries to suppress his laughter.

The Dodger is an older man, rail-lean, with a tall forehead and straight black hair going gray. He's got a poetic way of speaking when the mood is on him. Cowboy likes him—and trusts him, too, at least to a point, the point being giving the

Dodger the codes to his portfolio. He might be naïve, but he is not stupid.

Cowboy watches as the last pieces of cargo are stowed, making sure the panzer is trimmed, that all's ready for the run across what the Dodger, in an evocative mood, had once christened Damnation Alley.

"What's my cargo?" Cowboy asks. He smiles diffidently, wondering if the Dodger can see the thoughts behind his artificial eyes. The suspicions, the discontents. "Just for the record."

The Dodger is busy cutting a plug of tobacco. "Chloramphenildorphin," he says. "There's going to be a shortage on the East Coast. The hospitals will pay a lot. Or so the rumors say." He grins. "So be of good cheer. You're going to make sure a lot of sick people stay alive."

"Nice to be sort of legal," Cowboy says. "For a change."

He looks at the panzer, all angular armor and intakes, ugly and graceless compared to a delta. He owns this one but he hasn't given it a name, doesn't think of it in the same way. A panzer is just a machine, not a way of life. Not like flying.

Cowboy calls *himself* Pony Express now. It's his radio handle, another nickname. He wants to keep the idea alive, even if it can't take wing.

Cowboy climbs on top of the panzer, worms through the dorsal hatch, and sits down in the forward compartment. He studs a jack in his right temple and suddenly his vision is expanded, as if his two eyes were stretching around his head and a third eye surfaced on top. He calls up the maps he has stored on comp, and displays begin pulsing like strobes on the inside of his skull. His head has become a ROM cube. Inside it he sees fuel trucks spotted down the Alley, ready to move when he needs to be topped up; there is his planned route, with deviations and emergency routes marked, drawn in wide bands of color; there are old barns and deep coulees and other hiding places spotted like acne on the displays, all marked down by Arkady's scouts.

Cowboy fishes a datacube out of his jacket pocket and drops it into the trapdoor. The display flares with another series of pinpricks. His own secret hiding places, the ones he prefers to use, that he keeps up to date with scouting forays of his own. Arkady, he knows, wants this trip to succeed; but Cowboy doesn't know everyone in the thirdman's organization, and some of them might have been bought by the privateers. Best to stick with the places he knows are safe.

The panzer rocks slightly and Cowboy can hear the sound of footsteps on the Chobham Seven armor. He looks up and sees the Dodger's silhouette through the dorsal hatch. "Time to move, Cowboy," the Dodger says, and then spits his chaw over the side.

"Yo," says Cowboy. He unplugs himself and stands up in the cramped compartment. His Kikuyu pupils contract to pinpricks as he puts his head out the hatch and looks west, in the direction of the wine-dark Rockies he knows are somewhere over the horizon. He feels, again, the strange lassitude infecting his heart, a discontent with things as they are.

"Damn," he says. There is longing in the word.

"Yeah," says the Dodger.

"I wish I was flying."

"Yeah." The Dodger looks pensive. "Someday, Cowboy," he says. "We're just waiting for the technology to roll around the other way again."

Cowboy can see Arkady standing by his armored Packard, sweating in the shade of a cottonwood, and suddenly the discontent has a name. "Chloramphenildorphin," he says. "Where's Arkady get it?"

"We're not paid to know those kind of things," the Dodger says.

"In quantities like this?" Cowboy's voice turns thoughtful as he gazes across the gap of bright sky between himself and the thirdman. "Do you think it's true," he asks, "that the Orbitals are running the thirdmen, just like everything else?"

The Dodger glances nervously at Arkady and shrugs. "It don't pay to make those kind of speculations out loud."

"I just want to know who I'm working for," Cowboy says. "If the underground is run by the overground, then we're working for the people we're fighting, qué no?"

The Dodger looks at him crookedly. "I wasn't aware that we were fighting anybody a-tall, Cowboy," he says.

"You know what I mean." That if the thirdmen and panzerboys are just participating in a reshuffling of finances on behalf of the Orbital blocs, then the dream of being the last free Americans on the last free road is a foolish, romantic delusion. And what is Cowboy, then? A dupe, a hovercraft clown. Or worse than that, a tool.

The Dodger gives him a weary smile. "Concentrate on the privateers, Cowboy, that's my advice," he says. "You're the best panzerboy on the planet. Stick to what you're good at."

Cowboy forces a grin and gives him the finger, and then closes the dorsal hatch. He strips naked and sticks electrodes to his arms and legs, then runs the wires from the electrodes to collars on his wrists and ankles. He attaches a catheter, then dons his g-suit and boots, sits on his acceleration couch and attaches cables to the collars, straps himself onto the couch. While his body remains immobile, his muscles will be exercised by electrode to keep the blood flowing. In the old days, before this technique had been developed and the jocks were riding their headsets out of Earth's well and into the long diamond night, sometimes their legs and arms got gangrene. Next he plugs jacks into the sockets in his temples, the silver-chased sockets over each ear, the fifth socket at the base of his skull. He pulls his helmet on over them, careful not to stress the laser-optic wires coming out of his head. He closes the mask across his face. He tastes rubber and hears the hiss of anesthetic, loud here in the closed space of the helmet.

His body will be put to sleep while he makes his run through the Alley. He is going to have more important things to do than look after it.

Cowboy does the chore swiftly, automatically. All along, there is a feeling: I have done this too often not to know what it's about.

Neurotransmitters awaken the five studs in his head and Cowboy watches the insides of his skull blaze with incandescent light, the liquid-crystal data matrices of the panzer molding themselves to the configuration of his mind. His heart beats faster; he's living in the interface again, the eye-face, his expanded mind racing like electrons through the circuits, into the metal and crystal heart of the machine. He can see around the panzer a full 360 degrees, and there are other boards in his strange mental space for engine displays and the panzer systems. He does a system check and a comp check and a weapons check, watching the long rows of green as they light up. His physical perceptions are no longer in three dimensions: the boards overlap and intertwine as they weave in and out of the face, as they mirror the subatomic reality of the electronics and the data that are the dying day outside.

Neurotransmitters lick with their chemical tongues the metal and crystal in his head, and electrons spit from the chips, racing along the cables to the engine starters, and through a dozen sensors Cowboy feels the bladed turbines reluctantly turn as the starters moan, and then flame torches the walls of the combustion chambers and the blades spin into life with a screaming whine. Cowboy monitors the howling exhaust as it belches fire. On his mental displays Cowboy can see the Dodger and Arkady and the ground crew watching the panzer through the blurred exhaust haze, and he watches fore and aft and checks the engine displays and sees another set of green lights and knows it's time to move.

The howling of the engines beats at his senses. Warren's spent the last week tuning them, running check after check, making certain they will perform beyond expectations. They're military surplus jets, monsters. They aren't built to ride this close to the ground, and without Cowboy's straddling this mutant creature every inch of the way they're going to run away with him.

Inside the rubber-tasting mask his lips draw back from his teeth and he grins: he will ride this beast across the Alley and through the web of traps set up this side of the Mississippi and add another layer of permeable sky to the distance separating him from the lesser icons of glory that are the other panzerboys, more proof that the flaming corn-alcohol throbs through his chest like blood and that the shrieking exhaust flows from his lungs like breath, that his eyes beam radar and his fingers can flick missiles forth like pebbles. Through his sensors he can taste the exhaust and see the sky and the prairie sunset, and part of his mind can feel the throbbing radio energies that are the enemy's search planes, and it seems to him that the watchers and the escort vehicles are suddenly lessened, separated from him by more than a few hundred yards—he will be taking the panzer over the Line, and they will not, and he looks at them from within his interface, from his immeasurable height of radiant glory and pities them for what they do not know.

At the moment the ultimate beneficiaries of his run—the hospitals in New England, the thirdmen, his own portfolio, possibly the immeasurably distant, insanely gluttonous creatures who ride their Orbital factories and look down on the Earth as a fast-depleting treasure house to be plundered—all these fade down long redshifting lines, as if blurred by distance and the flaming jet's exhaust. The reality is here in the panzer. Discontent is banished. Action is the thing, and all.

He diverts a part of the jet's exhaust and another set of fans whine into life, lifting the ground-effect panzer with a lurch onto its inflatable self-sealing cushion. The Pony Express will deliver the mail or know the reason why.

Microwave chatter spins around his ears like gnats, and he wishes he could brush it away with his hands.

"Arkady wants to say a few words, Cowboy." The voice is the Dodger's, and Cowboy can tell he knows this isn't a good idea.

"I'm sort of getting ready here," Cowboy says.

"I know that." Shortly, sounding as if his mouth is full of tobacco: "Arkady thinks it's important."

Cowboy concedes, watching the green lights, seeing maps flash behind his eyes. "Whatever Arkady wants," he says.

Arkady has the mic too close to his lips. His *p*'s and *b*'s sound like cannon shots. Put the damn headset on your *head*, Cowboy thinks in irritation. That's what it's for, not to hold it to your fucking mouth.

"I've got a lot at stake here, Cowboy," Arkady says. "I'll be in the plane and with you all the way."

"I am comforted as hell to hear that, Arkady Mikhailovich." Cowboy knows Arkady will have laid off a lot of his costs with the other thirdmen, who wanted the Missouri privateers broken as much as he did.

There is a pause on the other end as Arkady digests this.

"I want you to come back," Arkady says. Cowboy can hear the sounds of temper as if from far away. The thirdman's voice drums on and on, every plosive a barrage. "But I fixed up that machine for a reason, and I don't want you to come back without it. And I don't want you to come back without having used it. Understand? Those fucking privateers are gonna get what's coming to 'em."

"Ten-four," Cowboy says, and before Arkady can ask what the fuck ten-four is supposed to mean, Cowboy opens his throttles and the howl, heard with utter clarity over Arkady's mic, buries Arkady's speech beneath its alcohol shriek. Though he can't hear Arkady anymore, Cowboy is fairly certain that the distant yammering he's hearing through his sockets contains a fair amount of abuse. He smiles.

"Adios, muchachitos." Cowboy laughs, and takes the panzer off the road. The farmer here, a friend of free enterprise and true, is getting paid for his wheat being trampled every so often, and Cowboy is going to have a clear run for the Line. The radar detectors pick up only weak signals from far away and Cowboy knows no one's looking at him.

The beast roars like the last lonely dinosaur and trembles as it gains way. Mental indicators climb their columns from blue to green to orange. Ripe wheat straw flies out behind in a plume. Cowboy has a steel guitar playing a lonesome cadenza somewhere in his mind. He cranks up the flame and is doing over a hundred when he blazes through some poor citizen's bobwire and crosses the Line.

His radar is forward-looking and strictly limited: it's to keep him out of pits and gullies and let him know when there might be a house or vehicle sitting in his way. It sends out a fairly weak signal and it shouldn't be detected by anything unless the detector is so close the first contact would be visual anyway. Kansas has most of its defenses out this way, and if he trips anything, it should be now.

The horizon is a blur of dark emptiness marked by an occasional silo. Any enemy radars are far away. The moon rises and the engines howl and Cowboy keeps his speed in check so as not to raise a dust signature that might be picked up on radar. He wants to save his systems for the real test. Missouri. Where the privateers crouch in the sky, snarling and ready to spring.

Cattle scatter from the panzer's scream. Robot harvesters sweep through the fields, standing like stately alien sentinels in pools of brilliant light, moving alone, unable to detect the panzer as it sweeps across the land. Cowboy gets a stronger radar signal to the north and knows a picket plane is coming his way. The panzer's absorbent camouflage paint sucks up radar signal like a thirsty elephant, but Cowboy slows and turns, lowering his infrared profile and making a wide swing away from any trouble. The picket plane moves on, undisturbed.

Mobile towers loom up like Neolithic monuments, awesomely expensive derricks built to inject a special bacteria into the bedrock below the eroded topsoil, bugs that will break down the stone and make new soil. Another eroded farm foreclosed by an Orbital bloc—no small farmer could afford to replace topsoil this way. Cowboy suppresses a desire to ram the derricks and snarls at them instead.

The panzer crosses the Little Arkansas south of McPherson, and Cowboy knows he'll make it across Kansas without trouble. The defenses are behind him. The only trouble will come if he rides right across the track of a state trooper when crossing a road, and even then the authorities will have to somehow scramble a chopper in time. He doesn't think it will happen.

And it doesn't. In the deep violet shadow of some crumbling grain silos near Gridley the panzer sweeps out of the darkness and scares the bejesus out of the sleeping kid in the cab of the fuel truck. Cowboy cycles his engines down and waits for the sweet cool alcohol to settle into the tanks. Already he can feel the pulsing radars questing out from the Missouri line. Stronger than anything he's seen yet. The privateers are not going to be easy.

"They're undercapitalized, Cowboy," Arkady had told him. "They can't afford to lose any equipment. They've got to score a lot of successes right away and get some cargo. Otherwise they're in trouble."

Since the Rock War, the U.S.A. had been balkanized far beyond the wildest dreams of the old states' rights crowd. The so-called central government no longer had its hands on interstate commerce and the result was a wild rush to impose tariffs all across the Midwest. In the West, close to the spaceports in California and Texas where the finished goods came down from the factories in orbit, the borders were free, but the Midwest saw no reason why it shouldn't profit from anything crossing its territory. A heavy duty was slammed on goods that passed through the states en route to elsewhere.

Which left the Northeast out of luck, as far as the distribution of Orbital-built products was concerned. They got some from the spaceports in the Florida Free Zone, but the Free Zone was under bloc control, and the Orbitals like to keep the market hungry for their product. Artificial scarcity was the name of the game, and the Northeast paid with its dwindling wealth for the scraps the Orbitals doled out. The West had more to offer the Orbitals, and the goods were cheaper and more abundant there—cheap enough to ship them to the markets in the Northeast at a fat profit, so long as there wasn't much duty to pay along the way.

And so the first atmosphere jocks rode their supersonic deltas across the Alley with their midnight loads of contraband. And the Midwest responded, first by sending up radar planes and armed interceptor aircraft, then, when the action shifted from planes to panzers, by strengthening their ground defenses.

And now, in Missouri, by licensing privateers. The states were unable to keep up with the changes in smuggling technology, and so they decided instead to license a local corporation to chase the contraband for them. The fact that the Constitution authorized only the federal government to grant letters of marque and reprisal had been ignored; the Constitution is a dead letter anyway, in the face of Orbital superiority.

The privateers are authorized to shoot to kill, and are rewarded by ownership, free and clear, of whatever contraband they can secure. Reports spoke of impressive arrays of airborne radar, of heat sensors and weird sound detectors and aircraft full of sensing missiles and bristling with guns.

From Gridley Cowboy moves slowly northeast, taking his time, mapping the flying radar arrays. They are drone aircraft, ultralights under robot control, solar-powered to stay aloft forever, rising with the sun and gliding slowly earthward at night, only having to return to base for servicing every couple of months or so. They are in constant microwave communication with computers on the ground, ready to scramble aircraft if anything suspicious pops up.

They are so light that radar-homing missiles can't find them to shoot them down, and antiradiation homers would be spotted as they climbed, in plenty of time for the arrays to switch off before the missile arrives.

Cowboy is aiming for the wide area between New Kansas City and the Ozarks. People in the Ozarks are friendly, he knows, with a tradition of resistance to the people they call ''the laws'' that goes back at least to Cole Younger, but the terrain is too restrictive. Cowboy wants a fast run over the flat. The fact that this part of the state is where the privateers have concentrated their defenses is just a pleasant coincidence.

The sensor drones are turning lazy circles in the air as they glide downward on battery power, and Cowboy thinks he sees a pattern building that will allow him to slide into a blind spot that might last until he's fifty miles the other side of the Missouri border. As his panzer slides down the crumbling banks of the Marais des Cygnes and tears across flat mudbanks and muddy water, it extrudes a directional antenna and spits a coded message to the west, to where Arkady and the Dodger wait in Arkady's aircraft, turning its own circles over the plains of eastern Colorado.

The answering signal comes quickly, a strong broadcast to Arkady's people on the Kansas-Missouri border. There are other panzerboys out there, standing ready by their vehicles, waiting for the word . . . and when they receive it, their own panzers will hit the plains, moving swiftly and then stopping, tearing through fields in zigzag patterns, sending dust signatures aloft, tracking radar and infrared patterns across the computer displays of the privateers. The laws will have to expend a lot of effort tracking them down and apprehending them. And when found, the decoy panzerboys will surrender meekly enough—since they carry no contraband and will only be fined for the amount of bobwire they flattened during their runs, and do a little time for reckless endangerment. Arkady will cover the fines and legal fees, as well as their generous salaries. If the worst happens, their widows and orphans will have the benefit of insurance. It's well-paid work, and a training ground for ambitious panzerboys who want to run the Line.

But after the signal to the other panzerboys comes the Dodger's voice, dry as the Portales plains. "Arkady Mikhailovich would appreciate a little more information, here, Cowboy," he says. "He wants to know why you didn't report earlier."

"They can trace a message these days, Dodger."

The Dodger is silent for a while, getting a lecture from Arkady no doubt, and when his voice returns, it is less good-humored. "A squirt transmission via microwave is next to untraceable," he says. "Arkady says you should have reported when you got past the Kansas defenses."

"Sorry," Cowboy says cheerfully. "But I'm damn close to the Missouri line right now and I would just as soon not have to keep up this conversation while I'm trying to work."

There is another pause. "Arkady reminds you that he has a big investment in your panzer, and he wants to be kept informed of what his investment is doing."

"I aim to give him a nice return on his money," Cowboy says. "I don't plan to waste time with a lot of chatter. I've got a window right now, and I'm taking it. See you." And he switches off, making a note to send Arkady some worry beads from the East when he gets there.

The panzer climbs out of the Marais des Cygnes and increases its speed as it begins its run east. The drumming of corn on the bow increases to a steady hammer. Engine gauges are running orange to red. Green lights everywhere else. Steel guitars sing like angels in the mind and Missouri wails a siren song in accompaniment. Delivering the mail is a splendid thing.

The decoy panzerboys are causing a stir, and more radar arrays are being turned on, the ones unused so far in the hope their sudden appearance will catch the smugglers by surprise. Cowboy's blind spot is still a blank. He throws caution to the wind and decides to red out the engines. A half-heard message from his body signals he is being punched back in his seat, but he's got other things to think about. The panzer is airborne half the time, tearing up the low hills and flying over the crests, throwing corn and scattering wire, its voice a madwoman's wail. Neurons flicker in Cowboy's mind, pulsing their messages to his crystal, keeping the craft stable as it punches up and down. He's deep into the face as the control surfaces invade his mind, riding the wire edge of stability, skating the brink. Cowboy knows there will be deep bruises under his restraining straps, even through the padding.

He crosses the Missouri line between Louisburg and the rusting monument to the Marais des Cygnes Massacre. Parched Missouri is waiting for rain, and his dust plume is towering a hundred yards, but there's no one to see it. The control surfaces are getting used to the buffeting they're taking, and the movement is easier.

And then radar pulses from directly above as a new sensor drone is switched into the array. Cowboy's blind spot has become pistol-hot and the dust signature must look like a flaming arrow in the night. Cowboy is shutting systems down from red to orange to amber and trying to make himself smaller, but the radar is right overhead and there's no way to get out of its way. He slows down the lunging panzer and dives over the banks of the South Grand. His water plume is a lot lower than the dust and he wonders if he's made a successful evasion, but then other airborne arrays begin to flick into existence in the nearby sky and he knows what's going to happen.

His own radar shows a fishing rowboat frozen in place on the still water, and the panzer lunges for the bank, avoiding it. He cools the engines from amber to green—best to save fuel for later. He decides it's time to listen to what the laws have to say and switches on his police-band antenna. The privateers' transmissions are coded but the state cops' are not, and with a part of his expanded mind he listens to their calls of frustration as they try, with four-wheel vehicles, to follow the panzerboys as they whip their way across country. Occasionally a privateer controller comes on the air to give them advice. Cowboy has the impression that the state laws are somewhat reluctant to cooperate with free-lance mercenary enforcement, something he more or less suspected.

The radars seem to be circling more randomly now, as if they've lost him at least part of the time. The panzer is into Johnson County before Cowboy detects a radar boring toward him from the east, low enough to be attached to an aircraft. He triggers the explosive bolts that release the shrouds covering his weapons pods; the panzer will be less aerodynamic now and will require watching at speed. Cowboy cycles his engine displays from green to blue and makes a wide swing to the south, hoping to avoid the craft, and for a moment it seems to be working; the aircraft continues on to the north, but then suddenly it jinks, swooping directly for the panzer.

Cowboy feels a wave of alcohol leaping through his heart as the engine displays rocket up to red, the panzer shuddering as it spits flame. For a moment it tries to climb aloft, the wind humming through the weapons pods like the southeast trades through a windjammer's rigging, but gravity pulls hard on its vector and the panzer crashes down onto its cushion. As the indicators max out, Cowboy looses a radar decoy missile and kicks the panzer into a shuddering left turn, its starboard side scraping soil as the panzer mashes its cushion down. The missile continues on a straight course, its wide wings extended, keeping low to the ground. It has no radar-absorbent paint and so its signature should look about the size of an absorbent panzer; and its exhaust should attract anyone looking at infrared.

Cowboy kicks on the afterburners and makes tracks for the Father of Waters. Behind him he can see flashes in the night sky as the aircraft fires off its weaponry at his decoy. He hopes there are no citizens below; those sheaf rockets look really unpleasant.

There are no explosions he can see; the privateer aircraft continues its course for a while, slowing, and Cowboy slows, too, minimizing his infrared signal. Strong radar pulses are still coming from right overhead. Cowboy hears from the state laws that two of the decoys have been caught, which means more resources available for chasing him. The privateer is beginning to circle back in his direction, and Cowboy sees the strange silhouettes of a metal forest on the horizon; he changes course again and dives into it.

It's a forest of rectennas, miles wide, receiving the low-energy microwave coming down from a solar power-satellite high above, a burning fixed star in the heavens that symbolizes the prostrate Earth's dependence on the Orbital power. Cowboy threads his way neatly through the metal web on night vision alone. He's probably confused any signal the enemy radars are getting, but the privateer craft is still getting closer. The panzer emerges into a clearing, where a metal maintenance shack rusts on its slab of concrete, and in that brief moment Cowboy fires a chaff rocket straight up and dives among the alloy trees once more.

The chaff rocket climbs three miles and bursts, and suddenly Cowboy's gear is picking up radar signals and low-energy microwaves bouncing from everywhere. The chaff, wafting gently down from altitude, is composed of aluminum strips, one out of ten of which are implanted with a minichip and a tiny power source that records and then plays back any radio signal it receives. On Cowboy's radar displays it looks as if a vast radio Christmas tree has suddenly bloomed above the prairie. The people controlling the power grid are probably going crazy. Once out of the rectenna forest, Cowboy kicks in the afterburners again. The aircraft's signal is lost in all the chaff and he figures it's time to run. His computer maps show a riverbed ahead. It seems a good time to go fishing.

The riverbed is dry and winding, but it leaves the enemy craft far behind. There's a lot of coded radio traffic flying around, each message echoed by the chaff as it slowly flutters down. There's a frantic quality to it, and there's one message from the privateers that requests assistance from the state cops, broadcast in the clear and repeated with endless, echoing lunatic efficiency by the chaff. Cowboy grins and climbs out of the riverbed, running northeast.

It looks as if the chase craft are all down and fueling because he's well across the Missouri north of Columbia before he runs into any more trouble. He is expecting it, cooling his engines on green and utilizing cover, because the police radios are telling him another two of his decoy panzerboys have been taken and the rest driven to ground. Suddenly there's radar pulsing from directly overhead again and another radar dopplering in from the northwestern horizon, as if it's just hopped up from somebody's airfield. Cowboy slows and turns away: no good. He looks for a piece of extensive woods and can't find one, and suddenly there's another radar signature arcing in fast from the south. He fires another chaff rocket and alters course once again. The two seem confused for a moment by the chaff, but then the southern one corrects its course, followed by the northern craft. The southern craft has probably spotted him on infrared and is vectoring the other one in.

Targeting displays flash like scarlet madness in the interior of Cowboy's mind. A snarl from his throat echoes the amplified roar of the combustion chambers, and the panzer gouges earth as it spins right, toward the oncoming southern radar source. Cowboy turns his own radar off to discourage homing missiles and navigates on his visual sensors alone, his mind making lightning decisions, neurotransmitters clattering against his headswitches like hail, the interface encompassing the whole flashing universe, the panzer and its systems, the corn thundering under the armored skirts, the blithering chaff, the two hostile privateers burning out of the night. His craft threatens to leave the Earth; its bones moan with stresses and the weapons pods shriek in the wind. The air is full of dismembered corn. Two fences are flattened, and the tall silhouette of a silo spears the blackness, the panzer's optics making it seem to curl in toward him, threatening. He can see the enemy now, a conventional helicopter speeding toward him at tree level, its minigun flashing. He fires an antiradiation homer right between the privateer's eyes just as the Chobham over his head begins to ring to the sound of cannonfire. Sparks flood his exterior displays and he flinches as he loses an eye.

Then he is past, and through the armor and the bucking of the vehicle he can hear the roar of the chopper as its blades flog apart the overhead sky. The antiradiation homer missed: too much chaff confusing things, or the copter got its radars off in time. But now there's another sound, the tone of a heat-seeker asking its permission to fly, and Cowboy triggers the bird and hauls the panzer to the left, feeling as from a dim distance the lurch as the craft slaloms over a hillcrest in a spray of corn dust, sliding sideways on its cushion.

The chopper dies in a flame of blazing glory, scoring the field in an eruption of fuel and weaponry. The silo stands in rearview like a tombstone, flickering red. There is mad chatter on the radio, a scrambled microwave screaming, still recognizably human, amplified and echoed to the point of yammering lunacy by the falling chaff. The privateer coming from the northwest has just seen what happened to his comrade. The panzer is trying to turn on a reverse camber, skidding on a bed of corn silk as gravity and momentum try to turn it over. Cowboy can feel the spin of the gyros in his head, trembling as the hovercraft rides the brink.

The privateer craft wails overhead with a banshee shriek and Cowboy can see its underbody reflecting the red flickering of its comrade's pyre. A coleopter, turbines throbbing inside the rotating shrouds that top the stubby wing tips. It's a light jet-fighter craft that can take off vertically and hover, combining the best qualities of a subsonic pursuit craft and helicopter, at a considerable expense in fuel consumption. Cowboy hopes to find a window to launch another missile, but the blazing fuel just over the rise is confusing his sensors and the coleopter suddenly banks into a swift turn, scattering thermite decoys that burn like miniature parachute suns, and the window that fluttered open for a second is gone. The panzer hurls itself above the rise again and skates along the edge of the red glare cast by the scattered chopper, heading for the spire of a silo in the distance.

Plans flicker through Cowboy's liquid-crystal switches with the fluid electric grace of heat lightning. The smartest thing for the privateer to do is to keep the panzer in sight and guide others in without risking itself. In that case, Cowboy will have to go after the coleopter; but on the other hand, radar is still hopelessly confused and the coleopter can't tell the infrared of the panzer from that of the wreck, and this is Cowboy's chance to fly. He decides to cycle up to red and run for the safety of Egypt on the other side of the Mississippi.

But the privateer pilot must have eyes like singularities, devouring worlds, or there's some remarkably fine equipment on the 'opter—maybe one of those sound detectors?—because the coleopter comes out of its bank and heads right for the panzer's exhaust. No error. Cowboy cuts in the afterburners and hopes there's some cover just over the horizon. His antiradiation homers won't work in the chaff, and neither will his radar-directed missiles. He can't get a good infrared signature from the coleopter's bow and so the heat-seekers won't be lucky, either.

The terrain is irregular, and suddenly the corn is replaced by hemp, high as an elephant's eye and bursting with resin. That will make the ground less slick than the corn did, maneuvers less critical. The enemy pilot is burning right for him in apparent anger over what happened to his friend, and Cowboy knows he can use that anger as an aikido master uses his opponent's kinetic energy against him—but first the engines have to max red, afterburners bleeding alcohol fire, and the panzer has to take some punishment.

Cowboy is airborne as he floats across the crest of a rise, and a tug on the controls slews the skimming panzer to starboard just as the coleopter triggers a weapons pod and half a dozen shaped-charge rockets set the hemp ablaze. There is pounding on the Chobham, and a blaze of red lights on Cowboy's displays tells him that one of his own weapons pods has been penetrated by a jug-sized minigun round that's wiped out a couple hundred K's worth of advanced electronics. The sensors aiming his own minigun are shot away just as he decides to trigger some rounds. The neurotransmitters clattering against Cowboy's brainchips are smoking with the sour tang of adrenaline, and the coleopter pilot seems to have tempered anger with caution because he's matching speed without overshooting, and so Cowboy has no choice but to rocket on across the good earth of Missouri, building momentum, jinking left and right, clawing against the hemp for the leverage that will send his enemy cartwheeling to the mat. The minigun hammers, hammers. The panzer's sensors flare and die.

And then Cowboy opens new floodgates of alcohol and his engines cry in anguish as in calculating fever he slams in his thrust reversers. Even through its chemical slumber his body wails as the straps dig in. Half the comp displays are frozen in utter shock. The coleopter staggers as it tries to maintain its position, but it's too close to the earth to stall in hopes of losing momentum and its flaps are already fully deployed. The pilot knows what's going to happen and is loosing thermite flares even before his half-controlled and thoroughly doomed craft whispers overhead and the tone sounds on Cowboy's aural crystal. Cowboy's missiles leap from his remaining pod, the port turbine explodes with red energy, and the coleopter whimpers in metallic pain and corkscrews in.

The panzer flees across the red-scored night. Egypt is near, but so is the dawn. Staggering systems reawaken; Cowboy gentles the engines and manages to keep them alive. Time to find a place to hide and wait out the day.

Cowboy gets across another fifty miles of country before being reined in by dawn and the sense of an approaching wave of enemy. There are thousands of abandoned farms and barns here, old privately owned places that couldn't compete with the Orbital-controlled agriplexes and their robot farms. Cowboy knows of quite a few where the old buildings, next to the robot-farmed cornfields, remain empty.

A new taste comes through the face mask as Cowboy's body is reawakened. A barn appears on his sensors, one of the long, narrow type, rectangular in cross section, designed to store baled hay in the days before the Orbitals built their big warehouses, one for every hundred farms. Carefully, with gentle precision, he shoulders aside the heavy double doors and guides the panzer into the concrete-walled barn. He remembers, just before he shuts off the engines, that he forgot to send Arkady a message.

Well, let him watch the news and find out that way. Cowboy will just tell him he couldn't get a signal through all the chaff.

With a touch of regret, Cowboy unfaces. Waves of delayed pain flame into his mind as the displays slip into night. His body is bruised and aching and slick with sweat. He takes the carbine from its scabbard and pops the hatch.

The barn smells like must and unburnt hydrocarbons. Cowboy turns the Kikuyu eyes to infrared and scans the barn. He can hear the scuttle of rats. With his hardwired nerves he can fire the carbine with perfect accuracy at anything the eyes can see.

And the eyes can see two people, huddled under some ancient straw in a concrete corner. Cowboy pauses for a moment, straining to find the signature of weapons, and then, keeping the carbine in his hand, he reaches below for a tradepack.

The cooling engines give out metallic crackles, and the doorframe, behind, is silvered with approaching dawn. Cowboy drags himself out of the hatch and climbs down the long frontal slope of armor, his boots sliding in the sticky hemp resin.

"Where you folks from?" he asks.

"New York. Buffalo." The voice is young and scared. Cowboy nears them and sees a pair of ragged kids of sixteen or so, a boy and a girl, the both of them huddled in a single sleeping bag atop a small pile of old straw. A pair of threadbare rucksacks sits in a forlorn heap near them.

"Heading west?" Cowboy asks.

"Yes, sir."

"I'm going east. Bet you're tired of living on a diet of roasting ears," Cowboy says. He lofts the tradepack and it thumps on concrete next to the pair. They flinch at the sound. "There's some real food in there, freeze-dried and canned. Some good whiskey and cigarettes. And a check postdated to next Monday, for five thousand dollars."

There is silence, broken only by the sound of breathing and the scuttle of rats.

"In case you don't get the picture," Cowboy says, "the check will only be good if I finish my run."

The two look at each other for a moment, then at Cowboy. "You don't have to pay us," the boy says quietly. "We wouldn't—we're from the East, you know. We know what you're doing. I wouldn't be alive if it weren't for some bootleg antibiotics."

"Yeah. Well. Just consider the money a goodwill gesture," Cowboy says, and turns away to place some remote sensors outside and close the barn doors.

Time for a rest.

Back in the panzer the cabin smells of sweat and adrenaline. Cowboy takes off the g-suit and removes the electrodes, then gives himself a sponge bath from one of his jerricans. He eats some prepared food that's heavy on protein, drinks something orange-flavored and packed with replacement electrolytes. He rolls into the little bunk.

The adrenaline still has him pumped up and all he can see behind his closed lids are the burning afterimages of maps and displays and engine grids climbing toward orange, of exploding fuel and rockets flaming through the night with pyrotechnic abandon. And, somewhere behind the neon throbbing visions, a little claw of resentment.

It has always been enough to run the Alley, to mesh his soul with throbbing turbopumps and wailing afterburners, bringing the mail from one free zone to another. There was an ethic in it, clean and pure. It was enough to be a free jock on a free road, doing battle with those who would restrict him, keep him bound to the Earth as if he were nothing more than a mudboy. It hadn't mattered what he was carrying. It was enough to know that, whatever the state of the rest of the country, the blue sky over his own head was the air of freedom.

But of late there has been a suspicion that adherence to the ethic may not be enough. He knows that while it is one thing to be a warrior noble and true, it is another to be a dupe.

Suppose you are an Orbital manufacturer, interested in keeping control of your markets on the planet. You've won all the political control that is necessary, and you've kept prices high by controlling supply. But still, you're smart enough to know that where there is scarcity, black markets will develop. Most of the stuff—the drugs and a lot of the hardware, anyway, if not the special alloys—can still be made Earthside, but more expensively.

If you know that the black market will develop anyway, why not develop it yourself? You can keep the thirdmen supplied with a trickle of product, enough to make themselves rich. You can afford enough muscle to keep the competition down, and in the meantime you are not only dominating the legitimate market, you are controlling supply in the underground as well. You can create and supply a demand in two separate markets, the legitimate and illegitimate.

Where does Arkady get his cargo? The question was beginning to have an important sound to it.

But now the adrenaline has burned out of Cowboy's body and his aches are dragging him down. He won't find any answers in a deserted barn in Missouri and his thoughts have become muddled. It's time to slip under the narrow wool trade blanket, marked with the line that means its value had once been equated with a beaver pelt, and prepare his mind and body for the last lunge across the Alley.

It's late afternoon before he wakes, and finds the kids gone. The postdated check flutters from one of the panzer's aerials. Cowboy plucks it from the spike and looks at it for a while, wonders about ethics and debts, symbols and actions, and the thing that in olden times they called honor. Somewhere near here, he knows, there is another piece of free and lucid sky.

He does his chores, replacing the sensors that were blown away by the privateers, scraping off most of the hemp resin along with the corn and wheat chaff that's adhered to it, spraying antiradiation paint over the dings in the Chobham. The minigun has really given the craft a working over, and it's lucky more systems weren't breached. He doesn't have much in the way of weapons left, but then there's only a few miles to the Big Muddy.

He sits in his padded couch and goes into the eye-face, listening to his sensors for a few minutes. Traffic seems normal. But then, as the day wanes, there's a lot of talk to and from some airport tower in the neighborhood. The place must be only a few miles away because he can hear each syllable clearly. The chatter is uncoded and seems innocuous, but a lot of the aircraft seem to have the same prefixes. Cowboy begins to find this interesting.

Suppose you were a privateer commander angry over a couple of losses the previous night. Suppose you'd worked out that the panzer you were chasing was beaten up, possibly disabled, and in any case couldn't have made it over the Mississippi before dawn. Suppose you wanted to get some revenge for your friends who had been burned beyond recognition in a Missouri cornfield the previous night.

You'd concentrate your forces on the airfield nearest to where the panzer is waiting for nightfall, and you'd have some picket planes move over the area with the best in detection technology, and the rest would be sitting on the runway apron ready to vector in on the panzer once it's spotted, and turn it into a lightly armored grease spot in some scorched little piece of prairie. That's what you'd do.

Cowboy puts a map on the display and finds something called the Philadelphia Community Airport only four miles away. It's far too small to have this kind of traffic coming in and out, and it's just over a ridge and through some woods. Cowboy begins to smile.

By dusk he's strapped in his couch and has the engines sweetly warming. He reverses them gently and backs out of the barn, then moves at low speed across some half-rusted bobwire and along the length of the ridge, not quite daring to put his radar signature, however briefly, on top of it. There's a dirt road here and he finds it, threads along it through a grove of pine that carries with it a memory of the smell and the sound of sweet breezes, the soft pillow of needles underfoot. He leaves the road and moves through a damp bottom, where the sound of his engines is muffled by leaves and moss. Then, moving in a roundabout track, he climbs a woody plateau, nudging young pine, until his expanded vision sees a little radar tower silhouetted against the sunset.

They are all there, a dozen or more warcraft squatting like evil metal cicadas, sunset flames reflecting off their polished bodies, the barrels of their guns, the pointed noses of the weapons in their pods. The airships have slogans and cartoons painted on their noses, evocative of swift mechanical violence, warrior machismo, or the trust of the gambler in the instrument of his passion: *Death from Above, PanzerBlaster, Sweet Judy Snakeyes, Ace of Spades*. There are a few techs walking about on the apron, tools in their hands. Cowboy permits himself a moment of adrenaline triumph before he cuts loose.

As the panzer trembles on the verge of the clearing Cowboy has a brief image of a runner poised on splayed fingertips, his feet in the blocks, his flesh molding the sinew in which the coiled energy waits, a faultless perfection, for the end of stillness. He unleashes the power and a covey of quail burst like scattershot from before the panzer's oncoming bow. The engines cycle from murmur to thunder to shriek, and Cowboy can see the techs stand for a moment of frozen horror as the panzer lunges from the trees, mashing down a fence like an armored cyclone, a piece of roaring mechanical vengeance straight from the Inferno, and then the men in coveralls scatter, crying warning.

Too late. The armored panzer is traveling at over a hundred across the flat ground before it brushes aside the first helicopter. The panzer is heavier by far and the *Ace of Spades* folds like the hollow death-white abandoned skin of an insect. Cowboy's popped up his minigun turret from beneath its armored cover and has it firing behind him into the wreckage, sparking off the fuel. *Sweet Judy Snakeyes* crumbles in front of the armored skirts, then a coleopter named *Death from Above*, then another called *Hanging Judge*. Through one of his sensors he catches a glimpse of pilots tumbling out of the airport lounge, coffee cups still in their hands, eyes and mouths wide as they watch the conflagration. Then burning fuel begins to set off ammunition and the pilots drop their drinks and scatter like the quail for cover.

Steel and flaming aluminum alloy storm on the Chobham. In the end Cowboy counts fourteen wrecks on the runway verge. He mashes down some more fence and follows the Salt River to the Father of Waters, crossing between Locks 21 and 22, unmolested by things that fly in the night. Though the sun is long gone, even from deep in Illinois he can still see the western horizon glowing red. He suspects he will hear no more of privateers.

The Illinois defenses face north against a breed of blond, apple-cheeked panzerboys who run butter and cheese across the Line from Wisconsin, and Cowboy expects no trouble. As he gentles the hovercraft up to a fueling barge on the Illinois River, Cowboy decides it's time to face the music and extrudes a directional microwave antenna and points it at the western horizon.

"Pony Express here," he says. "Sorry to be a little late with the report, but I got myself an antenna shot away." There is a kind of angry growl of static in reply, *b*'s and *p*'s like magnum rounds, and Cowboy grins as he turns down the volume and talks right over the voice.

"I'm not picking you up very well, but that's okay," he says. "I'm in Illinois right now, and I thought I'd mention that I've just about run out of Alley and that in the last twenty-four hours I've accounted for sixteen aircraft belonging to those undercapitalized bastards. You can read it in the papers tomorrow. Save me some copies for my scrapbook."

The buzzing sound in his ears is miraculously stilled, and Cowboy grins again. "Adios," he says, and he turns off the radio and sits in sweet and blissful silence while he watches the fuel gauges climbing upward, toward where he floats in the sky, a distant speck in the eyes of the other panzerboys, so high in the steely pure azure that to the mudboys and dirtgirls of Earth he is invisible, an icon of liberation. He has not simply run the Alley, he has beaten it, smashed the new instrument of oppression, and left it a mass of half-melted girders and blackened plexiglas amid a pool of flaming fuel and skyrocketing ammunition.

Kentucky is a state that figures to make more money from free-spending thirdmen and panzerboys than they can from taxing what they do, and it's an easy ride across Egypt to the Ohio. Burning across the river, he encounters none of the riverine patrol hovercraft that Ohio has out this way. Cowboy follows some nameless little creek up into the free state until it comes to a farm road, and then he makes another radio call explaining where he is.

What he's doing is legal in Kentucky, but the state does not appreciate large potentials for sudden violence within its borders, so all the stuff in the weapons pods is very much against the law. Cowboy has to wait up his little farm road for a crew to come along and pull them from the vehicle, and while he waits he takes the torn postdated check from his pocket and looks at it for a long while. By the time a truck full of mudboys comes bouncing along the corrugated road, he's got things figured out.

It matters, he decides. It matters where the chloramphenildorphine is coming from and it matters who bankrolls Arkady.

In Cowboy's hand is something that represents an obscure, indefinable debt to an anonymous pair of Alley rats, a debt as hard and cutting as Solingen steel, and the obligation is simply to find out.

It is no longer enough to be the best. Somehow, as well, it matters to be wise. To know on whose behalf he wields the sword.

And if he discovers the worst? That the thirdmen are masks worn by the Orbital power?

Then another debt is called. The interest alone is staggering, will take years to pay. But he's called himself a citizen of the free and immaculate sky too long to accept the notion that his world of air has bars on it.

There is a polite knock on the hatch, and he puts the check back in his pocket. The mudboys are telling him it's time to move. Somewhere in his mind, a steel guitar is singing. . . .

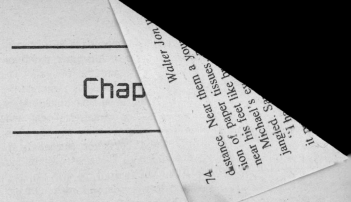

The city is melting, its outlines blurring in the August heat, the buildings swaying. Sarah closes her eyes and rests her temple against the cool metal frame of the window. Images of flame pulse orange and red on the backs of her eyelids. Just below the window frame, the cool air duct seems to whisper, to urge her in a strange, occluded tongue toward some course of action. She does not know what it wants. She shakes her head, feeling exhaustion beating at her.

"Cunningham's people are offering money for you, mi hermana." It is the soft voice of the Hetman. "I have let it be known that anyone who accepts their offer is no longer my friend. But that can only go so far. There are many who will do their job for them. And they have only to keep a watch on Daud."

Sarah opens her eyes. The city melts. "I know," she says.

She turns to face him. They are standing in a corner of the hospital waiting room, a circular chamber cantilevered high above the city in a corner of the hospital tower, its mirrored windows facing in a dozen directions like multiple insect eyes. A vid set blithers in a corner, stared at without interest by two Cuban women, sisters, each with vast makeup eyes and eyebrows painted like wings. Their father is in the last stages of viral Huntington's, his mind gone: he thinks they are harpies, come to eat his liver while he is chained to the rock of his disease. Passively they await his dying at a

...ng man cries softly into a succes-
...Twisted pastel colors litter the floor
...oken flowers.

...es are watery, red-rimmed. His gestures are
...ah suspects he's coming down from something.
...ve a job for you," he says. "It's not even illegal, and
...ays in gold, very well." He names a sum, and from the
size of it Sarah knows it has a high risk factor. Michael is an
honorable man, at least as thirdmen go, but charity is not one
of his traits.

Sarah walks to a chair and lets herself sink in it. Orange
plastic cushions, trying to be cheerful. She puts her head
down. The air is heavy with the smell of stale cigarettes.

"Who will I be working for?" Hopelessly.

Daud lies in a room a few doors away amid the blinking
eyes that are the LEDs of his machines. He is conscious now,
pain masked by doses of endorphins far greater than he took
even at the height of his addiction. His body is striped by
bright pink tissue, all factory-new, including a whole lower
arm. His legs are still swathed in gel, awaiting transplant of
tissue and muscle. And the transplants await new funds.

Sarah is running low on chloramphenildorphin. It was
supposed to be scarce and in high demand, but a new source
appeared just when she needed to pay for Daud's first bills,
the price plummeted. Normally she would have waited for
the price to rise again, but the hissing machines that kept
Daud alive were indifferent to market conditions. . . . She
had to put the 'dorphin on the street, even at the lowest value
in months. She wonders if Cunningham had somehow arranged it.

She is poison now, and knows it. Her usual sources of
income are gone. Normally she works as a bodyguard, but
who wants a guard who will draw fire? And as for the special
jobs . . . she hasn't had an offer. There is word that she
comes tangled up with matters no one else wants to touch,
that her profile is far too high. She can make a few street
deals, move things for other people who don't want to move
their action personally, but that won't pay for the hospital

and would also expose her, keep her too much in the public view, never knowing if any of the people she is hustling for will be eager to collect Cunningham's reward.

So. "Who will I be working for?" As if the answer mattered.

Michael the Hetman stares out the window, his face bleached by the sun. "For me," he says. "There is a job . . ." He screws up his face and shrugs. "There is maybe something wrong with it. I can't tell. Everything *seems* right, but the feeling is wrong. I want you to watch it for me."

Sarah looks up at him, wondering if this is another oblique warning like the one from Cunningham. As if Michael is maybe finding her too hot to shelter anymore, taking too much pressure from the people he does business with. Wants to move her out where she will be a target.

"Who's dealing?"

As if *that* answer mattered. She would have to take the job no matter how bad it smelled.

"I've taken delivery of a new shipment," Michael says. He frowns and moves to the next chair. His calf-high soft leather boots creak as he sits. "Crystal computer matrices," he says thoughtfully. "Fifteen thousand of them. High quality, from a source that's never delivered so well before. New boys just reaching the big markets, maybe. Or maybe thirdmanning for someone else. I can't tell."

"You want me to guard it?"

"Yes. Among other things." The Hetman sighs and rubs his chin. "Normally it would take me some time to move that kind of quantity. Months. But now there's someone up north, in Pennsylvania, who approached Andrei, wanting matrices in quantity. Will pay well for them." His liquid eyes turn to Sarah. "I can think of no reason not to sell. Andrei wants the deal badly. But there are too many coincidences here, mi hermana."

Andrei, Sarah knows, is one of the Hetman's lieutenants. She watches as Michael fumbles in his pocket for a Russian cigarette.

"Someone may be trying to set me up, but I can't think

who, or why." Crimping the end. Lighting it with a match that trembles. His hands are liver-spotted, old man's hands. "These people I'm dealing with are small men, and if they hijacked the cargo they wouldn't last long. Unless they have protection. But no one has that kind of strength, and right now I'm friends with everybody here on this coast. No sign that anyone's getting their moves ready. So maybe you'll be working for me for nothing."

"You don't feel that, Hetman," Sarah says. "Or you wouldn't be hiring me. Not at that price."

He gives her a long, expressionless glance, his eyelids jittering a nervous reply to Sarah's words, the cigarette smoke drifting ceilingward. Behind them the video begins to hype some new cocaine substitute, guaranteed nonaddictive, the audio filled with the tasteful hissing of compressed gases, the delighted exclamations of a young couple obviously in love. The cigarette flutters in the corner of Michael's mouth as he speaks.

"I'm hiring a panzerboy," he says. "If they're trying for a hijack and expecting to be able to knock out a truck, they'll be surprised. Andrei is handling the deal, the money. He'll have friends to protect him, but I want you to ride along in the panzer. Watch the deal, watch the panzerboy. You're hardwired for firearms?"

"Pistols and machine pistols." She shrugs. "Guns have no style," she says.

He smiles, a little wistful. As if he has heard this declaration many times, and knows that guns always seem to matter in the end. "I will get you a Heckler and Koch, seven-millimeter. You will practice with it?"

"When are we running?"

"Saturday."

"I'll practice tomorrow. If you can get me the gun by then."

"I will send a boy to meet you, take you to the range, then collect the gun when you are chipped in with it. Meet you when?"

"Tomorrow. The Plastic Girl, noon."

The Hetman draws on his cigarette and nods. Sarah can see the reflection of the vid in his eyes, hears the jarring resumption of a South American comedy, the canned laughter raucous in reply to shrill Spanish. "I hope I am wrong about this, mi hermana," says Michael. His voice is filled with Russian sadness that is no less genuine for its being theatrical. "I would be sorry to see another war. Just when things seem a little settled."

A war would mean work for Sarah; but she doesn't want it either. She knows that the only important war is already over, and that both she and Michael have already lost it, that any fighting here in the American Concessions is over the scraps the Orbitals had left behind, not thinking them worth the bother.

The Hetman rises to his feet. His hands make nervous movements. Sarah rises with him.

"I will go arrange for the gun," he says. A long worm of ash falls from the end of the cigarette, leaving a fingerprint of gray dust on his vest. If he is responding to pressure, Sarah thinks, if he is ready to betray her, then it will be tomorrow. When the boy comes with the gun, he will use it. She will try to be ready for it, poised to make her move, if that's what's really in the cards. She raises her hand to her throat, like a gypsy woman touching iron.

His eyes are unfocused, looking not at Sarah but at what will come, the future that, from the direction of his dreaming gaze, seems to be waiting above her right shoulder. She feels as if she should turn her head and see what is there.

"Thank you, Michael," Sarah says.

He turns his wise eyes to her, says nothing. She fights an impulse to put her arms around him, to seek a piece of comfort here in the sterile brightness, ignoring the fact that this is business and that this man may already have arranged for her death. . . . But it's a death she could almost welcome, feeling as if her own soul fled when she watched Danica's eyes turn to marble, that it is lost somewhere, with all the things that had seemed to give her meaning. Where does the shaped charge go when it has done its task? It flies apart, needles of steel each pursuing its own end. Scrap, seeking oblivion.

Once, she thinks dully, there was a purpose to this. Her life had intent, a wider focus. A direction, upward, out of the gravity well and into the black enveloping purity of airless space. Now the focus has narrowed. There is only the single imperative, Survive this Moment. The past scarcely matters; the future will be dealt with, instant by instant, as it arrives. Each tick of the clock, a new burden, a new application of the imperative. The Hetman will help her get through this moment, provide another brief imperative. Survive until tomorrow, attend the meet at the Plastic Girl. Then survive the meet, if possible.

The boy across the room weeps, shreds another tissue. "Clever of them," the Hetman says, "to go through Andrei, and not come direct. Knowing that Andrei would add his pressure to theirs." The voice is reflective, reaching into the ether for the enemy that may exist there, trying to know his mind.

"I'll meet your boy," Sarah says. And leaves, before the pain in her throat breaks free.

Daud is only a dozen doors away, sharing his room with an old man who is having his hips rebuilt. The flowers that Sarah and the old man's children have brought do not entirely mask the smell of chemical disinfectant. In an upper corner the video is showing the same graceless comedy that was playing in the waiting room. The old man is watching intently and does not acknowledge Sarah's presence.

"Hello, Daud," she says.

LEDs pulse green in Daud's corner, machines make ticking noises as they perform their obscure tasks. A vid screen shows a succession of jagged parabolas. He is breathing on his own these days, and his heart beats for itself. Over Daud's head gleams a mobile of stainless steel, the bars and weights that he is supposed to use to exercise his new arm. The chemicals he was taking to alter his hair color have been discontinued, and his hair, where it has grown in after being shaved, is brown; there is a bald spot on one side of his head,

pink with new skin. A gauze patch is taped over the eye
socket that will soon be filled with a Kikuyu implant. From
beneath the patch a wire trails to the computer on the headboard, keeping the optic nerve alive. The sheet is tented over
the stumps of his legs, and from beneath it come the tubes
that are keeping the tissue and bone alive in its coating of
gel.

Sarah bends over the bed to kiss him. She pulls a pack of
cigarettes out from her pocket, lights one for him, and puts it
in his mouth. His remaining eye is alert as it follows her
movements: he has developed a remarkable tolerance to the
doses of endorphin they have been giving him.

Daud swallows. There is a plastic button on his throat
where the tracheotomy went in, where the machine had fed
him air for weeks. His voice is ragged, forced up the damaged trachea, made harsher by the cigarette smoke. "Where's
Jackstraw?" he asks. "He told me he'd come."

"I haven't seen him." She doesn't want to tell Daud that
Jackstraw will probably not come again, will have long ago
found another boy to take Daud's place. For weeks Jackstraw's been just a voice on the phone that answers Daud's
calls without enthusiasm, that cuts him off with talk of
business, sudden guests, clients' demands. Anyone less iso-
lated than Daud, anyone less desperate, would have long
since got the message. When Jackstraw judges Daud can earn
money for him, he will visit.

"We can start building you legs now, in the next few
days," Sarah says. "One after the other, as soon as you're
strong enough. I just got a job." She tries to smile. "Would
you like the right first, or the left?"

He shakes his head. "Doesn't matter."

"I'll be gone a few days. From Saturday."

"On the job." He reaches up with his pink new arm and
flicks ash from his cigarette.

"Yes." Sarah can sense a fever behind Daud's eyes, some
desperate intensity building. He reaches up with his good
hand to one of the handgrips of the weight machine, clasping
it, then batting it away in frustration. When he speaks, he

keeps his teeth clenched on his cigarette, biting on each word.

"Jackstraw said he would try to get me some hormone maskers," Daud says. "Can you bring me some? Maybe tomorrow, before you leave?"

She looks at him in surprise at how desperate he is, how far from reality. She moves forward to sit on the edge of his bed, reaching for his hand. He snatches it away.

"*Will you bring me some?*" he cries.

She tries to speak calmly at the ache in her throat. "Daud," she says, "you can't suppress your hormones, not when you're trying to rebuild muscle tissue."

"You don't understand!" Desperate now. He is beating on the mattress with his fists, bounding from the mattress with each strike. A red warning light begins to blink from one of the machines, synching with a little mechanical peep. The old man in the next bed stirs restlessly, his comedy interrupted.

"I'm getting a *beard!* They *shave* me every morning now! I'm getting *older!*" He turns his head away, gasping for breath, coughing through the phlegm that coats his scarred windpipe. "They only want me young, my people," he says. "Jackstraw will only want me if I stay young."

"Daud." He is coughing too hard to speak. She takes his cigarette and stubs it out, then reaches for his hand with both of hers. He lets her take it now, holding it to her breast, stroking the hairs on its back with her knuckles. The warning peep dies, the light turns green again. "You'll be strong," she says. "You'll be young. You'll do fine. You have nothing to be afraid of." An incantation of hope, that she must repeat every day. Trusting that it will come true, or at least that Daud will come to believe it will come true.

"The ones who want cripples. I don't want to be with them." A breathy whisper, a last protest through the torn throat. Sarah kisses his hand, strokes the arm, says nothing. Says nothing at all, her language all mute strokes, comforting touch, until it is time to leave.

She calls a cab from the waiting room, tells it where to meet her, and goes out through one of the back doors, this one off the cafeteria. Her nerves are tingling as she steps near the loading dock where the food comes in, her eyes flickering left and right, looking for faces she hasn't seen before. She zips up her armored jacket and turns the collar up. It looks odd: the cafeteria workers have seen this behavior before, but still don't understand it. She ignores their stares, looks left and right, puts her weight on the metal door.

The heat almost takes the breath from her lungs. Instantly, it seems, her body is sheathed in sweat. Sarah dodges past a parked car to an alley, sees no one, moves quickly along the baking concrete. The hospital is huge and has a lot of exits: Cunningham's people can't cover them all.

The alley stinks of trash, urine, and frangipani. She stands for a moment, waiting, her eyes searching the blank windows above for sign of movement, for the foreshortening bullet. . . . The cab arrives within a minute: she almost flings herself into it. She feels herself safer here, though she knows it's an illusion. Last time they used a *rocket;* the fragile doors of a cab aren't going to stop their hardware if they really want to get in. She shouldn't even unzip her jacket, but she does.

Sarah looks over her shoulder as the cab speeds away and sees hurried motion through the rising waves of heat, an old piebald Mercury colored mainly primer gray, lunging from the curb before its passenger-side door can swing shut. . . .

Now she knows.

She is being hunted. Now, at this moment, not in some indefinite future. And Sarah's first feeling, to her surprise, is relief. The knot of tension at the back of her neck subsides; already her muscles seem to be easing, moving more fluidly. The waiting is over; she knows the situation and will be able to act.

But maybe she's being premature. First she should confirm things.

"Turn left here. Then right." The driver gives her a look in the mirror, but follows instructions. The Merc follows, keeping well back now that they have their quarry in sight. Sarah digs in her pocketbook for the control and turns on her police-band scanner, feeding the sounds directly into her audio nerves now that there's nothing else she needs to hear. Plenty of traffic, but none that sounds like it's from the Merc. She pops through a succession of channels. Nothing.

"Go straight." She's pretty sure the Merc is alone, that there aren't any backup cars. She lifts a hand to her throat, where her friend lives. *Weasel, I will call on you soon.*

"Left." The driver glances at her in his mirror again. They're heading straight for Venice.

Every coastal city has one, the low-lying district that was too big to dike off when the seas began to rise—only New York tried to keep the Atlantic at bay with its vast encircling wall, but the dikes were broken in the Rock War and now Manhattan is the largest Venice of all, fully half the island swept by gray waters at the spring tides, the boiling white wave caps climbing the empty streets, swirling among the broken ruins, snatching at the ankles of the people who still live there, who witness the slow erosion, the giving back to the sea, of the greatest city of legend. . . .

But there isn't much of a tide in Tampa Bay, just an inch or two, and the Venice here is more stable, the tranquil bay content to eat at the city only gradually, reserving its biggest bites for the summer storms. When the waters rose, the port was dredged and deepened but the residential and business quarters were allowed to fade away, the expensive beachfront property losing itself by millimeters to each tide. From the sea marches a progression of devastation, the farthest buildings out little more than rubble, perhaps a chimney or two; inland are the buildings that lean out to sea, as if in anticipation of the inevitable fall, or display their looted interiors following the collapse of a seaward wall. Some are almost untouched: the massive stone walls of some old office buildings remain upright, stained but defiant, and far inland, where the water only stands rippling a foot or two above the old pavement, the buildings stand intact, almost livable.

They have long since been gutted, of course, stripped of furniture, of wood and wiring. After the war the buildings were home to thousands of refugees come to undamaged, occupied Florida from the devastation in the North, and the desperate occupancy did not improve them. The refugees left some things behind on their own junk heaps, scavenged or homemade furniture, mattresses, rotting blankets, heaps of mildewed clothing. Things that could be of use to a new generation of refugees.

There aren't many who live in Venice now, only a few determined eccentrics, wanderers passing through to someplace else, and those on the run who have exhausted the other possibilities for places to hide. Runners like Sarah.

The taxi is on a road built above the tide line, a causeway looping out into the city of ruins and flanked by pellucid water, heading eventually across the bay to drowning St. Petersburg. Shattered windows seem to peer into the taxi. "Stop here," she says, and as the taxi's flywheel disengages, she begins shoving bills through the bulletproof shield. If it's to be her last, she thinks, let the tip be a big one.

The driver counts the money in surprise as Sarah skates down the embankment, warm water greeting her as radio conversations crackle and snarl in her head. Her ankles are embraced by water lilies as she walks down a shallow bay between a pair of apartment buildings. Behind her, not quite daring to look, she hears the Mercury's low hiss on the causeway. She steps through a doorway into an apartment foyer, the audio in her head dimming.

The room is full of darkness and bright, wet sounds. Silt rises around her feet as ripple reflections dance on the ceiling. Mildew crawls up ancient, defaced wallpaper, algae devour the scrawled obscenities of the last inhabitants. An imbecile fish strikes at her shin repeatedly, tasting something he wants. The elevator doors are open, revealing broken mirrors, a drooping cable. Walking carefully on the crusted carpet, Sarah takes the stairs to the landing and gives herself a two-second glance past a broken, dagger-edged pane.

The Merc has crawled another 300 yards down the causeway and pulled over to the side. Two heads are peering out as the traffic slices past. Sarah reaches for the control and turns off the voices in her head. The two are leaving the car, walking back along the highway verge. Sarah moves up the stairs.

Echoes of her childhood ring from the broken walls, from the litter lying on the landings. How many years did she live in a place like this? Hiding in the broken corners, playing in the glass-strewn hallways? Now to return, having—once again—no other place to run. Sarah, returning to the corridors of a childhood memory, come back to play another game of hide-and-seek.

The stairway is well lit through shattered windows, the walls streaked by every downpour. A mad profusion of fungus grows on each landing. Tired planks sag under the stained carpet. Sarah is leaving footprints in the sodden mess, a track for the two soldiers to follow.

It's an old trick, laying footprints down a hallway, then walking backward in one's old tracks. She moves with childhood ease, familiar scents and memories rising as she skates backward through the rubble. Then a leap to one side, into a darkened apartment, and wait, poised to move. A hiss of hardfire up each nostril to trigger her hardwired nerves, to make the neurotransmitters leap as they run jangling down the neural communications net. Listening. Tasting the sweat on her upper lip. Heartbeat and respiration climbing silently through the gears, ready to provide blood and oxygen to the tissues when the time comes. . . .

How many times had she done this as a girl? Hid in a dark room while the drunken hurricane that was her father raged outside, shouted his threats, banged on the doors, Daud's trembling arms around her while she tasted the scent of their mingled fear? But there are overlays on that childhood memory now, pictures of darker violence, of snagboys lying bloody in alleys next to their bags of merchandise, of runners caught in the sodium glare of police spotlights as their feet scrambled for traction on the wet concrete, of Weasel running its red cybernetic errands into the darkness of some terrified heart. But never anything like that earlier fear, the white nights with her father, the terror as the bedroom door finally gave way, the hinges tearing out amid pale moonbeam slivers of wood while her father stood silhouetted in the yellow hall light, the broken bottle in his hand. . . .

They are coming: Sarah can hear the brush of feet on the crumbling carpet. She blinks the sweat from her eyes, opens her mouth wide and tries to breathe deeply, silently. Weasel stirs in her throat, swallowing her tongue. It is possible that these two might actually have guns, and that will mean a very fast evaluation of their strength during the brief seconds they are visible to her, and perhaps a change of tactics. The drug is making her nerves leap, urging her to move. There are dim phantoms dancing at the peripherals of her vision. She forces herself to stand still.

The first one moves past, intent on the footprints, a silhouette for only a second—and Sarah sees a young man with jumpy eyes and a blond pompadour slicked forward, a sleeveless leather jacket, tattoos on the wiry upper arms, a club—no, a baseball bat—hanging loosely in the left hand. And then the next appears in the frame of the doorway, and Sarah is moving.

She sends the Weasel for his eyes, a straight-out strike like a flicker of lightning, but he's seen the movement out of the corner of one eye and manages to jerk his head around, and Weasel strikes a glancing blow to the cheekbone that leaves a red furrow. . . . But the strike has brought his hands up high to cover, leaving him open for the thrusting kick she delivers to his midsection with all the force of her moving body. He staggers, his arms flailing. The ice-gleam of a knife reflects shards of light over the carpet, disappears into the darkness. Sarah retracts Weasel and takes a gulp of air, already spinning toward the guy with the baseball bat. Both of these boys, she realizes now, are shorter than she is; she'll take whatever reach advantage she can.

A glance over her shoulder for a rear kick into the knifeboy's midsection that helps to propel her forward and the knifeboy back, he landing on his tail with an eruption of breath while Sarah flies like a spear to the target; but pompadour's too fast. The bat's swinging in a hissing arc before the boy even sees what's coming at him, and Sarah's moving forward and

knows she's going to be hit. She tries to buffer it with her
arm but takes it almost full force in the side, her armored
jacket spreading the impact but not enough. The breath goes
out of her in a rush and she slams into the wall; but as she
bounces she's already spinning inside the range of the bat.
She can smell the lilac scent of the grease on the boy's hair
as she goes for his eyes with her nails.

He drops the bat, which is what she wants, and grabs her
wrists, bearing down, hauling her arms apart, crucifying her
for the knife from behind. His tattoos ripple as he matches
her strength. She tries for his groin with her knee but he turns
a hip and takes the strike on his thigh. There is a grin on his
face now, partly just the rictus of combat, but Sarah can tell
that he's pleased he has a woman where he wants her,
helpless, spread across his front.

She puts Weasel through his left eye and the grin becomes
a bubbling scream. He falls, a bundle of random movements,
blood welling up into the ruined socket—Weasel may have
scarred part of the forebrain. Sarah's already retracting Weasel to strike again, spinning just in time to block a kick and a
punch from the knifeboy, but another punch strikes her breast
and she feels pain crackling up her all-too-efficient nerves.

He's wired—Sarah can tell that right away. The reflexes of
a second *dan* or so implanted in crystal in his animal brain,
hardwiring to boost his speed. But the reflexes of a five-foot-
two Korean do not necessarily adapt to a six-foot Occidental
without a lot of practice, and that kind of discipline is foreign
to most of the streetboys Sarah has ever met. . . . Sarah has
interwoven her own reflexes with those of her chips, making
the hardwired reflexes her own, integrating their patterns
with Weasel.

Their fight is sharp and close, the blood from his cut cheek
spattering her as they punch, grapple, butt. Weasel leaves
bloody weals on his forearms as he tries to block its strikes.
She comes in close and drives her forehead into his face, and
then she is standing over his unconscious body as she fights
for breath and listens to the sudden clamoring stillness.

Stars are flickering in the extremes of her vision. The pain that her fear had denied is having its revenge. Sarah massages her breast and ribs, breathing hard, leaning for a blessed moment against the mildewed wall. She finds the knife and baseball bat . . . and wonders, for a moment, what kind of message she wants to leave.

These are not Cunningham's people, obviously, just a couple of streetboys going for a reward, not fully understanding what league they were trying to play in. Vicious and stupid though they are, Sarah can't really bring herself to leave a pair of bodies here in the ruined hallway, but yet it might be politic to leave an example for other streetboys who might consider trying the same thing. A pair of high-visibility object lessons in plaster casts might work wonders.

The pompadour has lost part of his brain anyway, so Sarah settles for breaking his left arm with the baseball bat. The knifeboy will wake up with a pair of smashed collarbones. Sarah tosses the baseball bat through an apartment door, retrieves her pocketbook, and leaves with the keys to the Merc.

By the time Sarah climbs onto the causeway her ribs are throbbing with each step. The Mercury's seat is patched with duct tape and scorches her thighs with its baking heat. A Miraculous Medal hangs from the rearview mirror. She has to move the seat back to give room to her long legs.

She starts the machine and races up the causeway, heading for St. Petersburg, sweeping past the gutted shells of Venice. The sea breeze gusts through the window and cools her. She can feel the hardfire wearing away, her nerves slackening, the adrenaline wave teetering on the edge of a crash, and so brings the inhaler from her pocketbook and gives herself another rush to carry her across the waters of the bay.

In front of her a city is melting in the afternoon heat. She tastes the rushing wind as she arcs high over the water. Soon, Sarah knows, she will reach the peak, begin her fall. But not just yet. For now, she wants only to keep climbing.

Chapter Five

Arnold is a young panzergirl with wiry, muscled arms and dark hair cut short around her sockets. She's got a good reputation, has been running free-lance for years. For the last two days, she's been a member of Cowboy's party.

It's been a ten-day celebration, a series of binges up and down the Rockies, filled with a revolving-door succession of panzerboys, mechanics, thirdmen, retired deltajocks who could never learn the new technology . . . the large, loose, migratory network that likes to think of itself as the underground. They've been toasting their new legend, the man who opened Missouri to their midnight traffic. The party's current location is the bar of the Murray Hotel in Livingston, Montana, and it will probably stay here for a couple of days while people move in and out, buying Cowboy drinks and trying to absorb a part of his legend.

Cowboy's panzer is sitting in a hidden barn in West Virginia. It's too dangerous to bring it back, even on a legitimate run on the highways without cargo, so Cowboy took the bullet train west from Pittsburgh to Santa Fe, and since then he's been careening in his Maserati up and down the mountain states from one panzerboy watering hole to the next.

Talking to people, mostly. He's got reasons.

"Your last run had problems, right?" he says.

Arnold grimaces into her bourbon/rocks. Country hob thuds from the dance floor, where panzerboys and local ranchers are putting more energy into sizing each other up than into dancing. Some little blond girl has laser earrings that are tracking red fire on the walls and the other dancers, on the surprised face of the bartender. Cowboy can catch glimpses of her among the dance crowd.

"Two runs ago," Arnold corrects him. "One of the Sandman's fuel trucks didn't make the rendezvous. Had to hide the panzer in a fucking coulee for two days. With a town just over the next ridge. I could've been taken by a farmer in broad daylight."

"The Sandman ought to have paid you a bonus for that."

Her look is scornful. "Him? You kidding?"

"Someone," Cowboy says quietly, "ought to've made him."

The bourbon pauses en route to Arnold's lips. She puts the glass down and looks at him. "Who did you have in mind, Cowboy?"

The blond dancer's laser earrings track a dancing spot of crimson light across Arnold's cheek. Cowboy feigns nonchalance and signals the bartender for another round.

"Maybe *we* ought to've," he says.

She seems surprised by the notion. "The two of us?"

"The two of us. And some others."

Arnold glances over her shoulder, sees no one, and lowers her voice anyway. "What are you getting at?"

"Just that this business is getting real organized. The thirdmen have their networks on both coasts. They bribe people, run labs, work through cutouts. Hire people to hijack the stuff for them. They're not on the line themselves. The distributors all work for one another. The Orbitals have half the laws in their pockets. What risks are any of those people taking?"

"None," says Arnold. Just like Cowboy wants her to.

"We put ourselves on the line, Arnold," Cowboy says. "For piecework. We're work for hire. Sometimes we have agents working for us, like the Dodger, but if the Dodger cuts a deal that isn't enforced, he can't do anything about it. We're weaker than these other people, and sometimes we pay for it. You spent two days hanging your ass in a damn coulee, and none of it was your fault.''

The bartender brings the new round. Arnold looks over her shoulder again. ''I don't know if I should listen to this, man,'' she says. ''I'm in it for the ride, not the cargo.''

''I'm just suggesting that the people who take the risks ought to have something to say about what goes on.''

''You're talking union.''

''Nope. An association of independents. Just to keep the thirdmen up to the mark. To remind them that if it weren't for people like us, they wouldn't have their limos, their mountain homes, their cryo max.'' Cowboy jabs a finger into the bar to help make his point. ''We're the ones in the field making legends while the thirdmen are knocking back cinnamon vodka in their padded bar chairs.''

Arnold grins at him. ''Cinnamon vodka? Cryo max? You got a particular thirdman in mind?''

Cowboy figures she isn't ready, just yet, for what he has to say about Arkady. ''Not me,'' he says.

She shifts closer to him, leaning her elbow on the padded bar. ''If it weren't you saying this, C'boy, I'd turn around and walk right out of this bar.''

He smiles. ''Lucky it's me, then.''

Her artificial eyes look into his. ''How many people have you told about this?''

''Maybe half a dozen. I'm not broadcasting it.''

''You better not be. Shit.'' She tosses off the last of her bourbon, then reaches for the new glass. ''I still think I ought to walk out of here.''

''Walk then.''

She looks at him again, bites her lip. He holds her gaze for a long moment. She drops her eyes.

''I'll think about it,'' she says. ''That's all I'm saying.''

''Think about it as long as you need to. Think about it next time you have your ass on the line in some coulee.''

She shakes her head, laughs. ''If it weren't you, Cowboy . . .''

He grins, sips his drink. "It *is* me," he says. "It's lucky I exist."

Arnold's warning look appears suddenly as a pop-up minigun. She puts a hand on his arm. "Not so lucky for some people, if this actually works."

"I know."

"If these people find out about this, you won't live twenty-four hours."

"I told you. I'm being careful." He swallows bourbon "Who else do you think I should talk to? Who's safe?"

She looks over the room, chewing her lip. Red laserlight flickers in her eyes. "Vlemk, maybe. Ella. Soderman. Not Penn, he's too close to Pancho."

"Jimi Gutierrez?"

Arnold shakes her head. "Hard to say what that boy thinks. He's too crazy for his own good. He's got good instincts, but maybe he likes to talk too much."

A few more names come up, and Cowboy vetoes them. Arnold seems to take comfort from the fact that he doesn't take her every suggestion, that he really is being discreet.

The hob thuds to a finish, and dancers begin to disperse. Cowboy finishes his drink. "Think about it. Talk to me later," he says. "Right now, I think I'll dance."

"Yeah. Talk to you later." Her eyes abstracted, her face muscles tense. Thinking hard.

He walks up to the girl with the laser earrings. She's wearing a strange uniform coat across her shoulders and she doesn't look like one of the locals, but he's never seen her with the panzer crowd before. She looks up at Cowboy as he approaches, and he notes the curly hair, the inhaler in her hand. She fires a pair of torpedoes up her snub nose, then holds out the inhaler.

"Snapcoke," she says. "Want some?"

He takes the inhaler. "Is snapcoke your name?" he asks.

She gives a short, wired laugh. "Might as well be. But my name's Cathy."

The snapcoke numbs his nose and fires his nerves. Music begins to slam from the walls. Cathy turns out to be a

surprisingly energetic dancer, doing leaps and kicks that have
her laser earrings dancing red on the walls. They dance
the next two dances, then Cowboy offers to buy her a drink.
While they walk to the bar, he asks her about the uniform
coat.

"I'm a lieutenant in the Coast Guard," she says.

Cowboy's surprised. He didn't think the Coast Guard ex-
isted anymore. "No shit. Tell me more."

It turns out she runs a lifesaving cutter out of Norfolk,
plucking unlucky sailors from the forty-foot steel-gray chop
off Hatteras. She's on a three-week furlough, hitching across
the West and free-climbing vertical mountain walls just for
fun.

"I'm going to Yellowstone tomorrow. I'm climbing
Medlicott Dome." She looks at him. Her earrings dazzle his
eyes. "Want to watch?"

"I don't think I have any other plans."

But just then a new wave of panzerboys swarms into the
bar, just arrived from setting up a run across the Dakotas.
One of them is Soderman, and Cowboy particularly wants to
talk to him. He buys Cathy some more snapcoke and
apologizes.

"Business. You know."

She shrugs. "See you later, maybe." And fires a pair of
torpedoes to keep herself company.

Soderman's reaction is a lot like Arnold's. He looks at
Cowboy with a respect tempered with an uneasiness very
close to fear. "I don't know about this," he says. "If it were
anybody but you . . ."

Cowboy's heard this from just about everyone he's talked
to, and it's doing wonders for his sense of self-esteem. He
figures he's got enough prestige to put the machine together
and make it run, that enough panzerboys will think he's
making sense to join the association. But he also knows the
thirdmen won't like this at all, that they might consider it a
regrettable necessity to make sure Cowboy doesn't come
back from his next run. So he's spreading the word. Quietly.

Hoping to make the thing a reality before certain people find
out about it.

When he finishes talking to Soderman, he looks out on the
dance floor for Cathy and doesn't find her. These athletes, he
thinks, they keep sensible hours. So he dances with Arnold
and a couple of the local girls, and he accepts a white Stetson
somebody wants to hand him. He tips it back on his head and
walks up to his third-floor room.

A few minutes after he turns on his light there's a knock
on his window. He's surprised to see Cathy's grinning face
peering in, her snub nose pressed to the pane. She's free-
climbed the brick wall, hanging by fingers and bare toes. He
opens the window to let her in. "I like the hat," she says.
Her sneakers hang around her neck by their laces, and she's
stuffed a small bottle of bourbon in one of them. Cowboy
closes the window, and about fifteen seconds later they're in
bed together.

She's got a compact, well-muscled body, and he's surprised by her strength. "I hang by my fingernails a lot," she
says. "You'll see tomorrow, if you join me."

So the next day Cowboy moves his party to the Yellowstone, and he watches in hopeless terror as Cathy spends
most of the day free-soloing the granite face of Medlicott
Dome, her boots hanging in space while she supports herself
by her fingertips. She doesn't even use safety lines. When she
comes down, Cowboy goes to hug her and is appalled by the
state of her hands, the broken nails, the blood running down
her wrists. . . . He picks her up and carries her to a sink,
runs hot water and soap, then bathes her hands. "You do this
for *fun?*" he asks.

Her eyes smile up at him. "I do everything by the book
when I'm on my cutter," she says. "I've got the crew to
think about. But out here I like to climb everything without a
safety line." She puts her hands on his shoulders. He can
feel soap and water soaking through his shirt. "Everything I
can," she repeats, and she climbs up his front to kiss him,
wrapping her wet hands around his neck as her tongue slides
deliberately into his mouth. She's small enough so that he

can hold her without strain, and they complete the carnal act standing up, occasionally banging into bathroom fixtures. Later that night her unhealed cuts break open, and in the morning Cowboy finds bloodmarks on his chest and back.

A couple of days later Cowboy finds he can't watch as she climbs New Dimensions, so he spends the day in the hotel bar with his friends, keeping the party going. Cathy comes back in the early evening with a burrito in one broken hand and an inhaler of snapcoke in the other. They spend the night climbing each other, exploring chimneys, faces, crevasses. Cowboy thinks she's perfectly crazy.

It's not a bad party, though.

A week later Cowboy watches as a giant moon walks its slow patrol in the blue midafternoon sky, bracketed at this point of its beat by a pair of silver dots, power satellites in GEO, feeding their junk into the scarred veins of Earth. Below, the aspens writhe up the Western Slope, trying to caress the gibbous face, doomed by gravity to fail. Everything in orbit around Earth is assumed hostile, the aspens therefore are collaborators. It's an inescapable conclusion, sad but true. Cowboy shakes his head in sorrow and drinks another mescal.

His surroundings remind him of dependency, and that makes him sour. He's mixing beer and mescal on the terrace of a bar in Colorado with the remnants of the party. It had filled the place the night before, but now it's down to three.

Today Cathy's on a hike with Arnold, who's become her friend. Cowboy's staying in the bar, looking for the answers to some questions. He's been asking them these last weeks, quietly, as the party roistered up and down the Rockies, and pretending that the replies don't mean anything.

Jimi Gutierrez is eighteen, an up-and-comer with a brand new set of sockets planted in his head, the operation so recent that there's still a bit of shaved scalp surrounding each porcelain node. He grins through a mouthful of metal braces, watches the world through eyes fevered by speed. He's fast, the word says, but maybe too unstable to be trusted with major cargoes.

The other panzerboy is Chapel. He's burly, running to fat, nearing thirty. He drinks quietly and doesn't speak much. There's a black box on his belt with a wire that's studded into his head. A junkie of some kind, the electronic high something he can no longer do without.

Buttonheads make Cowboy nervous; he doesn't trust junkies in general and has a particular aversion to this kind—it's a near desecration, he thinks, an abuse of the interface. The point is to use the interface to reach out, to touch the remotes from the inside, to access the electron world . . . to feel yourself moving *at the speed of light!* The run across the Line is the only addiction Cowboy needs, and it's something real, not just an electronic stimulation of the lizard pleasure centers.

But Cowboy tolerates Chapel. The man runs almost exclusively for Arkady—these days he's a free-lancer only by courtesy—and maybe he's got a few of the answers Cowboy needs.

"Convoy stuff," Cowboy says. "Saturday, in Florida. No big deal, but the Dodger says they're offering a lot."

"When I started, I was running convoys across Utah," Jimi says. "Armored trucks, guys with no necks riding shotgun." He shakes his head, then splashes mescal into a shot glass. "Wouldn't do that now, though. Don't need it."

Cowboy hands him the lime. "The panzer's in the East, so why not?" he says. "I don't like it to sit idle for too long. Or me. Rev us up for a day, collect some gold."

"Yeah. Forgot you were in a panzer. That's okay." Jimi licks salt, drains the mescal, bites the lime. The blaze in his eyes grows brighter.

"I started right on deltas, of course," Cowboy says. "Didn't have to run convoys. But you should have seen the distribution networks back then. Flying out of blind canyons on the Indian reservations. Convoys moving without lights across old bits of state highway. It wasn't the competition that would hijack you back then, it was the refugees. Who could blame them? Half the time I'd be sitting on the runway apron past midnight, waiting for the delivery. And it wouldn't show, the whole mission would have to be scrubbed."

"Yeah," says Jimi, and starts off on a speed monologue, all rapping staccatos, about how the distribution is managed today. Cowboy smiles and raises a finger for another round of beers. He receives a quiet nod from the bartender, a Navajo and a refugee, still looking a bit bewildered behind the eyes. A man lacking a center, without a home, and no matter how many Ways are chanted by the Singers, it's not going to change things. Half of his reservation is as barren as the moon, strip-mined since the war by the Orbitals, and the rest is poisoned by the tailings piles, paved over into parking lots, or dry as the Sahara since the miners sucked off the water to run their operations. Texans, Cowboy thinks, leaving their goddamn dust bowls and their fairy high-heel bootprints from here to fucking Nix Olympica.

The drinks come and Cowboy sips his while listening to Jimi's stories. Asking questions here and there, but just mostly letting the man talk. Talk of midnight errands to Orbital loading docks, security people paid to look the other way, betrayal, fouled schedules, police raids on thirdman warehouses arranged by the thirdmen themselves so the laws could look good, the cargo quietly bought back later. Foul-ups, missed connections, real raids, treachery between thirdmen. Two thirdmen running their panzerboys across the same piece of territory on the same night, neither aware of the other until the blaze of radars from above pinned them both.

"Arkady, now," Cowboy says, "he's got his networks running smooth. Right, Chapel?"

"That's right," Chapel says. "Never missed a connection, far as I know." He's more closemouthed than Jimi but he seems to know a lot. Cowboy is beginning to build a picture. Large quantities of merchandise, all Orbital quality, moving out of California to the East. Warehouses spotted across the West. Arkady's floating entourage of helpers and assistants that turn up along the run, shepherding things along, just keeping an eye on everybody.

There's no way, Cowboy knows, that Arkady can be getting this kind of quantity without Orbital knowledge and cooperation. But who's using whom? Is Arkady just finding sources the others don't know, buying off the Orbitals' surplus and distributing it, or are they letting him have it, making sure the underground is their own, that they control both its supply and demand?

He tosses back another mescal and meditates for a bit, trying to stare down the unblinking eyes of the moon. Arkady's supplies seem to keep coming regardless of spot-market prices, so it can't be surplus. And that means he's got a mortgage on his heart, his hands and feet tied to strings that are hanging down from ice-cold fingers above the gravity well.

"It's a business," Chapel is saying. "Arkady just runs it like a business, is all."

Jimi turns his head away from Chapel, an expression of distaste on his face. Cowboy keeps his own face still. It didn't start as a business, he and Jimi know, it started as a cause. Locating the weak links in the Orbital system of distribution, finding people who were weak or bribable, who could be brought over. Feeding the system what it needed, not just the endless machine pleasure that the Orbitals wanted to jack into your head or push into your corroding veins. There were the problems of any underground market—territoriality, treachery, competition that strayed beyond the bounds of what was strictly friendly. There was, all along, the suspicion that the resistance might be an excuse on the part of some human lice to profit off a world's misfortune. But even if the lice were there, the mail still got itself delivered.

And it was a human mechanism, not a machine. Not the Orbitals, and not Arkady. Maybe a panzerboy association will help keep things human.

Cowboy has no plans to approach the lizardbrain Chapel. He's too much in the pockets of the thirdmen. And he's not sure about Jimi yet. He thinks the boy's too unstable to keep a secret for long. So he just listens, and pours more mescal.

From here, on the balcony, he can see Cathy and Arnold

wandering down the grassy slope in the shade of the aspens. Tonight's party will begin soon.

For now, Cowboy has another mescal and keeps trying to stare down the moon.

Chapter Six

Great, Sarah thinks. A buttonhead. She knows that only people who are serious about their addictions put sockets in their brains.

It's early morning. Cowboy is standing next to Warren and his panzer as the mechanic explains something, using his hands to diagram an auxiliary power unit that is sending spikes into the servos of an afterburner hydraulic system, explaining how Cowboy ought to avoid using it if possible. The panzer sits on broken blacktop cut by dunes, the asphalt already beginning to melt in the heat, here at the edge of the ocean just north of St. Petersburg where the gulf is turning an old housing development into a barrier reef, dark chimneys standing above the green swell to mark where fish swim among the old cinderblocks. Fore and aft are parked a pair of light trucks with warning flags—they'll be moving with the panzer till it reaches the interstate, as is required by law, ground-effects vehicles being able to travel very fast but having a problem with stopping.

The offshore wind plucks at Sarah's hair. She watches the conversation from a distance, standing by the Hetman's armored Packard with the unfamiliar weight of the Heckler & Koch on her hip.

She's chipped in with it now, having fired 200 rounds two days before. She's been hardwired with the generic chips for this type of weapon, but now she's got specific data in her ROM: when fired from the hip, the burst climbs this much, pulls so much to the right; when shoulder-fired, it behaves thus. Adding the suppressor does so. All worked into her reflexes. Ready, if the time should come.

And more important, she's survived. There's a livid bruise on her ribs, but it was almost worth it, seeing the expression on the faces of a few of her acquaintances when she walked into the Plastic Girl for her appointment—the first time she'd been there since her last meeting with Cunningham. She counted a number of double takes, a blunt stare or two, sudden whispered conversations in corners mixed with glances in her direction. People who knew her at least by sight, who'd heard of Cunningham's offer. Who knew, perhaps, a couple of streetboys who'd met with misfortune, and whose piebald Mercury was found driven into the surf near Tarpon Springs. Who watched her in the bar mirror as she drank a rum and lime, her back to the wall—no sense in being foolish—standing with her hip cocked as if there was already a gun on it, and a smile on her face that said that she knew something they didn't.

The boy had come, and she'd gone off with him, trailing that smile, walking in the smooth, confident stride that Firebud had taught her, walking as if there was no such thing as fear.

The boy's name was Lane. He carried the gun in the trunk of his car—if he'd brought it into the bar with him, the Plastic Girl's detectors would have screamed an alarm that would have had him in the crosshairs of a dozen automated systems. Lane opened the rear door for her and seemed pleased when she'd asked to ride up front.

He never made his move. He'd driven south to an old farm by the Little Manatee and brought the gun out of the trunk and showed her how to strip and load it, then stood by while she chipped in. Never knowing that she had figured he was wired himself, and probably with weapons, like the Weasel, that she couldn't see. Not knowing how ready she was, if he was false even for an instant, to fling Weasel into his face and claw for the right to remain standing, for that particular instant, on that particular patch of terran mud.

She had survived another slice of time, another Moment. She bought a bottle of rum to celebrate, and drank half of it in her hiding place—not in Tampa's Venice but across the bay in St. Petersburg, in a stately old office building with green deco bronze on the windows and a marble lobby scored by the spring tide. High above the city, where she could see the sun coming up over Tampa and watch it shine like spun gold on the arches that cross the bay.

Sarah has reason to be pleased. The Hetman's advance payment is in the hospital's account, and Daud will get a left leg tomorrow morning. Her final payment, on completion of her task, will pay for the other leg.

The surf hisses across the crumbling concrete beach. Another armored car appears, Andrei's. The Hetman opens his door and waits.

Andrei isn't fond of cryo max fashion, and instead dresses conservatively in denim trousers, boots, and a blue satin vest over his T-shirt. He and Michael meet, embrace, talk apart for a while, speaking in Russian. Michael insistent, Andrei reassuring. Sarah catches a word here and there. Their drivers and associates—bodyguards, mainly—watch from their vehicles. The Hetman is traveling in three-car convoys these days, and he's holding his neck stiffly, a result of the armored vest under his baggy blouse. Trying to be ready for whatever it is that he smells on the wind.

A five-ton truck, with its own escort, appears at the verge of the trees, lumbers down to the sand. The Hetman returns to the air conditioning of his Packard. The conversation between Cowboy and Warren ends, and they shake hands. Warren moves to his own car and drives off. The truck drops its loading gate and Cowboy begins supervising the transfer of the cargo. The Hetman, a figure of shadow behind his reflective armored glass, gives a wave, or a blessing, and then his car and escort pull out. Sarah stands alone, feeling the asphalt ooze beneath her boots.

She watches, trying to see what is important. Powerful people, she knows, have their own rituals, their own ways of doing things. A different stance, a different style. Firebud had shown her that, drilling into her the difference between the way a dirtgirl moves and the way a jock glides through her space.

The difference intrigues Sarah. She knows there are hierarchies building here on this corroded old thoroughfare, that power is being exchanged and validated. But she doesn't know what is important and what is not. Warren and the buttonhead shake hands, while Andrei and Michael give each other the abrazo. Does the embrace confer greater respect, or is the more elaborate ritual necessary in the more shadowy world of the thirdmen, where friendships exist as convenience dictates and alliances can crumble like Venice on a high tide, where more effort is necessary to convey the sincerity of one's allegiance? Perhaps it's just a Russian thing. She doesn't know.

The hydraulics of the panzer's cargo bay hiss as the gate closes. The buttonhead is staring out to sea, watching America crumbling into the Gulf. Sarah walks forward.

"My name is Sarah," she says.

Pupils like pinpricks turn to her. "Flattest damn country I ever saw." Sunlight gleams from the silver that decorates his head sockets. He frowns.

"Are we moving?"

"It's time, I guess," he says. "I'm Cowboy."

"I know."

Cowboy looks at her without any particular friendship. This dirtgirl's only an inch or so shorter than his six feet four inches, and she walks with a kind of arrogant strut that calls more attention than is strictly necessary to the gun she's wearing. Despite the mirrorshades, her face has a kind of clarity to it that he likes, a single-minded purposefulness like an old cutthroat razor that has been whetted half away but is still sharp enough to slice edelweiss; but though she probably came by those scars honestly enough, he doesn't like the way she uses them as part of an attitude, as if every glance was a challenge and every scar a dare. But still there's no reason to dislike her, so he concludes that things will be all right if she doesn't keep trying to prove things to herself all the rest of the day.

"This way," he says, and climbs the frontal slope of the panzer.

He doesn't turn and offer a hand as she climbs the sunbaked armor, and with Sarah that's a point in Cowboy's favor. The silken fingers of claustrophobia touch her nerves as she sees the interior, the passenger and control spaces crammed between the two engines, slabs of Chobham Seven armor, hydraulic and fuel lines. Rows of green and red lights glisten like a faraway Christmas. The place smells of stale air, hydraulic fluid, male humanity. There is, as it turns out, no passenger seat, only a narrow cot with straps that are intended to secure the passenger during high-g turns.

There is a carbine in a scabbard near the hatch, one of the light alloy ones, all metal and plastic, that look like they started out as golf clubs. "There's a headset in there for you," Cowboy says. "So you can listen to the radio or whatever." He points at a cabinet door. "Chemical toilet," he says. "Not what you're used to."

"Thanks." What she's used to is an old scrub bucket in a marble ruin in St. Petersburg, but she doesn't say it. She takes off the gun and rolls into the bunk, putting the Heckler & Koch in a far corner and raising the netting. She wonders what Cowboy has in mind for after the delivery, if he intends they should share the bunk. If that's what he means to do, he has a surprise in store.

The panzer, she decides, is a place only a junkie could love. A cozy cybernetic womb of masculine scent, soft blinking lights, the studs that feed one's addiction. Whatever Cowboy's is, she doesn't want to know. Porn mainlined to the forebrain, electric orgasms courtesy of induction, screaming synthetic highs circuited to the mind, technicolor power fantasies jabbed right into one's primal need. Sarah looks at the headset with sudden distrust. It might be tuned to Cowboy's channel, and if so, she isn't interested.

Cowboy strips unself-consciously and attaches the electrodes and a rubber urine collector. Sarah thinks of Daud, his insensate and lacerated flesh, no more human than an oozing, fresh-killed slab of pork. She tries to shrug deeper into her alcove. Pain chooses this moment to crawl over her ribs. She closes her eyes and puts her head on a naked pillow.

Pumps begin throbbing, hydraulic links hissing. There is the whine of a starter and the shriek of an engine. A lurch as the panzer rises on its cushion, a flutter in her stomach as it wheels and begins to move toward the highway. Sarah shifts in the bunk and the pain in her side fades. Weariness rises like a mist and she feels the tension drain out of her. She is cushioned in someone else's armored fantasy, being carried to someone else's destination. Her own armor, for the moment anyway, is superfluous.

The sound of the engine seems more and more distant. Sarah feels sleep beginning to ooze into her mind. It is, she realizes, someone else's job to get her through this next Moment. She decides to go to sleep and let him get on with his work.

Cowboy's deep in the face, paying no attention to Sarah once he's shown her the fixtures. Keeping watch on the columns of green, the video views of the exterior of the panzer. He keeps the escort aware of his intentions, listens to their chatter. Balances the panzer while it runs on only one engine, saving fuel as long as its speed is harnessed to that of the escort.

Once onto the interstate he says adios to the escort and starts the second engine. The surface is pitted and holed, the concrete of some bridges crumbled down to the rebar. Anything with wheels hugs the rightward lane and moves slowly, cursing the chuckholes. The ground-effect panzer rides smoothly on its air cushion, crossing the outer lanes of traffic to the two inner lanes reserved for vehicles moving over a hundred miles per hour.

Cowboy reds out the engines, mindful of his passenger and accelerating slowly until he's moving at over 200. He's a lot faster than the bigger cargo-carrying ground-effect jobs and slaloms around them with ease, hearing through his armor the low-dopplered sounds of their saluting horns as he torches past. The slow-moving automobiles are stationary objects. Trees are a continuous green blur. His concentration narrows to the tunnel ahead and the one behind, to the crumbling track over which he roars on his cushion of air, coordinating his video track with the readout on his forward-looking radars, the instantaneous radio echo, the fluorescent abstract images that might be anything, clouds or boxes or the spectra of subatomic particles in scintillators, superimposed onto his video display and resolving into other vehicles, the guardrail, stands of trees, the outskirts of sprawling cities impacted by war.

The border flashes by—no customs on the Georgia side but a long line of traffic going the other way into the American Concessions, waiting to pass inspection. He refuels in South Carolina and again in Virginia, robot pumps finding the fuel intakes, engaging without need for human intervention, without even a glance from the bored operator sitting in his bulletproof tower. It's early afternoon when he crosses the Maryland line and leaves the interstate, finds a patch of flat ground at a rest stop and deflates the cushion, waiting for his escort. He pulls off his helmet and unjacks.

Sarah, to his surprise, seems to be asleep. He had almost forgotten her existence. He disengages the urine collector, which he hasn't used, and pisses into the chemical toilet. Then he steps up the ladder to open the dorsal hatch and bring in some fresh air. He looks out at the rolling green countryside, the wide crumbling interstate slicing across it, eroding like an artery.

He said good-bye to Cathy two nights before. She had left his life the way she'd entered it, climbing out the eighth-floor window of his hotel room in Norfolk, grinning up from under the brim of the white Stetson he'd given her as she worked her way toward the four inches of brackish tide creeping over East Main. They'd said some things about keeping in touch, but he thinks if they meet again it will be another accident. He doesn't spend much time in Virginia and she won't be due for another furlough till next year. It's pointless to plan that far ahead. The laws might catch him in that time, or the sea might claim her. Best to have a clean farewell.

When he turns around, Sarah is awake and rolling down the netting on her bunk. Half asleep, she seems a lot less hard.

"Want some lunch?"

She nods, running her fingers through her hair. He opens a locker and brings some sandwiches out of the cooler. "What would you like to drink? Coffee? Orange juice? Ice tea?"

"Iced tea." She swings her legs out of the bunk, accepts the cool plastic container, peels off the top. "Gracias."

Cowboy leans against the ladder and opens a sandwich. He can hear birds calling through the open hatch. "Were you brought up speaking Spanish?" he asks.

"Spanglish, anyway. My father was part Cuban, part Gypsy. My mother was an Anglo." Now that she's awake, Cowboy notices, her cooler personality seems to be taking control, the look in her eyes abstracting off somewhere, not turning dreamy but seemingly involved in some intent calculation. The words "father" and "mother" seem to have some kind of negative charge, as if stripped of any emotional content.

"Did you lose them in the war?" Cowboy guesses.

She gives him a quick glance, as if sizing him in some way. "Yes," she says. The answer comes too quickly and Cowboy can't entirely believe it, but also can't figure out why she'd bother not telling the truth.

Sarah bites a sandwich and looks at him in surprise. "This is real ham," she says. "Not soy or anything."

Cowboy swallows chicken salad. "Pony Express riders eat only of the best," he says.

Cowboy conceals his amusement as Sarah gobbles down two more sandwiches. Jet engines and throbbing props doppler past on the freeway. There are some apricots for dessert. Cowboy looks at his watch. Their escort is a few minutes late.

"Mind if I look out the hatch?" Sarah asks. "I've never seen this part of the world."

"It's a nice-looking part. Civilized kind of country."

She straps on the machine pistol. Cowboy watches her.

"You hardwired for that?" he asks.

"Hardwired and chipped." Her look is challenging again, as if he had somehow questioned her competence.

"That'll be useful," he says, pretending he's glad to know he's so well protected. "Do you have the full Santistevan or an Owari?"

She gives him a glance, then dons her mirrorshades. Armor, he thinks, for the emotions, like the jacket, the strut, the attitude. "Owari," she says. That means the hardwiring needs a trigger, usually an inhaled chemical streetnamed hardfire, before it will work efficiently. His own more expensive job triggers on a command from his crystal.

Sarah squeezes past him in the corridor, climbs the short ladder, and props her arms on the edge of the hatch, watching through the heat shimmer of the cooling engines the low green hills, the close-packed corn across the road, a square white farmhouse that looks like something off a postcard.

"I have the Santistevan," Cowboy says. His voice comes up muffled through the hatch.

"What do you need it for? You do your driving through the face."

"I used to fly deltas. We needed arms, legs, fingers, crystal, eyes, everything."

Sarah hadn't realized that Cowboy was that much a veteran. He must be good at this if he's survived so long. She thinks of Maurice, the West Indian cutterjock with his old-model metal eyes and the military sockets on his wrists and ankles, his pictures of dead comrades on the wall. Lost in a past that was brighter than all his futures put together. She wonders if that is Cowboy's fate, retreating to some cool memory grotto when he finally bashes his panzer up against something that won't move aside for him, when the last bit of hope dies.

"I knew you had the eyes," she says. "Standing there in bright sunlight this morning without having to squint."

Shadows of cloud drift across the quiet landscape. Corn rustles in its rows. She finds herself oddly off-balance in this pastoral scene, not knowing what to expect. Her life is bounded by concrete, steel, ruins, flooded lands, the sea . . . . This long green horizon promises softness, melody, ease.

Sarah glances up, seeing the silver power stations in the sky, keeping watch on the planet for their masters, and then from over one of the low hills comes a robot harvester, a vast alloy machine with a cybernetic heart. No human tills this soil, and no human owns it: the pretty white frame house is either the residence of some employee who supervises the planting of this part of Pennsylvania, or the house no longer belongs to the farm at all, owned by a family that no longer controls the fields that begin just outside their window.

It's the same as the city, Sarah knows, the same hierarchy of power, beginning with the blocs in their orbits and ending with people who might as well be the fieldmice in front of the blades of the harvester, pointless, countless lives in the path of a structure that can't be stopped. She feels the anger coiling around her like armor. The chance to rest, she thinks, was nice enough while it lasted. But right now another fragment of time must be survived.

Three vehicles coil off the interstate, two flying red warning flags. Time for business. "Our escort," she says, and raises a hand in greeting.

Andrei has flown up from Florida with his guards and has rented a car along with the panzer escort. He leans a head out of the window as he drives onto the verge, and Sarah tells him all's well. Behind Andrei the harvester mows corn in its efficient, mindless fashion.

She slams the hatch down and dogs it, seeing Cowboy already in his seat, inserting studs into his sockets. Pumps begin to throb. Sarah rolls herself into the bunk as the starter wails. She hesitates for a moment as she looks at the headset, then takes it in her hands and presses it on, one hand guiding the featherweight mic on its hair-thin wire to its place at the corner of her mouth.

Distant music bounces indistinctly in her head, some radio program from far away. There is a selector switch above her ear and she turns it, hearing more music, voices hammering in some Russian dialect, a startlingly clear vid of some glittery drama set in, of all things, an African circus. A turn of the switch and she's into Cowboy's interface, jerking with surprise as the green walls of Pennsylvania rise on all sides of her, interwoven with columns, numbers, bright neon colors that are the panzer monitors, all of it seemingly painted on the inside of her skull, overlaid with the data of her eyes and ears. She's walled out from Cowboy's mind, a passive observer only, barred from the crackle of decision as Cowboy guides the panzer along the road. It's less vivid than it would be if she were getting it fed through sockets, like Cowboy, straight to the optical centers of her brain, but still the input is overwhelming, stunning her with its complexity, and she almost rips the set off her head to end the fluorescing burst of sensation.

But she's used to headsets and what they do, and after a moment settles in. She's been in simulations of things more complicated than this: orbital maneuvers, auto races, even combat. Voices echo in her head, Cowboy chatting with the escort, and she can feel, secondhand, the impacts of his decisions in the twitches of the big rudders, the movement of the jets, the emphasis placed on certain of the displays. After a while Sarah decides it isn't very interesting.

The panzer travels across twenty miles of decaying road, Sarah seeing a series of hills rising in the west, misty gray and shadowed in cloud. But here is a stake planted by the road with a pair of fluorescent orange streamers, marking the place to turn off. The escort trucks pull onto the grassy shoulder, the drivers waving their temporary good-byes. Andrei's limo slides into the turnoff. The panzer wallows across a ditch and follows.

The meet turns out to be at another picturesque farmhouse set among shade trees. The others are waiting—an unarmored ground-effects truck sitting under its four-bladed propellers and a pair of men leaning against a dark blue Subaru limousine. Cowboy's attention seems to switch to the terrain: there are close-up amplified views of the windows of the house, selected spots behind the trees, the low ridge of ground to the left.

Sarah, her mind strobing colors, reaches blindly into her pocket, finds her inhaler, triggers it once up each nostril. Her nerves burn with electric light.

The panzer moves next to the truck and spins, keeping its jet exhaust away from the truck's crew while training the off-load ramp toward the truck. Then the engines die and the panzer settles down onto its deflated cushion.

"Keep the headset, Sarah." Cowboy's voice pulses into her aural centers. "You can talk to me."

"Can you cut me out of your displays?" she asks. "They're too distracting."

Abruptly the video dies, the bright colors fading with only the lightest persistence. Sarah shakes her head and rolls out of the bunk. She zips her jacket to the throat and checks the pistol on her hip. She looks at Cowboy, the helmeted figure sitting motionless beneath the shimmering red and green, and hesitates for a moment at the bottom of the ladder.

"Cowboy," she says. "I think you should know something. The Hetman thinks we're being set up."

He turns in his couch and she can see his dark plastic eyes looking at her from under the brow of the helmet. "Thanks, Sarah," he says. "But I figured that from the fact that I'm here at all."

Sarah looks at him for a moment, surprise shimmering in her mind, and then she nods and pops the hatch, climbing the ladder while slipping on her shades. Sullen faces look back at her from the windows of the truck. She slips the Heckler & Koch from its holster and holds it just below the rim of the hatch. The farm smells of fuel, hot metal, and lubricant.

Sarah can feel her shoulder blades tense, as if in anticipation of a shot. Flame runs along her nerve paths. The Hetman sensed something wrong here, and she knows his antennae are good. Her interior landscapes are urban and she's not used to this kind of terrain, but she decides Cowboy's eye was intelligent enough and flicks her gaze to the farmhouse windows, the trees, the ridge behind them, then back to the farmyard.

The principals seem to be Andrei and a thin black man dressed in a gray silk suit. He wears a knit wool cap pulled over his dreadlocks and a Cantinflas mustache, just a strip of hair on either side of his mouth with most of the upper lip shaved. The abrazo is absent from their greeting—just a handshake and a quick, murmured discussion of business. The black man turns back to his car and gives an order, and two of his associates, one white, one black, open the trunk and bring out a heavy metal trunk. There is a jolt of recognition in Sarah's mind, thinking she's seen the white man before, but they're both wearing straw sun hats and big shades and she's met so many big guys without necks in her life that she can't be sure about this one. They look like men who spend a lot of time working with weights, but the trunk has them breathing hard by the time they get it to the middle of the yard.

The black man bends to open the trunk. Andrei squats down on his heels and inspects the contents while the black man stands back. Under the Cantinflas mustache is a superior smile.

Sarah can feel sweat trickling down her spine. Her gaze jumps from the yard to the faces of the men in the truck, to the yard again, then to the ridge behind, then to the windows of the farmhouse. Lace curtains flutter in the windows. She tries to remember if she's ever seen lace curtains in anything but pictures.

Andrei straightens and turns to give a signal to someone in his car, who raises a hand mic to his lips. Cowboy's voice rings in Sarah's head as he acknowledges, and then there's a gush of hydraulics as the panzer's armored cargo gate swings open.

Sarah's gaze flicks to the windows, the truck drivers, to Andrei and the black man walking toward the panzer. Things have separated too much for her to keep good watch. Her nerves are sparking like strings of fireworks. She forces the muscles in her arms to relax. She can feel her own sweat on the pistol grip of the Heckler & Koch.

Andrei and the black man step into the panzer. The black man will be opening boxes at random, checking the seals, checking that the comp matrices are there. Sarah's eyes flicker like lightning, ridge to truck to windows. She licks her lips, tasting salt.

The two men leave the panzer and walk into the yard. Andrei's two guards come out of their car to carry the gold payment into the trunk. The black man picks at a grease spot in the elbow of his silk suit as he walks toward his Subaru. On the far side of the truck a door opens, and the two men move to get out, to transfer the cargo.

Wrong, Sarah thinks. One of them at least should get out on this side.

"Cowboy . . ." she says, eyes flickering madly, neuro-transmitters firing along their paths, her mind trying to encompass the yard as the gold thuds down into the trunk, as the black man steps casually behind his car, as his two associates bend to reach into the Subaru.

The air is sliced apart by a rushing, hissing sound, and Sarah sees a silver needle leaping from the upper story of the farmhouse, arrowing straight to Andrei's car. To Sarah's hardwired senses it moves slowly, and her mind has plenty of time to scream as Andrei's windshield caves in, as the rocket burrows into the car and turns into a widening bubble of fire that erupts from the interior, and Sarah thinks, *Daud*. The bubble touches Andrei and his men and the three are thrown down as if there were no bones in their bodies at all. The scream builds in Sarah's mind, but she is already moving.

The machine pistol is up and already tracking onto the Subaru. She touches the trigger and the gun rattles, jarring her as she braces against the armor of the hatch. There is an echo to the scream in her mind but she pays it no attention. The bullets from the machine pistol make a metallic *spunk-spunk-spunk* sound across the trunk of the Subaru, and then the two men bent over by the rear door catch the rest of the burst, and the black man drops like a nerveless bundle of rags and his associate falls backward, arms thrown up over his head, one big hand holding the stock of an automatic shotgun. Spent rounds clatter like falling icicles on the Chobham armor. Sarah shifts and fires again, hearing more *spunk-spunk* sounds. The white man is sheltered behind an armored door.

The scream in her mind has become the scream of the starters, the big jets beginning to turn, and Sarah almost leaps out of her skin as a slab of armor just aft of her suddenly slams open and a turret rises with jackhammer quickness. There is an insistent hooting sound, a warning siren, as the cargo gate hisses shut. Cowboy's voice is clamoring in her head, "Behind you, Sarah," and she wheels around in the hatch and sees one of the two truck drivers peering out from behind his ground-effects craft, ready with a pistol to shoot her in the back. The Heckler & Koch yammers in her hands. She sees the fear in the man's eyes as he pulls his head back, as the bullets climb *spunk-spunk-spunk* toward him.

Kawham-kawham. Sarah turns again at the sound of an automatic shotgun concussing the air and sees dust leaping into the air around Andrei as the buckshot strikes. Andrei's body doesn't even twitch. The white man is firing over the Subaru's hood. A harsh purr resounds near Sarah's ear as the gun in the panzer's turret opens fire. Thirty-millimeter casings fountain into the sky, and Sarah looks up to see the entire second story of the farmhouse leap into the air in a storm of dust, as if every inch of paint had shed off the wood at the same instant. The turret gun tries to track down to the Subaru but fails—the realization snaps into Sarah's mind that the gun is meant to fire at aircraft and can't depress to ground targets. She snaps some rounds at the man behind the Subaru, but the bolt locks back and she has to reach for another clip, and she has to turn around again to watch the gunman behind the truck. The panzer gives a lurch as it rises onto its cushion. Engine din fills the air.

The upper story of the farmhouse is riddled, a round every few inches. Whoever fired the rocket can't have survived. Sarah slams a new clip into the machine pistol by feel, swaying across the hatch as the panzer begins to move. It's moving right across the yard, the armored bow heading the Subaru. Sarah crouches as the man with the shotgun begins to turn, as the shotgun keeps firing *kawham-kawham*. Pellets rattle off the armor. The man begins to run.

The panzer strikes the limo dead-on, pushing it ahead as if it were of no more weight than a bicycle. The man darts to one side, trying awkwardly to bring up the shotgun. He's lost his hat and shades. Sarah can feel her chips urging her to stand in the hatch, to bring the machine pistol up in both hands and trigger it. . . .

The white man spins as he falls, and Sarah can see the flaring agony in his eyes at the exact moment of her own jarring leap of recognition, and she knows she's met this particular man before, that she's looked into those eyes in the rearview mirror, as this particular white man drove Cunningham's car down the neon streets to her apartment. Cunningham's big assistant.

Then the panzer smashes the Subaru against the farmhouse and it crumples like a tin can, the panzer bounding off, heading for the ridge, its speed building. Cowboy's voice is ringing in her mind. "Get down inside, Sarah, you've done all you can." Sarah is still staring aft in shock, staring at the smoking, scattered tableau where Cunningham's driver lies like a sack of meal.

The turret gun begins to moan again, able to depress now that the panzer's climbing the ridge, and the unarmored ground-effects truck is riddled, the fuel tanks erupting in washes of flame. No sign of the two men who drove it; they're probably both chunks of shredded meat on the other side. Cunningham's man, she thinks. And the rocket. *Daud*.

The minigun is still firing as Sarah numbly climbs down the hatchway, trying to protect herself against the wild swings of the panzer. She dogs the hatch down over her head and dives for the bunk. Seven-millimeter casings roll jingling across the metal deck.

"Time to hide, Sarah." Cowboy's voice comes both in her head and ears.

"Time to find a deep hole and hide."

You can't, she wants to say. You can't hide from *them*.

She pulls the headset off, closes her eyes, and tries to escape into blackness.

Chapter Seven

TAMPA'S TOTALS OVERNITE, AS OF 8 THIS
MORNING:
22 FOUND DEAD WITHIN CITY LIMITS . . .
LUCKY WINNERS COLLECT AT ODDS OF 18 TO 1

POLICE DENY CHARGES OF FIXING
(RELATED STORY ON PAGE 3)

The panzer waits for nightfall in a narrow fold of ground between the Blue Mountains and the Tuscaroras, having followed a shallow creek between green bluffs into a quiet swale studded with pine. Cowboy sips some orange-flavored electrolyte replacement and squats on a fragrant bed of pine needles. His mind is cool and clear, but tremors are running through his limbs, the aftereffects of too much adrenaline. Through the trees he can see a hawk flying against the sun, wings spread to catch the thermals.

Lucky, he thinks. That the first rocket went for Andrei. That they assumed the panzer was unarmed except for Sarah in the hatch. Otherwise the first rocket would have been aimed right in his lap. Maybe it would have got through the armor, maybe not. His muscles tremble at the thought.

"Those people were trying to kill us," he says. "I figured if anybody's story survived, it had better be ours."

Sarah looks out into a dappled meadow and frowns. Her hand is never far from the gun on her hip. "Too bad about those truck drivers, though. They were just hired help."

"Then they shouldn't have tried to play with the likes of us," Cowboy says. He can feel indignation prickling along his neck and shoulders at the idea of being ambushed by a collection of shabby players like that. He frowns at the blue-green Tuscaroras. "This'll be all over the screamsheets in another few hours," he says. "Those escorts Andrei hired for the panzer weren't his people, right? Just some local escort service with a license from the police that'll be revoked if they get into trouble. They'll have seen the panzer go down that turn and then heard half the world blow up. No way they aren't going to tell the local laws."

"I've got to talk to Michael the Hetman," Sarah says. "This was a move against him, and it was by one of the Orbitals."

Cowboy feels shock prickling the hairs on his arms. He looks up at her. "How do you know that?"

"That white guy I unzipped," Sarah says. She bares her teeth in unconscious anger. "He worked for the Orbitals. One of their . . . security units. For a man named Cunningham. Cunningham had to have set this up." Cowboy stares at his silvered image in the mirrors over her eyes and wonders what he's stepped into, how high this dirtgirl's profile is. And how much he's been soiled by whatever it is she's mixed up with.

Sarah's voice turns soft. As if what she's saying is something so personal she can only speak of it in whispers. "And they've used rockets before. Fired one at me."

And now Cowboy knows. He's covered with Sarah's mess, and the smartest thing he can do is say adios and climb back into the panzer, stud into the eye-face, and fly away and never look back. Whoever is firing those rockets wants this scar-faced dirtgirl and doesn't care who gets splashed on the way to her. He represses an urge to look over his shoulder.

"Which Orbital?" he asks. "How strong are they on the ground here?"

She shakes her head. "I don't know. They wouldn't tell me."

"Wouldn't tell you when?"

She takes a breath and suddenly he can see the sadness in her, that in spite of the armor and gun and shades and swagger she's very alone here, sitting in some dead-end Blue Mountain valley and trying to think of a next move. A street animal lost and blind, running on adrenaline and instinct and knowing there are footsteps right behind her, each one bringing the enemy closer.

"When I worked for them," she says. And she tells him a story about how she was trained for a job and did it for them, and afterward they decided she was a risk and fired a rocket into her apartment and hit her brother. Who, according to her, had nothing to do with the original deal. Cowboy can tell there's a lot more to it than that, and tries to decide whether he ought to press her on it. There might be a detail that could save them both. But he knows she doesn't trust him yet, and decides to wait. He's out of it anyway, once he can get the panzer clear.

"So I've got to talk to the Hetman," she says. "Let him know what's happened so that he can make peace with those people." Cowboy watches her manner grow distant. She licks her lips. "Too bad," she says, "that part of his price for peace will probably be turning me over to them."

Cowboy shakes his head. "Don't jump to those kind of conclusions so early," he says. "He might not get his peace on any terms, and then you and Michael are in the same boat." He thinks for a moment, not liking this business of trying to see into a war where he doesn't know any of the players. His profile is suddenly higher than it's ever been, and he has no idea when or from where the next blow might fall. He finishes his drink and stands, crumpling the plastic cup in his hand.

"Still," he says, "I'd advise you not to tell him where you are. We've got his computer hearts and he'll want them back. He'll have to keep you alive until he can locate his shipment." He feels reluctant amusement bubbling along his spine. "In the meantime I'll call the Dodger—this friend of mine—and he'll send some transport to get us out. Or maybe even set up a run across the Line to Colorado with you as a passenger." He laughs. "Then the Hetman may have to pay me to run his crystal back."

Sarah looks at him without expression. "You just can't run across tonight?"

Cowboy shakes his head. "I can't make a legal run, because the laws will be looking. And I can't make a contraband run, because I don't have enough fuel, and also because that minigun's the only weapon I've got and I used up most of the ammunition. So we'll have to get some people working for us. Probably the best thing to do is hide the panzer here and arrange to pick it up later."

He stops and shades his eyes and looks at the sun. "Won't be dark enough for another three hours," he says. "Best to spend our time resting. We won't get much sleep tonight."

Sarah shakes her head and takes a deep breath. "I doubt I could sleep if I tried," she says.

He walks toward the panzer. "Up to you," he says, and climbs the frontal slope of armor.

He dumps the crumpled plastic cup in the trash and lowers himself into his contoured seat. He jacks a stud into his forehead and scans the channels, hoping to catch a news broadcast.

When he does, it's a local video screamsheet, and it's his own face that's rotating in the holographic presentation, a photograph he doesn't even remember being taken that's been enhanced to 3-D.

Wanted for questioning, the broadcast says. Statewide alert. Aerial patrols.

And Cowboy realizes that it isn't Sarah these people are looking for.

They want him.

NEW VIRAL HUNTINGTON'S CASES REACH 100,000 IN U.S. EPIDEMIC CONTINUES TO GROW

The panzer sits in a midnight creek just east of the main rise of the Allegheny range. Cowboy and Sarah have walked two kilometers into town and the only public phone they've found has been disemboweled by what appears to have been a chainsaw. Now they're watching a tavern and wondering if strangers would be noticed there.

Cowboy's been monitoring the newscasts and police broadcasts from the moment they turned interesting, and it seems that he's the only one they're looking for. There's no mention of another person in the panzer, and that means that even if the same people who are after him want Sarah, it's just an accident that she's with him. His description and a description of the panzer have been delivered to the police across the country, and he's so blazing hot that even though he's wearing the dark wig the Dodger made him buy for his emergency pack, with a visored cap jammed down low on his forehead, he can feel the crosshairs pasted over his heart. Sarah had to talk him out of wearing a plastic belly gun, guaranteed to pass the detectors about 60 percent of the time, pointing out that there was a 40-percent chance of the gun's getting him killed. But still he wishes he had the comforting solidity pressed against his stomach.

Sarah, on the other hand, is invisible, and Cowboy wants her with him. The enemy will be looking for a lone man, and she lowers his profile. She also knows at least some of the enemy's faces.

Still, he figures the odds aren't good. The Dodger's got to get him away from this war in the East before he's flown out in a body bag.

The tavern is called Oliver's and it's breathing a late-night Saturday crowd in and out with each pulse of the litejack music that's playing seven beats against sixteen from the inside. Cowboy and Sarah watch the place for a while as neon-colored holograms waver in the windows and the music begins to play eleven against four. The local cops pass by once without showing any interest in its clientele.

"Let's go before they come again," Sarah says. Cowboy nods but somehow he doesn't want to move. Sarah gives him a hard-alloy glance.

"Think of me as your bodyguard," she says. "It's something I know how to do."

The tavern breathes them in. Fluorescent holograms burn Oliver's ceiling and walls with cool, persistent fire. It is the only illumination except for a plain white spotlight trained on an expressionless man standing on the stage with five instruments plugged into his head, his monochrome shadow standing behind him like a male Medusa. He's playing all the instruments at once, five against seven now. People are dancing through his changes, even the zoned moving to his complex, compelling rhythms. "My heart is alloy," he recites, "I live in boxes." The voice is a breathless whisper that stands apart from the rest of the music, alone in ironic solitude.

Cowboy likes hearing old favorites, but mainly he's grateful for the fact that it's dark. Sarah is shrugged down into her jacket and has turned off the challenging swagger, and Cowboy's grateful for that, too. He and Sarah wander through the tavern without anyone seeming to pay any attention. There is a pay phone in a hallway leading to the toilet. Cowboy changes some bills at the bar into crystal money on a credit needle, and sticks the phone's optional audio stud into his head. It has a thin mic that trails to the corner of his mouth for a speaker.

It is the Dodger's wife who answers. Jutz is a wire-muscled blond woman who runs the Dodger's ranch while he's away, and she knows her end of the business well. She sounds as if Cowboy's got her out of bed.

"Jutz," he says, "is the Dodger there?"

"Cowboy," she says, "don't tell me where you are. They're probably monitoring this line."

Her timbre chills his nerves like liquid helium. There is a tremor in her voice, a well-controlled fear. Suddenly the little hallway seems very small.

"What's happened?" he asks.

"Listen carefully." Her words are carefully spaced and enunciated to avoid her having to repeat them. Fear overtones quaver at the hard edges of her consonants. Cowboy closes his eyes and presses his forehead to the comforting, solid reality of the metal phone.

"The Dodger has been shot. They tried to kill him in his car but he managed to get away. He's in the hospital now and I've got guards around him. Don't try to visit him, and don't call me again. Just find some safe place to hide and stay there until the situation clarifies."

The door to the toilet opens and Cowboy flashes a look over his shoulder, feeling his vulnerability. A man with bright glazed eyes steps out and gives Cowboy a friendly smile as he passes by. Cowboy hunches into himself and whispers into the mic. "Who's doing this?"

"Word is it's Arkady. That he's moving in on the other thirdmen and on the panzerboys. He wants you in particular."

A distorted dark-haired stranger, his reflection on the bright metal phone chassis, stares at Cowboy in cold-eyed anger. "He almost got me this afternoon," Cowboy says. "He's fighting his war here now. And he's given my face and name to the laws." Cowboy feels as if gravity is suspended, as if he were in a panzer soaring off the crest of a ridge that has turned into the lip of a black and bottomless canyon.

A tone sounds on Cowboy's aural crystal. He studs a credit needle into the phone and lets the machine take his money.

"Hide, Cowboy," Jutz says. "We don't know who to trust, and we can't set up a run to get you back West. Arkady's dealt with everybody at one time or another, and we don't know who are his men and who's on our side. So everyone's running for cover."

"Arkady's got a bloc behind him." Cowboy looks wildly to either side, afraid that his whisper will be overheard. "Tell everyone that."

"Which one?" But suddenly there is a click and Jutz is gone. Cowboy knows who's listening now. His lips pull back in a snarl.

"Too late," he says. "I'm gone."

He unjacks and steps out of the hallway. Sarah stands watching the dance floor. He gives her the credit needle. "Call the Hetman, but make it quick," he says. "We're compromised here. Your bloc has its thumb on communications.'' He stands outside the short hallway and watches. Plenty of time, he thinks. They probably traced the call, but the chance of their having any people sitting within a few minutes of this particular bar are nil, and they've got no liaison with the local cops. It'll take a long time to get through to anyone in this burg. But still he feels rushes of fear speeding up his spine, and his eyes count the exits. If the laws come in, he's got his escape routes planned.

"I have what you need," insinuates the voice from the singer. "I can keep the flames away."

Sarah is back in less than two minutes. "Couldn't reach the Hetman," she says. Cowboy is already moving toward the exit. "He's in hiding somewhere. But I talked to one of his people." She shakes her head. "It's chaos. There's a war going on, but the sides aren't very clear. Michael and most of his people seem to be safe for the moment, because he put the word out to be careful. Andrei was the only . . . casualty, aside from snagboys and the like."

Cowboy swings a fire door open and steps into an alley. His eyes adjust quickly to the light. There are rusting steel dumpsters complete with cats, and several people are sleeping uncovered in the August heat that radiates from the old concrete, glowing in Cowboy's infrared perception. Some drunk, some looking, some just lost. Like any small-town alley.

"They said to hide," Sarah says. "They'll pick up the computer hearts when things cool down in this part of the world."

"No way for us to get home?"

"None where we won't get assassinated the second we show up in the Free Zone. No one knows who to trust."

"Whom," says Cowboy.

He is walking fast for the far end of the alley, fists in his pockets, trying to keep his bootsteps quiet. One of the sleeping men stirs on his threadbare blanket and calls a name. His bulging, uncovered belly gleams pale in the night.

"We're on our own then," Cowboy says. He steps to the end of the alley and glances left and right. A woman's laughter echoes from the curb. He steps across the street and into another alley.

Sarah's voice behind makes him stop in his tracks. "I found out who Cunningham works for."

Cowboy spins in surprise. "The boy on the phone told you?"

"I told him the Orbitals were involved, and why. And he knew Cunningham, had dealt with him on some security matter."

The loathing in her voice is clear. Even in the darkness he can see the hatred plain in her eyes.

"It's Tempel. Tempel Pharmaceuticals I.G."

Cowboy hears the name and feels his heart quicken. Deep inside him he feels a howl building, a shriek of triumph like the panzer's jets as he opens the valves of pressured alcohol. Because, however little good it will do him right now, he finally knows the name of the enemy.

WOHNEN SIE IN LEID-STADT? ERLAUBEN SIE UNS IHNEN NACH HAPPYVILLE SCHICKEN!
—Pointsman Pharmaceuticals A.G.

Tempel Interessengemeinschaft, Cowboy thinks. The Fellowship of Interests Tempel. A lot of the Orbitals have I.G. after their names, and no wonder. It's such a perfect description of their state of mind.

He and Sarah are back at the panzer, sitting on its dorsal armor while the creek ripples across the ramming prow. Sarah is cradling the machine pistol in her arms, a cold and deadly child. Clouds are moving across the stars and they are alone in the darkness.

"I don't have any money beyond pocket change," Cowboy says. "I usually carry some gold in the panzer, to use if I have to buy some lawmen." He shakes his head. "But this delivery was supposed to be legal. No reason to suppose the cops would be interested." He gives an unamused laugh. "And I was supposed to be back in Florida tonight."

Sarah says nothing, simply shifts the weight of the machine pistol. She's got the long suppressor on the barrel, and the thing won't make so much as a whisper if she has to use it. He already knows she doesn't have a dime.

"I won't be able to access my portfolio," he goes on, thinking aloud. "If the laws are all cooperating, Arkady and his people will be able to follow every transaction, or even freeze my action. I've got gold cached back in New Mexico and Wyoming, but that's a long walk from here."

"We've got the matrices," Sarah says. Her voice seems loud after such a long silence. "They're worth a fortune if we can move them."

Cowboy looks up at her. "Do you know anyone you can trust with that amount of merchandise? I don't."

"We don't have to sell the whole cargo. Just enough to get us where we want to go."

Cowboy hears a mosquito dancing near his ear. His nerves are urging him to take the panzer out of here, telling him they are too near the phone that they used to call two compromised lines. But until he knows where they're going there doesn't seem to be any sense in moving. His fuel situation is too critical for wandering in circles.

Wait, he thinks. He looks up at the sky. Wait until the clouds move in.

He remembers the nights he flew the *Pony Express* through storm cloud, his crystal tuned to the weather bureau so that he could track the bad weather and hide in it, the delta diving past the rain that drummed on the canopy, through crepe blackness so complete, so tangible, that the world of the hissing aircraft, the softly glowing instrument lights, seemed to be the entirety of existence, the boundaries of the universe extending no more than an arm's length beyond the canopy and all his memories of an earthly existence now some fond, distant, entirely irrelevant hallucination, the only other thing existing in that world, besides Cowboy and the plane living in their interface, the echo of Cowboy's own breath in the confined space of his helmet. Remembering the sudden eruption of sheet lightning that turned the velvet sky brighter than

day, the delta a matte-black needle flung against the shimmering, streaming opalescent neverending electric dream
. . . A vision he could never share, never achieve anywhere
else. A belonging, a completeness, that he could never talk
about. Not even to those who flew with him. Just a shining in
his eyes, a glow in his mind. And sometimes, he could tell,
in the mind of others.

"Maybe I know someone," he says. "Maybe I know
someone who's been out of the game so long they won't be
looking for him."

HEARTS AND MINDS

It is late afternoon. The world has paused to catch its
breath, and the ice-cream streets melt slowly in the sun. The
people of Pennsylvania wait in the hush for the twilight that
will soften the tempered Gerber edges of their world.

The panzer is hidden in a half-flooded quarry, the old road
leading to the place now overgrown by brush so thick only
the badgers know the crumbling pair of ruts. Cowboy and
Sarah walk down the half-rural street that is called the
something-or-other pike, Cowboy with a cardboard box propped
on his shoulder, shielding his face from the traffic. Sarah
treads quietly behind, her footsteps smothered by the grassy
verge. Another pair of refugees with their rucksacks, not
worth a second glance, not even bothering to stick out a
hopeful thumb.

Since midnight they've been heading west, winding up the
Alleghenies, following the Youghiogheny River through the
passes of the western Appalachians, switching afterward to
the old Penn Central roadbed as it loops northwest to the city.
Pittsburgh is a boomtown now after decades of decline,
reviving as a transportation center and the new capital of
Pennsylvania, one of the places the blocs hadn't bothered to
smash to ruins. Cowboy has seen pictures of the new capital,
a granite fortress rising in halfhearted celebration of the old
city's luck, complete with a holochrome image of the Liberty
Bell, the original having been mashed flat along with Inde-

pendence Hall and then washed out into Delaware Bay by the
rising salt tide, swirling out as gray streamers in the murky
water along with the tons of stone and ash and blackened
bone that had been the City of Brotherly Love.

As night faded, there was only a few hundred miles' range
in the fuel tanks, and the landscape was growing too urban
for safety. After Cowboy found the old quarry, he and Sarah
slept the length of the morning and then began their hike, two
more walkers coming to the boomtown to find work, obviously destined to squat with the others in the shacks and
cardboard boxes that circle the city, staining the green walls
of the Monongahela valley with the smoke of their cookfires,
haunting the city looking for work and avoiding the dark
corners where people got murdered for the change in their
pockets.

One of Cowboy's old colleagues lives here in one of the
city's suburbs. Cowboy finds the address courtesy of direc-
tory assistance and wonders how much contact Reno still has
with the business. He knows Reno made a lot of money in
his days as a deltajock and hadn't seemed the sort of person
to lose it in the time since. If he's entirely on the legal side
now, that may even make things easier.

A wall surrounds Reno's house, and on one side an old
man with three days' growth of beard under a torn straw hat
waits next to his packstaff, smoking a cigarette and waiting
for the cool of twilight before continuing his pilgrimage.
Cowboy's nerves shriek an alarm, and he does his best to
silence them. Such sights are not unusual in this or any other
part of the world.

Reno's gate is a polished chromium alloy that reflects
Cowboy's image, standing spindly and haggard next to the
tall dirtgirl with the shades like an asphalt shimmer. In
answer to the gate's questions, he pulls off his cap and wig.
The gate's voice burbles in mirthless joy, the voice of something drowning. "I seem to remember seeing you on video.
By all means come in." The gate itself is soundless as it
opens.

The house is a hymn to the interface, a geometric singular-

ity composed of crystal and expensive off-planet alloy, suggesting the linkage of the human mind with digital reality.
Jagged antennas seek the sky, transparent plastic tubes, part
of some heating/cooling system, writhe over the house in a
complex arterial pattern, carrying brightly colored liquids of
exotic properties, streams of fluid insulated by bubbles that
suggest electrons speeding through their matrix. The walk-
way leading to the house is paved with millimeter-thin slices
of meteorite protected by hard, transparent gas-planet plastic,
the shining veins of nickel and magnesium bright against the
shadowy, unoxidized iron, spotted with flecks of chromium
and silicon. Other meteorites stand frozen in glass on alloy
pillars in the forecourt. The door is inset, more polished
alloy. It opens, like the other, without sound.

"Looks like an illustration from *Cyborg Life*," Sarah mutters. The dark laser-cut stone of the walls merges with bright
alloy beams like the wood and plaster of a half-timbered
house. Liquid-crystal art re-forms itself continually on the
walls. Cowboy recognizes one of the patterns as a giant-sized
schematic of one of his motor-reflex chips.

"Leave your guns in the foyer, please. I won't touch
them." Inside the house, the voice has a smoother quality.

Sarah has insisted on carrying the Heckler & Koch in her
ruck, and with a grudging smile she puts the ruck on a table.
Cowboy puts his belly gun next to it. They step into the next
room.

Soft gelatine-filled furniture glows Cherenkov blue from
internal light sources. Aquariums filled with genetically altered fish emit the same cold spidery light as a green computer display. Randomly generated tones sound in pointillist
pattern from concealed speakers. Reno enters the room from
an alloy-rimmed door.

"Hi, Cowboy. It's been a while."

"Hi, Reno." Cowboy looks at his surroundings in a studied way. "You seem to be doing well for yourself," he says.

Five years ago Reno's delta had sucked a missile into its
port engine over Indiana and then buried itself in some dark
West Virginia hollow, sending a potential 200-million-dollar

profit in pharmaceuticals skyward in a clean blue alcohol blaze. It was one of the last big delta runs and a turning point in the shift toward the use of panzers. Reno had got out of the plane before it screwed itself into Cheat Mountain, but he'd burned himself badly trying to horse the delta over the tree-crowned ridges to the landing field in Maryland, and his parachute hadn't developed properly. Parts of him had been scraped off the trees with a shovel. In Cowboy's world Reno's bad luck was still talked about in terms of regret

Cowboy had visited him in the hospital a few times, and talked by phone once or twice a year since. Reno's body had been put back together, Cowboy had been told, but there had been too much brain damage for it to work right; and that ruled out running the mail.

The rebuild job looks good. Arms and legs in fine working order. The blue eyes match. He looks fit in flannel pants and a Hawaiian shirt. Reno's face is young except for the fine networking of lines around the eyes, and his teeth gleam white and even in the twilit room. The dark sockets in his head are covered by shoulder-length brown hair.

"I keep up with my portfolio," he says. There is a strange vacancy behind his eyes.

"Reno, this is Sarah. Sarah, Reno." They nod at each other while Cowboy puts down his box of hearts. Cowboy reaches out to shake Reno's hand.

And it feels wrong. A little too warm, perhaps, a little too . . . dry. Even the best of palms are just the least bit moist. Cowboy looks down at the arm with his infrared eyes and sees that the heat distribution is uniform, which is not the case with any arm Cowboy has ever seen.

"A prosthesis," says Reno, seeing Cowboy's expression. "This and the two legs and other bits here and there."

"But you could have got real legs," says Cowboy.

Reno taps his skull. "I *got* real legs, but there was too much brain damage. My motor coordination was shot to hell, and my sense of touch was pretty much gone—I'd lost too much skin, too many neurons. But Modernbody was looking for someone to test their latest prostheses." He shrugs. Cowboy gets an odd feeling from the gesture, as if the shrug weren't real but rehearsed. Maybe Reno's given this explanation a few too many times.

"The arm and legs are hardwired in. There's a liquid-crystal computer replacing a damaged part of the brain. The feedback isn't very good on my sense of touch, but then it wasn't any good after the crash anyway. It's all experimental stuff, very advanced. Light alloy, lighter than bone and muscle. I'm a lot more mobile than I used to be. And if they go into production, the experimental prostheses will be cheaper than cloning new legs and regrafting."

"I didn't know," Cowboy says.

"Modernbody pays me a nice pension," Reno says. "It bought this house. All it costs me is a checkup every couple months, sometimes a rewiring with an improvement. And my new parts will last longer than the originals."

The coming thing, Cowboy thinks. Live forever in a bodily incarnation of the eye-face, not limited to the speed of artificially enhanced neurotransmitters but approaching the speed of light, extending the limits of the interface, the universe. Brain contained in a perfect liquid-crystal analog. Nerves like the strings of a steel guitar. Heart a spinning turbopump. The Steel Cowboy, his body a screaming monochrome flicker, dispensing justice and righting wrongs. Who was that masked AI? Dunno, pardner, but he left this silver casting of a crystal circuit.

To Cowboy, it sounds pretty good. If they can lick that feedback problem.

Reno looks at him with his old-young eyes. Eyes that were a lot younger until that port engine spewed its molten remains into the thin air of Indiana and the horizon began to do flip-flops.

"So," Reno says. "You people get caught in a crossfire?"

"That's about the size of it."

The eyes narrow. "From what I hear the crossfire extends all the way to California."

"I'll worry about that when I get West. After that, if you have any Tempel Pharmaceuticals stock in your portfolio, I'd sell."

Reno frowns into one of his crystal pieces of art. "Sit down," he says, "and tell me about it."

They sit next to each other on a pair of armchairs while Cowboy gives a brief recapitulation of what he knows. Sarah assumes a half-lotus on a glowing nuclear blue couch, not offering comment. Staying unobtrusive, as bodyguards should.

Reno rubs his chin. "So what do you need? Transportation west? A place to hide?"

Again Cowboy has a strange feeling. As if Reno is somehow cruising on automatic pilot. That, for all his apparent helpfulness, it's all reflex, that he's not really interested.

"We want to sell something." Cowboy reaches for his box of computer matrices and tears open the cover. Reno leans forward and peers into the container.

"We want to move a thousand of these," Cowboy says. "All perfect, all Orbital quality, made for Yoyodyne by their Olivetti subsidiary. OCM Twenty-two Eighty-ones, to be precise." There are matrices times fifteen K in the panzer, but he doesn't want to take more of the Hetman's property than necessary. He hasn't forgotten whom Sarah is really working for.

"Heart crystals," Reno murmurs. He makes a breathy sound with his lips. "So this is what that battle was over."

Cowboy feels he has succeeded in attracting Reno's attention.

They make the world go around, so central that the nickname "heart" isn't out of place, for if the hearts stopped, the body would die. Computer cores made of liquid crystal that can re-form itself in any configuration, creating the ultimate efficiency for any particular piece of cybernetic business that needs doing, shifting from storage of data to moving it to analyzing it and then altering to a form most efficient for acting on the analysis. Hearts that can make minds, from little bits of brightness in Cowboy's skull that let him move his panzer, to larger models that create working analogs of the human brain, the vast artificial intelligences that keep things moving smoothly for the Orbitals and the governments of the planet.

All in miniature potential, here in the cardboard box.

"Forty hearts per box," Cowboy says. "The other boxes are in a safe place. You get thirty percent for being our thirdman."

Reflected crystals gleam like rubies in Reno's eyes. "Let me check the market," he says.

He touches two places on the midnight-black table in front of him and a comp board glows in the interior, projecting its colors onto Reno's face. From underneath he slides a black box wired to the comp in the table and a box of crystal memories. He slips a memory cube into the trapdoor of the box, then unspools a stud from the box and puts it into his temple. He presses some of the keys on the deck face and leans back in his chair.

The fish tanks bubble in the far-off humming distance. Reno's expression softens, then hardens again. He is flying the face for a long time. Then his eyes flick to Cowboy, and his eyes show surprise.

"Tempel stock has gone up twelve points since noon." Reno's voice is dreamy, reluctant to unfuse with the interface. "They're moving against Korolev, a major takeover attempt. Korolev's vulnerable right now—they've made a lot of bad moves." Cowboy sees Sarah's startled expression from the corner of his eye and knows she understands more of this than she's been letting on, and that he'll have some questions for her later. But Reno's voice drones on from his chair.

"Tempel is strong in pharmaceuticals and mining, but their aerospace division is weak. Acquisition of Korolev would strengthen them. The market seems to be saying Tempel will win, but my guess is that it won't be a sure thing. Korolev has a lot of resources to call on . . . and they're so secretive there are bound to be some things Tempel doesn't know about."

Cowboy pictures the two Orbital giants grappled in their electronic conflict, using the paper value of the shares as leverage against each other, feeding on data more precious than gold, artificial intelligences and corporate minds scheming to manipulate the streams of numbers. Buying stock and futures through third parties they hoped no one knew they controlled. Both sides had resources that were almost unlimited, and victory would go to the most subtle, the one who manipulated the other through the most blinds, who had a better comprehension of the other's weaknesses. Reno seems to fade away, his mind moving back into the interface, sucking data through the filter of the memory box. Cowboy sneaks a look at Sarah and sees her, like Reno, turning inward, absorbed for a moment in her own inner landscape. Assembling a picture more complete than Cowboy's. He wishes she'd give him some of what she knows.

Reno unfaces. The glowing colors in the deep ebony table fade. He puts his crystal memory back in its file and takes a breath. "The borders are fading," he says. The voice is still dreamy, his eyes trancelike, staring a thousand yards into some internal landscape. "After the war, demarcation was clear—victors, vanquished, victims. Blocs agreed not to compete in certain areas, formed cartels to dominate other markets. Agreed-upon areas of exploitation. Sharing of data. Competition limited to nonvital areas.

"But the war created a lot of vacuums. Vacuums in power, in distribution, in information flow. The Orbitals got sucked into them, and there things weren't so neat. The borders were . . . less well defined. There the winners and losers weren't so easy to see. Now the blocs are tangled in those areas and the result is that the lines of demarcation are undergoing some adjustment. The system is beginning to undergo stress, to radiate fracture lines. Events taking place in the ill-defined areas are having consequences in the rest of the system. A little pressure put here and there, at a critical point . . . it could make a big difference." His eyes shift abruptly to face Cowboy.

"That, of course, isn't my concern," he says. "I'm planning on keeping in the middle, on the node of the standing waves. I've got some information and I've got a good sense of how things move. I can ride things out."

"Keeping in the middle gets you in the crossfire, Reno," Cowboy says. "Just like Sarah and me."

"You were never in the middle, Cowboy. None of the deltajockeys ever were. The thirdmen strive for the middle, but rarely reach it. And I'm in the middle." Reno's eyes are chill as he raises his prosthetic arm. "I'm in the middle by my nature, half one thing, half another. I can stand on the node and see the waves rising and collapsing around me. The deltajocks collapsed, Cowboy. You swam off to ride another wave, but it's going to collapse, too."

Who is speaking? Cowboy wonders. Reno or that mass of crystal lodged in his skull? Reno is living in the eye-face every moment now, and Cowboy wonders if he's lost himself in there, if too much of his personality has been sucked into the machine part of him, if control has shifted from his brain to the crystal.

Whiteout, it's called. Rapture of the comp. It's not supposed to happen to people like Cowboy and Reno, not to users who know the score, who fly the interface across the terrain of the real world, but it's a hazard for the theoretical types, artificial intelligence people and physicists, those who are lost in abstracts most of the time. They can confuse the electron image with the reality it images, diffusing themselves through the information net, racing at the speed of light along its patterns until their egos fade away, become so thin as to become intangible.

With a shiver Cowboy realizes that Reno is a ghost, a vacant-eyed collection of habits that have lost any purpose except to feed the crystal in his head with the data it needs. Whatever remains of the deltajock is pure reflex.

"These comp hearts are hot," Cowboy says. "You might want to sit on them for a while."

Reno shakes his head. "I'm not even going to sell them, not for a long time. I'll put them in a vault and use them as collateral for a loan from a face bank. I'll use the loan to enrich my portfolio, and by the time I've played with the money for a while, I'll be able to pay back the loan and then move the comp hearts onto the market. By then this war will be history."

Cowboy leans back in his chair. Reno seems to be thoroughly out of his trance now, and his plan for making use of the crystal seems as safe as any.

"You can move the hearts right to my place till I can rent a vault," Reno says. "I've got a double system of security here. The first one can be taken out if people know how. The second—well, they won't be looking for it. Anyone coming over my wall is going to get a firefight."

"Cowboy," Sarah says. He is startled by her voice, having got used to her as a silent half-lotus on the periphery of his vision. "We're going to need to get a truck to move the hearts here."

"Use mine," Reno says. "It's in the garage." He fishes in his pocket, brings out a key, a tiny crystal on the end of a stainless-steel needle. "This'll have the codes. I'll open the garage door and gate from here." He looks from Sarah to Cowboy. "Do you people need a meal?"

"No," Sarah says, and again Cowboy is surprised by the determined edge in her voice. "We should be getting back to the panzer. I don't like leaving the Hetman's cargo alone."

Reno points with his left hand. The fingertips are trembling. "Through there. Right, end of the hall. Kitchen's on the left if you change your mind." He reaches under the table, takes out a stud, puts it into one temple. His other hand reaches for the memory box. "I've got to talk to some people. See how much I can raise on this."

"Be careful," Sarah says. Reno pays no attention. His eyes are already abstracted. Cowboy rises from his chair.

Sarah uncoils herself like an angry cat, her dark eyes intent on Reno, her spine arched. She stalks away and Cowboy can see the ridged muscles on her arms. She comes back with her ruck and Cowboy's gun, and Reno doesn't react.

"Your friend's crazy, Cowboy," she says later as they take the truck south through the bright early evening. "His brain is so white I almost had to put on my shades to look at him."

Cowboy is driving the truck through the interface, feeling the hydrogen fuel cook in its turbine, the tires moving over the softening asphalt. "I know," he says. "He had a bad wreck."

"Now he thinks he's sitting on a node at the center of the cosmic dataflow," she says. "What happens if the celestial matrix tells him to turn us in?"

"He's an old friend," Cowboy says, unsettled. "We don't operate that way."

"What if he does?" Sarah demands. "Tempel would happily give him two thousand crystals instead of the single K we're giving him. And it wouldn't be a seventy-thirty split, either."

Cowboy feels his anger rising. "If he's a traitor, we're hardly any worse off, are we? I don't notice your friends offering to help."

Sarah's quiet fury is her only answer. Cowboy feels it as a silent, almost tangible radiation for the rest of the ride.

ARTIFICIAL INTELLIGENCES RIOT IN LENINGRAD DATANET KOROLEV I.G. OFFERS NO COMMENT ON SAFEGUARD QUESTION

In the four A.M. darkness Cowboy brings the panzer out of the quarry and he and Sarah load a thousand crystal hearts into Reno's light truck. Mosquitoes whine along their spiral tracks, aiming for wrists, necks, the hollow behind the ear. Sarah has made it clear she's going to scout Reno's neighborhood before she'll let the truck drive in.

The scouting turns out not to be necessary.

Fear moves like ammonia ice in Cowboy's veins as, from half a mile away, he sees the smoke rising like a slow gray phantom over Reno's house, the cloud's underside glowing the color of blood. Police wagons slice past, their sirens whooping up and down the register. Sarah rolls down the window, and a distant rattle of fire echoes hollow from the slate hills.

"That second defense system," Cowboy says. Something flares orange on the underside of the cloud and a second later Cowboy hears a muffled thump, and he can feel his teeth

drawing back as anger pours through him like alcohol fire.
He hauls the truck around and shoots hydrogen to the turbine,
feeling himself pressed back in the seat. He skids around a
curve and the cargo thumps in the back. If he can get to the
panzer in time, he might be able to get Reno out, the Pony
Express to the rescue. . . .

"Cowboy," Sarah says. "Slow down. We don't want
them checking our registration."

"I'm going to pull Reno out with the panzer."

Sarah moves toward him, her eyes glittering like dia-
monds. "Reno's blown, Cowboy. All he can do now is get
us killed. They'll be *ready* for a panzer. They know what
yours does by now. That turret gun won't surprise them."

"There's a chance."

She grips his arm and he can feel the pain skate along his
nerves. "He's alone, Cowboy," she says. "And so are we."

Cowboy can hear regret in Sarah's voice, and it surprises
him.

"We're alone," she repeats. "Just like we've been since
we left the Free Zone. The only difference is that now we
know it for sure."

There is a flash from behind them and the smoke turns
opalescent, shot through with white fire. Cowboy feels the
heat of it on his neck. There can't be anything left after that,
he knows. The turbine, seemingly of its own accord, lowers
the pitch of its quiet howl.

Dawn is just climbing over the Appalachians. The asphalt
is already beginning to melt.

Chapter Eight

TAMPA'S TOTALS OVERNITE,
28 FOUND DEAD IN CITY LIMITS . . .
LUCKY WINNERS PAY OFF AT 15 TO 1

POLICE BLAME RECORD HEAT WAVE

The cooling panzer engines crackle, sounding like someone knocking on the armor. Images of heat dance in slow
motion on Sarah's retinas.

"Tell me about Korolev," Cowboy says. Sarah looks at
him in surprise.

"You knew something about Korolev that Reno didn't
know," Cowboy insists. His expression is intent, angry. "If
I know it, I have a better chance of staying alive. I need you
to tell me. I have a right."

They have come another hundred miles west through the
slate hills and have found a dry brush-covered gully to hide
in, this one across the Line in Ohio, sitting in old National
Forest land amid timber too old and rotten to harvest. It's the
end of the line for the panzer, the fuel tanks laden with little
more than alcohol dew.

Sarah sits down on the passenger bunk. A seven-millimeter
casing rolls across the metal floor as she straightens her foot,

and she thinks of the sounds of fire echoing from the Pennsylvania ridges, that last white-heat flash that ended it. The screamsheets report that an armed party of unknown origin tried to break into Reno's place, got caught by his defense systems. Then the cops arrived and got fire from both the intruders and the automatics, and took out everything before it was clear what was going on. No survivors.

"Korolev Fellowship of Interests," Cowboy reminds her. Sarah can feel the words weighing on her shoulders like steel.

"All right," she says. Images flicker in her mind, Firebud's scornful violet eyes, the company patches on the zonedancers at the Aujourd'Oui, that last amber statement, RUNNING, burning forever in the corner of Danica's display as Sarah listened to the slow-dripping moments.

"All right," she says again. She feels the intensity of Cowboy's gaze and surrenders to it. History, she thinks. It doesn't matter anyway. "It was a penetration operation," she tells him, "targeted against the Korolev computer in Tampa. The outside security on the comp was too strong to break, so I was supposed to use this Korolev courier to get me into their compound and put a program into their system from there, once we got past the safeguards. I figured it was a data raid, but it looks as if it was sabotage. The program was aimed at smashing up Korolev's strategies, trying to weaken them for the takeover."

"What did the courier get out of it?"

Sarah feels Weasel throb, a heavy presence in her throat. She looks at Cowboy, daring him to react.

"He thought he was going to get laid. What he got was dead."

Cowboy holds her gaze. "Okay," he says.

"He deserved it."

"I never said he didn't."

In the end it is Sarah who drops her gaze. She plucks at the old wool blanket on the bed and smells the dense unmoving air, the sweat and chemical toilet and hot metal. Even the open dorsal hatch doesn't stir the air here.

"How'd you meet this Cunningham?" Cowboy asks.

"The Hetman gave him my name. I think they did business from time to time."

"Now they're trying to kill each other."

She shrugs. "It's business. Nothing personal. Cunningham isn't the type to mix the two, and even if he were, his company wouldn't let him."

Cowboy picks up his helmet from the back of his seat, holds it loosely in his hands. "Is it connected, do you think? Tempel's moving on the thirdmen and on Korolev at the same time?"

"I don't know. Could they be weakening Korolev by attacking you?"

"I can't see how. Nobody in this country uses Korolev engines or parts. My engines are Rolls-Royce turbines made under license by Pratt and Whitney."

Sarah leans back against the bulkhead and closes her eyes. She can still hear the roaring of the turbines, the vibration of the metal. Behind her eyelids Sarah can still see the amber message, RUNNING. She shakes her head.

"I don't see how it can be connected," she says.

"I've got to get out West, Sarah. I've got resources there."

She cocks an eyebrow at him. "Buried treasure?"

"Yes, as a matter of fact. And friends."

Sarah says nothing, just closes her eyes.

"Are you coming?" Cowboy asks. He sounds impatient. "Or are you going to try to get back to the Occupied Zone?"

"My brother's in Florida. I'm supposed to be taking care of him."

Cowboy stirs on his foam couch. "How old did you say he was?"

"I didn't say. But he's twenty."

"Then he can take care of himself."

Sarah opens her eyes and sneers. "You seem to need me to take care of *you*, Cowboy."

In one singing movement that is too fast for her eyes to follow, Cowboy slams his helmet down on his armrest. "*I'm a target, damn it!* They're looking for me! If I'm with you, it changes my profile. I'm safer."

Sarah laughs and shakes her head. "All that means is that I'm standing next to a target. Forget it, Cowboy. I can draw fire on my own."

He looks at her with his jaw muscle working. And to her surprise there's a hopeless look in his eyes, a vacancy filled only with desperation. "I'll pay you," he says. "Your standard rates for a bodyguard job. Payable when we get to Montana."

"Standard rates and a ticket to Florida," she says automatically, while her mind clicks into gear and she wonders whether she really wants this job. She thinks of Daud lying under the Christmas green LEDs of his automated bed, his eye dull with endorphins, waiting for Jackstraw, who would not come, having no one to turn to but the sister he fears. Wanting his old magic to return, the place in the street that was his own, knowing it was gone now because the rules have changed for him as well as for Sarah, that he will have to find a new pattern, a new source for what he needs. . . . She doesn't want him to be alone, having nothing to look into but the nullity of the endorphin haze.

But a job at this point would bring in some money, maybe make a down payment on Daud's replacement eye. Getting to Montana probably won't take appreciably longer than moving to Florida, and once she's paid, she can get past the border checks into the Occupied U.S. with fewer problems than if she were penniless. The Free Zone cops don't like to let in paupers.

With the fighting in Florida there will be work, but it might be too dangerous to go there right now: the Hetman might give her to Cunningham as part of a peace treaty. Business, of course, nothing personal. So—best to take Cowboy up on his offer.

And the look in his eyes has something to do with it, too, touching a part of her she doesn't want to think about. A part, she thinks, that doesn't want the next stage of the journey to be a lonely one.

Sarah haggles for a while about her "standard rate," not wanting Cowboy to think he was getting her easy. Cowboy ends up paying a little more than he would have otherwise, not as much as she suspects she could have got. In the end she stands up and shrugs. "Okay. You've got yourself a bodyguard. Now what have you got to eat?"

"Lurp rations are all that's left. Freeze-dried. Enough for three, four days."

Sarah grimaces. "Freeze-dried soy. My favorite."

"Unless you want to hold up a bank and buy the real."

"It's an option." She grins. She presses her hands to the metal of the low ceiling and pushes upward, feeling her muscles flex and strain, suddenly impatient to be on her way. Good to get outside of this Chobham box again, breathe some air. Good to have a direction to walk in, even if the goal was someone else's.

"It was a bank that killed Reno," Cowboy says. "He was trying to raise money on those hearts, and whoever he was dealing with must have tipped off Tempel."

If you knew where to look in the interface, you could find banks disguised as something else, trading companies or some kind of broker, that offered unusually high rates of interest and didn't inquire too deeply into the source of the cash, that either didn't report their transactions as required by law or cheerfully accepted a false name for their customers if they did. Uninsured, of course—sometimes the banks vanished overnight along with their depositors' funds. This was accepted as one of the risks of that kind of speculation, but it didn't happen often. And sometimes the bank was just re-forming under another cover, and the depositors would be contacted later.

"If the Orbitals are into the thirdman network, then they can be running a dozen eye-face banks and no one will know it," Cowboy says. "Maybe that's the connection. Maybe the thirdmen are using Korolev's banks and Tempel wants to take everything out."

Cowboy's speculation seems particularly pointless right now. Sarah begins field-stripping the Heckler & Koch. She plans on taking it in her rucksack. Montana might turn out to be full of somebody's army, and if it is, she wants all her parts in working order.

NOON RAID ON ARKANSAS BORDER HIDEOUT

Panzergirl Dies After Refusing Surrender
Fortune in Electronics Confiscated
M.B.I. Denies Use of Napalm

Shining across a sky the color of wet slate are the constellations of control, the Orbital factories, satellites, and power stations. A few early stars offer feeble competition. Sarah is deep in her own interface, her body oiled with sweat. Kicks thrust out, sword hands and fists flicker like heat lightning in the moist summer air. She conjures faces in front of her, aids to concentration as she wills her strikes into the imagined heart of the phantoms. She spins, cocks a leg, looks over her shoulder, spears an enemy. Beaten-down timothy provides sure traction for her bare feet. She's keeping Weasel hidden for the moment—no sense in giving away a surprise. Cowboy watches from the shadow of an elm, its leaves brown with the blight. He's tired from having walked most of the day, with a short ride or two to break the monotony. They're still in Ohio, keeping to the back roads, where the heat can't find them. They were hoping to find an old farmhouse to camp in but it appears that Ohio's been tearing them down so as to discourage transients.

"You're really into that, aren't you?" Cowboy offers. Sarah doesn't answer, merely strikes with elbows and hands against enemies to either side. Fighting an army of ghosts that rise before her, faces without names, as devoid of identity as Cunningham, their voices a rattle of dead tree limbs in the sluggish wind. Power flows through her muscles like quicksilver, and she flings herself into a sunburst of motion, spinning, kicking, leaping, her arms a blur.

And then stillness, poised in her stance, a hologram frozen in motion, while the army of ghosts fades. Sweat trickles the

length of her brows. The heavy air seems thick as honey in
her throat. On the decaying surface of the road, fifty yards
away through some bushes, a truck bounces across some
potholes. Sarah waits for the sound to fade entirely from the
deepening night.

She turns and faces Cowboy, gives him a smile. "Now I'll
eat," she says.

"Aren't you supposed to bow or something?" He pulls a
foil packet out of his ruck and tosses it to her. Her nerves are
still in overdrive and she plucks the packet from the air as if
it was in slow motion. She sits in front of Cowboy in a
half-lotus and tears the packet open.

Cowboy is looking at her with his dark artificial eyes. He's
taken off the cap and wig, and they lie on the grass beside
him. "Do you have crystal for that?" he asks. "Or did you
come up the hard way?"

She grins wolfishly and tears at a strand of meat analog.
"A little of each," she says.

"I'm not surprised." His pupils seem to dilate. "That scar
across your left eyebrow. Doesn't look like a knife or razor."

Sarah swallows the dry soy strand, shakes her head. History, she thinks. "Bottle," she says. "My father got drunk
and cut me when I was little."

"The one on your cheek."

"Knifeboy in a street fight. Years ago."

"Under your lip."

For a moment she sees again the mad eyes reflecting the
dim ruddy light, the dewy mouth repeating over and over the
words chanted as incantation, "Bitch, bitch," the razor held
in the white-knuckled hand. Her own knowledge, deep in her
spine, that she had lost control over this, that she had finally
met one of those clients who had a particular name, a name
that even the most hardened of her associates spoke of in
husky, fearful voices: "Thatch." And then her own reaction,
her catalyzed reflexes sending the chair blurring through the
air, the movement fanning her own blood across the room in
a jeweled crescent, tracking in a scarlet spray across the blue
pastel shirt of the madman, who in the next instant was dying

at the foot of the bed with a broken skull. And, as she stood over the body and the broken chair, her blood running down her throat and breasts and arms, the sudden knowledge, as deep and disturbing as the earlier realization, that she had found out what she was.

She looks up at him in feral anger. "What are we doing here, Cowboy?" she asks. "Writing history? Making a catalog of my mistakes?" She snarls and snatches the water bottle from the grass, wrenching off the top. "Each scar is a mistake, okay? A little misjudgment I made once upon a time. *But I don't make them anymore.* The stakes are a little higher this time around, okay?"

Sarah tilts back her head and swallows. The water is hot and tastes of plastic.

"I wondered why you didn't have them fixed," Cowboy says. Standing his ground, refusing to get angry. "That's all."

Sarah wipes her lips on the sleeve of her jersey. "Because it's good for business, that's why," she says. "Some people wonder if a dirtgirl isn't scared of making herself less pretty, or if she might be more frightened of getting hurt than a boy. So I prove my point, and prove it right out front. Satisfied?"

Cowboy smiles and Sarah is reminded of Cunningham, that tight-lipped expression of cold, superior judgment. "Satisfied," he says. "You don't mind letting people know what you are. Neither do I."

She looks at the sockets implanted in his skull, almost invisible in the growing darkness. "I thought you were a buttonhead when I first met you. Thought I was going to have to nursemaid a lizard."

"Out West the face sockets mean something different. But if people here want to make that mistake, that's okay. I can't see myself worrying over their opinions."

Sarah finishes the packet of soy product and crumples it. Somewhere to the south of them they can hear the moaning of a train and feel the deep vibration of it coming up from the ground. Cowboy turns his head toward the sound.

"In the old days we could have hitched a ride on the train," he says. "Been out west in a couple days."

"Huh? It must have been a long time ago if it was before cars with automated nerve darts and laser detection mechanisms."

"Not so long. In those days the only thing you had to watch out for were private cops called bulls. A friend of mine has some songs about it in his jukebox."

"A what box? Is that something else you have out west?"

He looks at her thoughtfully. "I guess so," he says.

Sarah's sweat is cooling on her skin. She takes another drink of water and wishes they hadn't run out of Cowboy's electrolyte replacement. Vitamin pills are all they have, that and the aspirin from Cowboy's first aid kit. She leans forward and stretches out her arms, feeling the suppleness of the muscle. She will sleep well tonight on her grassy pillow.

This, she thinks, might almost be a vacation. If it weren't for what was waiting at the end of the trip.

HOTTEST SUMMER IN HISTORY
SIXTH RECORD IN NINE YEARS

Record Heat Waves from Coast to Coast
(Climatologists' explanation, page 16)

The bikeboy is about seventeen, thin with a hollow naked chest, and his tan looks so inappropriate on his sickly body that it seems painted on. His matchstick arms are covered with tattoos that climb up across the yoke of his shoulders, blue circuit diagrams that at second glance form faces, devils, icons, women with slitted eyes and liquid-crystal tongues. His eyes are deep and more than a little mad. He's wearing only a pair of jeans cut off raggedly above the knee and heavy boots with blunt bronze toe caps.

"We'll take you," he says. His voice is almost buried beneath the sound of the turbine he's straddling. "We'll take you all the way to the big river."

They call themselves Silver Apaches, and their leader's

name is Ivan. He rides a turbine tricycle with a wirecutter
fixed to the front, looping up in a silver bladed arc. Others,
the men with the same kind of precise Escher tattooing,
women with the same type of designs printed on scarves that
wrap around their heads and breasts, are on trikes or gleaming dirtbikes with thick welted tires. Most are riding the face
but some steer manually. Sarah figures they don't spend a lot
of time on pavement.

"Get on, linefoot," Ivan says. "You can call us the
Silvers for short." He gives her an appreciative look. "That's
a nice piece of armor you're wearing. Somebody looking for
you?"

"Not since he found me, no," Sarah says. Ivan grins,
brown teeth webbed with metal.

Cowboy is talking to a black Silver whose dreads do not
entirely conceal the two rows of sockets in his skull, most an
extreme form of decoration since the five sockets Cowboy
wears are enough to handle any traffic with the eye-face.
Sarah looks at Cowboy, sees his shrug that means okay. She
climbs into the little jump seat behind Ivan. His shoulder
muscles flex under the tattoos as he digs into a pocket of his
jeans. "Nervewash, linefoot?" he asks, and holds up a plated
inhaler.

Sarah shakes her head. "No. Thanks." The combination
of speed and her hardwired nerves is too unpredictable.

Ivan shrugs. "Best way to appreciate a run. But it's up to
you, linefoot." He fires a torpedo up each nostril and throws
his head back, laughs. And the turbine cycles up.

The Silver Apaches move at full speed on more or less a
straight line, leaping ditches and slicing across fields of corn
or soy, changing course only for towns or occupied houses,
the chrome trikes with their wirecutters moving in front when
a fence crosses their path. "We're trying to bring back the
open range, see." Ivan laughs as the trike slices through an
eight-foot fence, the whiplashing wire gouging his arms,
drawing blood. Cattle scatter in lowing terror.

Sarah looks for handgrips as the trike crosses ditches and
creekbeds, sometimes rearing up on two wheels. She can tell

that the Silvers's style is supposed to be languid, lying back
in their seats and riding the eye-face, no more concerned than
if they were watching the vid—even the Silvers who are
driving manually try to move easily, without apparent effort—but Ivan's nervewash spoils the effect; he keeps tapping out rhythms on his bare knees, on the chrome keys of
the computer deck sitting across the useless handlebars.

In late afternoon Ivan cuts a fence into a pasture, but
instead of entering, the Silvers park their bikes and watch as
the black Silver steps off his bike with a short-handled sledge,
and with a single stroke drops a heifer in her tracks. "Fresh
veal, hey." Ivan grins. The Silvers draw skinning knives and
close in.

Bungees are holding bloody packets of beef to the bikes as
the Silvers rumble into a brush-strewn declivity on the east
bank of the Wabash. Two migrant families scatter for cover
before a chorus of jeers, the white legs of the children
flashing in the sun like the tails of startled deer. "*Our* river!
Our beach!" Ivan howls over the whine of his turbine as his
wirecutter slices apart a shelter made of canvas and driftwood. He jumps off the trike to loot the blanket rolls the
migrants left behind.

"Fucking losers!" His voice is an engine scream. "Think
I'm gonna sleep in your flea-ridden blankets?" He tears a
blanket in half with his skinning knife, crushes a corn doll
under his foot. "Outa my sight!" The others laugh or join in.

The Silver Apaches light driftwood fires and burn the last
of the migrants' scattered belongings before beginning their
barbecue. A few Silvers roll in the silty water, splashing
away travel dust. Sarah looks at the cool water, feels the
weight of the Heckler & Koch in her ruck, decides not to.

"Go ahead," Cowboy says. She's surprised that he's stepped
up behind her without her hearing. "I'll sit on the gun for a
while."

Sarah shrugs off the rucksack, pulls off the armored jacket
and her sneakers, steps into the warm water. Silvers howl
and splash nearby, but as soon as she submerges, the noise

fades, and it seems she can hear for miles through the water. The river buoys her up. She turns on her back and drifts, letting the Wabash hold up the weight of the world.

Later Sarah sits on the bank, leaning back with her ruck as a pillow, while Cowboy takes his turn in the water. The westering sun turns the river to quicksilver. The aroma of food is in the air. She watches Ivan as he marches up and down the beach, giving quick glances left and right like a general inspecting his troops. Laughing, every so often, for no apparent reason. Then Ivan sees her in the shade and grins to himself, walking to her.

"You got something nice in your little pack, linefoot?" he asks. "You running drugs across the Line?"

"If I were running, I'd be in a panzer from west to east," Sarah says. "Not hitchhiking in the wrong direction."

Ivan shrugs. "Not always, linefoot. We run the Line sometimes. We can only bring small quantities, but it pays for the upkeep of our bikes. Plenty of other amateurs in the business, too, some on foot. And it's kind of funny that you're wearing armor."

"The man who sold me this armor said it couldn't be told from regular cloth. And I'm not running drugs."

Ivan gives a little giggle. "Whatever you say. We all got secrets."

She looks up at him. "Is it a secret why you hate the migrants?"

He sneers, shrugs, twitches his shoulders. "Hey," he says. "They lost it, okay? Lost their jobs, their houses, cars. Everything." He leans close to her, grins with his brown metaled teeth. "But the stupid fuckers *want it all back*. They just got *given* their freedom, and they don't want it—they just want their house and a job with the company and a little patch of green for their kids to run in." He laughs and waves his arms. "When they could have this! *Freedom!*"

He fumbles for a pocket, pulls out his inhaler, fires a pair of torpedoes. "Blew my septum right into my hand the other week," he says. "Gotta switch to pills one of these days."

Ivan shambles off, his fingers moving in front of him as if

he were tapping a computer console. Sarah looks in the ruck
for the water bottle. There is another set of footsteps coming
and she sees one of the Silver women walking toward her,
carrying two bottles of beer. The bottles seem to be mis-
matched.

Her genes seem to be a graceful blend of black and Oriental, her kinky hair cropped close to allow access to the
sockets, and she's a little older than the rest. Her nipples are
standing out under the wet scarf she's tied around her small
breasts. She holds out a beer.

"My name is Sloe. As in gin."

"Thanks." Sarah takes the bottle and looks at it. "Where
do you get beer in bottles made out of petroleum plastic?"

"One of our part-time members brews the stuff. The bottles must be eighty years old."

"They're worth a fortune."

"We know. We just don't care."

Sarah tips her head back and swallows. The beer is dark
and just a little sweet. She nods her approval and wipes her
lips. One of Ivan's laughs floats up from the barbecue. Sloe
turns her long eyes in his direction. "Ivan's going to die,"
she says. "That's why we follow him." She turns back to
Sarah with a Mona Lisa smile. "We always follow the
doomed ones. The ones who show us the way."

"Ethical Nihilists?"

Sloe nods. "You've heard. Good."

"Sometimes they come down to where I live in Florida
and set fire to themselves or something. It fucks up the
nightly totals. Die with style, and hope the world follows,
right?"

Sloe's voice is soft, gentle in its certitude. "The world will
follow, no matter what. We just want them to accept that. Go
with a little dignity, a little forethought."

"You're a little old for this, aren't you?" Putting the
blades in her voice.

Sloe shakes her head. Shining through the tree leaves
behind her, the sunlight is printing moving data on her face
like a memory of Ivan's tattoos. "No. Just a little uncertain

of how I want to go. I can only do it once, and I don't have
Ivan's feeling for it.''

"Go down fighting, I'd say.''

Sloe looks at Sarah with her gentle smile. "That's not my
style,'' she says. She reaches out and takes Sarah's hand.
"Maybe I want to go out in the arms of a stranger. With
scars and a suit of armor and my scarf knotted in her hands.''
Sloe takes Sarah's hand and places it over her jugular. Sarah
can feel the pulse in Sloe's throat before she takes her hand
back.

"No," she says.

"That's all right,'' Sloe says. "If you don't want to.'' She
gives a sudden ferocious giggle. The lights of sunset dance in
her eyes. "Don't think I ask every stranger, either.''

"I know.'' Snarling. "It was love at first sight.''

Sloe's answer is soft. Her eyes are suddenly uncertain.
"Maybe it was.'' She rises, her glance drifting over the
encampment. Ivan is pouring beer down his throat. The
overflow runs in brown streams down his chest.

"His family were migrants,'' she says. "Lost their farm
between the erosion and the blocs. Walked all the way across
the country and back looking for work. Died, eventually. Of
bad luck, I guess.''

Sarah says nothing, stares stonily at the river. Cowboy,
shirtless, walks purposefully out of the water, his jeans plas-
tered to his long legs. His tan is deep and uniform over
whatever parts of his body she can see. She thinks about
tanning lamps and wonders if Cowboy has one, buried with
his treasure trove in Montana. She sips her beer.

Sloe wanders away, trying to look as if she has a destination in mind. Cowboy collects his shirt from a bush and
walks toward her.

"I'm getting good and sick of these people,'' she says,
and offers him her beer. Cowboy doesn't ask her why.

"I've been trying to talk to them about the war,'' he says.
"Tempel and Arkady and everything. Thought they could do
us some good.'' He sighs and brushes droplets of water from
his arms.

"But they won't," Sarah says. "They're Buzzard Cult, right?"

"Ethical Nihilists. That's their story."

"Has one of their girls asked you to kill her yet?"

Cowboy looks at her in surprise, then shakes his head. "Just wait," Sarah promises. She takes the beer from his hand and tips her head back.

There's a sudden roaring on the river, and Cowboy and Sarah both turn to see a pair of patrol hovercraft thundering south, flying Illinois flags and heading for the Ohio and tonight's panzer. Sun flickers red off perspex turrets. Cowboy looks at them with a slight frown, watching them in a cool professional way with his calm eyes.

"Old-fashioned pulse guns," he says. "Won't work on crystal, but before we shielded 'em they used to mess up our engines some. Those sheaf missiles are damned nasty, though, if they hit."

Sarah feels a sudden uprush of gratitude at his presence, the knowledge she isn't alone here—that he's calm and reasonably sane and smart enough to play his panzer across the country in the face of things like those thundering craft on the river, that he can gauge the opposition and play the odds and accept the fall of the dice.

It means she can relax from time to time, knowing he'll pull in the slack. She finishes her beer and puts the old bottle down. Her stomach is growling for its supper.

She stands up and moves toward the barbecue. She can feel her shoulder muscles easing, knowing there's someone looking after her back.

ARTIFICIAL INTELLIGENCE LOSES PATERNITY SUIT "MY LITTLE ANDROID HAS A NAME," SOBS GRATEFUL MOTHER KOROLEV I.G. OFFERS NO COMMENT

The Silver Apaches take them across the Wabash the next day, cutting straight across Illinois to the Mississippi. Ivan leaves them with a little barbecue in each ruck. Sloe, lying languid in her saddle, looks at Sarah with cool eyes.

As they stand on the bank Sarah sees that Cowboy is gazing toward Missouri like a man watching an enemy he respects. They cross the bridge into Hannibal, and the customs people, used to migrants, don't give them a second glance.

Their next ride comes from two men in a stretched-out truck filled with torn, cast-off furniture. Cowboy sits next to the driver in front, Sarah shares the cramped second seat in the back. The men are big, tanned, with callused hands. It turns out they want to talk about Jesus. Sarah only gives them a hostile glare, but Cowboy apparently knows their language and gives them hope of a conversion as long as the ride will last.

The driver wants to give them food and a place to stay for a few days and turns off toward his commune. He doesn't seem to hear Cowboy when he says they want to go west, not north. Sarah looks at the two men and wonders how far they're going to push this. She feels her muscles tingle and thinks about riding a stolen truck all the way to Montana. This should be easy, she thinks.

"Stop," Cowboy says. "We go west from here."

"Let me just give you a meal first." Sarah watches the back of the driver's thick neck and makes claws of her hands. Knock out the one in the back, she thinks, take the driver from behind. Then her eyes turn to Cowboy. Let him play it, she thinks. See what he does.

"No," Cowboy says. "We've got all the food we can carry."

The driver licks his lips, flashes Cowboy a nervous look. "You'll like it. Wait till you meet the Sir."

There is a flash of motion in the front seat, hardwired nerves responding with a motion Sarah's eyes can't quite follow. The short barrel of Cowboy's belly gun presses against the driver's ear.

"You can see Jesus later," Cowboy says, not bothering to

raise his voice or even look at the man in the back seat, "or you can see him in the next thirty seconds. Your choice."

A minute later, as they stand in the truck's dust and watch it face toward the vanishing point, Cowboy smiles and puts the gun back in his belt. "I heard about them," he said. "Barracks and bobwire, towers on every corner with guards they call the Hounds of Christ. I would have been working in the fields all day and you would have been putting old furniture back together until their Sir got you knocked up."

"Sorry I missed it. I could have given their Sir a surprise or two."

He gives a laugh. "One of my friends, a guy named Jimi, took his panzer through their place one night. Knocked down a couple towers, trampled their wire. I heard a lot of their converts took the chance to run for it." He shakes his head. "Jimi's a crazy man. It wasn't even his fight, just something he did for fun."

Cowboy adjusts his ruck and looks at her with amusement. "Hey. I thought you were my bodyguard. Supposed to keep me out of situations like that."

"You were doing fine by yourself. I would have kept the truck, though." They start their hike along the rutted dust.

Cowboy shakes his head, a little negative twist of the chin. "No. Don't want to attract any attention in this state. If I get picked up here, I get shot."

"Mind if I ask why?"

"Because some weeks ago I blew up sixteen privateers, and they're kind of upset about that."

"You're *that* panzerboy?"

Cowboy says nothing, just watches the horizon from under the bent brim of his hat as he walks. Sarah tries to decide whether or not she believes him, concludes it's the only way things make sense.

"No wonder they're after you."

"I've got friends," he says.

"Friends like Reno? In your position friends don't happen, Cowboy. The most you've got is allies."

Cowboy doesn't answer. Sarah watches him as he walks, seeing the sweat running down his neck from under his dusty wig, still feeling the flush of surprise at this revelation, seeing bits of the mosaic falling into place. He'd become too powerful, and even the people he'd been useful to had seen that. And they'd quietly moved to swat him before he realized just how much power he had. Even now he had enough to last a while against them, maybe even cut a deal that would let him retire with his life.

But not enough to win. Sarah knows she's walking behind a man who's about to lose his first, his biggest war. She feels the dry, cool fingers of sadness touching her. No way to win without becoming one of *them*.

Sarah wonders if he knows it, if he's just playing on because it's all he knows how to do, or if he really thinks he has a hope. In a strange way she wants him not to know, to keep believing in his own star for a while longer, so as not to lose it all at once, all he ever worked for or dreamed. . . . She knows too well how that feels.

But then she remembers that look he had only once, that last day in the panzer, the knowledge of his own hopelessness and desperation, and she knows that he's entirely aware of what's going to happen to him when he gets where he's going. He's playing a game with himself, pretending that there's only friends and money at the end of this trip, and a fighting chance . . . that he's walking west because it's the only way he knows to go.

For a long moment she hopes the trek will last forever, that the destination, the hopeless, losing war both in the West and Florida, will forever recede. She looks again at Cowboy, seeing his long legs marching to the destination they both see too clearly, and feels her heart turn over.

Cowboy raises his head, watching the sky from under the brim of his cap. He seems to sniff the air. "It's going to rain," he says.

And walks on.

IF IT'S HOB, IT'S REAL . . . IF IT'S REAL, IT'S MARC MAHOMED

There aren't any more rides that day, and through the early afternoon they watch vast tumbling thunderheads coiling up above the prairies like cobras rising and spreading their hoods. The afternoon darkens, and lightning begins to jump from one cloud to another like the ball the team kicks around before the game.

"I think I know a barn near here," Cowboy says, but he's a little out of his reckoning, and the rain begins to come down in warm waves, trying to beat them down, drive them into the mud. Sarah feels the breath knocked out of her by the impact. They walk blindly through the featureless black, and it's only a lightning flash that reveals the long concrete ruin they're looking for. Further flashes reveal the roof beams packed with the mud nests of swallows, the corners filled by the dung of rats. The farm to which it once belonged is crumpled like a house of cards, fallen into its basement. They find a dry place near the door and stretch out their sleeping bags. The darkness closes around them like wet felt. Leaks pour onto concrete in the interior, molten gold streaming in the black.

"Sorry. Thought it was closer." Cowboy's disembodied voice echoes from the concrete walls.

"Not your fault. Do you know every old barn in Missouri?"

"I'd better, if I want to survive." A small pause in the black emptiness. "I'm used to traveling across this country at a higher rate of speed, though."

Thunder explodes over their heads and Sarah sees the silver sheet of water pouring down outside the broken barn door, Cowboy slumped against the wall with a rueful smile, the buttons in his head reflecting the lightning in blue-white pattern, silver and turquoise, like eyes gazing inward, into his head. Sarah feels a sweep of sadness for Cowboy, the dispossessed panzerboy, his boots leaving tracks in the dust above which he once flew with his mind flicking at the speed of light. She reaches out to take his hand, sees in the night the blue of Daud's eyes, the azure of Danica's soft sheets, the translucent inexorable color of the long Gulf rollers as they sweep slowly onto the darkening land.

"You'll ride your panzer again," she says. Her throat aches at the words.

She can sense him leaning forward, reaches out another hand blindly and touches his neck, feeling warm skin, cold rain. She laughs. "It's not fair," she says. "You can see in the dark and I can't."

"Talk to me," Cowboy says. "Tell me why you're doing this." His voice is very close. She can feel the touch of his breath on her.

"It means we're walking west," Sarah says. "And at the end of the trip we've got things to do. Alone."

"Okay." He hesitates for a moment, and she can hear his throat working at words that won't come. "Are we friends, Sarah?" he asks. "Or just allies?"

She feels a laugh coming, low in her throat. "A little of both, Cowboy."

"I'm glad."

He leans forward and she can feel his cheek pressing against her neck. His arms come around her and he holds her, not moving. She runs her fingers through his short hair, seeing again the blue of the Gulf, yearning for the touch of that wide endless purity.

Cowboy's hands begin to move. Sarah accepts the salt azure comforting touch.

Chapter Nine

The Rockies are sweating in the afternoon heat, cleft by deep shadows. The still air is filled with clouds of gnats and the scent of sagebrush scrub. Cowboy studies the old line shack and feels the presence of the belly gun stuck in his jeans.

Sarah crouches in cover fifty yards away, the machine pistol focused on the weathered paint of the line shack. Cattle at the water hole behind them call to one another. Cowboy knows the next move is up to him.

He shrugs and takes a long breath of the laden air, then stands and walks down the slope to the shack. It's a frame building shingled with cedar and painted the color of red sand, built low to the ground against winter winds. A cord of wood is stacked neatly against the west wall. There's a four-stall stable standing empty nearby. Cowboy unspools a stud from the metal doorframe, puts it into his head, and gives the lock the code.

Inside there's a metal cabinet holding tools, chairs and a table, a pair of narrow cots lying on their sides against the wall. An old metal stove with a coffeepot on it, cooking implements hanging on the wall, shelves holding cans of sugar, flour, lard, coffee, beans. He steps out into the sun and waves Sarah toward the shack.

"The lock says no one's been here since spring," he says. "I don't think it's been fooled with. I doubt they'd find this place, and I don't see why they'd bother bugging it anyway."

Sarah glances around uneasily, sweating in her armored jacket that's closed up around her throat. "Whatever you say. This is your country, not mine."

He steps back and lets her into the shack. She puts the Heckler & Koch down on the table and pulls off her jacket, fanning her jersey against the heat. "This place is only occupied in winter," Cowboy says. "People come here to look out for the cattle that use this water hole."

She looks around the small room. "Let's clean the place and take the shutters off," she says. "I don't like being blind in here."

"First things first." He walks to the tool cabinet and takes out a pry bar, nails, and a hammer. He moves the old metal frame of the cot and raises a pair of floorboards. He takes out a flat metal box and opens it.

Traveling money, documents identifying him as a man named Gary Cooper who was born twenty-five years ago in Bozeman, and a bright needle on a silver chain. He raises the key and smiles at the crystal that gleams on its point. "Safety deposit box down in Butte," he says. "Where Mr. Gary Cooper keeps his spare funds."

Sarah is looking among the supplies on the shelf and finds an old bottle of whiskey, half full. She blows the dust off it, looks at Cowboy and grins. "Looks like a party," she says.

Cowboy puts the chain around his neck and takes a heavy knife from its place above the stove, then walks back to the metal cabinet. In the corner stands a rifle in its case; he takes the rifle out, smelling oil and the lanolin of the lamb's-wool lining of the case. Curled magazines lie in a box on the upper shelf. Behind him he hears Sarah unscrewing the cap on the bottle.

"I'll get us some steaks," he says.

He snaps a magazine into the rifle. The cattle are half his anyway.

Moths dance their kamikaze spirals around the sunset flame of a kerosene lamp, battering against the blued glass of the ancient flue. Cowboy lies with Sarah under a red trade blanket, staring at the rugged cedar beams of the ceiling and surprised to find he's missing the presence of the midnight stars.

Beside him he can feel Sarah's body spasm; and all at once she sits up, the blanket falling from her breasts as she reaches for the machine pistol. "What's that?" she whispers.

"Nothing."

"Thought I heard something."

She listens carefully, her eyes moving slowly from one corner of the room to another.

"Nothing," Cowboy says again. "I was awake."

Sarah listens again, then Cowboy can see her shoulders relax and she settles back against the pillow. He considers putting an arm around her and decides not to. There are moments when she doesn't want to be touched, and from the hard expression on her profile this is one of them. She seems to be listening, still partly on guard.

"Ah, fuck it," she says, and reaches for the machine pistol. He watches while she reaches into her pocket for her inhaler, triggers it once up each nostril, then pads to the door on bare feet. She listens for a moment, the flickering glow of the lantern light making her seem to be in motion as she stands poised, then Sarah opens the door and glides into the night.

Cowboy raises his head on his arms and waits. After a few minutes Sarah slips back in the door, propping the gun's folding stock on her hip as she stands on one foot, brushing soil from the bottom of the other. Her eyes are distant, unforthcoming. Cowboy admires the way her muscles play under her dark skin. Without a word she brushes off the other foot and slips under the blanket.

"You're not going to be able to sleep after those torpedoes," Cowboy says.

"I know." Staring at the ceiling. "I should do a workout."

Cowboy reaches above his head for the bottle, takes a short pull. He holds it out to Sarah and she shakes her head.

"Making plans?"

"Trying to." She decides to take the bottle anyway and

props herself on one elbow while taking her drink. She puts the whiskey down on the blanket between them. "I figure I'll enter the Free Zone at Havana. Then I won't have to go through customs at Tampa, just take the domestic flight. Once in Tampa I can hide until I talk to some people and find out if it's safe to come out. I think I'll be okay—the Hetman's in too deep to back out by now, and he'll be wanting soldiers. And we know by now the war's not being fought over me."

"Yeah. And we know that out here it is being fought over *me*."

She gives him a look. "Yes. In a way."

Cowboy rests his head on his hands and smiles, pieces of the panzer interface shuttling through his mind, gauges flaming, monitors searching for the hovering enemies. . . . Nice not to miss this fuss. Hate to have a war fought over your body and not show up for it. He thinks of Elfego Baca calmly cooking his breakfast tortillas while the bullets of a mob of Texans chip away at the mud walls of his shack, the buffalo hunters at Adobe Walls steadying their Sharps while Quanah Parker's Indian coalition come wailing out of the night, Lieutenant Christopher Carson slipping past Pico's lancers to bring Commodore Stockton and his marines to the rescue of Kearny's column. . . . However this comes out, Cowboy thinks, he's going to be remembered out here for a long time.

"I figure to be an Apache for a while," Cowboy says. "Keep light, keep moving. Keep my people doing the same. Arkady isn't going to have a snagboy or a runner who can move without guards."

"Do you know that much about Arkady's organization?"

"It won't be hard to find out. We'll know where to look." He laughs. "There's supposed to be a little Apache in my family," he says. "But that wasn't respectable in my part of the world for a long time, so nobody knows for sure. Guess we'll find out."

Sarah looks at him intently, starts to say something, then falls silent. Then she looks up again. "Cowboy," she says, "always leave yourself room to run. You don't have to win all the time."

"I've spent my career running. And winning, too."

Her tone is hard. "Just know when to cut a deal, Cowboy. Know when it's time to go."

Cowboy looks at her, feels sadness pooling up in him. "You don't think I'll win, do you?"

Sarah turns her head away. And that's his answer.

Cowboy lets the whiskey touch his tongue again. A chill is settling in his spine and the warmth of the drink dies at its touch. "You figure Michael has a better chance?" he asks.

She shrugs. "He's got more resources, more contacts. Better able to deal."

"And in Florida you'll see your brother."

"Yes."

He sits up, crossing his legs and sipping whiskey again. He looks down at Sarah, her broad shoulders, the catlike muscle stretched over the ribs, the breasts that would have seemed large and out of proportion on a woman who wasn't so tall. He flips to infrared and watches the heat moving through her muscles, the pulsing flood of warmth through her throat.

She looks at him impatiently. "Look at it this way, Cowboy. Once this trip ends, we're just allies again, and maybe not for long. I get paid off and go home, and after that our troubles are our own."

"I know it. I'd just like the time to regret it for a decent interval, if that's okay."

"Just don't get sentimental."

He flips back to normal vision and watches the hardness in her face as she rolls over on her stomach, pillowing her chin on her forearms, her head turned away. "It seems to me," he says, "that I need a bodyguard out here more than on the hike across the Alley. Someone who can't shop me to the opposition because they want her as much as they want me."

"No. There's Daud."

"You could bring him out here."

She looks at him over her shoulder. There are razors in

her voice. "Look, Cowboy, from here it's just business. The sex isn't a part of the service anymore, and my standard rates are going up as of tomorrow."

"If I'd known sex was part of the service, I'd have taken advantage of it a little earlier."

Her face turns to stone for a moment. Then it softens. "Sorry, Cowboy," she says. She looks at him. "It's been fun, but I can't have any attachments to people I do business with, and you know why."

"I guess." Cowboy takes another drink, seeing the lantern glow reflecting in the heart of the bottle like a sunrise in the midst of ragged clouds, and for a moment he recalls the sky, the deep blackness and steady stars behind as he brought the delta arrowing across the Line and into the dawn. . . .

Sarah settles back against her pillow, her eyes black as a delta's cockpit and glowing with the same kind of subtle light. She's turning hard again, Cowboy thinks, and she has a reason: she's going back into a place where she has no friends, where there is no one to guard her back but herself. Where she can't afford to trust anyone, except perhaps this Daud in his hospital bed. . . .

Not unlike himself. He thinks he can trust more people than Sarah can, but the one he trusts most is recovering from bullet wounds somewhere.

In the distance coyotes begin to make their weird yelps. Next to him he can feel Sarah stiffen, then relax. At the familiar sound Cowboy caps the whiskey bottle and leans back, his mind flickering through the long series of plans he's made while walking across the country.

First thing, he's got to get himself some wheels.

Cowboy is riding the interface again, the notes of a steel guitar running up and down his spine like a winter storm. It's only a Packard midsize with a four-wheel option but it's still the eye-face, still moving down the torn ribbon of asphalt under a free and azure sky, and Cowboy is cherishing it, monitoring the turbine revs, fuel line, engine temperature as if he were coddling his panzer's Rolls-Royce jets.

Sarah sits in her bucket beside him. They're heading for the train station and the Butte Bullet that waits to take her, at 200 miles per hour, to New Kansas City. From there she'll hop a plane to Havana in the Occupied U.S.

She's armored again, back in her freshly laundered blue jacket with the collar turned up, mirrorshades masking her eyes. Scarred, caustic, hard-faced, sometimes flexing her hands in an unconscious way, as if they were clasping someone's windpipe. Cowboy can almost watch the streetgirl memories coming back, the reflexes she'd slowly eased out of in the last few weeks.

Survival time, he thinks. Strange to think of a hike across the country as a vacation. But it was, and now's the time to get serious.

The Bullet terminus is underground, beneath the streets of the city. Cowboy takes the Packard into a deep garage, feeling the echo of the humming tires moving along his nerves. His mind shuttles at the speed of light. It's the *face*, and it's been too long.

Reluctantly, he turns off the turbine. The spinning flywheel hums gently deep in the car's body as he unfaces and looks at Sarah. She's already half out the open door. Cowboy follows her example.

She waits while he opens the trunk. Her bag, just bought in Butte, is heavy with gold, but not as heavy as it had once been—the Heckler & Koch won't make it through the detectors. Written on a slip of paper is the code that will open the panzer cargo bay so that the Hetman can get his hearts back.

Cowboy holds out the bag, feels her cool fingers taking it, thinks of high-mountain air flavored with aspen, the astringent touch of desert wind in winter, the warm quicksilver touch of her body as they rode the sexual interface, her skin glowing white in his infrared eyes, dusky red-orange breath flowing from her mouth like streamers of sunset cloud.

"I don't plan on being sentimental," she says.

"If you need to get hold of me," Cowboy says, "you can leave a message at the number of Randolph Scott, in Santa Fe. I'll open the number in just a few days."

"Randolph Scott. I'll remember." The shaded eyes seem to glance skyward for a moment. "You can leave a message for me at a bar called the Blue Silk." She smiles to herself. "The owner's a friend."

"Okay."

She holds out her hand. "It was good doing business, Cowboy."

"Maybe we'll be allies again." Cowboy figures he can play this game as well as anybody. When he takes her hand, she steps forward and puts her arms around him. He feels the crushed armor against his chest. She kisses his neck and steps back abruptly. Past her dark mirrors he can see her eyes blinking rapidly. She smiles grimly to herself, tugs her armor firmly into place, and turns away.

Cowboy feels a draft on his neck and looks behind him, seeing no one. He closes the trunk of the Packard and steps into the driver's seat.

Time to head south, he thinks. Montana is getting to be a lonely place.

Chapter Ten

TAMPA'S TOTALS OVERNITE, AS OF 8 THIS
MORNING
22 FOUND DEAD IN CITY LIMITS
LUCKY WINNERS PAY OFF AT 3 TO 1

The *Pony Express* crouches in the big hangar like the ebony carving of a panther frozen at the moment of its spring. The Wurlitzer's colored spotlights gleam red, yellow, blue across the beams of the ceiling, and the Texas Playboys boom loud in the cavernous space, brass ringing off the metal walls, bass throbbing deep in the concrete. Cowboy feels the familiar scent of the cockpit rising around him as he eases into the couch and adjusts the weight of the Heckler & Koch on his lap. He puts the studs into his head and wakens the delta's sensors, his expanded vision overlapping like transparencies in his head, seeing only the dead empty hangar and waiting deltas set wing to wing.

He lights the weapons displays, seeing red lights only, missile pods in storage somewhere, no ammunition in the dorsal and belly minigun. Okay, he thinks, that's no surprise. The Heckler & Koch will have to do.

He hears the whine of a car turbine outside and knows

someone has arrived. He zips up the gray armored jacket he bought in Boulder and turns the collar up to protect his neck, then puts the helmet over his studs. The door opens and on his displays he can see a single figure enter the hangar, the sound of his footsteps on the concrete covered by country swing.

Pony Express can see the intruder on infrared and night cameras both, the images overlapping, red and chrome white, a hard-edged shadow silhouetted against the juke's brilliance. It's Warren, Cowboy sees, moving slowly and cautiously with a carbine in his hand. Cowboy had triggered some of his electronics simply by driving here, and Warren's come to investigate.

He's still alive, Cowboy thinks. Maybe things aren't so bad.

Cowboy triggers a belly light, and now a red revolving strobe rockets along the walls, keeping time to Smokey Dacus's drums. Warren pauses while he looks along the row of deltas, then moves toward *Pony Express,* keeping in the shadow of its wings. Cowboy turns on his Santistevan nerve boosters and leans his head out of the cockpit. "I figured they might be watching your house."

Warren looks up from beneath the brim of his cap. "Hi, C'boy." He lowers the carbine and grins with stumpy teeth. "Some people have been here looking for you."

"What did they have in mind?"

"They didn't say. In my personal opinion, I think most of them wanted to kill you." He puts the carbine on the ground and climbs the wheeled ladder to the cockpit. "Arkady came in person. He's offering twenty-two hundred common shares of Tempel for your body."

Amusement trickles into Cowboy's mind. "I wonder how he came by that figure?"

"One of Arkady's people came by just last week, just to snoop around. Chapel. You know, the lizardbrain. Delivered the warning again, made the offer for the reward again. What you'd expect. I told him I was trying to stay out of it. Maybe it satisfied him."

Cowboy snaps off the sensors and the belly light. "Chapel," he says. "Okay. Who else does Arkady have working for him?"

"It's mostly a battle between thirdmen at the moment. The independent panzerboys are trying to stay clear. As far as the thirdmen go, Pancho and the Sandman have joined Arkady. Georgi and Saavedra got assassinated right at the start. Faceman, Haystack, and Dmitri the Arrow are fighting Arkady right now, but they're not doing so good. Most of their panzerboys are loyal, at least right now. And the Dodger's boys are hopping mad."

Cowboy feels a shiver of tension running along his arms at the mention of the Dodger's name. He takes a careful breath. "How is he?" he asks.

Warren looks at him. "He'll be all right. He's at his mountain place now, with Flash Force guards and electronics. Arkady won't get near him, not unless he decides to come out."

Cowboy feels the tension dissipate. "I've got to see him."

"It can be arranged."

Cowboy pulls off his helmet and reluctantly unfaces from the delta's systems. Red monitors fade from his mind's eye.

Warren watches him with a frown. "Not all my visits were from Arkady's people," he says. "Jimi Gutierrez came by a couple times. He seemed to think I'd know where to find you, acted like he didn't believe me when I said I didn't. He says he wants to join you, and asked me to pass the message on."

"Okay. It's passed."

Warren seems amused. "Jimi's okay. Pretty crazed, though."

Cowboy looks at Warren carefully, feeling the touch of anticipation on his neck. "Warren," he says, "I've got to know if you're willing to help me in this."

Warren looks at the floor. "I got a family," he says.

Cowboy feels sadness settling in his spine. He frowns at the bank of instruments in front of him. "That's okay. I understand."

Warren glares at him, his eyes glittering on either side of his beaky nose. "I didn't say I wouldn't. Just meant it was a consideration." His mouth tightens to an angry line. "Jutz said you called to say the Orbitals were involved."

"Tempel is, anyway. Arkady's fronting for them."

Warren makes a contemptuous noise at the back of his throat. "So that's where he got his stock offer. Cheap bastard."

A laugh rises from Cowboy's heart. He grins at Warren and raises a fist, bashing the canopy frame in triumph. "You don't want to miss this," he says "We can take care of the family, Warren. Hide them till it's over."

Warren's mouth twists with amusement. "How many years do you figure that's gonna be, C'boy?"

"Not long. Not with the Orbitals involved. They've got too many resources, and they'll win if the war goes on too long."

"Yep. That's how it looks. You got a way to keep it short?"

Cowboy looks up at Warren. "I need a couple things right away. I've got to get a crystal jockey to free up some of my funds. Then a talk with the Dodger. And you, Warren." He watches as the older man rubs his stubble. "I want you to stay out of it for the moment. Let Chapel and Arkady think you're keeping clear. But I'd like you up here, working on the deltas. Making sure *Pony Express* is ready to ride."

Cowboy sees the shock running through Warren's face. "The deltas?" Warren asks. "Are you going to fly the Line again?"

"Maybe." Cowboy settles back in his seat, feeling the delta as a matte-black extension of his body, ready to soar. "Arkady likes to supervise his runs from a plane," he says. "Flying out over Colorado and Wyoming."

He sees the comprehension grow in Warren's eyes. It dawns slow and pretty as a sunrise.

WAREHOUSE FIRE IN ORLANDO
SEVERAL LIVES BELIEVED LOST
Police Deny Reports of Firefight

Marc Mahomed whispers from concealed speakers, his voice a subaudible message amid the subtle cries and rhythms of hob. Maurice looks expressionlessly at the photographs on the wall, as absorbed as if they were a vidscreen. His metal eyes turn toward Sarah as she enters, and a slight smile crosses his face. "Rum and lime?" he asks.

Sarah nods, feeling the cool conditioned air of the bar chilling the sweat on her brow. She smiles gratefully at the Blue Silk, its familiarity easing the tension in her.

She looks around the bar, seeing only a pair of customers she's seen before, two sad-eyed Russian women who, to judge by the names that punctuate their conversation—Lenin, Stukalin, Bunin, Trotsky—are engaged in the usual discussion of where the Soviet Union had gone wrong in its mission of civilizing the rest of the world. The old argument, Sarah knows, being fought by the Russian exiles all over the world. She ignores it and takes a frosted glass from Maurice.

"Have one yourself. On me," she says.

Maurice nods and reaches for the White Horse with the slow, precise grace of a mime defining an unseen object. "Haven't seen you lately, miss," he says.

Sarah sips her drink. "I've been out of town. Business. And I've been trying to stay away from some people."

"That Orbital gentleman?"

She gives a shrug that means yes. "Don't like those people. They don't seem to know when to let a person alone."

"They look for you here. That Cunningham fella. I tell him to get the hell out."

Sarah gives him a grateful smile. "Thank you, Maurice."

"Every so often I see someone who might work for him, but I can't be sure." He shakes his head. "Haven't seen anyone funny in weeks, Sarah. I think Cunningham's gone home."

"I hope so. But I doubt it."

One of the Russians raises a hand for blue vodka, and Maurice pours it into frosted glasses and delivers it to their table. Sarah feels the rum gently warm her throat. The door opens behind her with a blast of September heat and she casts a swift glance over her shoulder, seeing a wheelchair holding a middle-aged white man with metal eyes, his legs a pair of padded stumps shorn off above the knee. One of Maurice's old service friends, someone she's seen before. Sarah thinks his name is James. She stares into her glass, hearing them exchange soft-voiced greetings.

Maurice makes James a drink and puts it on his table, refusing payment over his protests. Sarah has the impression they've been through this before. Marc Mahomed chants a lament for missed chances, the loss of love, of meaning. James maneuvers his wheelchair toward the rest rooms in the back. Maurice returns to the bar, to his endless, unblinking stare at the photos on the wall, his drink untasted in his hand. Sarah finishes her White Horse. She signals for another.

"Maurice," she says, "you live upstairs here, right?"

"That's correct, miss."

"Do you have a spare room?"

The featureless Zeiss eyes rise to meet hers. "Why do you ask?"

"I'd like a place in Tampa," she says. "Where Cunningham and those friends of his won't be able to find me. I'll pay you rent, Maurice. In advance."

Maurice looks at Sarah evenly, while she wonders if she's pressed his buttons, if the mention of the Orbitals will swing it. "No dealing in my place," he says. "Nothing against the law, no people I don't know. Don't want no trouble."

"No trouble, Maurice. I only want a place to sleep."

He puts her drink on the bar. "Okay, then," he says. "One week. Then we'll see."

Sarah feels relief easing her limbs. She raises the drink and gives Maurice a faint smile. "Thank you, Maurice. You're a friend."

The rest-room door opens and James threads his chair between the tables to his place. Maurice looks at him meditatively. "A good man, once, the captain. Crazy for years, 'cause he can't fly."

Sarah looks at James over her shoulder, feeling the sadness

that is the touch of memory. "Yeah," she says. "I know someone like that."

ASSASSINATION ATTEMPT IN CASPER MAYOR ANDREIEVICH ESCAPES WITH MINOR INJURIES

Claims, "I have no enemies in the state of Wyoming." Police Baffled.

The Dodger's house occupies a minor mountain on the east face of the Sangre de Cristos, looking down on the eastern plains for a hundred miles, and not coincidentally sitting in a nice military position, with a view of everything that happens below and a near-unassailable ridge behind. Strangers have never been welcome in this part of the world, and any watchers would not go unmarked by the locals.

Cowboy rides the face south, the Heckler & Koch resting in his lap as he pushes the Packard to its limits on the high road, where the sky seems close enough to touch. Dawn graces the long eastern plains. Pine rises tall around him, young trees planted after a wholesale harvest a few years before, their growth boosted courtesy of Orbital chemicals.

The Packard glides along the interface between mind and eye, sky and earth, dawn and the last cool touch of twilight. Cowboy's eyes flicker to the windows of the rare cars and trucks, looking for familiar faces, surprised looks, cunning glances. Nothing but the faces of families heading to early mass in town.

The Dodger's gate features a pair of guards standing in camouflaged military armor, wearing bulky night vision and infra scanners over their eyes that give the same advantages as Cowboy's implants. With his infrared sight Cowboy thinks he can see a pair of figures in a camouflaged trench nearby, with what looks from its profile to be a shoulder-fired rocket. Cowboy moves the machine pistol from his lap to the seat next to him.

He parks in front of the gate and turns off the turbine. In

the quiet of the dawn, the electric whine of his descending
window seems loud. Cowboy looks into the protruding scanners of the approaching man.

"I'd like to see the Dodger. Tell him it's his old friend
Tom Mix, from the Portales rodeo."

"I'll need that piece first."

"Just take care of it. I like the feel of the thing." He hands
out the Heckler & Koch, and the man tucks it under his
elbow. Cowboy looks at the Flash Force patch over the
man's pocket, marking him as one of the best and most
incorruptible mercenaries in the business. The merc reports
Cowboy's message through a throat mic and presses his
helmet over his left ear to hear the answer. He looks at
Cowboy and shakes his head. "You must be an Angel of the
Lord, man," he says. "I'm even supposed to give your gun
back."

"Thank you kindly."

The turbine whimpers into life as the guard signals for the
gate to rise. The Packard spits gravel, climbing the switchback ruts. There are some patrols he sees on infrared, but
he's not supposed to notice them, so he doesn't. When he
parks in front of the long log-walled house, he leaves the
machine pistol in the front seat and tosses his wig on top of
it.

Jutz steps out of the door with a grin turned ruddy by the
sunrise, then yowls and jumps forward, wrapping her arms
and legs around Cowboy as he stands with a slow smile on
the cindered path. "Bastard," she says, ruffling his short fair
hair. "We missed the hell out of you." She peers at him with
her lined blue eyes. "You been fed right? You look okay."

"I'm just fine. Had to walk across most of the country, but
I had a bodyguard the whole time."

She drops to the ground and hooks a thumb in her Concho
belt. Cowboy puts an arm around her as they walk to the
door. "How's the Dodger?" Cowboy asks.

"Getting better. He's asleep right now, so let's get you
some siege posole and talk trash till he gets up." They pass
under the scanning lintel and no red lights blink, no hard

tracking-laser voices command them to halt. This is the Dodger's vacation place, not his working ranch: the place has the look of a building that is taking a lot more traffic than it's used to.

There's a twenty-gallon pot of posole on the stove in the kitchen, available at any time for any of the Dodger's people who are living on an irregular schedule, and a pile of foil-wrapped tortillas sitting in the warming oven. Cowboy collects some of each and plugs some quarters into the jukebox he'd bought Jutz and the Dodger for Christmas a couple years ago. The juke's bubble tubes cycle in time to western lightjack as Jutz brings him up to date.

Cowboy mops up the last of the posole with his tortilla. It sounds as if the troops are being worn away. The thirdmen need money to fight the war and so they're shipping more product, and the northeasterners are stockpiling. The price is dropping in the Northeast at the same time as it's rising in the West due to increased demand. Panzers are making the runs so frequently they're beginning to show signs of wear: break-downs, decoy panzers missing runs because they're sitting in police impoundment. One of the Dodger's people had to sit with his broken, shot-up panzer in a barn in Missouri for six days before his machine could be fixed and his escape run set up.

"They've been trying data raids, coming in on the phone lines, even once by microwave from a plane out over Wagon Mound," Jutz says. "But we keep our data in our heads, of course. That's why they tried to kill the Dodger."

Cowboy feels the unfamiliar touch of guilt. "I think it had a little something to do with me," he says.

Jutz looks at him with a quiet smile. "Yeah. We figured that out."

He feels uncomfortable under her gaze. "I'm sorry I started it," he says.

Jutz laughs and pats his hand. "Would have happened anyway. Maybe if you hadn't scared them, they would have set things up better and aimed straighter."

Cowboy hears the sound of footsteps and turns to see the

Dodger walking in. He's wearing a sheepskin jacket over blue silk pajamas, and he looks frail, pale, and thinner than ever, his hair disordered with sleep, walking with care on the Navajo rugs. At the sight of him Cowboy feels an uplift of joy so overwhelming that he breaks into laughter.

The Dodger scowls at him. "I know I look ridiculous," he says, "but you don't have to be so offensive about it."

Cowboy has already jumped out of his seat and run to shake his hand. He would have hugged him but he wasn't sure whether he might be damaging his stitches.

The Dodger's eyes widen with pleasure. "Damn," he says. "Good to have you back."

"I've got some ideas. And some news."

"Okay, I'll listen. But let me drink some coffee first."

"Right." Cowboy feels himself grinning like a buttonhead on his first charge of the day. He turns and follows the Dodger into the kitchen. As the Dodger draws his coffee, Cowboy puts more quarters into the jukebox. He feels like dancing.

They return to the front room, and Cowboy explains his notions as the Dodger sits in his comfortable chair, his eyes narrowed as he listens hunched in his sheepskin jacket with his mug of coffee clasped in both hands. From time to time he nods or asks for clarification. The Dodger pours himself a refill, drinks it, leans back in his chair with his eyes closed. "Yeah," he says. "We'll try her."

"Crystaljock first," Cowboy says.

"Right."

There's a simultaneous bleat from a pair of radios, one on Jutz's belt, the other in the Dodger's pocket. The Dodger takes his and answers.

The voice comes through distinctly. "This is Lockyer at the gate. There's a Jimi Gutierrez to see you. Says he's got news."

A look of distaste crosses the Dodger's face. "Okay. Clear him and send him up."

"Right."

The Dodger puts the radio back in his pocket. "Damn. I'm too old to deal with punks like him."

"He's on our side, Dodger," Cowboy says.

"That's what he keeps telling me. But he says it with that crazy smile, and I keep thinking he's on my side the same way as a pet bobcat, till he gets my hand confused with his dinner."

Another security man appears to clear Jimi through the detector in the lintel, and then the panzerboy is shown into the room. He's got a twitchy grin on his face, and his eyes are as dilated as the barrels of a twin gun. He's wearing an armored jacket and cutoff jeans, blue tennis shoes over bare feet. He sees Cowboy sitting in the corner and he laughs in triumph. The metal braces flash between his lips.

"Finally caught up with you, Cowboy," he chatters. "Hey, I want to join. Remember that day on the Western Slope?"

"Yeah. Sit down and tell us the news."

Jimi's too excited to sit, and instead he jumps in place, a human pogo. Jutz watches his performance with tolerance. "I got ten thousand K's worth of Arkady's antibiotics sitting in the cargo bay of a panzer a hundred miles north of here," Jimi says. "D'you think you could use 'em, Dodger?" He spins in glee, his arms held high, his feet jittering in a hardwired victory dance. "And I got that bastard Chapel. Blew his ass halfway to Mexico."

Cowboy looks at Dodger with a widening smile. The Dodger turns his face away from Jimi and closes his eyes. "Sit down, Jimi, before you give me a heart attack," he says. "And tell me what happened."

Jimi looks at the Dodger without any apparent loss of enthusiasm and perches himself on the edge of a chair, his rubber soles still beating little rhythms on the floor. The Sandman, one of Arkady's allies, had hired him to run across the Line from eastern Colorado. Chapel had shown up at the loading and so Jimi knew that Arkady had at least a part interest in the run. Jimi started his panzer, turned his guns and rockets on his support crew, and blew up the

Sandman, Chapel, and the fuel truck before running for the Rockies and someplace to hide.

"Got myself ten million bucks in cargo, a brand new panzer, and cleaned up a couple pieces of slime all at once," Jimi says, and then jumps up from his chair and claps his hands over his head. "Do you figure that makes me a part of the team?"

"I figure it does, Jimi," Cowboy says.

Cowboy watches as the Dodger capitulates to the inevitable. "Yeah, Jimi," he says. "I reckon you did good."

Jutz stands and puts an arm around Jimi's shoulders. "Thanks," she says. "It's good to know we made a few friends."

Jimi grabs her and whirls her in the air. Jutz whoops with laughter, while the Dodger looks sourly out of one slitted eye.

"I'll go put some more quarters in the Wurlitzer," Cowboy says. He looks over his shoulder as he walks toward the kitchen. "Hey, Jimi, you want some posole?"

Jimi puts Jutz down and reaches in a pocket for a transparent flask of mescal. "Sure," he says. "Glad to be aboard, you know."

"I know," Cowboy says, and walks toward the bubbling jukebox light, his hands groping in his pockets.

NEW UKRAINIAN PRESIDENT ELECTED WILL MAINTAIN NEUTRALITY IN ESTONIA-MUSCOVY CONFLICT

Sarah walks into Daud's room and sees a Russian priest standing by the bed of a new roommate, whose arms and legs are tied to the bright metal rack of the bed by leather straps. Viral Huntington's, she thinks, mind and body both eroding. Past the contagious stage now. The priest doesn't turn his eyes to her, just gazes down at the dying man from out of his bearded face.

Daud has two eyes now, one circled by the bruise made by the implant operation that he had only yesterday, paid for by the funds she'd wired from the Bullet station in New Kansas City. He looks at her as she passes the priest, and his face dissolves. "Sarah," he says.

"I'm here."

He reaches out a hand and she takes it, presses it to her. *"Where have you been?"*

She looks at him, the way his face is warring with itself, gratitude mixed with resentment. "I had to run, Daud," she says.

"You left me alone." She strokes his hand gently, the new pink flesh. "Damn you," Daud says. "Why did you go? You said it would only be a couple of days."

"Things went wrong."

She tries to kiss him on the cheek. He twists his head away. She pulls back and holds onto his hand.

"They're cutting my dose," he says. "It hurts. My legs, everything. I can't do the exercises they give me."

Sarah looks down at him, seeing the outline of the thin new legs under the sheet. "They can't let you out of here till you can walk right," she says.

"I can't walk at all unless I get my dose."

"Daud," she says, trying to keep her voice gentle. "I'm not bringing you anything. Not hormone maskers, not endorphins."

Daud pulls his hand away. Sarah tries to talk to him, but he refuses to answer. She watches his throat and cheek muscles working and feels her own anger and frustration rising. She reminds herself that these kinds of games are all that Daud has left, that he's playing them because he wants to know she still cares enough to put up with them, but the anger rises too quickly, and before it explodes she turns and stalks away.

The cool corridor air whispers to her, and this time she knows its message.

The city is closing in, and there is no one to guard her back.

TEMPEL PHARMACEUTICALS ANNOUNCES HUNTINGTON'S CURE
TEMPEL STOCK GOES WILD IN MARKET

Cure Described as "Search-and-Destroy Virus"

Thibodaux is a crystaljock, an intense thin man who crouches over his deck in Cowboy's car, deep in some inner trance as he frowns and taps at the keyboard in his lap. Cowboy knows him slightly from a few years ago, when Thibodaux had a panzerboy lover who'd later got himself blown away in some South Dakota wheat field. "Okay, man," Thibodaux says "That holding company in Montevideo has been alerted. We're ready to move."

"Go," Cowboy says. He takes a stud from the Cajun's deck and faces in.

The trick, Cowboy knows, is not moving the funds—that's easy, once he gives Thibodaux the codes. The trick is losing the tracers that the laws have put on his accounts in order to follow his every transaction and alert the police to his location.

They're operating from Cowboy's car with Thibodaux's deck studded into a public phone standing on its aluminum post on West Alameda in Santa Fe. The laws might be good enough to trace the series of commands, and Cowboy doesn't want to use any of the lines to which he has regular access.

There's already a close smell in the car, nerves beginning to spark with adrenaline. Thibodaux clicks into the eye-face and calls Cowboy's robobroker. Cowboy releases the first code from his crystal and within a period of two seconds all of Cowboy's stock holdings are dumped in a complicated and seemingly random way onto the markets of Singapore, London, and Mombasa Nova.

Approximately three seconds later they have all been traded for other stocks. While the sales are being completed, Thibodaux gives Cowboy a signal and Cowboy gives the second code from his chips. Cowboy's titles to various deposits of precious metal, actually held in deep Bastille security in various banks throughout the western U.S., are shuttled onto the commodities markets in Tobago.

The data strings representing Cowboy's new stockholdings, bought in three different places, are encoded and bounced off geosynchronous Earth satellites owned by Mikoyan-Gurevich, Toshiba, and the Gold Coast Maximum Law Corporation I.G. Then they are sold at three more different exchanges for Mexican pesos, CFA francs from Bangui, and Icelandic kronur.

Meanwhile, Cowboy's gold and silver have been traded for Ugandan shillings, shillings that are shuttled to Manila, where they are deposited in a face bank disguised as something called the Greater Asian Trade Company. The shillings are used as collateral for a loan, the loan being taken on something like 99.999 percent of the value of the shillings. The duration of the loan is ten seconds.

Cowboy gives Thibodaux a third code, and his shares in luxury apartment buildings in the Lightside Development on the Mitsubishi Permanent Orbital Environment at Lagrange Point Four are sold, at a moderate profit, to an investor living in Zürich. The payment, in Swiss francs, is shuttled to a face bank in Melbourne, where again it is used as collateral for a loan of ten seconds' duration.

While the codes representing the Swiss francs are received in Melbourne, the three separate strings of information representing Cowboy's stock sales are bouncing at the speed of light off a series of satellites and ground stations. The program Thibodaux has created is self-contained, traveling with the data, and needs no instructions at this point, but this is not necessarily the case with the tracer programs the laws have placed on them—with each bounce from Earth to satellite and back again, another fraction of a second is added to the lag time between the instant the program sees a transfer and the time the main tracer program, sitting in the cold crystal heart of a large computer on the ground, is able to perceive the transfer and act on it.

During the course of its leaps from Earth to space and back again, each data string passes through a receiving station sitting on a former oil-drilling platform off Big Sur. Thibodaux waits on a separate direct line to the drilling rig, and as each data string passes through, Thibodaux adds a new program, a string of new data that attaches itself to the first message, mimicking it in shape and form. . . . The new program is called, in the trade, a caboose.

Cowboy's loans are shuttled in separate movements to the

Singapore and Mombasa Nova exchanges, where they are used to purchase stock in the Greater Asian Trade Company. This stock is then shuffled to Manila, where it is sold at face value back to the Trade Company, all for Ukrainian konings, which are moved to Patagonia to buy cattle futures.

The pesos, CFA francs, and kronur burn at the speed of light to a receiving station on the island of Ascension, where another message from Thibodaux is waiting. Each string of data breaks in half, the caboose, by now mimicking the original program, peeling off and blazing a trail high into the late evening sky, with any luck taking the tracers with them. The data representing the money, meanwhile, is bounced off a Korolev-owned satellite and burns straight for Montevideo and an interface post box labeled "Holding Company No. 384673." The holding company computer counts the money, deducts Thibodaux's fee as well as its own, and alerts a human operator, a middle-aged and bored woman sitting next to an old computer deck in a battered one-room office overlooking the dike built to hold back the combined waters of the Atlantic and Río de la Plata. The human operator opens another phone line and begins tapping in code.

While the woman bends over her keyboard and taps, the Greater Asian Trading Company's main computer realizes that the ten-second loan has not been repaid, and forecloses. It is hoped that in addition to Ugandan shillings the face bank has collected a police tracer that was unable to follow the loan transfer.

The Patagonian cattle futures are sold in Namibia in exchange for South African rubles. The rubles commence bouncing from Earth to ground in the same way as the earlier data strings, also passing through the Big Sur offshore station and having a caboose attached in the same way.

The bank in Melbourne forecloses on the second loan and collects Cowboy's Swiss francs. The woman in Montevideo has finished her laborious task of transferring the funds by hand to the Sony Bank of Uruguay, from which Thibodaux immediately transfers them to the Chicago exchange in a complicated and apparently random series of stock purchases.

The caboose attached to the South African rubles fires itself toward Lagrange Point Five, while the rubles themselves peel away and head for Montevideo. Another string of data appears in the main computer of Holding Company No. 384673. The woman bends again over her deck and thinks about her next cigarette as she types.

The cabooses appear in the NewsData offices in various Orbital complexes, presenting themselves under the FOR IMMEDIATE RELEASE banner as a copy of a Reuters dispatch concerning Marc Mahomed's triumphant tour of Malaysia.

Thibodaux withdraws the rubles from the Sony Bank of Uruguay for another series of stock purchases in Chicago. There is a sheen of sweat on his upper lip. He unfaces from his deck and looks at Cowboy. "Okay," he says. "Slug in your codes on the stocks."

Cowboy fires out a series of codes, then Thibodaux pops a crystal cube up from its trapdoor and hands it to him. Cowboy unfaces and takes the cube.

"Any official heat shouldn't have been able to follow that. They should have been stopped dead when the money went into the banks as collateral for a loan—they very likely wouldn't have been able to make the jump from following our collateral to following the money the face banks loaned us. With the long lag we put on them after that, they shouldn't have been able to tell our real data from the caboose, and so they should have followed *that*. And I can't see any way they could have got through the holding company in Uruguay, not with a human operator working through two different computers that lack an interface." Thibodaux reaches in his pocket for a cigarette and grins. "I think you even made a profit on those stock transfers," he says. "A couple thousand dollars, looked like."

"It's not official heat I'm worried about," Cowboy says. "It's an Orbital tracer I want to keep off my neck."

"Even *they* can't travel faster than the speed of light," Thibodaux says. "And in any case, they would have been stopped dead in Uruguay. That program would have had to have the smarts to check every phone link at random in the whole city, just to see which one your money was moving on." He shakes his head. "Hell, the surest thing for them to try would have been to break in and steal it during one of the transfers—their stuff's good enough to do it, if they put their minds to it." He looks at Cowboy with a grin. "You'll find out for sure, anyway, when you try to move some of that stock."

"Yeah. Thanks." Cowboy plans on trading all his stocks before he lets Thibodaux out of his sight, and then on putting new codes on all of them. Thibodaux has a reputation as an honest face rider, but there's no sense in taking any chances.

Thibodaux brings down the Packard window and reaches out to stud his deck out from the phone. Cowboy faces into the car. The turbine ignites in near-silence, a vibration felt through the car's frame.

Thibodaux frowns down at his deck. "You know, maybe there *was* some Orbital heat on you. There was more than one tracer, that's for sure. I was riding with the program early on, during the first moves, and I felt them trying to hang on."

"Yes?"

"One of them was kind of funny, though. More like a message label." His eyes cloud for a moment, then he looks up. "Do you know anybody named Reno?"

Cowboy feels the touch of something cold on the back of his neck. He gazes at Thibodaux while fear moves through him like a wave of hydraulic shock. He shakes his head. "Reno's dead," he says.

"You sure? The only part of the message I could read was COWBOY CALL RENO, over and over."

"Nothing else?"

Thibodaux grins. "Nothing I bothered to read. You hired me to move your money, not to figure out the programs that were on its tail."

"Right." Cowboy licks his lips, tries to drag his attention back to the traffic moving down West Alameda. He picks his opportunity and moves out between two cars.

"It was some kind of trick, I think," Cowboy says. "They wanted me to answer so they could trace me."

"Probably. Funny way to do it, though."

"Funny. Reno was a funny sort of man."

Cowboy's pupils contract to pinpricks as he turns to face the morning sun, high above the faraway green of the Sangre de Cristos. He feels the chill crystal presence of Reno's ghost, lost somewhere in the interface, reaching out with spidery metal fingers from which uncoil long hieroglyphic streams of data. . . . No, he thinks. It was a trick.

Had to be.

KOROLEV RETURNS FIRE
NEW-MODEL JOVIAN DRONESCOOP ANNOUNCED
PRICES OF GAS-PLANET PLASTICS EXPECTED
TO EASE

Sarah looks down at the panzer sitting abandoned in the gully. Broken branches have fallen across it, leaves have drifted beneath its lee side. Sadness riffles through her like a gusting Montana wind. Something began here, a journey in which the city and the street melted away in the late-summer sun, and she had been free to be something other than an armored dirtgirl scrabbling for her ticket.

She looks from behind her shades at the Hetman's four men who have driven from Florida with her. "Okay," she says, "let's get our crystal."

She steps into the gully and taps the code into the panzer's cargo bay. The hatch swings up with a pneumatic hiss.

The hearts lie waiting, their armor stripped away.

DEMEUREZ-VOUS AU PAYS DE DOULEUR?
LAISSEZ NOUS VOUS ENVOYER À HAPPYVILLE!
—Pointsman Pharmaceuticals A.G.

Cowboy's awareness slides out of the eye-face when Jimi comes into the room. Jimi's just returned from running his own stolen antibiotics to Kentucky and is coming down from the high he's maintained for the last three days. There are bruises on his neck and arms from the pressure of the restraining straps during his high-g maneuvers, the result of a 200-mile drag race with the Nebraska heat that ended with one chopper forced down in a cornfield and a coleopter that seems to have sucked a bale of aluminum chaff into an intake and had to stagger home on one engine.

"Hope the poor bastard made it," Jimi says, "He was a hell of a pilot."

The exhaustion is beginning to catch up with him now, weariness showing in his posture, in his sagging eyelids. He accepts a whiskey and water from the Dodger and sags into a seat.

"I'm pleased to tell you that you got paid well for your bruises," the Dodger says. "Your owner's percentage and your delivery cut came out to over five million."

Jimi is too exhausted even to reply. Cowboy knows how he feels, having just come back from a four-day trip north and west, a pair of Flash Force mercenaries sharing the back seat of the Packard, standing over him as he met with panzerboys by ones and twos, trying to get them to agree to put the brakes on Arkady's war. Some seemed willing to make the jump, but none wanted to be the first. Cowboy knows he's got to get some kind of organization formed, a program under way. Right now he thinks he's making headway, but he knows a single piece of bad news can undo everything.

"If I hear that 'In it for the ride, not for the cargo' again," he says, "I'm going to break someone's nose."

The Dodger looks at him. "You used to say that yourself."

Cowboy takes a drink of his lukewarm coffee and hopes the caffeine will keep him going for another few hours. "Since then I've seen the light," he says.

Jimi rubs his neck muscles. Cowboy wonders if it's time to tell him about the Dodger's chat with the executive from the Korolev Bureau, who had come up the mountain at Dodger's invitation to discuss a united front against Arkady and Tempel.

The woman had coldly refused to deal unless the Dodger agreed to terms that would amount to total surrender—becoming a subdivision of Korolev instead of a part of Tempel, and doing it without a fight.

Korolev's interests were not being threatened here on the ground, she'd pointed out, and if they were to get involved, they'd want it to be worth their while. The Dodger had turned her down and concluded Korolev was perfectly happy to see Tempel divert its funds to a war outside its attempted takeover of Korolev, but that the company would probably never agree to financing a popular movement against one of the blocs, even a bloc that was an enemy.

The panzerboys would have to fight without bloc backing. Cowboy thought it was just as well. In his view, accepting an arrangement with Korolev would have made him no better than Arkady.

Cowboy finishes his cup of coffee and knows that another cup isn't going to help, that he's already turning fuzzy, and if he turns on his hardwiring, he'll blaze bright for maybe an hour, and then after his reserves are used up he'll crash and burn. So he decides to give it one more try and glides back into the interface, seeing the colored framework, the girders and stanchions and interweaving lattices that represent Tempel Pharmaceuticals I.G.

Thibodaux has built this structure, a four-dimensional representation of the Tempel bloc and its subsidiaries. Most of it's on the public record, but some of it—particularly the connection with Arkady—is built up out of inference. The totality of it is enormous, Tempel's skeletal cool fingers straining several thousand different dishes in search of its profit. Tempel is so diverse that it's difficult to get a grasp on any one operation; it blends in with a hundred more, and its tracks disappear among the others. Astronomical amounts of private-issue currency flash through the files, pour down a thousand chutes, disappear into some nameless laundry and then reappear elsewhere, no clue as to their origin. Names fly up for brief periods and then disappear into the fourth dimension, moving timewise through the network, not following what Cowboy can discern of the organizational structure. Cowboy begins following individual names, trying to get a glimpse of the way the top people move through the net. Some guy named Marcus Thorn, a name picked at random, begins in the experimental drugs division in old Earthside New York, transfers to the Orbital Research Group when the main drug action climbed out of the well, then shifts with the title of vice president of personnel to something called Acceleration Group Maximum, run by an up-and-comer named Henri Couceiro. After six years in Maximum, Thorn shifts to the Luna Division of the Pathology Department. There Cowboy finds another name, Liu McEldowny, who had been with the Acceleration Group before moving to the Luna Division a year before. Just before the Rock War, according to the movement flag in the Luna Division box, McEldowny moves back to the Acceleration Group, stays for a month after the surrender and then heads downside to the Orbital Freeport Control Commission, which Cowboy knows was the blocs' organizing group for setting up the Florida, Texas, and California Free Zones.

Thorn stays on the moon for another two years, then becomes chairman of the Solar Power Satellite Building Committee, which, despite its name, seems mainly concerned with personnel. Here he reports to Couceiro, who has popped up again as chief executive officer of the entire pharmaceutical Division. From the SPS Building Committee Thorn moves laterally to a vice presidency in the Security Division before, two months later, being called to the board of directors upon Couceiro's assumption of the chairmanship of the whole organization. On the board, Thorn holds a number of portfolios, including Development and, once again, Freeport Control. One of his cohorts, big surprise, is none other than Liu McEldowny.

Cowboy traces McEldowny downward through time, finds another connection with Couceiro when the two were numbers one and five, respectively, in the Erosion Control Subsidiary, which was busy mortgaging and then foreclosing on tens of thousands of acres of eroded Ukrainian farmland.

Cowboy wanders up the time lattice again and watches the composition of the board of directors shift, seeing a flurry of activity around the time Couceiro became chairman, the whole board contracting from twenty-four members to fifteen, with a minor reshuffle among those who remain. He follows each of the departing members and discovers that three die and several of the rest are transferred to major positions elsewhere in the company—positions that are, nevertheless, in places like Antarctica and Ceres. Some of the others are shuttled out when they undergo a crystal-medium brain transfer into another body, taking demotions until the board can determine if their performance has been hampered by the transfer. Cowboy concludes that Couceiro is at this point consolidating his hold on the board and keeping his opposition divided by sending them out into far-off assignments in the field.

There is another flurry of movement on the board just two years later, directors swapping portfolios back and forth, another director shuttling out entirely. Cowboy can see a pointer floating in the lattice indicating a news item culled from a MediaNet screamsheet report. He follows the pointer and absorbs the report, discovering that this latest movement represents the collapse of an attempt by the old chairman, Albrecht Roon, to regain his office, a move that fails by only a single vote. Before Couceiro's assumption of power Roon had been chairman for eighteen years, before getting his brain shunted to a new body at the age of seventy-nine and being demoted to the Asteroid Resource Commission—a major post in a bloc stronger in space transportation, but at Tempel the equivalent of Siberia. From there Roon attempts his comeback and fails, one of his supporters on the board being retired permanently and replaced with one of Couceiro's people, Roon himself being moved downside to head South American Marketing.

That suggests a major fall from grace, from chairman atop the gravity well to exile in South America within the space of a few years. Cowboy follows Roon's career up and down the Tempel construct, then follows Couceiro's, something he's done before. The available information doesn't seem very forthcoming. He's going to have to dig deeper.

He lets the interface fade from his mind and discovers that the Dodger is gone, probably for his afternoon nap, and that Jimi has fallen asleep in his chair, his drink sitting between his thighs, collecting dew. Cowboy quietly leaves the house and gets into his Packard, then cycles up the engine and moves down the switchback paths to the old town of Cimarron, built long ago by that cheerful old scoundrel Lucien Bonaparte Maxwell, friend to Christopher Carson and William Bonney, the whole town built because Maxwell owned the largest land grant in the history of the world and thought there ought by rights to be a town on it. Cowboy studs the Packard's computer into a phone line and starts calling libraries.

The data's easy enough to find now that he knows what he's looking for in the library crystal. Roon was born in Bonn, went to school in Leipzig and collected a degree in chemistry, then joined Tempel Pharmaceuticals I.G. in the same year it began building its first orbital drug factory. His first assignment in space was shortly thereafter, and the company kept him busy shuttling up and down for a decade or so, before the company headquarters went into orbit and Roon went up with them.

Once he was Tempel's chairman, he pushed for independence for the Orbitals, at one point ordered his jocks into the asteroid belt in defiance of the Space Control Commission, something that took a lot of nerve considering the fact that Tempel wasn't a major mining company and had only a few ships to send. Roon was a founder of the first Orbital Bloc Congress, second in power only to Grechko. It appears that many of the Bloc Congress programs originated with Roon, but he was willing to stay out of the spotlight and let Grechko take the heat for them. After the Rock War, Roon was behind the policy of the balkanization of the major Earth powers and the establishment of the Free Zones under Orbital supervision.

Henri Couceiro was born, of Brazilian parents, in orbit when Roon was still on Earth working to finish his degree. He was proud of the fact he'd never set foot on Earth, and one of his more controversial public statements, uttered shortly after his assumption of the chairmanship, called the planet ''just another big asteroid.''

Making that statement seems to have been one of Couceiro's few impolitic moves. The precise movements of his career seem occluded from time to time, but he seems to have spent the early period moving from place to place in the big Tempel structure as something of an executive troubleshooter, rearranging programs and structures, making executives toe the line, firing incompetents. His big break came with his becoming the head of Acceleration Group Maximum, which Cowboy is no longer surprised to discover was a liaison team with the other blocs, dedicated to decreasing the Orbitals' dependence on Earth by the sharing of resources and the creation of new technologies. It was also Group Maximum that developed the military plans that led to victory for the blocs in the Rock War and the sharing of the spoils afterward.

Acceleration Group Maximum seems to have made Couceiro's name. He stayed out of political positions after Group Maximum's policies were put into place, concentrating instead on developing a working knowledge of the bureaucracy, eventually moving to head of the Pharmacological Division and a seat on the board. From there he arranged the board's refusal to allow Roon to continue in his seat following his brain transfer—apparently the vote was taken after Roon's mind was already in its crystal matrix—and the first of Roon's demotions was assured.

Cowboy drifts out of Thibodaux's model and thinks for a moment about Couceiro and Roon, the split between the architect of Orbital independence and the man who helped implement Roon's schemes. He'll have to run through the model again, picking out each man's allies on the board and in the bureaucracy, trying to see if there might be some leverage there.

But now, to Cowboy's surprise, there seems to be some movement in the complicated architecture of the model, red figures appearing along the eye-face lattice, pulsing in rhythm, resolving into letters that march along Tempel's girders and supports. . . .

COWBOYHELPRENOCOWBOYHELPRENOCOWBOYHELPRENO

Adrenaline shrieks up Cowboy's neck. He screams and yanks the studs from his head, the interface snapping out of his mind. Looking at the silent crystal display in front of him, he sits in the Packard and hears his heart crashing in his chest. He reaches a trembling hand out of the car window and yanks the comp's cable from the telephone.

They've found him, he thinks. There are people on their way to kill him, and he hasn't brought a bodyguard with him. He looks over each shoulder, trying to decide whether to head straight back to the Dodger's or try an evasive pattern through the mountains.

He leans back against the cushioned headrest and puts his hands on the instrument panel in front of him, straightening his arms, trying to stop the trembling. He's got to face in again to get the car moving, but he doesn't want to touch the studs, to see those glowing crystal letters pulsing out their message.

Cowboy moves forward and clears everything out of the car's RAM, which should take care of any more ghostly communications from Reno, then reaches out and takes the studs in his hands. The trembling has almost gone away.

He puts them in his head. He's heading straight back to the Dodger's, at the fastest possible speed. He's pretty sure he can run any pursuers off the road.

Time to find out, anyway.

MODERNBODYMODERNBODYMODERNBODYMODERN

Stay in Touch with Your Portfolio,
No Matter Where You Are

NBODYMODERNBODYMODERNBODYMODERNBODY

Michael the Hetman lights a cigarette with a match that trembles. His eyes are deep and rimmed in red. "Too bad," he said. "I was afraid my source might not be genuine. I'm sorry I was right."

"Those people were good," Sarah says. Fear rushes along her nerves in little packets, prickling the down on her arms. She stuffs her hands in her pockets to control her own shaking. Her mouth is dry and longs for the touch of cool citrus, tastes instead the dry refrigerated air of the Hetman's study.

Michael reaches for a squeeze bottle of vodka, lets it fall in a thin silver stream into a pair of glasses. "It seemed worth a chance," he says.

Sarah has spent the night huddled in a doorway with only her heartbeat for company, that and the taste of her own sweat. Earlier she'd been waiting with five other people for the Laffite snagboy that was supposed to come by with an attaché case of pharmaceuticals and only a single amateur guard, but either the information was part of a setup or the snagboy had smelled something in the air, because suddenly there were two big armored cars wailing down the street with muzzles pointing from the black reflective windows, gunfire echoes ringing from the hard surfaces of the buildings as teflon-coated bullets drilled the concrete and turned brick to powder. The people inside the cars were hardwired and fast, and though Sarah was careful enough to choose a post with an escape route, it was still only luck that she got away, the cars chasing others while she ran through a night that had become a shadowy monster with humid compost breath and infrared scanners for eyes, its laugh like the chatter of an automatic weapon. The fight had lasted only a few seconds. The rest of the night hours were spent in the doorway, feeling the moist urban grit of the sweating wall against her cheek, waiting while the cars patrolled the broken streets, looking for survivors.

She should put some money down on tonight's body count. It's going to be higher than usual.

Sarah takes the glass of vodka from Michael's hand and lets it ease slowly down her throat, a cold alcohol fire. "It could have bought me another week," Michael says, and sits in a deep chair of chrome and black leather. He looks at her with his liquid spiderwebbed eyes.

"I've got it worked out," he says quietly. "I've got eight months before everything falls apart. Your bringing back those crystal hearts gave me one of those months."

He leans back in the chair, gazing at the dark acoustic tiles of the ceiling. Even holding the arms of the chair his hands tremble. "Tempel cut off my sources, but I can get by with hijacking for a while, bribery, running things out of my labs—all that and what I have stored. As soon as the war started I borrowed as much as I could, because I knew my credit would never be as good. I wanted to be in debt to a lot of people, I wanted me to be worth something to them alive."

Sarah closes her eyes, seeing night, sudden movement, spotlight glare, the sheen of laser holograms reflecting off the polished, speeding hood of a rushing car.

"I can fight the war unimpaired for six months," Michael says, his soft accent the only sound in this soundproofed fortress. "After that I won't be able to pay off the police anymore, and then they'll start raiding me. Income will start to decline. After seven months I won't be able to pay my Maximum Law guards and I'll have to hire nonprofessionals. Sooner or later one of my friends will decide I'm hurting him too badly just by staying alive."

Sarah opens her eyes to see Michael looking at her, an amused expression on his face.

"You're the only one I can trust with this," he says. "You're the only one who can't betray me. They want you, too."

"I can't help, Hetman," she says. "I can't change reality."

"I know you can't," the Hetman says. His gaze turns from her, becoming the eyes of a gambler focused on the wheel as he waits for the silver ball to find his slot. "We can just keep moving," he says. "Just keep things in the air. And when they fall"—he gives a little shrug—"we'll try to run, and we can hope we no longer matter enough for them to come after us."

Sarah looks into the vodka glass, seeing it reflect Michael's dark refrigerated interior. Try not to matter, she thinks, perhaps they won't notice and they'll let you live. Matter the way Michael and Cowboy matter and they'll take you down. Only the rats survive, never the lions.

And rats never guard each other's back.

ORBITAL COPS RAID TEXAS WAREHOUSE HOME-BUILT WEAPONS PLANT UNCOVERED ROCKETS BELIEVED USED IN SMUGGLING

Pony Express, a piece of the night in motion, glides along its parabola like a bow over a violin, making delicate music. Cowboy's in the eye-face again, feeling the cold air whispering over the matte-black fuselage of the delta, his nerves thrilling to the wind-whisper of liberation as he lofts high over the Rockies. His metal eyes search the night sky for infrared signatures.

This isn't a mail run. Cowboy is hunting.

He had driven home like a madman after the day in Cimarron, feeling Reno or whatever was behind Reno clawing its way up his back like a rush of adrenaline. He'd seen no one that day, no one following, not even a suspicious glance. No sign of an enemy in the next two weeks. He hasn't faced into a telephone since. Whatever was behind that message, it is more than Cowboy wants to deal with.

An amber blip flashes in Cowboy's radar display, and Cowboy looks at it carefully. One of the rare commercial flights, he concludes, it's too high to be Arkady's plane.

The delta cuts neatly through the air, its vast power muted, under careful control. Arkady's plane is small and the *Pony Express* radars aren't very efficient and have a limited range—until now Cowboy's been much more interested in detecting the location of enemy radars than in using his own. But he knows Arkady's up here somewhere. The airfield receptionist, on the Dodger's payroll, has passed on the information that his plane took off just before sunset, and that he was on it, his hair still rising and changing colors every few seconds.

Neurotransmitters tickle Cowboy's crystal, and the *Pony Express* banks and sweeps eastward over Medicine Bow. Electronic ears are extended for the sound of microwave transmissions. Distant radars pulse weakly on the delta's absorbent skin. Inside the seamless black hood of his helmet Cowboy can hear only the echo of his own breath, taste only rubber and anesthetic gas.

Cowboy's mind rejoices, feeling the delta's power vibrating under his control. His nerves tingle pleasure. It's been too long since he possessed the sky.

A silver-white dot moves against the wheeling star field and Cowboy looks closer. It's an infrared signature all right, and he tilts the delta's nose upward to give his forward-looking radars a peek, g-forces tugging at the skin around his eyelids. An amber dot appears on the displays, outlines uncertain. Cowboy pictures himself as a falcon, narrowing its wings as it prepares to move upon its distant prey.

A steel guitar plays in Cowboy's mind as he floods the engines with fuel, the big plane climbing toward the diamond stars. The whimper of wind turns to a hiss. Cowboy's spine can feel delicate vibrations moving fore and aft along the plane's structure as the frame absorbs the additional stress. Arkady is blind to this, he thinks, and can't know what it's about. Can't come near the top, thinks only in terms of money and fashion, the cryo max clothes that he hopes will buy him a ticket into the world where things really happen, and all the while the panzerboys are building and living their legend and Arkady is frozen outside, trying to pretend he matters.

The infrared signature is nearer, glowing white in Cowboy's vision. Two engines. He's above and behind the target now, at the top of a long parabolic arc, and he lowers the delta's nose and throttles back, the engine noises dying away almost entirely, left far behind in the craft's wake.

The target is very close now. Cowboy lowers *Pony Express*'s flaps, feeling the plane fight the brakes, jarring. The infrared signature is close, cat's eyes in the night. Cowboy takes his eyes off infrared and can see the dark silhouette nearing him. He has to be certain this is the right one.

Neurotransmitters flick a switch, and electrons race along the cable to snap on the quartz-iodide brightness of his landing lights. Suddenly the night is afire with the form of a white fuselage pinstriped with blue. Arkady's plane, the right configuration. Cowboy can see heads peering out the windows. The plane cocks one wing up and tries to fall away.

Too late. The plane is already exhaling, air gushing through the holes in the fuselage made by Cowboy's humming dorsal minigun turret. A wing breaks away, an engine flares and breaks into pieces, spitting fire and melting alloy. *Pony Express* arcs over the falling craft, turning cockpit-down so Cowboy can watch it fall away. He knows it will be at least half an hour before it impacts the earth somewhere on the Nebraska line, falling amid a tumbling hail of thirty-millimeter casings, Arkady's hair standing on end every few seconds, turning orange, green, blue in pointless fashionable sequence. . . .

Cowboy watches it fall, slow regret already touching his mind. Arkady's dead, but it was all too easy. The thirdman was in a defenseless civilian jet, up against a maneuverable armored monster. Cowboy's nerves are still blazing, still ready for a fight, not realizing it's already over.

He can feel Damnation Alley's radars trying to touch him

with furious microwave claws, and deep in him there is a yearning to run the Line again, feel the delta's airframe moan with the stress of supersonic turns, dance among the lances of enemy missiles, feel the blue alcohol fires erupting behind him to drive him clear. . . . This simple interception and destruction wasn't worthy of *Pony Express*, wasn't fitting as the flaming climax of a battle.

Cowboy turns the delta's nose downward and works out his course toward Colorado. He's done his job he's taken Arkady out of the picture so that the Dodger and his allies will have a breathing space.

He takes comfort in the fact that this isn't the final battle. Tempel backed Arkady, and they'll return soon enough with someone else.

He's just created a respite, and he hopes it will grant him enough time to organize his embassy to Albrecht Roon.

MARC MAHOMED TELLS YOU WHO YOU ARE

Sarah slips through the back door of the Blue Silk, seeing the cases of liquor and drugs stacked in their frozen cardboard rows. She closes the door silently and pockets the key.

Her room upstairs has only a desk, a telephone-linked comp deck, a single chair, a plastic cooler chest, and a narrow mattress set on the floor. Music throbs up from the bar, a disconnected bass track. She's been imitating the rat, hiding while the terrier sniffs overhead.

She pulls off her jacket and shirt, and reaches for a towel, dabbing off the sweat. She's just been to visit Daud, spending an hour with him while he complained about the hospital and the treatment, how the therapists were working him too hard and cutting his dosage, how Jackstraw wouldn't return his calls and had some new boy answering the phone, someone whose tone Daud didn't like. . . . It was a long monologue that poured out of him at every visit, like a loop of tape that could only replay the same event over and over. Sarah feels drained.

She throws the towel down and opens the cooler for a beer before she notices that there's a message light on her deck.

She opens the foil bottle top with her teeth while reaching to touch the button that will display the message that Maurice has relayed up to her, and as it flashes on her monitor she can feel a rush of warmth along her nerves, as fine and real as the inhaled mist of a fine drug:

> TOMORROW, THREE O'CLOCK, BLUE SILK.
> LEAVE MESSAGE IF YOU CAN'T MEET.
> RANDOLPH SCOTT.

Chapter Eleven

Cowboy sits restlessly in the back of the car and watches the wind tugging at the broken leaves of the dying palm outside the Blue Silk. White noise hisses from the radio receiver that sits on the seat next to his Flash Force driver. The dark mirrored windows of the bar reflect the baking street, the laser glowing image of the three-dimensional holographic phantom that parades the bar's name past the eyes of passersby.

There's another Flash Force man inside the bar, trying to sniff out an ambush. Cowboy shifts nervously in his seat and hopes the guard won't spook Sarah, that she isn't already dodging through the alley behind the bar with images of assassination in her head.

Two short bursts of noise crackle from the guard's receiver as the merc in the Blue Silk breaks squelch twice, the all-clear signal delivered from the transmitter buried in his skull. The driver moves the car forward along the narrow sidewalk and parks in front of the bar. He scans the crowd once and nods, and Cowboy bursts out of the car and lopes through the cool inviting Blue Silk doors.

Sarah's not inside the bar, only some businessmen soaking up a late lunch, a man in a wheelchair gazing down at the place where his legs used to be, and Cowboy's Flash Force guard sitting quietly over his Canadian and water, his back to the wall, where he won't have to watch his own spine.

Cowboy walks to the bar and orders a beer from the quiet black man with the metal eyes.

By the time the beer comes he's seen the pictures on the wall and figures he knows what the bar's name stands for. "Did you know a man called Warren?" he asks. "He was a crew chief at Vandenberg during the war."

"No sir," Maurice says. "I rode my cutter out of Panama."

"You were with Townsend? You must have done some good, then."

"Not damn near enough." It's the man in the wheelchair talking, his chin jerking up with reflex pride at the mention of Townsend's name. Cowboy looks with surprise into a pair of Zeiss eyes that glow with a twisted, grudging fury that seems less than entirely sane.

"I got burned early and never climbed the well," the man says. "Crashed here in Florida. Maurice was one of the people who took out the Chinese SPS, but got burned on his way down and force-landed at Orlando."

Cowboy turns to Maurice. He knows that only about a dozen made it back from the SPS fight. "That was some good piloting," he says.

"The war was over before we even left the ground. We just didn't know it." Maurice's soft voice is edged with weary bitterness. Cowboy thinks of that voice coming over the controller's speakers at Orlando, quietly calling in his mayday landing as his burning cutter draws a line of fire across the hot Florida sky.

Cowboy sips his beer. "I'm a pilot. Air jockey."

"I thought you were." Maurice raises a finger to his blank metal eyes. "I saw you had all the equipment."

They talk flying while Cowboy drinks half his beer. Then he looks up at Maurice and lowers his voice. He can feel anticipation warming his nerves. "Is Sarah here? Could you tell her that Randolph Scott wants to talk to her?"

Maurice jerks his chin toward the Flash Force guard nursing his drink in the corner. "Is he yours?"

"Yes."

"Good. Thought he might be, ah, the other people again.

One moment, sir." He turns to his cash register and punches some code on its keyboard with his fingernail. His eyes reflect an amber message on its screen.

"Okay, Mr. Scott. Go back through the door to the toilets, take the door marked PRIVATE, go up the stairs."

Cowboy drains his beer. "Thanks. Talk to you later."

He walks to the door without glancing in his guard's direction and pushes through the door into the back room. He can hear the electric lock snapping shut behind him. There is a muted smell of hashish. Crates of liquor and legal drugs stand dimly around him. He walks up some narrow stairs and sees Sarah silhouetted against the light of a bare bulb on the landing.

She's wearing a red T-shirt with the sleeves ripped off and soft white cotton jeans above her bare feet. Her hair has grown out, strand tips touching the junction of neck and shoulder. As he steps onto the landing she grins and reaches out to feel the shoulder of his armored jacket. "I see you've been to my tailor."

"Coat and two pairs of pants."

Sarah turns and begins to move down a hallway crowded with more crates of liquor. "Let's go to my room." He watches her wary panther strut as he follows her.

He's surprised at the narrowness of the little place, the lack of furnishings in the room with its white walls and bricked-over window. He takes off the heavy jacket and sits on the only chair. Sarah offers him a beer from the cooler, then sits in a half-lotus on her little mattress. She rips the foil lid off her own beer with her teeth and looks at him. "So why are you in Florida, Cowboy?"

"To talk to Michael the Hetman."

"What about?"

"A way to win the war."

She laughs. "Good. I was afraid you were just getting sentimental."

That game again, Cowboy thinks. Okay, he can play it well enough. "Sentimental for the Silver Apaches' beer, maybe," he says. He looks at her carefully. "You're still working for the Hetman, right? Not changed sides?"

A brief shake of the head. "We're still on the same team. The other side wouldn't have me anyway."

"So we're still allies."

Sarah allows herself a quiet smile. "Yes. I guess we are."

Point to me, Cowboy thinks. He sips his beer. "When can you put me in touch with Michael?"

"I happen to know he's out of town. I won't be able to get a line to him till tonight."

Cowboy takes a long drink of his beer, then puts the bottle down. He switches his eyes to infrared, seeing the blood burning silver in Sarah's cheeks.

"Arkady's dead," he says. "I shot down his plane."

Sarah considers this, patterns of warmth shifting across her face. "Good," she says. "But that won't put an end to things in your part of the world, will it?"

"Probably not, considering who was behind him. But we'll have some time." He clicks back to normal vision. Sarah's dark eyes are watching him carefully.

"Time for what?" she asks.

So he tells her about Tempel, about Henri Couceiro sitting in his Lagrange habitat and looking down at Earth with cold spaceborn eyes, about Albrecht Roon feeding his mind through the crystal matrix and into a new, young body, about portfolios and offices and lattices of control, about Cowboy's sense of the votes on the board that could be swung if certain things happened, the stockholders whose proxies held the balance of power. It's all pure intuition, simply Cowboy's ideas about the people he's been studying, but he thinks he's right about them.

The whispery cadences of hob music throb up through the floor while Sarah listens quietly in her half-lotus, barely sipping her beer. After Cowboy finishes, she stares down at the floor for a long moment. "If it doesn't work?"

"We lose more quickly than we're losing now. We cut a deal and run."

Sarah looks at him. "So long as you know when to cut,

Cowboy. Daud and I aren't planning to commit seppuku with you, and I don't think the Hetman will, either."

"You can pull out whenever you want. I can't stop you, and I won't try."

She looks at him for a long while, her face intent, then she nods. "Just so you know."

Sarah uncoils her long legs and stands, moving to the bricked-up old window, leaning a shoulder against its sill and gazing into the distance as if the frame still held glass. "Do you think we can win this war, Cowboy?" she asks. Softly, almost as though she's talking to herself.

"Yes. If Roon gives us what we need."

"I wasn't planning for a win. I just wanted to hang on long enough to get Daud a ticket into orbit. Then . . ." She shakes her head. "It didn't seem to matter what happened after. I would have tried to run, I suppose, when our side fell apart."

"A place in the sky. That's what you want?"

Sarah turns to face him, her body slumped against the wall. "Shit, man. I sold my *soul* for a ticket. Turned out the people I sold it to didn't even want it. Too dirty for them, I guess." A bitter skeleton's grin twists across her face. "They'll take Daud, though, if he comes with enough cash. They'll wrinkle their noses at the smell, maybe, but they'll take him."

"Is that what *he* wants?"

A shutter falls across her face. "That's what's best. If he stays with me, he'll die."

Cowboy feels the chill plastic bottle in his hands, the condensation trickling down his thumb. "You might not be doing your Daud a favor sending him up the well, Sarah," he says. "Those aren't our people up there."

She laughs. "*Our* people, Cowboy, are losers. They lost twelve years ago and they haven't stopped losing yet."

Cowboy feels his jaw muscles tautening, his hands turning into fists. He looks at Sarah. "We can win this one," he says.

Sarah raises her eyes, looking at him for a long moment. A

long bass line threads up from the bar to fill the silence. "Yes," she says. "We might. For once we might come out ahead."

Cowboy can almost see Sarah's hackles rising at the sight of the two Flash Force guards, but she greets them with a terse nod and steps out of the bar into Cowboy's rented car, her head turning each way to look at the slow-motion figures moving down the shadowed street. Cowboy follows her into the back of the car and the driver smoothly pulls away from the curb.

"Secure phone," he says, wishing he was faced into the car and driving himself, but the driver glides easily through the traffic, his eyes flickering to the mirrors to check for tags. He heads for a public phone standing by an old twenty-four-hour bank, where they will be covered not only by the Flash Force but by the bank's own security system. Sarah leaves the car, jingling change in her pockets. She leans into the phone, punches numbers, talks in an undertone.

She gives Cowboy a ragged smile as she steps into the car again. "He was getting high with some of his Russian friends, but he said he'd see you tomorrow morning. I figured in the morning he'd either be hung over or still in orbit, so I made an appointment for the afternoon. He'll be more receptive then, I think. Suit you?"

"To the ground," Cowboy says. Sarah closes the door and the automatic security locks *chunk* shut with the cold sound of impervious alloy, the closing of the cage called Security.

"Take you back to the Blue Silk?" Cowboy asks. "Or shall I buy you dinner first?"

Sarah's eyes flicker to the Flash Force people in the front seat, forming a question.

"In my room at the Ritz Flop," he says. "They won't let me out in public anyway."

She leans back in the padded seat, her fingers sliding along the grain of the simulated leather. "Fine," she says. The flywheel engages smoothly and the car slides away from the crumbling curb.

Glittering alloy alternates with obsidian glass at the Ritz Flop, a smooth series of parabolas, half buried, low and close to the ground without a single straight line anywhere, a Lagrange world come to terms with gravity. In Cowboy's room, like the others, there are no right angles, only smooth curves meeting one another like clouds in a dream of night flight. The dark wood in the furniture turns out, at a touch, to be cool alloy, vibrating faintly against Cowboy's fingertips, as if with a fast hummingbird life existing in the ultrasonic, just beyond the realm of human perception.

He snaps on the computer on the headboard of the bed and orders western beef, guaranteed not to have been plexgrown in a vat, and a bottle of Cryo White. One of the Flash Force shadows comes in with room service and Cowboy can see Sarah's scowl as their meal passes its electronic examination. She seems to relax after the guard leaves, shrugging out of her jacket, shaking her hair. She looks at the dark gray matte of the curved ceiling.

"I was a lot less obvious when I was guarding you," she says, her mouth twisting. She reaches for the White, and thick chips of frost fall from the metal flask as she holds it over her goblet and presses the nitrogen trigger. White foam splatters over the goblet lip and lands on Cowboy's knuckle. He lifts the finger to his lips and feels the chill shock move through his nerves, his teeth.

After dinner he goes in his luggage for an inhaler of softglow, a chemical high that won't tangle with hardwired nerves. Sarah finishes the last of her Cryo White and then breathes in a pair of torpedoes. She tosses her head back, shakes her hair, grins. Cowboy triggers the inhaler twice and feels a windblown grassfire burning up each hemisphere of his brain.

"Do you remember . . . ?" Sarah says.

"It's good being allies again."

Then they're tangled on the bed, Cowboy watching her body on infrared, seeing the blood rush to the skin in rivers of silver, forming bright pools in her breasts, her groin, little glowing snake tracks following his fingertips wherever he

touches her. He reaches into one of the headboard compart-
ments for a headset and some studs, faces in, fits the headset
over her temples. Her dreaming eyes grow suddenly wide
and her hands jerk up to yank off the headset.

"No, Cowboy."

There is fear in her voice, and he feels a chill surprise. His
eyes click back to normal. Sarah's face is deep in shadow. "I
thought we could share our heads," he says.

He can feel Sarah give a quick shake of the head. "No."
She takes a deep breath, presses her hand to his cheek. "I'm
not . . ." She shakes her head again. "There are things in
my head you don't want to know about," Sarah says. She
presses her forehead to his, looks straight into his eyes.
Speaks regretfully, plainly. Her breath flutters against his
lips. "Things from my past, things that don't have anything
to do with you. It's just that . . . sometimes they're there.
Even when I don't want them to be. And you wouldn't like
it."

"I've been places," he says.

"Not these kinds of places. Otherwise you wouldn't have
tried to put us both into the same face."

Cowboy slowly reaches up to his head and takes himself
out of the face. Sarah slides her arms around him. He can
feel the warm silk of her thigh riding up his hip and switches
to infrared, seeing the silver and rust build glowing patterns
in the darkness. He thinks about Sarah's little room above the
bar, the single chair, the bare narrow mattress. He knows he
will not be invited into that bed, that the sex between the two
of them must always remain on neutral ground. Because she
will always need that little place, the bare little room where
she can hide and nothing can touch her.

He rolls atop Sarah and enters her, seeing her glowing
against the sheets, her skin ablaze. Her eye sockets are a cool
cyanide violet, the windows to her mind firmly shuttered.

A few hours later Cowboy wakes to find Sarah deep in her
own rhythm, her nerves triggered and her body a blur of
kicks and punches, running her pattern of makebelieve vio-

lence in the center of the room, locked in battle with the
night, with the phantoms trying to reach her.

He watches her move in the dimness, feeling the vibration
of the Ritz Flop rising through his spine. Wondering what
she sees in front of her as she launches her attacks, what
faces are conjured in the legion of invisible enemies. If his
own face is among them, to be kept always at bay.

And then he sees the flicker of darkness from between her
lips, and coldness touches him with spiderweb fingertips. He
snaps his vision to infrared and sees the cybernetic lash that
is Weasel, the cybersnake running its swift deadly patterns in
combination with her hand strikes, flashing out against the
ghosts that fill the room.

Fear fills him, cold touching his fingertips. He watches
silently from his pillow, realizing that she's always had this
face in her mind, a piece of cold alloy and plastic madness
incarnated in her throat, hidden beneath her warm, humid
tongue. . . . Cowboy's heart thrashes in his chest, urging
him to run. He thinks about facing with the cybersnake by
accident, feeling its cold crystal mind through his sockets. . . . *"There are things in my head you don't want to
know about."* In her head, aye, and her throat, her heart.
Hidden behind her cyanide eyes.

She finishes her work and sucks the Weasel back in her.
Cowboy closes his eyes and hopes she will think he is asleep.
Sarah pads quietly to the shower, giving Cowboy time to get
his breathing under control.

When she comes back to the bed, he moves over and gives
her plenty of room.

Chapter Twelve

Sweat gathers on Daud's upper lip, on his forehead. His blue eyes are glazed with pain. The muscles on his upper arms bunch as he tries to support his weight on the gleaming metal rails while his new pink-fleshed legs take a few careful steps.

"That's it, Daud. You got it." The blond bodybuilder therapist, standing close by in case of a fall, urges Daud on. Sarah adds her own encouragement as Daud walks slowly the length of the rails, then turns and moves torturously back to his wheelchair.

"That was good, Daud," Sarah says later, as she pushes the chair to the elevator. "The best yet."

Daud's head lolls back against its rest. "Can we stop for some cigarettes?" he asks.

"I've got some with me." Back in his room she helps him climb into his bed and then opens one of the two packs of cigarettes she's brought with her. She puts the other in a drawer where he can reach it. The neighboring bed is empty and Sarah sits on it.

A thin bearded nurse comes in with a basin for Daud's bath. "You shouldn't be smoking in bed," he says mildly. He carefully begins to stack towels on the bedside table.

"I'll wash him," Sarah says. She slides off the bed and reaches for the basin in the nurse's hands. The nurse looks at her in surprise.

"Daud and I have some talking to do," Sarah says. "In

private." The nurse's nervous eyes flicker to Daud, and Daud nods.

"Doesn't matter to me," the nurse says, and shrugs. He looks at Sarah. "You're not supposed to sit on the beds."

"Won't happen again."

The nurse leaves, and Sarah pulls down the sheets covering Daud, unbuttons his pajama tunic, exposing the slack white chest mottled with pink shrapnel scars. She washes him while Daud stares at the ceiling, the cigarette in the corner of his mouth.

"You should exercise more, Daud," she says. "You used to exercise all the time when you lived with me. You'll be walking a lot faster."

"It hurts too much." He blows smoke at the high acoustic ceiling. "They keep dropping my dose."

Sarah washes the long legs, the thin white calves weightless in her arms.

"I've got to leave again, Daud," she says. "I don't know for how long."

Daud blinks, his eyes still upturned. "I knew you were going again," he says. "All those afternoons when you were at meetings and couldn't see me." She reaches for his cigarette and taps the lengthening ash into his tray.

"I have to pay your bills, Daud," she says.

He swallows hard. Sarah watches the cords in his neck. She gives him his cigarette.

"Don't go," he says. "Don't leave me here again."

"Roll over on your side." She washes his back, the deep white hollow between his shoulder blades.

"There's a number where you'll be able to leave a message," Sarah says. "It's in New Mexico. Maybe they'll be able to patch you right through to me, maybe not. But I'll get the message and call you from wherever I am. Okay?"

"Whatever you say." Dully, pretending not to care.

"I'll give you the number," Sarah says. "You're going to have to memorize it. I can't ever write it down. And you can't call from this room. Your phone might still be monitored. You'll have to get in your wheelchair and go down to the waiting room and use the phone there. I'll give you a credit needle so you can use it. Understand?''

"Yes. I understand." Daud's voice is a whisper. He reaches to the table for a towel and snatches it, but he's using the new left arm and the movement lacks precision. The towel unfolds and Sarah sees the flash of crystal and metal in the instant before a vial strikes the floor and dances under the table. The cold rattle of glass on tile seems to last for a long time. Sarah feels the chill touch of metal on her nerves.

"No," Daud says. "It's mine. Don't look."

He gives a little moan as she reaches for the vial, as she brings it up to the light. Polymyxin-phenildorphin Nu, solution of 12 percent. At his old level, it should last him about a day. Less now. Not a surprise, now that she thinks about it.

Daud whimpers as she searches the towels and the bed, finding another new vial and one near-empty vial under his pillow. "No," he says. "Look. Joseph was just doing me a favor." He looks at the coldness in her face and falls silent.

"You don't have any money, Daud," she says. "How'd you pay for it?"

He clamps his mouth shut and shakes his head. Sarah feels the towel in her hands, and she flicks it in his face. He jerks his head back, his lips trembling.

"Tell me."

He swallows, tries to turn his head away. Sarah flicks the towel again. It makes a hard sound in the air.

"Look," he says, "they just add the cost to the—the hospital bill. Disguised charges. Joseph has a friend at the desk. You would never have known." He begins to talk fast. "I've been making such progress since, Sarah. I really have."

"I'm moving you out of this place. A recovery hospital somewhere. You don't need full care anymore."

"Sarah."

"*Don't.*" She raises a hand clenched around a towel, feeling the anger making her fist tremble. She balls the towel up and flings it into a corner of the room, then spins and stalks into the corridor.

She finds Joseph in another room, washing the gaunt

corded muscles of an accident victim who has both his legs
raised in traction. "Hey, Joseph," she calls, and sends one of
the vials at his head. He ducks, his eyes wide, and the vial
splinters against the wall. The room fills with a glycerine
chemical smell.

Sarah's moving too fast for him to dodge. The first kick
catches his midsection; the second, his face. He goes down
and she stands astride him, her hands seizing his collar,
holding it tight, cutting into the skin around his neck. "Joseph," she says, "I should fire the rest into your veins.
How'd you like a nice endorphin overdose, hey?"

The accident victim is scrabbling with his one good hand
for the emergency cable. Sarah drops the bearded nurse and
gently takes the emergency cord and puts it out of reach.
Joseph puts a hand to his throat and gasps for breath.

Sarah turns to him. "Stay away from my brother, Joseph," she says. "He doesn't need you, or the things that
you hide in your towels."

"I was just—"

Sarah slaps him hard across the face. She can feel the man
in the bed flinch at the sound.

"Just follow instructions, Joseph. My brother doesn't get
any of the drugs you're selling, and the price of what you've
sold him comes off my bill. Don't say anything, just nod yes
or no."

Joseph looks up at her, gives a slow nod.

Sarah straightens, takes the emergency cable and puts it in
the hand of the accident victim. "Sorry," she says. "I just
had to reach an accommodation with the local 'dorphin dealer."
She looks into his surprised eyes. "Check your bill carefully
before you pay it. Joseph here may have added some of his
disguised charges."

She turns and leaves the room, the smoldering anger turning to sadness. She can't keep Daud away from the endorphins,
not even if she stays with him. They're a part of what keeps
him alive now. He's got nothing to look forward to but the
next injection, nothing but a visit from his sister—and Sarah
wants only to make him feel again, to bring him back to the

world of pain, where nothing stands between him and the city. No wonder, she thinks, that he made his deal with Joseph. She's a part of the city, the city that wants him. Joseph was his only chance to get away.

Chapter Thirteen

"Dodger?" Cowboy looks at the phone in surprise.

"Who else?" says the Dodger.

Cowboy grins at the sound of the Dodger's voice. "I'm glad to hear you're out. I hope your Flash Force people are keeping as good an eye on you as they are on me."

"Nothing to worry about there." Cowboy hears the sound of chewing tobacco being shifted from one cheek to the other. "Some of their mercs tried to set up an ambush down Mora way, on old Bob Aguilar's land. I must've heard from half a dozen people about it, Bob in particular, so we hired an extra platoon for one afternoon and took them out. A wired fight, lasted about ten minutes all told. Had to lock Jimi in the bathroom so he wouldn't jump in his panzer and join the war. I don't think our friends'll be coming into the mountains again. Strangers are too conspicuous up here."

Cowboy laughs and offers his congratulations. He's talking from a public phone at the Orlando port of entry to the Randolph Scott accommodation link in Santa Fe. His phone-in time was set up in advance, giving the Dodger's people time to instruct the Randolph Scott number to forward the call to Mora or Eagle Nest or whatever public phone the Dodger was standing by.

"The meet with Roon's still set up for tomorrow," Cowboy says. "I've got a cube holding the instructions for the treaty we're going to cut. Ready to receive?"

"Anytime, Cowboy."

Cowboy snaps the trapdoor shut over the cube and fires the data to New Mexico. Dodger's voice informs him that he's got the treaty in his crystal.

"Michael got hit bad last night," Cowboy says. "One of his people went over to the other side, took his crowd along and a warehouseful of hearts and antibiotics."

"We've been doing a little better thisaway." In spite of the news the Dodger's voice seems full of good cheer. Probably, Cowboy thinks, because it's the first time he's left his house in months.

"The, ah, express riders are about to split from Arkady's group." A pulse of slow delight flares in Cowboy's mind. The panzerboys, following his lead. They could shut Arkady's machine down cold. "After Jimi did . . . what he did . . . Arkady started insisting on one of his people going along on every run, riding shotgun inside the delivery vehicle. That didn't sit well with the drivers. And after Arkady's plane crash his people got even more nervous. It seems Arkady's replacement showed up real quick."

Cowboy's lips draw back from his teeth. Tempel was showing its hand. "Anyone we know?" he asks.

"A man from orbit, looks like. Name of Calvert. People had seen him with Arkady from time to time, but they didn't know who he was. He's not Russian, and Arkady's Russians don't like him."

"Think they'll change their minds about who the good guys are?"

Cowboy can sense the Dodger's shrug in the sound of his voice. "The Russians are so paranoid and treacherous that I reckon anything could happen. But Calvert knows Arkady's people too well, knows where they live and who they associate with. They're vulnerable to him, but they don't know him at all, or how to touch him. He's a bad man, this Calvert. Nobody wants to cross him, not after they've met him. And he brought a new crowd in, Orbital people. He says he'll start his own people running across the Line if the regular express riders stop working for him."

"Then he'll lose a lot of cargo."

"It's pocket change to these people, Cowboy. If they figure there's a profit in the long run, they can afford to lose for years and years. We can't."

Cowboy rubs his chin. He feels a warning prickle on the back of his neck. "What does this Calvert look like?"

"Medium height. Real hard. Talks in a kind of whisper. Looks like he started out as a mudboy before he went up the well."

Cowboy's eyes rise to Sarah standing five yards away, kicking absently at the passenger port's granite paving while she waits for Cowboy to finish. "I think this boy's known as Cunningham out here, Dodger," he says. "He's working this side of the war, too."

"That possibility had occurred to me, Cowboy. If it's true, he's a busy man."

"We'll try and make him busier."

"That we will." The Dodger clears his throat. "Warren says to tell you he's got the sixth delta ready to fly. Word has it that Arkady's people are trying to put deltas together from whatever spare parts they can find. Nice of you to corner the market before you flew against Arkady."

"Nostalgia has its uses," Cowboy says. On the display over his head he can see the blinking light that means his shuttle is boarding.

After he says adios to the Dodger, he waves good-bye to the Flash Force guards at the gate.

Roon has promised them his protection, but Cowboy figures he knows how much that's worth. If Roon is treacherous, he and Sarah will die. The Flash Force won't make a particle's worth of difference, except in the number of bodies.

Chapter Fourteen

Roon's home, Cowboy thinks, is a tesseract, coiling in on itself with the logic of a neverending nightmare. A black and silver dream invading Cowboy's mind, burning through his crystal. Imposing its architecture upon him, *its* logic, *its* pattern. He is lost in it, helpless in the swirl of time.

"Earth," Roon says. His kohl-rimmed eyes are moist. "I was born in the well. Matured in orbit. Was reborn in crystal. Until then I did not understand."

Across the table Cowboy can smell the foulness of his breath. Roon reaches out a trembling hand to touch the short fair hair of the little girl that holds his wineglass. Cowboy sees her start, sees her eyes widen, her mouth open in a hushed intake of breath, prelude to a scream that never comes. "I understand how we may work together," Roon says. "You and Earth are the past. I and the sky are the present. You are mud, I am vision. I wish to mold the Earth, to form it in the proper image. Build an architecture for the future."

The sweat of fear gathers under Cowboy's collar. He looks at the crystal glass in his hand, pictures the ease with which he can bring the glass down on the edge of the table, the way the cut glass will sing as the shards skate across the polished hardwood and between the priceless petroleum-plastic dishes, the razor-edged fragments inverting the world as they mirror the shadowed airy ceiling, the look in the little girl's wide, fearful eyes, the pulse in Roon's throat as Cowboy lunges across the table with the sharp crystal in his hand, finally the bright arterial blood as it pools on the table, welling up around the scattered crystal worlds, extinguishing each miniature light in a rising scarlet tide. . . .

The anticipated movement quavers in Cowboy's hand. He tightens his grip on the glass to end the shiver. The water in the glass trembles, reflects the lights above in a crescent like the rim of a distant world.

He looks up at Sarah, seeing her impassive face, her carefully veiled eyes. Thinks of the murderous thing in her throat and the madness it implies. Madness of the world, or Sarah's? Both at once? He wonders what she would do if he makes his move, whether the cybersnake would flicker out at Roon, or in Roon's defense.

He lowers the crystal goblet to the table, pulls his hand back to his lap, clasps it with the other to stop their shaking. What difference will it make? he thinks, and knows that he has made his first compromise with this madness, this horror.

"What I do I do with love," Roon says. He strokes the hair of the little girl. Tears trace kohl down his beardless cheeks. "I love you all, as a father does his children. I love you very much."

*   *   *

The long tube of the Florida-Venezuela Free Zone suborbital shuttle is full of Orbital executives riding for free, jocks in their blazoned jackets moving from one free port to another, and a blend of Occupied America drawn from professions wealthy enough to afford air travel, hustlers and gamblers wearing cryo max, snagboys with a feigned nonchalance and booby-trapped satchels handcuffed to their wrists, officials of the collaborationist governments who sit in sweating isolation between the indifferent bloc execs and the hustlers with their carnivore smiles.

Cowboy looks down at the curving horizon against the black sky, the blue ceramic rim of earth softened by the translucent haze of atmosphere. Below him are clouds in implausibly neat rows, wedged above a warm front moving in on the Lesser Antilles, the dusty island brown and green perched on the edge of the glowing turquoise sea. When the shuttle begins its slow fall to Earth, he can feel his body straining against the straps, trying to continue its climb, but the well has the shuttle in its grip again, and his body, too, begins its fall. He turns to Sarah in the next seat, seeing the yearning in her dark eyes as she gazes out of the port, a desire that matches his own longing for the black airless purity. . . . "Damn them," she whispers, shaking her head, and he knows without asking who she's talking about.

The shuttle buffets slightly as it arrows to its landing in La Gran Sabana, the high Venezuelan plateau near the equator where the Orbitals have built their largest spaceport. The green land seems wrinkled as a baby's skin, cut by rivers that look like drops of quicksilver strung on a necklace. Cowboy can see the long jagged mesa edge of Roraima bulking off the port side as the shuttle drops and touches gently on the concrete and alloy floor of the well.

*   *   *

"The architecture of earth always strove for the heavens. Think of the ziggurats of Babylon, the pyramids of Egypt. The cathedrals of the Middle Ages, the pagodas of China. Fingers pointing out of the well, toward liberation." Roon shakes his head. "It's no longer necessary. Humankind has reached for heaven and has found it. But those who live in the sky have become divorced from those who still live in the soil. A new vision is demanded, and with it a new architecture. Like this place, a metaphor for the fusion of earth and sky. Dominating even the mountain upon which it rests.

"Architecture has become my passion," Roon says. Cowboy and Sarah follow him down the coils of his home, along humming alloy corridors, beneath the holographic eyes of Earth's children. Roon raises a finger. "Architecture in all its forms. Including the architecture of the perfect crystal, of the data in the heart of the machine. There is the true medium. In the past humankind has been inhibited by the sympathy of flesh for flesh, by each person's sympathetic understanding of another's own organic weakness. Now we can integrate our consciousness with the immaculate perfection of data. The barriers of Earth are dissolved. No flesh can stand before the supremacy of numbers. Sympathetic action is no longer a possibility. The crystal recognizes only the logic of necessity.

"Necessity," Roon repeats, and he looks at them with his painted eyes. "Necessity is the same, in the crystal world, as inevitability. All that is necessary will become, whatever your feelings, your actions." He smiles. "As my return to power is inevitable. As your own crystal hearts are wise enough to tell you."

*　　*　　*

Roon lives far to the west of the landing port in La Gran Sabana, across the country in the Cordillera Oriental. For Cowboy and Sarah he's laid on private transport, a jet painted as black as the Orbital sky save for the blue Tempel logo above each canard. A dirtgirl in a uniform rushes to carry their bags to the craft. The pilot is a jock with a spaceborn gliding walk, a cold slight man with the company patches on his jacket and pebble Japanese eyes, he looks at Cowboy with a frigid contempt and talks in monosyllables. Cowboy's anger rises; he can feel the crystal burning in his brain while his shoulders ache as if with the tension of wrestling a delta, and he wants badly to meet this man in the sky, to match *Pony Express* against the jock's Orbital cutter. Cowboy can see Sarah's face going rigid, her hands coiling as they try to become claws, and he knows she's thinking of the sweating streets of her own city, placing the jock amid the humid monster of the night.

The flight lasts only twenty minutes, the plane arrowing straight across the country in a quiet so absolute it seems as if the air itself can't touch its mirror-obsidian skin. Cowboy feels envy for the craft, wishes to feel her studs in his skull. Sarah rises from her seat to investigate the aircraft's bar.

Cowboy shakes his head at her offer and she comes back
with a rum and lime, drinks in the silence, the clink of ice the
loudest sound in the plane. Cowboy looks down at the dark
green land blighted by the brown of erosion, the silver rivers
choking, turning dark with topsoil. The black needle threads
through cloud. From above the Sierra Nevada, Cowboy can
see Roon's palace shining silver among the tall green slopes,
a piece of Orbital alloy and crystal jacked into the earth.

A peak interposes: the gleam is gone. The plane is banking
among mountains, twisting silently down a valley. Sarah's
ice cubes sing at the touchdown, but Cowboy can scarcely
feel the impact. He looks up at the surrounding mountains for
the flash of silver and sees Roon's beacon gleaming through
the trees. . . .

                    *   *   *

Through a holographic door that evaporates as it senses his
presence, Roon has taken them into a room alive with holo-
graphs of crystal, changing, growing, interlocking. Their
brightness gleams in Roon's eyes, in the eyes of the two
children who stand motionless before a comp terminal. The
girl is about ten, olive-skinned, wearing a white dress. The
boy is in a white shirt and dark trousers. Both are barefoot.
Their dark hair is cut short around the sockets in their heads.
Tutorial programs flicker on the crystal displays.

"This is Lupe," Roon says. "I named her for her wolf's
eyes. Her brother is Raul." He looks down at them and
smiles.

"They are my oldest acolytes, here in my temple," Roon
says. "I found them in the streets, living like little rodents.
Not a human existence at all. Their parents were dead, their
relatives were indifferent. Chances are they would have died
of malnutrition or disease before they grew to maturity. If
they lived, they would have been on the fringes, turned crimi-
nal, addicts, perhaps sold themselves. The girl might have
borne half a dozen children before she was twenty." He
shakes his head. "Now their possibilities are . . . unlimited.

I feed them, educate them. Impress upon them the pattern that they, that the Earth, must follow." He looks down again at the children.

"Raul was born just after the war. Has lived his whole life amid the new order. New clay, to be shaped by Orbital hands." His eyes rise to look at Sarah and Cowboy. "The older ones—they've absorbed too many of the obsolete views of their parents. Their minds resist the new teaching, the will of the teacher. With these . . ." He smiles down at them sweetly, proudly, as he raises his hands in a gesture of benediction, of possession. Tutorials flash out from the matrix. "These can lead Earth through its time of changes. To its new relationship with the heavens."

He looks up at Cowboy. His gelid eyes gaze out of kohl-rimmed skull sockets. "You have seen the upright way I have taught them to stand," he says. "Like soldiers at attention. Disciplined. Obedient, but proud in their subservience." His eyes radiate joy. His foul breath drifts in the room. "The new relationship," he says. "The pattern to which the future will adhere."

*   *   *

The jock doesn't even look at them as he steps from his cabin and presses the button that opens the pressure door and drops the spindly alloy ladder. He pushes his fists into the pockets of his jacket and steps out on the ladder, heading for the pilot's lounge. Sarah looks up. "Hey," she says. Her voice cuts the air like a razor.

The jock turns and stands half in the door.

"You forgot our bags," Sarah says.

The jock's face is stone. Cowboy feels a grin tugging at the corners of his mouth.

"It's not my job," the jock says.

"It's your job to keep Mr. Roon's guests happy," Sarah says. "Mr. Roon's guests do not. Carry. Their. Own. Fucking. Bags." Her eyes are colder than the drink in her hand, her grin a tiger's.

Blood rises into the jock's face. He hunches into his jacket and reaches into the baggage compartment. Sarah stands and smiles with frigid sweetness. "Thanks very much." Cowboy follows her out.

Waiting just outside is a helicopter, a cold black and silver stork folded onto the alloy runway apron. Smoking a caffeine stick and leaning on the car is what Cowboy can recognize by now as a mudboy mercenary bodyguard, a broad-shouldered man dressed neatly with matching handkerchief and braces. He opens the cargo compartment and watches the jock push the bags inside.

Sarah drops a silver coin into the jock's hands and sees his jaw muscles clench. Cowboy can't help but grin. As the jock stalks away Cowboy can hear the sound of metal skiddering on the surface. The mercenary seems to be amused by the jock's anger.

"I'm Gorman," he says, and opens the helicopter's door.

*   *   *

"Infiltration," says Roon. "Interpenetration of attacker and target. The coiling of subtlety into subtlety. It has become the metaphor of our age. Action is crude, foolish. A waste of energy."

He sighs, holding his crystal goblet to the air. Cowboy sees the holographic stars in its beveled edges. "Couceiro and his Acceleration Group people have no understanding of this, no subtlety. They treat everything as if it were war. War is what they understand. Their attacks are direct, savage, aimed always at the obvious target. Never realizing that if the ground is properly prepared, no direct strike will ever be necessary. Only the Acceleration Group would try to fight on two fronts at once, against Korolev and the thirdmen at the same time. The war on the thirdmen had been in preparation for some time, and the plans wouldn't have been damaged by a delay."

He raises an eyebrow. "Like viral Huntington's," he says. "Diseases that operate by crude assault are too easily dealt with—to survive these days, a disease has to be subtle. Infiltrate the target years before the assault, lie dormant in brain and nerve tissue. Then turn contagious, spreading its offspring to people who have no warning, before coming alive at once, a nest of viral saboteurs, to bring the target down. The disease was in the population for years before we were even aware of it. Spread by the aftereffects of the war. Millions have been exposed who don't know it." He laughs.

"We could only cure it by being more subtle than the disease. By creating a tailor-made virus, a tiny infiltrator that can mimic the Huntington's virus. That uses the Huntington's numbers against itself. That can approach the target, then inject the enemy with a lab-born DNA strand that will ligate with their own and mutate it. Turn it from black to white, from a Huntington's virus to one of our own. So that the infected cell becomes a new infiltrator, changes its allegiance to the side of life." He smiles in satisfaction. His eyes turn to Cowboy.

"I like your plan for its subtlety, Cowboy," Roon says. "I like the idea of using this viral cure as a way of bringing down Couceiro. Turning his biggest triumph against him." He caresses the back of his cupbearer absently, not turning his eyes toward her. "I will put your plan into my crystal," he says. "Match your logic against the logic of data." He smiles with brown teeth. "Then we shall see whether your architecture is worthy of the sky."

*   *   *

Gorman pilots manually, not facing in even through a headset. He wrestles with the chopper as if it were an alligator. Cowboy winces at his clumsiness.

From the air Roon's place is as much sculpture as dwelling, a twisted hyperboloid driven into the soil, the surfaces— silver lattice supporting black glass—stretching toward an impossible singularity. It's built of patterned Orbital alloy in reckless Gaussian curves that seem only conceivable outside of gravity; no terrestrial metal could possibly support the design. The grounds are bare of life, dark metal threaded with silver, as if the building had spread itself thinly across the earth surrounding it. Cowboy thinks of the four-dimensional model of Tempel built by Thibodaux, its own complex geometries and interrelationships. Brought to Earth, here, an analog of Orbital power.

Gorman wrenches the helicopter to a landing, fighting a gusting wind. As the blades whimper to a standstill he looks over his shoulder and reaches in his pocket for another caffeine stick. "Mr. Roon will tell you his house is a metaphor," he says. "Agree with him."

Cowboy shrugs. "Okay. If it's important."

Gorman's unobtrusive artificial eyes look into Cowboy's. "Dirt walks carefully here. That was a nice trick you pulled on Hideo, but don't even think of something like that around Roon." He unbuckles his safety harness and opens the door, blowing mint-scented smoke. "If he doesn't like you," Gorman says, "he'll probably have me kill you. And since I don't get paid extra for things like that, I'd really rather not."

Cowboy looks at Gorman curiously. "Would you do it quietly in the basement, or would Roon want to watch?"

Gorman considers. "Depends on what lesson he was trying to give. He's big on lessons."

Cowboy and Sarah step out of the chopper. Cowboy finds the metal yard cool under his bootsoles, even in the afternoon sun. There must be some kind of heat absorption underneath. He's surprised to see a pair of children, nine or ten years old, walking quickly to the helicopter across the metal yard. They're dressed alike in dark pants and crisp white shirts, their hair cut short. They have to get close within a few feet before Cowboy can tell the boy from the girl. Another wave of surprise rises through Cowboy at the sight of sockets in their heads.

"You're Roon's people, right?" Sarah is asking Gorman. "Not company security?"

"Company security's run by Couceiro. You know who he is, right? Roon doesn't want those people around."

"Glad to hear it," Cowboy says. The boy and girl walk up to the helicopter, open the cargo door, take out their bags. Begin their silent return to the house.

Gorman closes the chopper door behind them. "Follow the boy and girl," he says. "And give thanks to God you were born before the war."

"It's never occurred to me that I should be thankful for that," Cowboy says. He watches the bright white backs of the children recede across the silver threaded metal, then another thought strikes him. He turns to Gorman. "Do you pray a lot, then, Gorman?"

The mercenary gives a low, angry laugh. "Here? Just every goddamn day."

*   *   *

Cowboy's window looks east. He stands gazing out at the pale predawn, and above the shadowed mountain peaks can see a diamond scratching a line across the glass sphere of sky. The exhaust trail of a rocket rising from La Gran Sabana, turning in the cold thin air to crystals that refract the sunlight, climbing toward the last dim stars and the high constellation of Orbital worlds. He can feel things out of place here, shifting under his feet.

"I don't know." He shakes his head. "I don't know what's going on here. The children, the way he talks. This place."

They've cleared his room of the mics Roon had planted. Jammed any they'd missed with the electronics Flash Force had provided. This is as safe a place for conversation as Roon's place will ever be.

"You really don't know what's going on?" Sarah untangles her long limbs from the bed sheets. "You don't know what he's doing?" She comes up behind him, puts her arms around his shoulders. He can feel her cheek resting on his shoulder. Thinks of the thing in her throat. Watches the rainbow contrail, feels the longing rise in his heart. . . .

"He's fucking them, Cowboy," Sarah says, and he can

feel his mind fill with ice. Her voice is soft, gentle, all the streetgirl hardness gone. "He's fucking all those little boys and girls. And he's studding himself into their brains so they can't get away from him, not even into their own heads. That's what his religion is about. That's this new arrangement he wants to make with the children of Earth."

The knowledge rises in Cowboy's gorge like bile. He takes a breath, swallows. The sockets in his head burn at the thought of an alien mind riding him.

He shakes his head. His voice quavers. "I'm not dealing with him."

"You can't help them."

"That doesn't mean I have to help *him*."

He feels her step back. He braces for her whipcrack voice, but her tones are still low. "He and Couceiro and those other people . . . they killed millions. They killed almost all my family and they put scars on me and on my brother. If I could, I'd shoot Roon and Couceiro and Grechko and the others in the guts with soft-nosed bullets and toss them onto anthills to die. But I can't do that."

"I won't . . ." He shakes his head again, the words fading away completely.

"There's only one difference between Couceiro and Roon, so far as I can see. Couceiro wants to kill us. Roon will let us live." He feels Sarah's hands on his shoulders again, heavy as iron, heavy as the Earth.

"That's not it," he says. "I want to stay . . . clean."

"Lucky Cowboy." For the first time the edge of sarcasm is in her voice. Her voice drifts lazily to his ears. "Lucky Cowboy and his clean hands. By chance you had a talent somebody wanted, and now you're able to afford principles. Good for you."

The weight comes off Cowboy's shoulders and he can hear her pacing behind him. Her words come in little bursts, run together like gunfire, obeying some internal sense of rhythm. "There are better ways to live than fucking old men, but there are some that are a lot worse. Let me tell you. . . ."

She steps up behind him, so close that he can feel her breath on his neck. He tries to control a tremor.

"My brother is a whore and a junkie. He had some surgery and took a lot of hormone suppressants to look young, because that's how his customers like them. The hormone blockers meant he couldn't respond very well, but even that appeals to a certain kind of taste. But there are other kinds of tastes on the streets . . . let's call one of them a taste for reality." The words come slowly, unstoppably, each with its own impact. Slow bullets. Cowboy wants to shudder with each one.

"Whores offer fantasy. They get good at figuring out what their customers want, and how well they latch onto those fantasies has a lot to do with how well they get paid. It's fake, but most of the customers don't notice, or care. These other people, the ones who want reality—they care. They want things to be real. Real sex, real orgasms. Real love, even. And when they don't get it, they get mad. They want what happens between them and their boy to be real. Even if they have to torture him to death to get a real reaction. People like that are called thatch."

"I've heard the word."

"Yeah. You just don't know what it means." He can feel her stepping back. "Some people are thatch, and that's bad. Some people get killed or hurt by a thatch, and that's bad. You know what's worse?" She waits for him to answer. The silence beats at Cowboy's ears. "What's worse," Sarah says, "is that a thatch has no end of victims. Because there are people who are so desperate, or so tired, that they don't care anymore. They don't take any kind of precautions, because it's just too much trouble to hang onto a life that's become a pointless, endless misery. Some even go with a thatch, half hoping they'll die, when doing what's necessary to stay alive is just too much trouble, because life's just become a pain that won't stop."

There is another heartbeat of silence.

"That's my brother," Sarah says. "That's Daud."

Cowboy stares out the glass, seeing the long rainbow

fingernail-scratch of the rocket fading, vanishing in the high winds. He finds his voice. "So," he says, "Lupe and what's his name, Raul, they're in good shape, huh?"

"No. They're victims. Roon is evil. I'm just saying my brother would trade places with either one of them in a minute. And once upon a time, I would have done the same."

The last of the contrail vanishes. Cowboy takes a deep breath and turns to face Sarah. She stands deep in his shadow, her hands cocked on her hips. Watching him with cold eyes.

"I want to kill him," he says. "Kill Roon. I've never wanted anything more." He's surprised at it. Even Arkady had never seemed worth the trouble of hating—just a Russian thirdman who was foolish enough to stand between Cowboy and his legend. But Roon is something else, a shadowy foul-breathed evil hovering in his silver-laced Gaussian nightmare. . . . A creature worth the killing.

Sarah tosses her hair. "So kill him. I won't stop you. Two months from now."

"After he's out of the well, where I can't reach him."

"Kill Couceiro first. He's the one that's trying to kill you."

Cowboy moves through the connecting door to Sarah's room, to the white plastic bar that stands outlined with holograms of old neon tropical images, green palm trees, blue water, girls in oscillating grass skirts. He reaches for a bottle and feels the cool glass against his fingers, sees the holo images glowing through the crystal, distorted, nightmarish. He drops the bottle, tastes sweat on his lip. He realizes that he's shifted into a hardwired state, that impulses are screaming through his Santistevan nerves, the dark room seeming to bend in toward him as the rushing adrenaline distorts his vision. . . .

He closes his eyes and looks up. Sees behind his lids the twists and turns of the wire and crystal world, the victors drifting out of the well, building their architecture of power, contemplating the earth with artificial raptor eyes. Earth's billions in their ratholes, scrabbling for their diminishing portions while the air grows hotter, the grip of the blocs stronger, the pressure of numbers greater. In the black night alleys of the war of all against all, Sarah's cybersnake is only logical, a piece of cyborg cunning that can kill only those trusting enough to come close. They're the only ones she can reach. The others fly too high, out of her sight. That she is desperate enough to have such a thing marks her as a victim before it marks her as anything else.

An alliance with Roon? Easily done. A few children will lose their childhood, and who's to say they wouldn't have lost it anyway, here or in the streets? At least they're being fed well. For dirt.

He opens his eyes, seeing the cold and brilliant hologram of the night sky that covers all the ceilings here, the burning stars and the stationary platinum beacons of the geosynchronous robot factories. "You've lost your choices long ago," the constellation whispers, "and whatever moves you make are the ones we let you. And Cowboy—we do not permit innocence as an option. That is the first thing you give us."

Cowboy is aware of Sarah standing in the doorway, her body in shadow, her eyes concerned but still demanding a choice. Whatever innocence she once possessed had gone long ago, cut away by the razors of the streets. The cybersnake is less a horror now, more a pathetic attempt at defense, at making a place for herself in the dark new order.

He tries to tote up the debts he owes, to Sarah and the Dodger and Warren, to a couple of kids huddled in a single sleeping bag in some decaying barn in Missouri. To the children here in Roon's palace. To his own burning dreams.

"All right," he whispers. His eyelids flutter, an old reflex made obsolete by his plastic eyes and his amputated tear ducts. "All right. We'll do it your way."

She walks up to him slowly, putting her arms around his neck, laying her cheek to his. "I'm sorry, Cowboy," she says. "I'm sorry."

He clings to her for a while, lets her lead him away into the night of her own scarred mind, torn life, dark choices.

He lived free in the air, once, on the last free road. It's a tunnel now, growing ever narrower and blacker, and he never saw the walls rise till he was deep inside. Moving faster than light down this narrowing, echoing, darkening pathway.

He'll have to watch Sarah carefully. She knows how to survive in this place.

* * *

Roon's new body has only been worn for eight years and shouldn't look any older than thirty, but there are lines around the eyes that can't be entirely hidden by the kohl, and they proclaim how hard Roon is using himself. His scalp is shaved entirely except for an oiled, curled scalp lock over the left eye. Diamond chips glitter in his head sockets. It looks as if he's never brushed his teeth. He laughs, reaches for his drink. Cowboy can feel his own eyelids tremble, fear racing up his spine.

"The well has been a barrier for both our peoples," Roon says. He reaches for an inhaler, fires a pair of rockets, throws his head back and sniffs. His voice drones on, unchanged, directed at the starry hologram of the ceiling. "Consciousness has evolved differently for those outside of gravity. But crystal bridges the gap, burning in our heads, burning away the imperfection. Leaves us helpless before the inevitability of its logic."

He reaches a hand out, touching one of Cowboy's temple sockets. Cowboy tries not to flinch. Roon's corpse breath enfolds him. Cowboy can see Sarah across the dinner table, her face a mask as she watches. "It is the perfect architecture of crystal that bridges the gap between us, Cowboy," he says. "The barriers of Earth and its well can be dissolved. A new relationship created. The union of exploiter and exploited, cosmic and earthly, predator and prey."

The hand falls away. Roon turns to Sarah, his eyes looking at her aslant, and then he leans toward her, cupping her face in his hands. Cowboy's nerves begin to scream.

Roon's words were slurred, drunken. "It was forced at

first, our new relationship. The war—it was made inevitable by the stupidity of the leaders of Earth. Even now you try to resist us. But soon it will change. You will come willingly. Become prey to our vision, our ecstacies. The crystal will draw you."

He smiles, reaches for his drink again, leans back on his couch, closes his eyes. Cowboy watches as his breathing deepens, as the drink slides from his fingers to bounce soundlessly on the deep carpet. Lupe and Raul motionless at either side of his seat, exchange covert glances.

Cowboy rises from his chair, his head swimming with hatred. Sarah's eyes rise to him as he stands, flicker to Roon, then turn back to him as she makes her decision. She follows him as he begins to walk toward their suite.

They're only partway there when they hear the cry, the blow. Cowboys nerves trigger as he spins in the dark metal corridor and begins his run through the alloy corridors of Roon's dream.

Raul lies unconscious on the deep carpet, the side of his face reddening. A table knife lies by his hand, a jewel of red trembling on its tip. Roon stands astride him, wrapping a napkin around his arm. Blood streams from his hand onto the smooth white surface of a petroleum-plastic dish.

"A foolish act of rebellion," Roon says. His breath comes in pants. "Tried to cut me while I slept." A pair of guards burst through the kitchen door with their armored coats pulled up around their eyes, weapons in hand. Gorman is right behind them. Roon turns his head. "The boy," he says. "I handled it."

Cowboy kneels by Raul. His eyelids are flickering, his head lolls from left to right. Regaining consciousness. He looks up into the terrified eyes of Lupe, still standing at her place by Roon's couch. Gorman is calling for a medic on his radio. Tears are spilling silently down Lupe's cheeks. Cowboy stands up and puts his arm around her shoulders. He can feel her trembling, but she's too scared of Roon to leave her stance.

Raul begins to open his eyes. Cowboy looks at Roon.
Feels his heart thundering in his throat. "What will you do
with him?"

Roon looks down at the boy. His expression is mild.
"Nothing," he says. "Put him outside the gates. Let him live
outside of the communion with the sky." He looks at Cowboy, and there is a sweet smile of genuine sadness on his
face. "It's the worst thing that can happen to him, really. To
be barred forever from the future that could have been his."
One of the mercenaries reaches down, drags Raul to his feet
by his collar.

"Poor fool," Roon says. "I love him still." He looks
down at Lupe and puts a hand on her trembling forehead.
Drops of blood patter down the starched white dress. "The
sister will stay, of course. I will not shun her for her brother's sin." He seems to become aware of the scarlet stream
running down his wrist.

"Where is the medic?" He frowns, and walks away,
toward his rooms, leaving a speckled, darkening trail.

Cowboy watches him go. Raul hangs by his collar from
the guard's fist, passive now, ready to accept the consequences of his revolt. His cheek is glowing red where Roon's
hand struck.

Gorman looks at the guard, shrugs. "You heard the boss.
Put the boy outside."

The two guards march away. Cowboy strokes Lupe's head,
trying to give comfort. Hoping she doesn't think it a pirate
caress. Gorman shrugs, his hands on his hips, then looks at
Cowboy—and for a moment there's a reflection of Cowboy's
own hatred there, before the mercenary can choke it back
down.

Then Cowboy's fishing in his pocket for a credit spike and
holds it out. "Can you see he gets this?"

"Raul?"

Cowboy nods. "Tell him who it's from."

Gorman takes the needle with its little jewel of crystal at
its tip, then puts it in his pocket. He looks into Cowboy's
eyes for a half second, and Cowboy can't tell what he's

reading there. Gorman nods slowly. "Yeah. Okay," he says. He calls into his radio for the guards to wait, then walks briskly away.

Cowboy feels Sarah's gaze on him. "How much was in that?" she asks.

"A few thousand. Something like that."

"In dollars?"

Cowboy says nothing. A grin twitches at Sarah's lips. She turns to look at Gorman's receding back

"Dollars aren't worth much back home, but they're worth a lot more here. The little bastard'll be rich . . . if they don't think he stole it." She reaches to the table for a napkin, crouches in front of Lupe, blots her tears. Now that Roon and the guards are gone Lupe breaks her stance, throws her arms around Sarah. Sobs.

Cowboy keeps stroking her hair, not knowing what else to do. Adrenaline pulses in spurts through his ragged nerves. He looks at the door where Raul had gone and tastes envy on his tongue. Knows he should have done it himself, should have broken the glass and gone for Roon's throat with a piece of the crystal in his hand. Let the act become one of the metaphors Roon's so fond of.

He will never do it. He's too caught up in the matrix of darkness, here, the compromises he's made have wedged too far into him for him ever to see clearly again.

*   *   *

As Sarah and Cowboy come nearer, parts of Roon's building seem to curl out of sight, as if moving like Thibodaux's model into the fourth dimension. A warm canyon wind brings dust hissing in elegant scouring tracework over the building's black skin. There is no door, no interface between the geometrical Orbital fantasy and the courtyard; they simply walk under the bright pretzel girders and into an area of cool, still air, hushed like the place is holding its breath, the sun's light, refracted by the curved crystal above, shining down in falling sheets of green, violet, blue, touching sculpted metal furniture with delicate pastel-colored nails. . . .

"Must be a metaphor, huh?" Cowboy says. Sarah's laugh echoes harshly from the silent metal.

They follow the two children down a metal runway that turns into a curving hallway. Cowboy's bootheels sink deep into the carpet. This leads to a pair of linked rooms, all shadows and curves, just like the Ritz Flop, but with a hologram image of some space habitat rotating slowly near one ceiling corner. Cowboy feels an urge to use the softglow inhaler in his pocket, feeling that a sense of unreality might help in coping with this place. Sarah walks through the irising connecting doorway.

"We're deep in Fantasyland here," she says. "You know about Fantasyland, Cowboy? Where they built the spaceport at Orlando?"

"Never heard of it."

"A place for children. Where they could learn how nice the future was supposed to be." She laughs. "They sure got that part wrong, didn't they?"

*   *   *

The sitting room has a holo of a refugee kid in the corner, all ribs and eyes. Cowboy doesn't like to look at it.

Roon enters the room quietly from behind, and Cowboy can feel his hackles trying to rise at the man's scent, the sweet pomade he uses on his forelock, the scent of corpses on his breath. Roon, moving in silence behind Cowboy's chair, lowers his pale hands to the iron muscles in Cowboy's shoulders. Cowboy looks at the opaque expression on Sarah's face as she curls in a half-lotus on a settee.

"I have considered your plan," he says. "My crystal tells me it is sound. I will accept." He pauses. "I will make the arrangements for secure communication lines."

The tension doesn't leave Cowboy's neck. "Thank you, Mr. Roon," he says.

Roon's thumbs drill into Cowboy's neck with considered

pressure, as if trying to loosen the hard muscles there. Cowboy remains as still as one of Roon's children at the table. "You are blessed," Roon says. Corrupt breath floats in the room. "You will help me to regain heaven. From there I shall impose my crystal dreams upon the Earth."

"We're only messengers," Cowboy says. He can feel prickles of sweat on his scalp.

Roon doesn't seem to be listening. "I shall send Couceiro to Earth," he says, his voice drifting on, locked in its own madness. "To the surface of the planet he hates. Perhaps it will redeem him, perhaps the people of Earth will teach him to love. Who can say?"

He takes his hands away, and Cowboy can feel relief filling his muscles. Roon walks toward Sarah. Cowboy can see the white bandage on his arm as he takes her head in his hands and bends to gravely kiss her lips. "I thank you," he says. "I thank you both." He turns and fixes Cowboy with his blissful smile. Liquid nitrogen fills Cowboy's heart. "You have made possible all my dreams."

*   *   *

After waiting for an hour, Cowboy and Sarah decide to go exploring. They poke into things at random, finding the same kind of soft, shadowy rooms lit by tinted sunlight. Beds, chairs, tables, computer access seem to be strewn more or less randomly; few of the rooms appear to have any definite purpose in mind. Hologrammatic images of star fields, ships, industrial colonies move silently on the walls, the ceilings. There are also pictures of children, wide-eyed barefoot refugee kids, standing like appeals to charity in the midst of the plush, silent rooms.

In the end they find Roon by accident, wandering into the room where he sits on a tall white chair, faced into a portable computer deck held in the still arms of a small, absolutely motionless girl-child standing next to him in a white dress. By now Cowboy's beginning to doubt anything he sees and it takes him a moment to realize the picture isn't another hologram, that the man with the long laser-optic cable reaching up to the socket on his temple is breathing slightly, that his closed eyelids are trembling with reflex eyeball movement as his optical centers scan the data.

The black-rimmed eyes open, move dreamily across the room. Find Cowboy and Sarah, focus on them. His look sharpens. "I love you," he says. "As if you were my very own children."

The black and silver singularity twists into cold n-dimensional space. And the collective nightmare, Roon's and Cowboy's, begins again.

Chapter Fifteen

The flat green border of the Florida peninsula, scalloped where the sea is coming in, lies canted up on edge before them. Clouds seem pasted to it like construction-paper cutouts. The returning gravity presses on Sarah's chest. She swallows hard and feels Weasel lying like a rock in her throat.

In Roon's house she hadn't dared relax—she was either watching Roon the whole time or riding Cowboy to make sure he didn't flip. The time in Roon's house had felt like a century, and she's surprised it was only five days. Before the shuttle left she mixed rightsnap and alcohol in the port bar, the first relief she'd allowed herself, and walked onto the shuttle in a blaze of warm internal light. Now the drugs move sluggishly through her veins, softening the razor edge of reality.

She looks at Cowboy and frowns. He's been faced into his computer for most of the trip, and even when he's had his head out of the crystal his eyes have still had that far-off look, as if he was trying to make sense out of something . . . like maybe the latticework of his three-dimensional holo construct of the Tempel bloc, the way Roon was worked into it, the girders and networks of its architecture studding into his sockets, the way Cowboy and Sarah are now extensions of those networks, a tunnel through which Roon communicates with all the lattices and powers outside of the Tempel organization. Cowboy's trying to make sense, Sarah thinks, of the way Cowboy and Roon are linked, and what that means to the world that Cowboy's lived in for so many years, that implausible vision of himself that she's been able to glimpse from time to time, all jet-powered hardware and burning crystal escaping into black night corridors, the outside sensors filled with flaming rockets, alcohol fire, screaming pumps—and all this mechanical violence in the unlikely service of some kind of transcendental, personal sense of justice, life lived in service to unspoken codes of honor and existence. . . . Sarah figures Cowboy's been living alongside evil people all his life, but just never let one touch him before.

Lucky man, she thinks, and sips her rum and lime. Gravity squats on her chest, and she sees the bubbles that rise in her glass slow down, then hang in the cool solution, waiting for the well to free them. Her head presses back against the padded rest.

"You think he'll be okay?" Sarah can't decide whether Cowboy's muttering to himself or to her.

"Who?"

"Raul."

She closes her eyes, seeing growing patches the color of blood on the back of her lids. "Yeah," she says. "He'll do good." Maybe it's even the truth, though Sarah suspects that Raul's throat will most likely get cut the first time he tries to use the American dollars Cowboy gave him. She wishes he'd given the money to her—she'd have found a good use for it, better anyway than scattering it among the knifeboys of some Cordillera shantytown.

"Maybe I can find him again. Bring him to the States, let him stay with my uncle. He can always use a willing hand."

Sarah can feel the atmosphere whispering against the outside of the shuttle. She opens her eyes. The clouds over Florida have risen at an angle oblique to the land, like a layered transparency lifted over a map. Shadows pox the land below. The pressure in her throat lessens. "If you want to get into that kind of business," Sarah says, "there are homeless kids a lot closer than Venezuela."

He doesn't answer that, just stares forward and fades into

the matrix again. Sarah sips her drink and closes her eyes. The shuttle begins to buffet and the Free Zone rises to claim them.

"Michael will meet you tonight." That's the word from the Flash Force man who waits at the security gate. "In the meantime, we'll drive you where you need to go."

The sun hammers at them as they step onto the concrete. "The Ritz Flop," Sarah says, but out of the corner of her eye she sees Cowboy shake his head.

"No," he says. "Someplace else." She looks at him in silent surprise. Sweat dots his forehead like a constellation of extra sockets.

"Where?" she asks.

Cowboy shrugs. He looks at the long car with its opaqued windows, then at Sarah. "Your place, maybe. Above the bar?"

She's about to refuse but something stops her. His look, a sixth sense, something. A knowledge that to say no would be wrong—not unwise, just a piece of unnecessary cruelty.

"Okay," she says slowly. "But you'll be by yourself. If we don't meet the Hetman till night, I'm going to spend the afternoon with Daud."

Cowboy shrugs again. "Blue Silk, then," Sarah tells the driver, then ducks into the car's back seat.

Cowboy's quiet on the ride back to Tampa, drawn into himself. Sarah stops in the Blue Silk long enough to tell Maurice that it's okay if Cowboy stays for the afternoon, then lets the Flash Force take her to Daud.

She's moved him out of the hospital and into a recovery house in a Tampa suburb, a place out behind the howling limited expressway that connects Tampa with Orlando. He's got a room that's more like a dormitory residence than a hospital room, and Sarah doesn't think any of the attendants have the look of a Joseph, with a syringe hidden in the towels.

Daud is sitting up in a chair when she enters his room. He looks better simply by virtue of the fact he's out of hospital clothes, and he's lifting a dumbbell with his weak arm. It's the first time she's seen him exercise voluntarily, and she smiles as she walks toward him.

"Hi, Sarah."

She bends to kiss him. His blue eyes smile up at her from beneath an unscarred brow. Sarah straightens in surprise. "Daud . . ." She blinks at him. A cold needle begins to stitch her nerves. His smile broadens as he works the weight. "How . . . ?"

"The body designer took off the face scars two days ago. With her laser." He's beginning to breathe hard from the exertion. His tone shows the strain.

She leans back against the wall, crosses her arms. "Who paid for it?" she asks.

"This . . . guy I met. His sister is in here with . . . terminal Huntington's. He's rich." Daud's smile turns shaky. The cords on his neck stand out. He lifts the weight twice more, then lets it down. He leans his head back and takes a breath.

"What does he do?"

"Something in shipping. He's from southern Africa someplace. He's just here because his sister is a patient here." He raises his head and looks at Sarah. His smile is hesitant. "He thinks he might want me to go home with him."

"Well." Sarah can feel a harshness in her tone that she doesn't want. She swallows and tries to control it. "This is fast. A romantic African from across the seas. All in five days."

A wary look clouds Daud's eyes. "I think you'll like him," he says.

"Is he here now?"

Daud mutely shakes his head. "He left about an hour ago."

Sarah wants to grab him, hold his arm out, tear up his sleeve to see if there are puncture marks. Shake him till his teeth rattle. Instead she makes herself smile. Knowing how badly he needs this new bit of hope, and that she doesn't dare destroy it unless she knows for certain it's a phantom.

"Can I meet his sister?"

"Sure. But she's paralyzed with viral Huntington's. Can't talk."

Sarah feels apprehension warring in her system with the rightsnap. She moves to sit on Daud's bed. Tries to smile again. "Daud, I hope you're being careful. Because this man may be aimed at me."

She sees the jaw muscles clench, the anger flaring behind the coldness in Daud's eyes. He turns to her. "You can't believe in things that aren't connected to you, can you? Everything has to revolve around you, even me and the people I know." He throws up his hands. "Can't you stay out of my life?"

"I'm just trying to keep you from getting hurt, Daud. If this man turns out to be one of the people that are after me."

"He's not. He cares for me. He really does."

"I'm glad. If . . ." She lets the sentence fade away.

"If he turns out to be real." Daud's voice blazes defiance. "That's what you were going to say, right?" He shakes his head. "You didn't even ask his name, did you? It's Nick Mslope."

"I don't want to fight, Daud."

"Nick Mslope. Say it."

"Yeah. Fine. Nick Mslope. Who may or may not be real." She looks at him. "Can you say that?"

He turns away, fumbles in his pocket for a cigarette.

"Can you, Daud?" Her voice is as gentle as she can make it.

"I don't have to take this," Daud mumbles. "I don't have to say anything I don't want." He lights the tobacco. "I don't have to depend on your money anymore. Nick will take care of me."

"I hope he will," Sarah says. "But tell him something first. Tell him you saw me, that we had a fight and you'll never see me again. And then if he'll still take care of you, fine." Smoke rises over Daud's averted head. Sarah leans forward. "Will you tell him that, Daud? Will you take that chance?"

Daud's jaw is trembling. "I don't have to," he says.

"I'm only interested in making things clear. For everybody. If Nick wants to help you through this, fine. I'd enjoy not having to pay for it. But don't question him too close till you get all your parts back."

He looks at her out of the corner of his eyes. "Damn you," he says. "You can't leave me with anything."

"I don't enjoy this."

"So you say." He tries to make his voice cut, but he can't do more than choke on the words. She reaches out to touch him, feels him try to flinch away, then accept her.

Feeding people realities. That seems to be all she's done lately, and she feels a sickness at it, like bile stirring in her stomach.

She comes closer to Daud, putting her arms around him, kissing his cold, compliant cheek. "Take care, Daud," she whispers. "Take care." Knowing that he won't, that he doesn't care enough to do more than take whatever comes. He'll hang his hope on it, whether it exists or not.

Chapter Sixteen

The bottom of the bottle makes a cold circle on Cowboy's chest. He feels hot, unable to sleep. Something is working at him.

Sarah's little room is a box and suddenly he can't take it anymore.

He stands, finishes the beer, pulls on a shirt. He walks down the stairs and lets himself out the back so that he won't have the Flash Force tagging along. The alley steams after a short rainshower. He steps out of the alley and the city oozes up around him, smelling of frangipani.

He thinks about getting high, but drugs won't do the job. . . . He has to get *really* high, in a delta, float in the whispering night, before *high* will do him any good. Even sitting in his abandoned panzer would help. He wonders if it's been found yet, sitting in its gully in Ohio.

People on the street are looking at the sockets in his head, and he realizes he's forgotten his wig. He glares at them, and they look away, their curiosity turning covert. *I'm not a junkie*, he thinks at them, *I'm a pilot*. The sidelong looks continue. Cowboy gives up in disgust and goes into the first bar he finds. It's full of potted palms and tasteful holograms floating above businessmen drinking away their expense accounts. Cowboy can't take this, either. With no idea other than acquiring some privacy, he walks into a phone booth and closes the door.

A little fan whines into action on the roof of the booth,

sounding like an anemic turbine. Cool air brushes Cowboy's face. He studs the phone into the socket over his right ear and decides to call Norfolk and talk to Cathy, his Coast Guard lieutenant, see if she's able to get away for another weekend, somewhere up on the Western Slope, where the lowlands are far away and the clean winds move through the aspens like a cutter through the thin air, but he's told that she's at sea and they won't patch him through. He stares at the phone, clenches his fists, and decides he's tired of being careful, of being told he can't help people if he wants to.

He calls Reno's number in Pittsburgh.

"Cowboy. Cowboy, my god."

The voice is that of a lost child, but it's Reno's, a little toneless maybe, but still good enough to send a wave of liquid oxygen rushing over Cowboy's skin, a pulse of fear, cold yet somehow invigorating.

"Cowboy, what happened? I can't remember."

"They came down on us, Reno," Cowboy says. Reno's brain was white, Cowboy remembers. In the eye-face all the time. The personality fading almost visibly. Unless it's a Tempel trick. Unless they've got a program jacking along the lines, identifying this phone, sending out their hard men with their robot eyes and crystal-guided deathware.

"We had a talk, about hearts you wanted to sell," Reno says. "I remember that. And that tall girl you had with you, the one with the gun. Then I can't remember anything, not until . . . I remember fire all over the place. Intruder alarms. Never knew who was out there. I was faced in, trying to call for help." There is silence for a moment.

"I think I died, Cowboy." The voice is hesitant. "That's what I read in the screamsheets, that I died. They didn't mention you."

Cowboy can feel his sweat going cold. Fear is making his teeth ache. He reaches out blindly, touching the brushed aluminum front of the phone. "Reno," he says. "Reno, where are you?"

"I'm in public crystal, Cowboy. In Pittsburgh, in Maryland . . . I've got parts of me all over. Libraries, minimum security datafiles, unused telephone addresses. Banks where I've opened accounts and had the passwords." The voice wanders on. Cowboy can feel his hackles rising. "I was faced through my house crystal, through memory boxes. I've got all that data. But I'm so scattered out I can't use it very well. And I've lost so much else." Reno's voice is a child's whimper. Cowboy thinks of Lupe, of the scream bottled in her throat at the touch of Roon's hand.

"Cowboy," Reno says, "I've forgotten things. I've forgotten how to be a person. I remember it boiling away. My brain boiling in the fire. Help me, Cowboy."

Cowboy can feel Reno out there, just on the other side of the socket. Trying to pour himself out of the crystal, become a person again. Cowboy makes a fist, punches the glass wall of the booth. Bar patrons look at him, then look away. "Listen," he says, "we can get you out. Into a body. They do crystal transfers every day."

"I don't think there's enough of me left. I'm losing more pieces all the time. Getting little bits of data lost in tranfers. Sometimes people find me in their crystal and erase parts of me before I know it, before I can get away." Reno sounds as if, wherever he is, he's crying. "Why didn't you call sooner? You're one of the few people I can remember. I tried everything to get hold of you. I tried calling, following your accounts. I think I got you once, in a library matrix in New Mexico, but you unfaced. Everyone's shut off."

"There's a war on, Reno. You were killed. Everyone else is hiding."

"War? With *who?* Who killed me, Cowboy?"

There is a knock on the booth's door. Cowboy glares up to see one of the waiters, a tall South American with cold eyes and a curled lip.

"Interruption here. Excuse me." Cowboy opens the door.

"Who killed me, Cowboy?" The voice sounds on Cowboy's aural crystal. It's growing distorted, as if Reno's losing control of the pulses that are creating his voice in Cowboy's head.

"This telephone is for the convenience of our patrons only, sir," the waiter says.

"So bring me a drink. Beer. Any brand." Cowboy slams the door.

"Cowboy?" Reno's voice is almost inaudible below an uncontrolled fluctuation of white noise. Cowboy winces at the volume. "How did I die?"

"Tempel killed you. Tempel Pharmaceuticals Interessenge-meinschaft. They and their friends."

"Tempel . . . Tempel." Reno's voice grows clear again, as if understanding has somehow cleared up his interface problem. "I've still got a lot of detail about Tempel—it was faced into my memory box when I died. And I talked to you through that Tempel model you had, and I've got the model in my memory now. When you were in my house, did we talk about Tempel, Cowboy? I remember talking to you about something."

"Yeah. We talked about Tempel. About the war."

"It's all so long ago. I measure time in picoseconds now."

Cowboy thinks again of the hard men in their armored cars, their faces cold planes, their eyes ice, metal in their hands. "Reno," he says. "I need to know if you're real. You might be a trap."

"Cowboy. *I'm real. Help me.*"

"Tell me something only we know about. Tell me something, Reno."

"Cowboy." Reno's soft cry is buried in white noise. "I don't know. I've lost so much."

The waiter is coming with Cowboy's beer. Cowboy's knuckles are white as he grips the frame of the phone booth. He gulps the cool air fanning slowly down from above.

"Cowboy, listen." White noise crashes like the sound of Oahu surf. "I remember a time we were playing poker. In that little cammo shack Saavedra set up by the Dakota line. You'd just brought the *Express* back from a run and you decided to stay around and be part of my ground crew later that night. You and I were there, and Saavedra dropped in for a few hands, and there was another jock. Begay, the big

Navajo. The one who got killed by his brother in that accident. He took all our money, gave us all cigars. Remember?''

The waiter is standing by the booth with a beer in his hand. Cowboy has no strength anymore, just leans against the transparent plastic. Sobs try to force their way up past his throat. "Jesus, Reno. My god. It's you. It's you."

He would cry if he could. Saavedra and Begay are both dead and there is no one else who could have told Tempel about that poker game. Reno's caught somewhere in the crystal, what's left of him an electronic ghost caught in an endless loop between two worlds, going nowhere at the speed of light. Cowboy smashes the back of his head against the booth, seeking the clarity of pain. The waiter looks at him in disapproval, a buttonhead junkie going mad in his clean palm bar.

"Look, Reno, we'll get you out." Cowboy tastes blood in his mouth. He swipes his forehead with the back of his arm. "The Dodger and me. We'll find a body for you."

"I don't have the money, Cowboy. I've got most of my accounts, but the money isn't near enough."

Cowboy laughs. The sound is vast in the small booth, and the echo comes back tinny with the overtones of hysteria. He wants to keep on laughing but manages to stop himself.

"Hell, brother, you're halfway there." He realizes he's shouting and lowers his voice. "You're already out of your body and in the crystal medium. It's only the last part we've got to pay for. Bet we can get a big discount."

He swings open the door and takes the beer from the surprised waiter. "Some snacks, too," he says. "Nachos, if you have them. Peanuts'll be okay, though."

"Cowboy . . . Cowboy." Reno's voice is fading in and out of the white noise.

"Yeah, Reno. I'm still here."

"Thank you, Cowboy. Thank you so much. Everyone I called was dead or hiding. It's like I killed them or drove them away."

"Reno, I'm here." He gulps air. The little booth smells of

beer. "I'm here." Cowboy tries to speak comfortingly. "I'm here," he says.

But where are *you?* he thinks. A lost program, stealing comp time where he can find it, hiding from the system that will kill him without knowing what he is. Running forever, losing bits of himself in inefficient transfers until there's almost nothing left, just a ghost wind touching the interface with its electron breath.

"I'll take care of you," Cowboy says. And thinks of the little girl trembling under Roon's hand, the two kids in the barn in Missouri, all the burdens he's failed to carry, and how much good he's done any of them. . . .

"I'll figure a way out," he promises, and in some part of his own mind sees a monochrome image, himself and Reno, Raul and Lupe, Sarah looking as if she's been lit by von Sternberg and bearing a resemblance to Louise Brooks, all in some improbably large delta cabin, sailing against a background of gray watercolor-wash clouds pierced by the bright swords of sunbeams, a happy silver nitrate ending glowing on the screen of Cowboy's closed lids, and he has a feeling he can work it somehow, flick a switch and things will turn out that way, if he just knows what switch and when.

There is knock on the booth door. It is the waiter with his peanuts. Cowboy looks up at him, the thin disapproving face with its tracks of broken veins high on the cheeks, the clipped graying mustache, the careful contempt somehow enhanced by the twitch of one lower lid. The gray mindcolor fades, no THE END marching across the sky in a sudden Alfred Newman swell of triumphant music. Cowboy's lost his grip on the switch; instead, he's trapped in the sweating plastic walls of a tiny room in a little Florida bar, stuck here with all of Earth's lost children, and can't seem to find his way out. . . .

Chapter Seventeen

LIVING IN THE DEAD ZONE?
WE GUARANTEE A PAYOFF!

When Sarah gets back, Cowboy is sitting with crossed legs on the mattress, shirtless, wearing only a pair of cutoff jeans. A half-dozen empty beer bottles are scattered around him. He's lubricating his eyes, rolling them up into his head while he attaches the nipple on a bottle of silicon gel to the little reservoir in the bottom of each implant.

When he finishes and looks at her she can see that his eyes are rimmed by violet shadows. There are cords in his neck that weren't there before.

"Cowboy," Sarah says, "you look like death."

He looks down at the floor, swallows. "Yeah."

She walks over to him, squatting on her heels and putting her hands on his shoulders. His skin is moist. She feels a trickle of gratitude that he doesn't flinch, like Daud, from her touch. She looks into his eyes. "Anything happen while I was gone?"

"Just . . . ." he begins, then shakes his head. "No. Nothing."

"You sure?"

"Yes."

She kisses his cheek, feeling bristles against her lips. She stands up and shrugs out of her jacket. "I'm going to take a shower," she says. "Want to join me?"

The shower is in an old battered stainless-steel tub, down the hall in a bathroom Sarah shares with Maurice. Pebbled glass doors seal in the mist, fill the tub with soft, ambiguous luminescence, patterning their skin with diffused nebula light. Cowboy stands under the running heat for a long time, soap and water pouring in translucent waves down his chest while Sarah reaches up to work on his muscles, finding them strung like steel wire with all the unvoiced screams of the last five days with Roon, each shriek encoded on the muscle pattern like data in crystal. She takes her time, works on each muscle in turn, feeling him grow alive again under her fingers. Then she turns the water cold and watches a shudder run up his back. His eyes come alive for the first time in days.

Sarah turns the water off and Cowboy puts his arms around her, presses his cool skin against hers. With her cheek she blots the droplets on his shoulder. Standing on the scarred reflective surface of the tub, they are moving against each other before either of them quite realizes it.

She's uncertain when Cowboy picks her up and carries her toward her room. Sarah can't tell if he really belongs, if he's sufficiently a part of things here. . . . There's a difference, she thinks, between letting someone into your body and letting him into the place where you live—but then she realizes that she wants him here, that he's not a false note in her walk-up hideaway. She puts her arms around his neck, surprised to find herself excited by the fact of someone tall and strong enough to carry her so easily, freeing her from gravity in the cradle of his forearms. She watches water droplets appearing from his nape hair, running down the thick muscle of his pilot's neck. Feels his hard pectoral against her shoulder. Lets her head hang back, shaking it, feeling the water flying from her hair in parabolic rainbow trajectories. Laughs. Decides to let things happen.

The both of them together have a tendency to overflow her narrow mattress, their long legs and arms tangling on the dark polished floor, heads lolling to leave wet beaded traceries on the polymer. . . . It doesn't seem to matter much. Eventually they're facing each other, sitting up with Sarah in his lap. Their motion is slow, almost imperceptible, a renewed acquaintance of near-frictionless membranes sliding slower than the tolling chimes of breath and heartbeat. Window light patterns his chest with distorted crossword patterns; she reaches out to touch them, fill in the bright squares with an alphabet of her own invention, touches, nail-scratches, brushes with the backs of her knuckles or the pads of fingertips. Cowboy looks at her with a silent intensity, and she finds this unnerving until she begins to feel that for the first time he's all here, not drifting in and out of some strange space hidden behind his artificial eyes, but looking at her as if there's something there he hasn't seen before. She gazes back at him, into the hard dilated pupils that seem to absorb her, absorbing the radiance she has become, bottomless singularities planted in Cowboy's head. . . . She reaches for him and comes, Cowboy's face dissolving as if a sheet of gelid rain had fallen before her unfocused eyes, the breath bottled in her throat, burning her lungs.

Sarah lets the air out a sip at a time, feeling Cowboy's eyes still on her. She runs her fingers through his short fair hair. They're moving a little faster now they've become acquainted. She reaches forward and pushes him onto his back, crouching over him. Sunlight warms the side of her face. Her thigh muscles are as taut as bridge cable, an arch spanning his hips. He reaches up to touch her breasts, cupping them, raising his head to lick the nipples. Sarah throws her head back, feeling hair ends tickling her shoulder blades. Packets of energy rush along the highways of her nerves, sirens dopplering up and down, their speedometer needles twitching, rising higher, climbing toward the speed of light. Cowboy leans back and she feels the touch of his eyes. . . . She comes again, superliminal.

Impact, splash, into the heart of a star. Sarah is a pulsar, flinging burning photons in widening circles. . . . She's surprised her binary's flesh is still cool, that she isn't giving him sunburn. He's on top of her now, their orbits having

swung round each other. There's a crumpled wet towel under
her left shoulder. Slow music throbs up from the bar below.
The room is beginning to blueshift again. Sarah raises her
hands, clasps Cowboy's head. He comes a half second before
she does, a mutual gravitational collapse. She folds her arms
around him, drawing him toward her, cherishing the touch of
his breath on her neck.

The music crawls slowly beneath Sarah's spine. Cowboy
raises himself again. Her arms still wreath his neck. She
wonders if this is someone she could get sentimental about.

His storm-cloud eyes rain down on her. She can feel parts
of herself coming to life. His voice is slow, like a recording
at half speed. "Reno's alive," he says. "I just talked to
him."

TEMPEL PROMISES DELIVERY OF HUNTINGTON'S
CURE IN 6–10 WEEKS
ANTICIPATION MOUNTS

Two sets of purposeful figures move through the confusion
of the bullet station, the square Caucasian jaws of Cowboy's
Flash Force guards thrusting against the current set up by the
suspicious black faces of the Gold Coast Maximum Law
people that Michael the Hetman is sending to New Mexico to
help establish a secure communications link. Mercenaries
can't afford overlong memories, but these two groups have
tangled in the past, and though neither is being outright
hostile, they're obviously not going to make friends anytime
soon.

Sarah can feel the tension. Cowboy is already looking
unhappy at the prospect of sharing a ride to Sante Fe with
this crowd. He pulls up his jacket collar and glances around
the platform.

A hawker wanders by, selling drugs from a cart. A disconnected female voice, in three languages, announces schedules, tracks, numbers.

"I'll see you in a couple weeks," Sarah says.

"See you then."

The faces circle, black and white, weaving their invisible pattern of defense, of power, moving outside of Sarah's volition like Orbital constellations involved in some vast and vastly subtle game of positional strategy. . . . Their presence inhibits her. She tries to shrug off their influence, fails.

"You'll like the mountains," Cowboy says.

"I'll look forward."

Spanish numbers accumulate in the air, flitting like birds around their pointless spoken banalities. Fuck it, Sarah decides, and grabs Cowboy by the sleeves of his jacket. "Hey, Cowboy." She looks up into his lean, impassive face. "Are we friends, or allies?"

A cold smile twitches at the corners of Cowboy's mouth. "I guess we're friends," he says. "When we can afford to be."

A chime of steel amusement vibrates through her. "Yeah." She nods slowly. "That's how it looks from here."

"Call Reno when you can," Cowboy says. "He's lonely where he is."

She remembers the white-brained cyborg zombie in his dark, glowing little Pennsylvania womb, then imagines his disembodied spectral voice coming out of some disconnected piece of crystal, pulsing into her ear. . . . The man was ghost enough when he was in his body, no sense in asking to be haunted. She shrugs. "I'll try. But the guy spooked me enough when he was alive."

Cowboy frowns a little. "He can help. He's got a lot of money stashed away."

"Okay. I'll call him. Promise."

They say good-bye. Sarah watches his tall form, orbited by his black and white satellites, fading down the fluorescent-lit platform, moving down the tunnel toward the vanishing point, and wonders if it's a good idea to see him again. She could arrange it easily enough, simply talk the Hetman into sending someone else out to the Dodger when the time came. . . . There are commitments she has made, to herself, to her brother, and they allow no indulgence in sentiment. Letting people into the places where you live, she knows, gives them a license to injure you, and she's had injuries enough as it is.

Her Maximum Law guard is looking impatient. She rates a bodyguard now that she knows the Hetman's plan—this boy's probably got orders to kill her if he can't keep her from capture. After this he'll take her to a hotel, where she'll be easier to keep secure: she won't be visiting her hideaway at the Blue Silk anytime soon. She turns her back on her guard as the drug vendor comes by and buys a whiff of snapcoke. Well-being coils in helixes of pleasure along her veins. She buys some cigarettes for Daud and begins to move toward the exit.

She'll feel good when she visits Daud, at least until the drug wears off.

MODERNBODYMODERNBODYMODERNBODYMODERN

Tired of What You're Seeing in Your Mirror?
Let MODERNBODY Give YOU a New Face!
Special This Month on Celebrity Physiognomy!

RNBODYMODERNBODYMODERNBODYMODERNBODY

Daud has visitors. There's a woman body designer with vast unblinking owl eyes and cheekbones sharp as broken glass. She is removing the jagged pink scars from Daud's chest with a humming laser, watched with a benevolent look by a middle-aged black man.

"Nick Mslope? I'm Sarah."

He glances up with a pleased smile. He's small and soft, dressed in pressed white cotton jeans and a tropical shirt. There's a partly eaten candy bar, its white envelope carefully folded, sticking out of the pocket of the shirt. "Pleased to meet you," he says. His accent is unfamiliar.

Disintegrating scar tissue rises from Daud's pale chest in a wisp of gray smoke. Daud opens his eyes and looks at Sarah.

"Hi. Look at this, will you? Miss Deboyce says you won't be able to see the scars without a microscope."

"Don't talk," says the body designer. She brushes ash from his chest with a gloved finger. "Don't breathe, if you can help it." She adjusts a pair of magnifying lenses on her nose and bends over him with a frown of concentration.

Mslope lights a cigarette, then puts it between Daud's lips. Anger, dulled by the snapcoke, flickers in Sarah's mind. Mslope gives her a quick look and then steps around Daud to stand by her. She looks at him cautiously.

"Thank you for all this," she says. "Daud and I are grateful."

"I am very happy to be able to help." He watches as the red beam lances a scar, turns it to vapor. "Daud seems a very worthy young man, and . . . I am glad I can be of some use, you see." He shakes his head. "My poor sister—I cannot do anything for her."

"There's the new cure," Sarah says. Discomfort settles in her, in the interface between what she knows and Mslope doesn't.

"Too late. It would halt the progress of the disease, but her mind is already gone. Death will be a mercy, when it comes."

The laser licks Daud's chest with its scarlet tongue. Sarah looks from Mslope to Daud and back again. "What sort of business are you in, Mr. Mslope?" she asks.

"Please, call me Nick."

"Nick."

"Shipping. We move goods by hovercraft from the landing port at Cape Town."

A cryogenic smile tugs at Sarah's mouth. "I know some people in that business."

"I think—" Mslope looks at Daud. "I think I can find a place for Daud there. If he wishes to join me."

Sarah feels the scrape of a razor on her nerves. "As what? Daud isn't skilled."

"My secretary. I'm certain he could learn the job quickly."

She grins at him, wondering if it's an answering cynicism

she sees in Mslope's smile, or whether it's a reflection of her own. She can feel Daud's blue, opaque eyes on them, watching helplessly as they battle for his heart, as the tug of war develops over his future.

"I'd hate to be that far away from him," Sarah says. "If it doesn't work out, he'll be so far away."

Mslope reaches for the cigarette in Daud's mouth, flicks the ash into the tray, returns it. "I take my responsibilities very seriously, Sarah. I would never bring a young man all that way without providing the means to return home if he becomes unhappy." He looks at Sarah. "Perhaps I could help you, too. I know some people here at the port. And if you came to Africa with us, I could certainly find work for you."

"As what?"

His look is imperturbable. "I'm sure you would know best."

Sarah laughs, the snapcoke and her own spring-steel mirth rising in her veins. The laser hums again. Smoke rises, the color of gunmetal, pain transformed to vapor.

PANZER HIJACKED IN NEBRASKA
PITCHED BATTLE FOUGHT
POLICE REPORT NO SUSPECTS

"This is Sarah. Do you remember me?"

"Sarah. Yes." The voice seems to bubble through a hundred miles of water before it reaches Sarah's ear. The sound prickles her skin. A line of dying palms flickers past the car's windows, brown against a steel sky. She's calling from the mobile phone in her Maximum Law car, not yet convinced this isn't some form of elaborate trap. Staying mobile seems to be the best way to keep from getting ambushed.

"You were with Cowboy," Reno says, "just before I was killed." A chill rides up her nerves at his words, at the calm with which he accepts his own fate.

"That's right." Gutted Venice buildings rotate slowly in

the background as the car climbs the St. Petersburg causeway. "I helped him get away to his people out West."

"I'm glad you escaped. Do you work for Michael the
Hetman?"

"Sometimes."

"I think I may have met him once. I don't remember
things very well." Reno's voice hesitates for an instant, then
rushes on, his words earnest. "Thank you for calling, Sarah.
I'm very alone where I am."

"Yeah." Sarah gazes at the water below, dark and sluggish, filmed with oil. Thinks of Daud's cool, faithless eyes,
the explosion of water and wind against long Missouri concrete walls, Cowboy recessing forever down the length of the
bullet platform, moving toward the supersonic horizon.
"Lonely," she says. "I know how that can be."

"WE'RE RECLAIMING EIGHTY THOUSAND SQUARE MILES OF FARMLAND EVERY YEAR!"
Mikoyan-Gurevich Feeds the World

Sarah sees Mslope every day. When she's alone she finds
herself thinking about him, about his gentle voice, the way
his soft hands seem to reach out for her but always stop
short, the small kindnesses—lighting Daud's cigarettes, fetch-
ing her a chair, offering her one of the candy bars he always
carries in the pocket of his inevitable tropical shirt. . . . It's
as though there's some kind of strange courting ritual going
on between them, a seductive dance with Daud as the focus,
progressing in slow motion toward the inevitable payoff, the
contents of which Sarah thinks she knows.

"I understand your concern, believe me," Mslope protests, and opens an attaché case to show her a contract ready
for Daud's signature. A ticket to and from Cape Town on the
Havana suborbital shuttle; a year's wages guaranteed regardless of performance; lodging at Mslope's expense. . . . "And,
of course, I'll see he gets all necessary medical attention,"
Mslope says with a smile. For a moment Sarah's suspicion

wavers and she wonders whether he could possibly be genuine, then decides that things like this just don't happen in real life. Where did They find this man? What pressures are They using? Or has he been one of Them all along? There *is* a real Mslope, she assumes. They wouldn't be that careless. And the real Mslope has a sister who is dying, and whose dying comforts will be provided by Tempel Pharmaceuticals I.G. if Mslope agrees to let someone else use his identity for a while.

It's flattering, Sarah thinks, that They want her so badly They created a plan this elaborate. "The contract's good," she tells Daud. "Sign it if you want." But she and Mslope are watching each other, their eyes meeting over Daud's bed. It's not Daud, after all, that They are after. He's almost irrelevant by now.

"Perhaps I can introduce you to someone," Mslope says in his gentle voice. He reaches into his pocket for his candy bar and peels away the wrapper. "I know a lot of people at the port. You could get good work."

"I'd be happy to meet somebody," she says. "Here, for preference." How much is Mslope willing to break his cover? No real port boss would interview an employee in a place of her choosing.

"I don't know if that's possible," Mslope says. Sarah shrugs. Daud scrawls his signature on the contract.

Mslope bites his candy bar. "I have a meeting here in Tampa tomorrow," he says. "Perhaps, after the meeting, I could bring one of the people I know. . . ."

"That would be nice, I'm sure," Sarah purrs. Daud gazes up at her tone, wondering what's happening here. His look grows bewildered. Sarah puts a comforting hand on his shoulder. "Miss Deboyce will be in tomorrow, yes?" Sarah asks.

Mslope gives her his most reassuring smile. "Of course. My company takes good care of its employees. Better than anyone in this area, I'm sure."

Sarah can hear the songs of alloy strings in her mind, love's old sweet song. She's useful to them again, and they're willing to pay for her services. If she can avoid what might happen at the moment when her usefulness ends—the rocket

or bullet or cold steel needle laden with its silent overdose—
she might be able to get what she wants.

A pair of tickets. Maybe they've finally figured it out.

She glances out the window at the long dark Maximum
Law car. She'll have to carry out the negotiations under their
watching eyes.

"What would be a good time?" she asks.

Mslope's eyes meet hers again. "Two o'clock," he says.

The minute she sees Mslope's friend, waiting for her in the
patients' lounge in the front, she knows it's not going to be
easy. Steve Andre is hard, his body all rigid planes thinly
disguised by a loose shirt and baggy parachute pants—clothing
ideal for street fighting, she notices that right away—and for
a moment she wonders if he actually plans to drag her off by
force. Cunningham was inconspicuous, a civilian, an agent
living in the shadowy interface between sky and Earth. Andre
is different, nothing ambiguous about him. A soldier. Everything about him proclaims it. She assumes he's wired, with
God knows how many chips, and his eyes' stainless-steel
irises proclaim his enhanced perception. Sarah's thoroughly
grateful for the fact the halfway house has advanced detectors
in its doors—Andre won't have been able to bring a gun
inside in his little document case, and the Weasel might give
Sarah an edge. If it comes to that.

"I'll visit Daud and leave the two of you alone," Mslope
says with a smile, and as he turns toward Daud's room he
reaches for the candy in his shirt pocket.

Sarah sits down on one of the plush lounge chairs and
gives Andre a grin. Behind her a couple of elderly patients
complain in Spanglish about their doctors. "How's Cunningham?" she asks. "Or Calvert, or whatever he's calling himself these days?" A jab, she figures, maybe set the boy off
balance.

Andre's eyes barely flicker. "He's fine, Sarah. He has
nothing to worry about. He's on the side that's going to win."

"Be sure to give him my regards. I haven't seen him since
before you people started shooting rockets at me."

He gazes at her for a moment. It's Cunningham's style, she

recognizes, that quiet, arrogant assumption of superiority. But Andre's not Cunningham; he can't bring off that tempered razor menace, not quite.

"You were a danger then," he says. "Any knowledge you have of our operations is now obsolete. Policy's changed."

"How do I know it won't change again?"

"I am authorized to offer guarantees."

Sarah laughs, throwing her contempt at him. She can tell he's irritated; he's not used to having dirtgirls find him amusing. "Guarantees backed by *what?* Your word of honor as a killer in the employ of a bunch of mass murderers?"

Andre's mouth tightens, as if he's just bit into a lemon. "We are not here to discuss politics."

"We're here to discuss your company's habit of killing people who are no longer of use to them."

Andre fidgets with the case in his lap. "What sort of security would you require?"

"Tickets out of the well for myself and my brother. To a bloc of my choice. You can take it as given that the bloc will not be your own."

"That's expensive."

"Not to you people. Issue me some stock. I'll trade it for what I want."

Andre leans forward. She can see his cold chrome pupils dilate as he looks at her like a sniper through his scope. "We want the Hetman," he says.

"You'll get him. If I get my guarantees."

"Understand," Andre says. "You're not that valuable to us. The Hetman is losing anyway; he's only got a few months at most. We only want to end things quickly, just for the sake of convenience."

"If I'm not that valuable, why are you talking to me?" She leans toward him, giving an intimacy to her mocking tone. "Or haven't your owners given you the authority to make a deal?"

Andre reaches into a pocket for a cigarette. During the time it takes to light it a hovercraft shrieks past, doing 200 on the limited expressway behind the hospital. "I'm not sure if Michael the Hetman is worth what you're asking."

"Better talk with your masters before you draw that particular conclusion." She leans back, giving him an insolent grin. "Understand," she adds, "I'll feed you the Hetman, but I'm not going to make it easy for you by letting myself get caught in the crossfire when it starts—I'm going to be far across town with my own guards. I'll let you know where the Hetman is staying, or when he's moving from place to place. After that, you can fire your own rockets."

Andre stares at her dully. "I can't guarantee any of this now," he says.

"Let me know when you can. You know where I can be reached."

Sarah stands up and walks toward the hallway that leads to Daud's room. She struts slowly, making her exit last as long as possible. She can feel Andre's gunsight eyes on her all the way.

"I CAN BREAK A BHICK WITH MY IMPLANT CRYSTAL!" SEZ VIDEO RANGER KNUT CARLSON, PLEASED WITH HIS NEW HARDWIRED KARATE REFLEXES

Just in case, she uses her inhaler in the car before she steps out to visit Daud. Her nerves crackling with hardfire, Sarah walks into the building and sees Andre sitting in the lounge. She knows she has him hooked. She peels her lips from her teeth in a carnivore smile.

"Was it the shuttle, Andre?" she asks. "Did that push you over the line?"

That morning a panzer broke through the perimeter at Vandenberg and shot up a Tempel shuttle with thirty-millimeter rounds. Further details were unclear. It appears the panzer got away.

"I have nothing to do with operations on the West Coast," Andre says.

"Lucky for you." Sarah sits on a chair, cocking a leg up over the arm. "Still think it's going to be any easier here?"

Andre looks at her stonily. A turbine whines into life, heard in the distance from the limited expressway behind the hospital. "I've been authorized to give you your guarantees."

Hardfire moves through her veins like a flaming silk caress. Out of the well, she thinks, she and Daud surrounded by nothing but the clean velvet blackness. "Thank Cunningham for me," she says.

Andre's chrome irises dilate. "We want something besides Michael."

She shrugs. "Tell me. And then I'll tell you if it will cost you extra."

"No. This is a two-for-one deal, Sarah. It should be easy for you."

"Like I said, tell me."

"Michael's moving his money around. We can't trace it entirely, but the pattern is very odd. Communications people have come in from the Gold Coast. We want you to tell us what he's planning."

Cold touches her palate. She forces a slow, superior smile. "That *will* cost extra."

"You know what it is?" His answer is instant, and she knows that Tempel wants it badly.

She shakes her head. "Maybe I can find out."

"You don't know, Sarah? You're high enough in Michael's organization to rate a bodyguard, but you don't know his plans?"

"I rate the bodyguard because I'm liaison with the Dodger out West, not because the Hetman tells me his plans. But maybe I can find out."

"I'm not sure 'maybe' is acceptable."

"I'm not sure that I understand what it is that you want," Sarah says. She taps her fingertips on her knee. "Is it the Hetman, or his plans, or both? What if I can deliver one without the other?"

"It's the same fee, either way."

She shrugs. "Okay. Then I've got no reason to put myself to any more trouble than necessary, do I?"

Sarah decides to let Andre chew that one over for another twenty-four hours, and walks away. The next day, as Sarah walks in, her nose numb with hardfire, he has documents ready for signature atop his little briefcase.

"Stock in Daud's name," he says. "Enough to take him wherever he wants to go."

Sarah crouches down on her haunches and looks over the old-fashioned paper certificates. She counts them in her head and smiles a cold smile—what she's wanted all along, cool and dry in her hand, the textured paper worth more than money.

"Good," she says. "When do I see mine?"

"You'll get an equal amount of stock for the Hetman, as soon as you call us and tell us where we'll be able to take him out. Half again as much if you can tell us his operational plans."

"You didn't hear me, Andre," Sarah says. "I asked when, not how much."

"We'll transfer the stock to your portfolio as soon as we get a call from you."

"Stock first, so that I can confirm it over the phone. Then the information."

A minute hesitation from Andre, less than an eye blink. "Very well," he says.

She folds the stock certificates, puts them in her pocket, and smiles. "Thank you," she says. "It's been nice doing business. Just so long as you remember that if you want me to trust you, you'd better make sure I stay free, and that I get paid in advance for anything I do."

He looks at her sullenly. Her smile turns to ice. "See you in the sky," she says, and walks to Daud's room.

Daud is smoking a cigarette and watching the vid. When he sees her, he reaches for the control and turns off the video. "What's happening?" he says. "Where's Nick?"

"Nick? I don't know." Sarah pulls cigarette packs out of

her jacket, dropping them into Daud's table. "Has Miss Deboyce been in to see you today?"

He shakes his head. "Later this afternoon."

Sarah leans against the table. "If she doesn't show up," she says, "I want to know."

Daud looks up at her in surprise. "What's going on?" he asks. "Why wouldn't she show up?"

"Nick's friend. I've been talking to him. He wants something from me. I just want to make sure he's keeping his part of the deal."

"Yeah? What does he want?"

"Something I can find out for him."

Daud's pale eyes prowl restlessly over the room. One hand rubs slowly along his jaw. "Nick's friend is paying for my body designer? But . . ." He stubs out his half-finished cigarette. "I thought Nick . . . was paying . . ." His voice trails away, his face reflecting his growing realization.

"Neither of them have any money, Daud," Sarah says. "It's their employer who's paying for Deboyce, and for a few other things."

Daud stares at her for a few moments, his eyelids twitching. She takes the stock certificates from her pocket. "I've got your ticket, Daud," she says. "Your ticket out of this life." Tell him now, she thinks, while he's desperate enough to say yes.

Resentment crackles in Daud. "What did you do to earn that, Sarah?" he demands. "Who did you sell? Yourself? Someone else?"

"That's my action," she says. "Not yours."

"Your fucking action keeps wrecking my life!" Daud is shouting now. "You keep . . ." He chokes on his rage, tears spilling from his one organic eye. "I can't even meet some guy," he says. "Not without it being someone who's really after you."

"I warned you. I told you Nick might not be real."

"I don't care if he's real. I just want him to be *here*."

Sarah steps forward and reaches out for him. He doesn't resist. She drops the stock certificates into his lap and presses him to her, holding his head against her abdomen as he weeps. She tries to concentrate on her tickets, on the vision of the clean alloy places floating in space, limitless in room, in resources. The life that can be lived there, free of the soil of Earth, of the taint of gravity. So far away they are visible only as bright stars among the constellations of the sky.

But another star intrudes in her thoughts, a bright blue fire against the sky, propelling a needle darkness in defiance of Orbital power. Cowboy, his plastic eyes reflecting the diamond stars of Sarah's vision, riding his delta high in the cool thin cloudless air, his awareness spread out from the crystal in his head to the long polymerized bones of the big aircraft body, the hydraulic muscle, laser-optic nerves . . . Sarah looks down at the stock certificates lying in Daud's lap and wonders about her debts.

Michael, she thinks, would understand. He knows the life she's lived, knows what she's wanted these long years, knows that what she needs is beyond his ability to deliver. Realizes that she owes him nothing, that every service she's done him has been paid for, that she can't say no to her heart's own desire.

It's different with Cowboy. He's tangled up in loyalties of his own, ideals that she can't afford. His plan to bring down Couceiro, she thinks, is too unlikely. It depends too much on Roon's unstable desires, no more to be trusted than the rest of them. Best to deal with the one who's paying cash up front. If Cowboy doesn't know any better than to run for it when things fall apart, then it's his problem.

No sentiment, she thinks. Cowboy said it himself. Friends when we can afford to be.

She looks down at Daud, stroking his short dark hair in whorling patterns. A hovercraft moans past on the limited expressway behind the hospital. "I've got us our tickets," she says. "I lost them, but now I got them back."

We've Got the Thing That People Are Looking For . . .
We've Got What People Are Talking About . . .
We've Got the Look That People Demand . . .
We Call It
COOL STONE

"Sarah." It's Reno's drowning voice. "I want to help. I want to join the war."

She's in the car again, moving along the torn Florida streets. She gazes up through soundproof glass to see her guard's eyes flicker in the rearview mirror, looking for tags. "How can you?" she asks. "What can you do? You're so vulnerable."

"I've learned some things, living where I am. About breaking into computer systems. I can try to crash into their communications, or into their files. Find out what they're planning."

"Their computers are too well protected, Reno. They're not like the government computers you're living in—the Orbitals can afford the best security. If you were a programmer, I'd say go ahead. The worst they could do is trace you, and by then you'd be gone. But you're *living* in there. They could wreck you."

"Sarah, I'm learning things. I've got every available piece of data on Tempel in my memory. The patterns are beginning to make sense. I know where they're weak. All I need is access."

"Access." Sarah laughs. "Getting access has been the problem all along, Reno."

"*I could be stuck here forever.* If you people lose, there's no way I could get out."

The desperation in Reno's voice twists something in Sarah, cutting short her laughter. She feels the blast from the air conditioning chilling her skin. "What do you need, Reno?" she asks.

"Get me into their system. If you can't break in, buy somebody at Orlando—there's enough dirt working there, some of them have to have access."

"We've been trying that all along, Reno. Yeah, okay, we can get you into their outside crystal. But there are only a couple dozen who have access to the main Tempel comp. And they've got ten wired guards apiece and hardly ever leave the compound."

"I don't need that. Once you buy somebody, that doesn't

mean he knows what to look for. There's too much data for one person to correlate.

"Sarah, listen." Reno's voice rises coldly from the receiver, like bubbles in liquid oxygen. "Florida is one of the places where the Orbitals are all tangled up, where their lines of demarcation don't apply. Tempel has a lot of action here, and it's not all public. They're not hiding it from us so much as from their competitors. If I got into their system, I could start putting things together. A chit for truck rental, and the fact of a shuttle coming down, and a telephone record of a call to Pittsburgh, and tickets for some high-priority security people coming down the well—that all adds up to a shipment heading north, Sarah. A *person* wouldn't see that, wouldn't have the time to sift through the data. But I could. I could find out for the Hetman where they're hiding their shipments, how they're distributing the merchandise to their thirdmen, maybe even the routes they're using."

Sarah remembers the white-brained ex-pilot drifting in and out of the interface, talking in a dreamy voice about nodes, systems, the way the Orbitals fit together. If it doesn't work, she thinks, Reno's no worse off. If it works, he puts pressure on Tempel.

Sarah likes the idea of the Tempel people under pressure. It will make her more valuable to them.

"Okay, Reno," she says. "I'll talk to the Hetman about it."

HOPE IS OUR BUSINESS

Sarah is surprised to see Mslope sitting quietly by Daud, sharing a cigarette with him as the laser hums and the scars on Daud's back turn to ash and mist. "I couldn't stay away," Mslope says, reaching down to touch Daud's nape. "They said I probably should. I changed their minds about it."

There is something in Daud's look that stops Sarah's reply. They know, she thinks, how useful it is to give Daud hope. But now that he has it, she can't take it away.

"Good," she says. Her hand comes out, touches Daud's cheek. "I know he's missed you."

FROM OUR WEIGHTLESS PLATFORM WE ENCOMPASS THE EARTH WITH TWO HANDS. OUR MINDS TURN TO HOPE AND SORROW.
—Mitsubishi I.G.

Maximum Law people sniff the salt air like attack dogs, alert to the scent of violence. Sarah can only smell the Pride of Barbados hiding the Hetman's bungalow from the ocean, that and the tension in the air. Tonight one of Tempel's mudboy employees is going to give Reno a window into the Orbital crystal.

Michael, not trusting anyone, is alone except for Sarah. He leans over his home deck, chain-smoking Russian cigarettes and firing torpedoes of snapcoke into his brain. Sarah stands behind him looking out the sliding glass doors, hoping to see a glimpse of blue past the screen of poinciana.

"There's a lot of traffic going in and out," Reno reports. His hollow voice, blending at times into a continuous background hiss, comes out of Michael's comp. "There's good security even on their low-level crystal—I've tried to ride in some incoming data, but I always get cut off."

"It's six o'clock," Michael says. His eyes glitter like old glass. "He should be calling." He puffs on his cigarette. Sarah watches the sun casting hard-edged baroque shadows through the wrought-iron patio furniture.

"Give him time," she says. "He's got to be alone when he calls."

Sarah turns around, seeing the Hetman in profile as he turns to his ashtray. Lined eyes, trembling hands.

A dead man, she thinks. Cool sorrow whispers through her. She turns away, watching the heat roll up off the patio in waves.

I can't afford not to, she thinks. Michael would understand.

"I have the call," Reno says. "I'm going."

THERE'S A NAME FOR WHAT WE DO.
WE CALL IT CYBORG PRIDE.

"My people are getting impatient," Andre says, his voice reaching Sarah through swirls of angry hardfire. Sarah has begun to notice things about him: a little scar by one ear, disappearing into the hair, a once-broken knuckle he probably got in a fight. That all his shirts have plastic pocket protectors built into the pockets. That he always carries exactly three pens.

"I'm doing what I can. Michael isn't an easy man to catch."

Andre's face is stone, relentless. "There is a time limit on our offer. It's getting closer."

"If you're suspecting a traitor, you're right," Sarah says, and watches Andre's face as he tries to absorb the shock. She knows why they're suddenly so impatient. Reno found two shipments and deduced the location of a major drug warehouse in his first few hours in Tempel's comp. Michael's people took all three seamlessly, without a loss.

Andre's eyes fix her within rings of stainless steel. "I need to know who."

"It's someone deep," she says. "Someone with a lot of access. Michael turned him, or her. I don't know how." Which should keep them chasing shadows for weeks.

Then: "How do you know?"

"I saw Michael last night. He was high, very pleased with himself. He let it slip."

Andre looks at her for a long while. "What were his exact words?"

Sarah shakes her head. "I was high myself, Andre. Exact words I don't recall."

"Think. Tell me what you remember."

Sarah looks at the floor, feigns concentration. Her nerves jitter with hardfire. "Yeah," she says. "Okay. He said, 'I've sent out our friends. Three hits. I've turned one of their execs and I know their every move.' "

"Are you sure that's all?"

She looks coolly into the stainless-steel irises. "That's it. After that he looked like he realized he was saying something he shouldn't, and changed the subject."

"No names?"

"No names."

"Where did this happen?"

She gives the location of the house by the beach. His lips tighten. "It looks to me like you're stalling. Why didn't you tell us Michael was going to be there?"

"I didn't know myself. The driver just got orders to pick me up at the hotel."

"If you're not telling us the truth . . ." Andre leaves that thought unfinished. Instead, he reaches into a pocket, comes up with a recorder. "If you're thinking there's a way back, I'm telling you there's not. I've made recordings of every conversation we've had. They can be sent to Michael."

Sarah's wired nerves flame with fury at her own idiocy. She looks at Andre in white anger.

These people expect us to trust them, even though they will betray us, even though we know the betrayal is coming. Because we have no choice but to trust them. Because they are our only hope.

"I'm not turning back," she grates. "But you've got to give me room."

Andre puts the recorder in his pocket. His look is softer now that's he made his point. "You'll have your room," he says. "But soon the walls will start getting closer. I'm just telling you."

"I'm listening," Sarah says. Despair tugs at her. Perhaps up to this point she hasn't really believed in the deal she's cut, in what it means. She thinks of Cowboy doing loops in the night sky, of the Hetman shrouded by poinciana, of Reno, a pattern of burning electrons, circling desperately in his world of wire and crystal. The cost of her ticket.

I'm sorry. But they didn't leave me a way out.

And hates herself. Because she knows it's not true.

ANYWHERE, ANYTIME
YOU KNOW WE'RE WITH YOU

The voice makes her think of sagebrush, of long prairies and the purple eastern face of mountains staring up at the sky. "It's cool where I am, Sarah. The summer's dying here."

She tries to think of Daud, of the humming laser and who's paying for it, of Daud's ticket and her own. The body designer finished with him that afternoon. His body is healed, beautiful, just a little weak.

"The aspens will be turning soon. I hope you can see it."

"It sounds good," Sarah says. She reaches into her pocketbook for her inhaler, wanting hardfire, needing desperately to be high.

"I heard from Reno. I told you he'd be useful."

Sarah fires the torpedoes, throws her head back. Her hardwiring screams as the neurotransmitters multiply. Reno had broken open the entire Tempel distribution net on the East Coast, from Havana all the way to Halifax. Half their people had been assassinated within a two-day period, the other half were running and wouldn't be doing business anytime soon. Michael's people had raided so many warehouses they were at a loss as to where to put the stuff. News datalines screamed the statistics on every street corner, while officials ducked for cover and offered no comment.

"They're getting desperate," Sarah says. Her hands tremble and she reaches for the table edge to steady them.

Friends, she thinks. When we can afford to be. She is going to have to give them the Hetman soon. And give him as well the nature of Roon's part in the Hetman's plans, which will be the only piece of pleasure in this sorry business.

"Michael says that Reno's given him another four months," she says. "Reno's in his tank now. The Hetman paid for it. Have you heard?"

"Yeah. He called me from there."

Reno's tank is a crystal matrix in Havana, ready to move into a cloned body as soon as DNA can be found to approximate his original appearance and a new body grown from it. He was beginning to feel paranoid living in the Tempel computers, knowing that sooner or later they'd start looking for an intruder program.

At least Reno's body and the operation is paid for in advance. When Michael falls, Reno will be out of the way.

"Our friend in South America is almost ready," Cowboy says. "He's got the date."

Sarah feels ice form in her veins. The deadline is coming. "When?"

"Five days from now. We figure on moving you out by bullet in three days."

"I'll have to prepare Daud," she says. "And arrange to see the Hetman."

That, she thinks, is when it will have to happen. Feed them Roon at the same time. And then, a part of her thinks, a call through secure lines to Cowboy to let him know that he's just crashed, that all his plans and hopes are going up in flames on some mountainside labeled Reality, that it's time to say good-bye.

"Say hi from me," Cowboy says. Sarah remembers the way he looked a few months ago, when he was sitting in the armored cabin of his betrayed panzer outside Pittsburgh, the fear and bafflement and anger in his eyes . . . When the news comes, will the look be the same? Sarah wonders.

When we can afford to be. The operative phrase.

After the conversation she decides that she needs the hotel bar. Her guard isn't happy but allows it. She sails down the elevator and submerges herself in thudding litejack, shouted conversation, dark rum served neat, a softglow high out of the bar inhaler that smooths the hardfire jitters. She looks at the single men in the room, wondering about the possibility of letting one come to her room, of letting the high she's feeling peak in orgasm, in the necessary obliteration. But when one approaches her, she brushes him off. There's plenty of time.

She notices a crowd around one of the games at the other end of the bar. She picks up her drink and wanders over, hearing the hum of laserfire, the rush of missiles. Delta, the game is called. A black man is strapped into the seat, his head obscured by a sensory helmet that feeds him information, letting him feel the jar of missiles cutting loose, the pull of g-stresses. A wide-screen video unit above the machine gives other customers a glimpse of his play.

Government liteweights pounce from the sky. The sun glitters off the rotating fins of turning missiles. Radar displays scream for attention. Liteweights dodge, leap, explode in flaring ruin, draw charcoal fingers across the sky.

Sarah loses interest and decides to go back for another round of softglow. She turns to step away and meets the metal eyes of a man in a wheelchair. Memory jars her.

"Is it Maurice who's playing?" she asks.

The man nods. His eyes stay on the display above his head. "Yes. It's the closest we can come."

"Tell Maurice hi." The video cockpit gushes flame as an enemy missile strikes home. Sadness wars with the softglow in Sarah's veins. She wonders if Cowboy will end like that, endlessly rerunning the war he fought and lost.

Maurice tries to eject, fails, tumbles to the earth like a broken dragonfly. Before he can raise the sensory helmet from his face, Sarah turns and drifts away with the murmuring crowd.

LIVING IN PAIN CITY?
LET US SEND YOU TO HAPPYVILLE!
—Pointsman Pharmaceuticals A.G.

Andre is dressed in tailored jungle fatigues, even to the cap. His stainless-steel irises gleam from the shadow of the brim. His inevitable pens are fixed to the breast pocket with camouflage velcro straps.

"We don't think," he says, "that you've been entirely candid."

Sarah cocks her hands on her hips. "Que?" she says softly.

"We think that you know more than you're giving us." His voice is soft, his inflections unhurried. As if he's made some decision. He takes a step toward her.

Sarah's mouth is suddenly dry. She runs her corrugated tongue over her palate, sandpaper on stone. She looks left and right, seeing patients in bathrobes and pajamas. "What do you think I know?"

"We're not sure. More than you're telling." His eyes are wide, unblinking, focused on her like a pair of gunsights. His calm voice drones on. "We're going to make you disappear for a few hours. Give you a few drugs, let you talk. You won't be hurt."

Sarah tries to calm the hardfire pulsing adrenaline messages through her body. A cold inner voice, a soulless inflection like Reno's, tells her he's got more chips, more talent. If she fights, she'll lose. "I've got a guard, Andre. The Hetman will know."

"We have a story ready for Michael. We tried to snatch you. You got away."

She shakes her head slowly. "He's not going to believe that."

Andre takes another step toward her, only inches away. Her flesh prickles. She can feel his breath against her face, taste spearmint. "Turn around," he says. "Look out the window. He'll believe the evidence."

She can feel the hairs on her neck erect as she turns. He can hit her from here, and she has only instinct to tell her where and when.

From the front window she can see her Maximum Law escort car stretched out by the curb, the color of blued steel. The windows are mirrors, but she can see the driver as a vague shadow behind the silver glass.

A girl is coming down the street in a bicycle. Brown-skinned, young, her hair in pigtails braided with yellow ribbon. She's reclining in the bucket seat of an alloy bicycle, feet first, low to the ground, moving fast behind an aerodynamic shield. In her lap is a woven basket with artificial daisies plaited around the rim. She's wearing a white blouse with bright red patterns. As she rides she laughs to herself. Her teeth are white and contrast brilliantly with her dark face.

She passes the car to streetward, out of Sarah's sight, but still Sarah senses a movement. And then the bicycle is skimming past and there is a thud, hardly perceptible to Sarah through the double panes of window glass and the insulating walls of the hospital. The driver's window of her car flies outward, brilliant bits of mirror gushing up in a sunlit expanding funnel . . .

"Sticky bomb with a half-second delay," Andre says. His tone is low, conversational. "Put a shaped charge right through the window glass. I don't think your driver got out of the way."

Sarah is suddenly aware that she hasn't been breathing. She lets the air out of her lungs, breathes in. Neurotransmitters are multiplying, racing from her crystal. Her veins are smoking with adrenaline. The cybersnake waits coldly, uselessly in her throat.

They're going to get it all, she thinks. She knows she won't get paid, but maybe they'll let her live. And Daud has his ticket, that's something.

The last bit of mirror flutters to the pavement. Another car pulls up behind the Maximum Law car. Two men in summer suits get out, walk to the shattered window. Facing the car, visible only from the chest up as they draw pistols from their belts, they look, ludicrously, as if they're getting ready to piss on the polished blue finish.

"Silenced pistols," Andre says. "If your driver has a head left, he's going to lose it."

Spearmint whispers coolly into Sarah's nostrils. Behind her in the room there is a low murmur of patient conversation. The assassins zip up their pants and start walking up the drive. Their car pulls away from the curb.

Sarah sees government liteweights bursting on the screen. Cowboy's head under the sensory helmet. The look in his eyes, the look of someone whose dream is broken and is desperate in search of another.

There is a smile of pleasure in Andre's voice. "We're going to wring you dry, Sarah," he says. "You have no choice. We've bought you and we're going to have you."

Sarah lets her head fall, gulps air. She knew all along, as soon as she saw Andre, that this was going to happen, and that she was going to let it. That Andre would enjoy it. That his stainless-steel irises would dilate with satisfaction as her struggles ceased and the drugs took hold of her mind, as she began babbling her every thought into their cold, waiting crystal.

"Come along, Sarah," Andre says. "Time for your ride."

It's the tone that does it. Sarah has sold herself, and she can live with that, accept the consequences. But the idea that the man who has bought her will take such pleasure in it . . . Something in her screams outrage. She remembers a droning voice, a razor, a blur of movement, abstract patterns of red, like paint. Weasel stirs. Her chips are spitting instructions and the neurotransmitters are multiplying along their chemical pathways before she even knows she has made a conscious decision.

She takes a step back with her right foot, toward Andre. Her fists cock up toward her chest, where she knows he can't see. Then her weight shifts back and she is spinning, her right arm lashing out with a back-knuckle blow aimed at Andre's temple, the torque of her upper body behind it.

Andre blocks it, of course. Foolish to think otherwise—he is wired himself. But when his hands come up, she changes her movement from a blow to a sweep, gets her hands and forearm over both his hands, driving down his guard. Follows it up with a lash from Weasel, aimed at Andre's throat. . . .

From somewhere there is a dry steel *click*, like a hammer going back. . . .

And her weight is already shifted forward to the right foot, her left coming up in a wheeling kick aimed high, a kick he can't even see because when it was launched Sarah's fist and his own two hands were in the way. By the time Andre sees the blur to his right, the only thing he can do is to try to hunch down into his shoulders and roll with it.

Too late. The kick has all of Sarah's weight behind it, all six feet three inches torqued in by hip and shoulder and concentrated along a few square inches of Andre's reluctant skull. Sarah's shin impacts Andre's temple with enough force to send shards of pain shrieking along Sarah's leg. Andre falls like a sack of sugar, his every nerve misfiring. Something extrudes from between his lips.

Sarah recovers her balance, steps forward with her left foot, and delivers a rising kick with her right boot-tip square between Andre's eyes. Andre's head bounces back, hits the floor, bounces again. A cybersnake flails uselessly from his mouth, a glistening metal whip looking for something to kill. Maybe Andre is dead. Sarah doesn't care.

One eye is open, one shut. Sarah stares into the open eye, ignoring the whipping cybersnake, seeing something wrong. The stainless-steel iris is dilated wide and there is a hole where the pupil should be, and Sarah remembers the sound of that *click*. She looks down at herself, sees the steel needle stuck in her armored jacket, and feels the fear begin, clamping on her in a wave of nausea.

Andre's eyes, like gunsights because they *were* gunsights. A spring-loaded dart gun, snapping up into place on command, firing through the porthole pupil. Sarah reaches a hand to the dart, pulls it out, feels a tug in her flesh. The dart is slippery and squirts from her fingers, leaving a trace of something like oil on her fingertips. It went through the jacket, slipping through where a blunt-nosed bullet would be stopped cold. Less than a millimeter into her flesh, she suspects, but maybe enough.

Sarah raises her fingers to her nose, sniffs, smells a faint medicinal scent. Drugged, then. It didn't penetrate very far, so maybe she didn't get a full dose.

"Who *is* that?" An elderly patient, staring through thick glasses and stammering in outrage. Andre's cybersnake is beating itself to death against the sound-deadening carpet.

Sarah is already moving, running down a pastel corridor to Daud's room.

He's exercising, lying back on his bed while he works with the weights, letting Mslope watch his muscles move under the pale skin. "Daud," Sarah breathes, skidding through the door.

Mslope is rising from his seat, his eyes wide with alarm. "Out," Sarah says, and she can see pain forming in the man's eyes, the knowledge that his moment is over.

She pays him no attention. She runs to Daud, seeing the alarm entering his face. He lets the weights go and there is a crash.

"Things have gone wrong. They tried to kidnap me." She presses her cheek to Daud's, whispering in his ear. "If I get away, call me at the same number as last time. Randolph Scott, Santa Fe. Don't call from here; this phone is not secure."

"Sarah." His eyes are wide with fear. "I thought things were set. I thought—" She takes his head in her hands and kisses him, a fierce kiss that maybe he'll remember through what is going to come.

"I love you," she says, and is running again. Abandoning him as he cries her name again, as he tries to catch her clothing with a hand. Sarah tries to blot out his voice. She can feel the first delicate touch of whatever drug was on the needle, something wrong with her nerves, the feathery pat of a kitten that has not yet unsheathed its claws.

She's mapped out the hospital and knows where to go. Down the green pastel corridor, left at the pink pastel intersection. Daud's last cry is ringing in her ears. Her shin aches with each step. She reaches a steel door, takes a last breath of cold air, and, keeping her silhouette low, rolls out into the furnace of afternoon.

A truck turbine dopplers past on the limited expressway. Her brain whirls as she staggers to her feet and runs clumsily for the truck stop behind the hospital. If she can get across the expressway, she'll be able to lose herself in the rows of residential flats behind. The drug has just dug in with its claws and each steps seems to wade through gelatin.

SARAH THIS IS CUNNINGHAM. . . . SARAH YOU CANT GET AWAY

Suddenly there are amber lights above her vision. Someone's broadcasting to her on her optical-tagged radio, her crystal translating the spoken words into moving print. She doesn't have the control for it and can't turn it off. "Go the fuck away," she mumbles.

ALL WE WANT IS COOPERATION SARAH

She snorts her disbelief. "Go away. You're not even Cunningham I bet." A truck turbine begins to whine by the automated fuel pump, its tone rising. Sarah shakes sweat from her eyes and hops a low cinderblock fence, catches a foot, almost falls. Then something smashes her between the shoulder blades and she goes down.

Concrete bites her breasts, her cheek. She has lost her breath and can't find it. Her hands flail out, scrabble at the concrete. She realizes she's just been shot. Someone behind at the hospital, with marksman's crystal and a pistol.

STAY WHERE YOU ARE SARAH WE WILL FIND YOU WE ONLY WANT TO HELP

"Bullshit," she says wearily. She finds that she can't stand, that she can only crawl. She feels the touch of grit against her palms. She creeps, slithers, rolls. Feels her shoulders tensing for the next shot.

It's only then that she realizes that it's lucky she couldn't stand up. She's been hidden from them behind the cinderblock wall. But she knows they're sprinting for her, that the two assassins in their summer suits will be appearing above the wall shortly.

Turbines are shrieking within an inch of her skull. Tires crunch gravel and something comes between her and the sun. A robot tractor-trailer rig, backing slowly away from the automated pumps. The assassins are on the other side of it, she realizes, and she rolls to her feet, falls to one knee, staggers up again. As the truck cab passes her, still in reverse, she seizes the safety bar and steps up onto the ladder leading to the observation cab.

The turbine whimpers. Gears clatter. The truck begins to lurch forward, almost throwing Sarah off. She hugs the safety bar, then moves a foot up on the ladder. Moves a second foot. Seizes the emergency door latch and pulls on it. There is the sound of a warning buzzer, very loud in Sarah's ears.

"This is an unauthorized entry," a voice recites. "Trespassers are subject to penalty upon discovery."

GIVE IT UP SARAH. . . . WE DONT WANT TO HURT YOU

"Entrance may not be made safely when the tractor is in motion. This is an unauthorized entry. Trespassers are subject to penalty upon discovery."

JUST LIE DOWN WHERE YOU ARE WE WILL FIND YOU

"Shut up." The truck lurches through another gear change. Pavement is moving by at a faster rate. Sarah's vision contracts, her head swimming with the drug. Her arms tense on the safety bar, pulling her up. Pain cries through her arms, her spine. She kicks out and hauls herself blindly into the cab, draws a breath, reaches behind her to pull the cab door shut. She can hear the solid chunk of electromagnets drawing shut a pair of metal bolts. The turbine howl is muffled.

"This is an unauthorized entry. You have been secured in the cabin until the tractor reaches its destination, where you will be turned over to the authorities. If this is a genuine emergency, you may contact the police on the red telephone located on the dashboard."

The message repeats itself. Sarah gives herself over to pain. She can feel blood trailing warmly down her neck. She coughs phlegm from her throat, spikes of pain driving into her back, where the shot blunted itself on her armored jacket.

WE SAW YOU GETTING INTO THE TRUCK WE ARE COMING AFTER YOU

Sarah fumbles for her inhaler, finds it, triggers another round of hardfire. Her heart goes mad, trying to pound its way out of her chest, but pain and the new round of stimulant fights whatever drug was on Andre's needle and helps to clear her head.

THAT TRUCK IS A ONE-WAY RIDE TO ORLANDO. . . . ORLANDO
IS OUR TOWN SARAH

Sarah's vision clears slowly. She's lying across a pair of
bucket seats in front of an instrument board filled with green
glowing lights. The observation cab is where safety inspectors ride, or where emergency operators work the truck if the
tractor's crystal brain isn't working. There are no controls as
such—the truck's supposed to be worked through the face.
Sarah looks across the panel and under the seats, fails to find
a headset. The truck's owners apparently don't want stow-
aways running off with their truck. Not that she knows how
to drive a turbine-tractor anyway.

She settles herself into one of the seats and looks out the
cab windows, seeing the blurring posts of the limited highway, the shining, stubby radio beacons that control the robot
traffic. The tires whine over concrete. A hovercraft, its props
throbbing, soars by at 200 miles per hour in the fast lane. She
swipes at the blood running down her neck. Presses a button
and feels a blast of hot air that soon turns cold. Her head is
almost clear. Time to figure a way out of this. She brushes
sweat from her eyes and looks at the instrument panel.

Green gauges glow coldly. The red phone on the instrument panel beckons her. She pulls the phone from its cradle
and listens, hearing the normal dial tone. She leans back, the
tone moaning in her ear, and wonders who she wants to talk
to.

The Hetman, she decides. Maybe he can arrange for some
of his cops to pick her up on the way. He won't have got any
of the recordings yet, and she can try to figure a way to
explain those later.

She dials the only number she has, finds it's been disconnected in the last twenty-four hours, the normal shifting of
interface addresses to prevent monitoring. She calls the Gold
Coast Maximum Law number and starts as the telephone
screams at her. Whoever owns the phone isn't about to pay
for a transatlantic call.

SARAH WE ARE JUST BEHIND YOU WE ARE COMING UP

She slams the phone down, looks wildly in the rearview

mirrors. Sees only a hovercraft coming up on the left. "Fuck you, Cunningham," she mutters, and reaches for the phone again.

WE ARE GOING TO HAVE TO BLOW YOUR DOOR LOOK FOR COVER SARAH

She presses Reno's number and scans the rearview mirrors again. Adrenaline flows through her blood. She snaps upright, represses an urge to bounce the phone off the windscreen. There's a long black car coming up on the right, racing along the expressway's shoulder. It's a car she recognizes.

The voice on the phone bubbles in her ear. "This is Reno."

Sarah's voice sounds like the shriek of a cornered animal. She can scarcely recognize it as her own. "Reno, this is Sarah! I'm trapped! They've killed my guard and now they're after me!"

The car is coming up fast on the edge of the expressway. The road is limited to robot traffic, and cars are forbidden here because the trucks and hovercraft can't see them, but the car should be safe enough on the shoulder. Sarah sees a flash of color near the car.

Reno's voice doesn't change expression. "Sarah, where are you?"

Sarah tries to calm her runaway heart, takes a deliberate breath. "I'm in a robot truck on the limited expressway, moving from Tampa to Orlando. They're following in a car." Sarah can see the blur of a dark face in the mirror, pigtails streaming with yellow ribbon. "They're just behind me, Reno!" Her voice cracks on the dead man's name. She bounces in her seat, her fist pounding the instrument panel. Rage boils in her. "I'm locked in the truck! I can't get out! Call the Hetman. Have him send his people out."

SARAH WE ARE GOING TO BLOW THE DOOR ON YOUR RIGHT. . . . GET IN THE LEFT SEAT AND COVER UP. . . . WE DONT WANT TO HURT YOU

"What's the truck's registration number? It should be in the cab somewhere." Reno's voice patterns over the letters of Cunningham's message that are rolling past Sarah's expanded vision. She can see one of the doors on the black car opening, the girl in the patterned blouse leaning out against the blast of wind, something in her hand.

Sarah wants to shriek. "Jesus, Reno, what does it matter? They're just behind. Get Michael now!"

"The registration number. I need it to find you. Tell me."

WE JUST WANT TO TALK TO YOU. . . . GET IN THE LEFT SEAT AND COVER UP

"Oh, fuck, Reno. The registration. All right." Droplets of her sweat and blood pattern the instruments as Sarah searches desperately for a number. She finds a metal plate, reads the contents into the phone. The black car fills the lower half of the mirror. She can see the whites of the dark girl's eyes, the bright, sunny smile, the same smile of innocent pleasure she wore when she slapped the charge on the guard's window. Sarah can see someone's thick wrist, holding her by the belt as she leans out with the bomb in one hand, the other hand clawed to reach for the safety bar.

"Where are they now, Sarah?" Reno says. The calm in his voice drives her to frenzy.

"They're right beside me! *Reno help me!*" She screams the last words, seeing only a blur in the mirror now, white smile, black metal, windows reflecting the blue of Daud's altered eyes. . . . Then there is a loud overwhelming electronic moan, filling the cab from the truck's speakers, and she shrieks in outrage and fear and drops the phone, huddling in the left seat, scrabbling for her collar to pull it up over her head, wondering if the truck somehow senses the oncoming violence of its impending violation.

The electronic moan fades. Lights on the instrument panel flick from green to red. There is a lurch that throws Sarah against the door, and the amber lights above her vision are screaming silent panic: OH GOD LOOK OUT FOR THE . . . And then Sarah feels the kiss of metal, only the lightest brush, and she looks in the mirror to see a pinwheeling form, bright print blouse and yellow hair ribbons, flying like the corn doll before mad Ivan's foot, and then there's a wheeling car that snaps a radio post like a toothpick and flies off the embankment. An impact, a silent gush of flame in the ever-receding distance. The amber lights, the written version of an assassin's last cry, finish their track across Sarah's vision.

Magnetic bolts thud open in the doorframes.

"I've taken command of your truck, Sarah," says Reno's voice, his tone faint but clear from the dropped phone spinning on the metal floor. "I'll be calling the Gold Coast people to meet you at an underpass. I'll park the truck there. The laws will find it."

Sarah's heart hammers in cold emptiness, the panic still bottled in her throat, lost without its reason for existence. She scrabbles for the phone. "Reno," she calls. "Reno, thank you."

"I'm glad to have something to do, Sarah."

Sarah's hands tremble with adrenaline shock. A blinding pain is forming behind her eyes.

"You've got to wipe your fingerprints off the truck, Sarah," Reno says. White noise flitters in the background of his voice. "Do that now, and then sit back and don't touch anything."

"Just let me catch my breath." She leans back and gulps in the cool air. Her nerves flash hot and cold.

"Reno," she says. "I've got to talk to the Hetman. Tempel is going to send him some tapes. They had my voice from the job I did for them, and . . . The tapes are doctored. They said they'd send them to Michael if I didn't cooperate."

"I'll connect you," Reno answers.

Dimly, from far away, Sarah hears the sound of a phone ringing.

Chapter Eighteen

The *Pony Express* waits under camouflage nets a quarter mile behind the Dodger's place, surrounded by a blizzard of security and passive electronic countermeasures. Warren, wearing a headset, his cap stuffed in a back pocket, is feeding a program into the crystal heart of a radar-guided missile, making sure the missile knows its job. Cowboy stands under a ponderosa nearby and listens to the breeze high up in the trees. Here on the ground the air is still. Tension without a name crouches in his body, touching his muscles and mind, letting him know of its presence.

Down the slopes Cowboy can see Jimi Gutierrez walking with Thibodaux. The panzerboy and the crystal jock are lovers now, devotees of the face. Thibodaux is still here, trying to stay close to Jimi, even though his job is more or less over. No one's raised any objection. It keeps Jimi out of people's hair.

Cowboy's eyes flicker at the sight of another movement and he sees Sarah coming up the slope. There's a machine pistol on her hip, the Heckler & Koch. Her new scars are worn with the old defiance, but he can see there's something else there, a kind of fever behind the eyes. As if there's a fear there she hasn't got over. Cowboy begins walking down toward her, his bootheels making crescent marks in the bed of needles.

"Sorry I couldn't meet you," he says. "Warren needed me for something."

"Yeah. That's okay. I was surrounded by security anyway. The Hetman didn't want to take any more chances." While she speaks she puts her arms around him, her last words breathed out against his neck. Cowboy exhales, and part of the tension he's been feeling goes out with the stale air, seeing Sarah here, knowing she's away from the things in Florida that have been putting their claws in her. He takes a step back and takes her chin, looks at the gouge marks on one cheek. The swelling has gone down but the bruises are still bad.

"Another fucking mistake," she says. Her mouth twitches in anger. "Another goddamn fucking mistake."

"Mistakes get made."

Cowboy can see her clenched teeth. "Not by me. I can't afford them. If it wasn't for Reno saving my ass . . ." She shakes her head.

"You're allowed to be human, Sarah," he says.

"What I'm not allowed to be is *stupid*." She puts her hands in her pockets, begins walking upslope. He can see the self-contempt in her as he walks by her side. "I'm keeping these scars, Cowboy. So I can look at myself in the mirror every morning and know not to be stupid today."

"You were ambushed. It can happen to anyone. How does that make you stupid?"

She gives him a sidelong look. "Maybe I'll tell you someday, Cowboy. But not now."

"How's your brother?"

She stiffens slightly, her gait slowing. "Okay. Looking for an apartment. They let him alone—he's not useful anymore."

Cowboy gazes up at the smooth matte nose of *Pony Express* lying under the nets. His heart lifts. "Reno said that Cunningham might have been in that car."

"No. Three men, one woman. None of them were Cunningham. One of them just said he was."

"Too bad."

She gives him a skeletal smile. "Yeah. Too bad."

The camouflage net prints patterns on Sarah's face, merging with the bruises. Warren squints as he looks up at her from his bench. "Sarah," Cowboy says, "this is my friend Warren. He keeps the deltas flying."

"Hi, Warren."

"Howdy." He looks at the dark bulk of the crouching delta. "Not bad for a home-built job, hey?"

Sarah grins. "Not bad." She reaches out to touch the port canard, brushing it with her fingertips. "How do you build something like this in your backyard?"

"Out of odds and ends," Warren says. He squints as he looks up at the dark panther shape. "The engines are ex-military. They're the expensive part, because they're made out of Orbital alloy and they have to be pulled for overhaul every three thousand hours or so. Everything else we make ourselves. We've avoided alloys in making the airframe and used something cheaper and almost as good—composites made of epoxy resins and a few other things. The landing gear and some of the hydraulics are the only things made of metal."

Cowboy points out the nearly invisible seams of the cargo doors on the delta's smooth belly. "Deltas are made to carry cargo, and they have to have a lot of onboard fuel to get the necessary range," he says. "So they can't be as fast and maneuverable as a government liteweight. We try to make up for that by carrying a lot more electronics, armor, and weapons, and by using lots of redundancy in the plane's systems."

Sarah looks down at a rack of missiles, seeing one of them open, revealing its components to Warren's scrutiny. "You make those at home, too?"

"Yep," Warren says. "They're easier than anything—everything we use can be bought in an electronics store except the propellant and the explosive, and those we brew up in a garage lab."

"We've been putting those missiles together all afternoon," Cowboy says. "That's why I couldn't meet you in Santa Fe."

Sarah ducks under a wing, walks along the length of the plane, gazing up at the smooth black epoxide, her fingers trailing along the rivetless surface. Cowboy follows. "I'm flying to Nevada tomorrow morning, just before dawn. I figure to be landing just as the dawn breaks over the base.''

She steps out from under the delta's tail, straightening and looking out over the small mountain meadow to the green peaks beyond. Cowboy follows her, watching the camouflage patterns on her hands, her face. "The Dodger's given me a room in the back,'' he says. "You could join me there tonight, if you don't mind me getting up early.''

She gives him a sidelong grin. "I'm glad you said that, Cowboy. I had my bags put in your room.''

"That's fair.'' The tension he's felt all day seems to whisper out of him. "Have you seen the jukebox yet?''

"The what box? Oh. No, I haven't.''

"Let me help Warren finish up here. Then I'll show you.''

She nods, shifts her balance to relieve the weight of the gun on her hip. "I'm guarding you now,'' she says. "So don't blow yourself up.''

"I won't.'' Cowboy watches Sarah's profile as she looks out on the high meadow, the tall trees beyond. Sees the sudden look of what might be relief or gratitude that suddenly blazes out of her, through the cracks in her armor. He wonders briefly what it's about.

But *Pony Express* is waiting. Cowboy turns and steps under the wing of his black polymerized obsession.

Chapter Nineteen

Sarah's armored limo whispers across the flats of north-western Arizona. She's sharing the back with two Maximum Law communications specialists, who assure her that the phone link is secure. It's as good a time as any to place a call.

"Yes?" She feels her nerves begin to crackle at the sound of the voice. She tries to control her shock.

"Is Daud there?"

"Yes. Just a moment."

There is a moment's silence in which Sarah fights a losing war with her amazement and anger. "Hello, Sarah," Daud says.

"Was that Nick?" she asks.

"Yeah." She can see the way Daud's eyes would flicker, the way they would look away. "He's stuck here. They won't send him back. They say he abrogated their contract when he didn't try to stop you. As if he could have. And they made me sign away my contract after you ran. So we're both out of money."

"Listen. He may still be working for them."

"Maybe he is. I don't care. He's stuck here and we're going to look for a place." Sarah can hear Daud sucking briefly on a cigarette. "His real name is Sandor Nxumalo. I have a hard time not calling him Nick."

Sarah can feel Daud drifting away. Tries to hold him, remembering the man's soft body, his cynical gaze over

Daud's blind head. "Daud, I want you to be careful. He may try to get into our communications. If you need to talk to me, call from—"

"I know that. Yeah. Anything else? We were going to go look for a place."

For a moment Sarah thinks, just a word to the Hetman and the man is dead. But Daud would know, would throw it at her. Despair trickles into her heart.

"Just be careful, Daud." The line goes dead. She thinks how they know just how to give her brother hope, how they know, as they knew with her, that if they promise certain things there is no choice other than to obey, even though obedience means leaving them all the opportunity in the world for their inevitable betrayal.

"Daud, take care," she says to the telephone. It cries back at her in a language she does not know. A warning, she knows, but not of what.

Chapter Twenty

A song bends steel notes through Cowboy's mind. He calls it "Face Riders in the Sky." *Pony Express* is climbing high above the white, wheeling eye of a low-pressure system about to impact the Pacific coast; the sun glows off the delta's black cockpit struts. The sky above is a brilliant blue, just beginning to go dark with the promise of space. Cowboy tells his helmet to lower his visor as he climbs toward the sun. He tastes anesthetic gas as he whistles through his teeth.

"Reno." Cowboy doesn't bother to verbalize his message, just sends it through his chips and keeps whistling. "Tell them I'm in position."

"Roger." Reno's got his electronic fingers stretching across microwave relays from coast to coast, keeping the communications net together more efficiently than the Dodger's mercenaries.

Cowboy runs automatically through the displays, seeing the engines idling at blue, the rest of the columns green. From far below he can feel California's radars reaching out for him, touching the skin of *Pony Express* with feeble paws, not able to bounce a strong enough reflection from the delta's rounded surfaces and absorbent antiradiation paint. These aren't as powerful as the Midwest's radars—no need for them to be. They aren't used to deltas running illegal missions high over the Pacific.

"Cowboy? Are you busy?" Reno's distant voice, bubbles rising slowly in crystal.

"Just circling. Waiting for our friends."

"I found out something. I've been poking around in the crystal here at the labs."

"Isn't that likely to cause, ah, a termination of your contract?"

"I'm bored, Cowboy. There's nothing to do here."

"It's dangerous, Reno."

"No. Their outside defenses are pretty strong, but once you get into their system, their security isn't very good. Their stuff would have been adequate ten years ago, when they set up, but now it's easy enough to break. I borrowed an intrusion program from our Maximum Law friends when they weren't looking."

Cowboy thinks what could happen if the lab people discover the tampering and freeze Reno's crystal. An unavoidable accident, they'll say. "You're taking chances, friend," he says.

"I had a good idea of what I was looking for, once I saw how this place is put together. It isn't exactly a black lab, but they're into a lot of gray areas. That's how come Michael knew about them, and knew they'd take someone like me, just a mind over the phone without a body. They're used to dealing with customers who have a lot of money for one reason or another, and who want to appear with a new face and identity."

"Even more reason to stay out of their comp, I'd say."

"Have you ever heard of Project Black Mind?"

Cowboy thinks for a moment while he runs over the engine and weapons displays. "No," he says finally. "Can't say as I have."

"I'm not surprised. I never heard of it, either, before I got in here. It's an intruder program of the worst sort. Developed by the U.S. National Security people just before the war. The same people who set up this lab, years ago. And who are still running it."

No surprise, Cowboy thinks. Intelligence types like to keep their fingers in many pies. Used to run lots of interface banks to launder money for their operations, and when the face banks made money, they looked for places to invest. When their government was flattened by the blocs, they just kept on doing what they knew best.

"Okay. So what does it do?"

"Sets up a mind in crystal. Then goes into another mind, a live mind, and prints the first mind on top of it. Imposes the first personality on the second. Backs up the program."

Cowboy feels the crystal in his head turn cold. This time he forgets not to vocalize, blurting into the mic in his face mask. "God, why? What good would it do? The guy wouldn't have the target's memories to draw on, or anything."

"He might, he might not. Brain transfer is an inexact science."

"There are safeguards. No program can jump from crystal into someone's head."

"Black Mind says different."

Cowboy thinks of someone swarming into his mind through his sockets, destroying his memories, his personalities. His body, his remaining mind, turning into the puppet of someone else. Worse, Cowboy thinks, than what Roon is doing to those kids.

"Fuck," Cowboy says. Horror clutches at his heart. "Stay the hell out of that crystal, Reno. We don't want to have anything to do with this."

"The intelligence people intended to use Black Mind against the Orbitals. The plan was to have a few fanatic assassin types intrude on the minds of key Orbital personnel. If all went well, they'd start giving orders that would leave the Orbitals open to a preemptive attack from Earth. They'd suicide if they were discovered—the original assassins would still be alive down on Earth, remember. Even if the plan didn't work perfectly, at least the key Orbitals would go psychotic or something, and there would be confusion at the top. Nobody would dare use the eye-face for comumnication. It was a good plan."

"So what went wrong?"

"The Orbitals preempted the plan and attacked before Black Mind could be put into operation. But the point is,

Cowboy—*Black Mind is still here*. It's sitting in the computers of this lab, and maybe other labs. Blacker labs. The Orbitals—hell, *anybody*—could get hold of it. We've got to wipe it out.''

"Shit, yes."

"After this run, I'm going to start looking. Find out who else might have Black Mind hiding somewhere." There is a pause. Reno's tone changes. "The shuttle's on time, Cowboy. You should see its signature at about two-seven zero."

Cowboy turns his head to port, sees a brightness in the darkening sky. "Confirmed, Reno. High and to port, about eight o'clock." *Pony Express* begins a slow bank to the left. Engines cycle from blue to green. Cowboy can feel his veins opening as the alcohol fuel pours through them. Black Mind is forgotten in an instant as Cowboy's electronic nerves extrude into the delta, into the wings and engines, the smooth composite skin studded with sensors and the cold cybernetic hearts of the missiles that wait, shrouded protectively by the curved black wings.

"Hey, Cowboy." It's Sarah's voice, speaking from the base transmitter down in Nevada. She sounds a little nervous. "Thumbs up. Good hunting. I don't know what you people say at these sorts of times."

"You said it just fine. Thanks."

"I'm taking myself out of the net for now. But I'll be thinking sentimental thoughts about you."

The words stir a warmness in Cowboy, but it's washed away by the surge of data swarming into his crystal, his extensions. His turbopumps moan, pouring fuel into the combustion chamber of his shrieking heart. Neurotransmitters pulse to a steel beat like Smokey Dacus's drums. "Thanks," he says, his eyes flickering in and out of infrared perception, tracking the glowing path of the shuttle in the sky. The leading edges of the delta warm to the onrushing air. *Pony Express* twists in the air, banks, falls onto a new path. Engines climb to orange. Coming down above the shuttle, out of the sun.

"Cowboy." It is an uninflected voice of pure crystal,

purged of personality. Someone faced in through a vast computer heart, part of a gigantic cybernetic mind. "This is Roon. I'm faced into the net. I'm going to run with you. I want you to be my eyes and ears. Maybe I'll be able to offer some suggestions."

Cowboy's anger flares like a bloom of chaff over Damnation Alley. He's not one of the little boys and girls who have no choice but to let Roon ride their minds, their bodies, sucking sensation like a vampire studding into a vein. "The fuck you will," he says, and cuts himself out of the net. He thinks for a moment about what Roon could do with the Black Mind program and hears a mutter of terror in his expanded mind.

He can feel microwave pulses from over the Sierras frantically trying to reestablish contact. He fends them off. The cargo shuttle is coming down now, fast, a silver alloy brightness in the sky. Cowboy is punched back in his couch by the thrust of the afterburners. Engines red to max. The g-suit clamps on his veins, trying to keep the blood from pooling. He can hear the shuttle pilot chatting with Vandenberg ground control. Runs through the weapons check again. Thinks about the shuttle's cargo, the cryogenic pods containing billions of the mutant spaceborn viruses tailored to destroy the epidemic called viral Huntington's, the cure into which Tempel has sunk part of its massive research budget for eight years.

Pony Express buffets as it strikes the shuttle's slipstream. The shuttle is vast, 200 meters long, occupying half of the forward view from the delta's canopy, pounding through the atmosphere at twice the speed of sound.

He's been over the shuttle specs, and it's immensely strong, with multiple redundancy built in, able to absorb implausible amounts of damage. Cowboy figures he'll have to shoot it down about eight times over, and he's got less than two minutes before touchdown at Vandenberg.

Microwave squawks from Nevada batter his sensors. Cowboy ignores them. First, he thinks, the thrusters. The shuttle can out-accelerate him if he doesn't cripple it. He falls into the shuttle's trough, decelerates, fires a radar-homer. Pushes the delta into the sun again.

"What's that signal?" one of the shuttle pilots asks, his passive sensors having picked up the radar pulse from the missile. His answer comes soon enough. Flame blossoms at the shuttle's base, among the clustered rockets.

"Himmel!" says the same voice. Cowboy pushes another radar-homer out of its fairing.

"Ground, this is Tempel one-eight-three. Report we are under attack. . . ." The boy twigs fast, Cowboy thinks. The second missile plunges into the shuttle's stern and sends molten metal spewing through the thruster compartment. Cowboy is already feeding alcohol into the afterburners, slamming back into his couch again, diving under the target. The shuttle is twisting, trying to make its escape. Too slowly, too big to miss.

"Tempel one-eight-three, say again?" Ground doesn't seem to be very quick on the uptake. Cowboy looses another missile in the direction of some cargo doors and pops out his dorsal minigun turret. Thirty-millimeter rounds riddle the shuttle's belly. If he knocks out enough hydraulics, they won't be able to drop their landing gear, and even if the shuttle gets away, it might crash on landing. Sparks stitch a bright trail along the shuttle's vast belly as pieces of alloy shielding are torn apart. Freon pours like mist into the sky from broken coolant veins. The pilot isn't waiting for the people on the ground to figure things out; he's making maximum use of his maneuvering thrusters and flaps, and is dropping like an elevator, trying to swat the delta with his entire craft. Cowboy dodges easily, fires a missile into a riddled part of the ship, and hopes it will cause structural damage. His dorsal minigun is empty and he retracts the turret.

He burns forward along the massive ship, inverting himself, the belly gun slamming out of its faired hatchway. He begins firing the minigun up into the command section, aiming for the control crystal and the pilot. An oxygen tank explodes with a puff of frigid gas. He can see electricity arcing between broken cables. He fires another missile into the wreckage and suddenly the shuttle's frame screams in pain, a sound Cowboy hears as attenuated shock waves that rock the *Express*. Pieces of metal begin peeling off from the base of a fifty-foot canard, little bits of chaff whipped by the thundering slipstream.

"She's coming apart under us," the pilot reports, and it's true. *Pony Express* twists out of danger as the canard rips away, as hydraulic fluid spurts like arterial blood into the air. At Mach two there isn't much leeway for a shape that loses its aerodynamics. The shuttle lurches, slews to one side, begins to crumple.

"Tempel one-eight-three . . ." the pilot begins, but then there's a final, echoing *click* as the transmitter flattens against a wall of air and suddenly there's nothing on that channel, nothing but the feeble sound of ground control trying to regain contact, talking to no one but himself. The shuttle is a silver blizzard of alloy, twisted structural members, wings, canards, tumbling cargo drums, all spinning toward a final engagement with the Pacific hidden under the vast swirl of cloud below. *Pony Express* banks over the metal storm, its engines cycling down toward green, and begins its long descent toward Nevada.

Cowboy feels his neurotransmitter hail begin to slacken. He flips a mental switch and fires a quick-burst transmission toward Nevada. "This is Cowboy. Mission accomplished. You may applaud at will."

"No time to cheer, Cowboy." It's Reno's waterlogged voice. "Everyone's too busy right now. Would you like to listen in?"

"So long as you keep that white-brained pederast out of my head," Cowboy says.

"I don't think he wants to talk to you anyway. He seemed kind of upset."

Pony Express stoops like a hawk over the Mojave, shedding speed as it loses altitude. Reno cuts him into the commo net and suddenly his mind is a babble of voices. The Dodger's people in the West, the Hetman in the East, and Roon's people everywhere are all feeding news releases to the interface screamsheets. "Tempel Cure Down in Flames." "No Relief for Sufferers of Viral Huntington's." That's the first news.

Then the news reports begin to target on specific screamsheets. *NewsFax* receives a report that the Tempel flight was shot down. *Seconds* is told the Tempel shuttle was sabotaged. *MedNews* gets reports that the cure might have had unforeseen side effects, that all the Tempel money went down the drain. *MarkReps* receives a report that Tempel is overextended in its takeover bid, a report fleshed out with a lot of Roon-generated statistics. *MedNews* gets confirmation from a "high Tempel official" that the Huntington's cure was worthless. *NewsFax* received an "unconfirmed report" that Tempel sabotaged its own shuttle in order to prevent the news about the cure from leaking.

While the reports storm into the screamsheet offices, Roon, the Dodger, and Michael are beginning to dump Tempel stock on the Chicago exchange. The sell orders are laundered through a few hundred robobrokers, concealing the fact they're coming from only a few sources. The robobrokers are monitoring the screamsheet traffic and "Tempel" is coming up a lot. Red lights begin to wink on the computer decks of the robobroker's human supervisors. News about the sell orders hits the screamsheets, and the panic begins.

Tempel stock falls, triggering automatic sell orders from thousands of automated brokers. Nervous stockholders jitter to their monitors. Tempel had been hovering at 4,500 when Cowboy's miniguns began hammering the shuttle, now it's down by nearly 800. Screamsheet stories reflect Tempel's lack of capital reserves, its research budget wasted on a useless cure, the rumors of the self-sabotage, the possibilities that there will be no dividend this year or the next. Michael and the Dodger feed the panic with a continuous round of small sell orders. The market goes crazy.

Pony Express whispers across the Nevada line, a black cursor descending, like a graph of the values of Tempel shares. More warning lights flash in Chicago. Tempel execs are denying the screamsheet reports, but no one believes Orbitals anyway, and all it does is feed the rumors. Tempel shares have lost 56 percent of their value in about twelve minutes. Chicago exchange officials begin feeling heat from outside the well, and trading in Tempel stock is frozen "pending confirmation of outside reports."

That only fuels the action elsewhere. Roon dumps large blocks of stock onto the Osaka and Singapore exchanges. Tempel shares are falling so fast in Mombasa that Roon doesn't even need to interfere there. In Osaka, Tempel is down under 900 before trading is shut off on orders from the Exchange Master Program. Singapore doesn't follow the regs and Tempel continues to decline.

The Orbital begins its response, declaring an immediate 5-percent dividend. The plunge begins to slow as *Pony Express* begins to circle its base. People are beginning to look more carefully at the rumors. Roon tries to counter by ordering a screamsheet report that Tempel can't pay its declared dividend, that all its capital is tied up in the Korolev bid. The United Orbital Soviet announces the combined pharmaceutical bloc is funding Tempel's dividend, which appears simultaneously with Couceiro's personal announcement that Tempel is divesting itself of all Korolev stock, that the takeover bid is concluded unsuccessfully, but that all profits will be used to guarantee the dividend. With the dividend guaranteed by two different sources, Tempel stock begins to stagger upward. Michael tries more screamsheet rumors, but people are thinking twice about any more unsubstantiated Tempel stories.

A cold pulse moves over the net, firing at the speed of light from Roon's big crystal AI. Cowboy cringes at the sound, tastes a phantom foulness in his mask. "We've hit bottom. Start buying. We'll sell at fifteen hundred and hope we catch a profit-taking storm and drive it down again."

Cowboy rotates the delta's exhaust, hovering over the Nevada desert. Buy orders swarm out through the robobrokers. Tempel's recovery is faster than its collapse. At 1,500, sell orders go out again, but there are more eager buyers than sellers. Prices hover uncertainly for a few seconds as profits are taken, but there is another announcement from Couceiro.

The reserve supply of the Huntington's cure will be brought down from orbit within days, accompanied by Orbital cutters to prevent attack. The screamsheets begin printing releases about the safety and effectiveness of the cure. Prices roar upward.

The Chicago exchange reopens trading in Tempel at 2,000. The Dodger and Michael have exhausted their available funds. The proxy from every piece of stock they've acquired is sent at once to Roon in Venezuela. *Pony Express* hovers over its pad, slipping toward the ground as its landing gear slides smoothly out of its fairings, as Tempel prices seem to stabilize around 3,000.

The ground crew runs for the delta, carrying their camouflage net. Cold despair gnaws at Cowboy's heart. The message that Roon sends through the network only serves to confirm Cowboy's intuition.

"Your proxies are not enough to force Couceiro out. If I demanded a stockholders' vote at this stage, I would only call attention to my part in this."

"Gutless bastard!" Cowboy shrieks. Pain burns in his awakening limbs.

"I can try to change some minds on the board, but I suspect Couceiro will have gathered more admiration than enmity for his work today. I suggest we take our profits and consider it a lesson."

"Afraid to make yourself a target, Roon?" Cowboy demands. "Afraid to play your games with grownups?"

"He's out of the net," Reno reports. "He can't hear you."

"I should have killed him when I had the chance," Cowboy says. He unstraps, pulls off his helmet. Sweat trickles down his forehead. The canopy rises with an electronic whine. Desert heat takes his breath away, even with the camouflage netting occluding the sun. He feels the crystal in his head burning, his anger a roaring combustion in his heart.

"Don't start breaking down the net," Cowboy says. "We're

going to need it. I'll explain later." He unfaces and stands in the cockpit, legging down the ladder as hands rise to his assistance.

The headquarters here is a bubble tent draped in camouflage nets. Fuel trucks and a pair of panzers stand nearby, wavering in the heat. Helmet in his hand, Cowboy stalks into the tent.

Sarah meets him at the doorway. He sees a stricken look, eyes shadowed by despair. There's a red crease across her forehead from the headset she was wearing when she was tied into the net. She reaches out, wraps him in her arms. Cowboy lurches to a stop. She presses her cheek to his neck.

"We almost did it," she says. "We came so close."

"It's not over," Cowboy says. "Where's the Dodger? I don't want the net closed down."

She pulls back and looks at him. "What are you talking about?"

"We have a lot more stock now, we made a big profit. We're in a lot stronger position."

Sarah shakes her head. "What good is it? We don't—"

Cool air blows fitfully against Cowboy's forehead. The g-suit seems to clutch at him, dragging him down the well.

"I shot them down once," he says. "I'll do it again."

For a moment Sarah seems suspended in time, her face a mask of shock. "The escorts. They'll have escorts this time."

"Fuck the escorts." He takes her hand and leads her through the big bubble tent, toward the comm section set up in the rear. The Dodger sits there amid the ruin of the plan, the communcations gear being broken down, the Flash Force specialists watching the bustle with cool professional interest. Cowboy thinks he's never seen the Dodger look so old.

"Dodger," he says. "Listen. It's not over." He can see the heads turning toward him. "I want to make a run."

Already the steel guitar is bending notes in his mind.

Chapter Twenty-one

Sarah lies naked and restless on her pallet in a section of the bubble tent sealed off by an opaque hanging of Jovian plastic. Her arms and neck are red with sunburn from the hours she's spent in the sun assembling homemade missiles, the sunblock she'd brought from Florida having proved to be less than useful in the Nevada desert. Cooled air whistles through the duct but does not ease her discomfort. She reaches for her beer and presses the cold bottle to her forehead, feeling the chill in welcome contrast to her burning skin.

"Where are you going to get pilots, C'boy?" The question had been Warren's. "We got five deltas, six if we don't keep one in reserve for spare parts, but we only got three pilots." Warren's head shook slowly from side to side. "Most of the pilots died crossing the Line. And a lot of the survivors are hiding from both sides in this war."

Then Sarah remembered the pictures on the wall of the Blue Silk, the few that weren't swathed in mourning ribbons. She blurted out what she knew, and a call to Tampa was made. Maurice was coming west, with 30,000 in gold guaranteed. Attempts had been made, one successful, to contact a pair of old cutterjocks Maurice had recommended. Raw material for missiles were brought in by chopper. Fuel and explosive were being cooked up day and night under a waving camouflage net.

"It's me." Cowboy's voice. The velcro room seal rips

302

open with the sound of torn linen. He steps in, sealing the door behind him. Sweat pours down his face. He's in a pair of worn coveralls, his forehead and hands bright with sunburn.

"Hi." He kneels by her side and bends to kiss her nipple. Sarah hands him her beer. He sits, crosses his legs, drinks. "I've got to ferry in a delta from Colorado tonight," he says. "The chopper's taking me out."

"When are you going to get some sleep?"

Cowboy wipes sweat from his forehead with his palm, then wipes the palm on his thigh. "On the chopper flight," he says. "I'm not piloting."

"Shit, Cowboy." She scowls and props herself up on her elbows. "You need rest. Take off your clothes and come to bed."

He grins. "I don't know just how restful that's going to be."

She moves over to make room on the pallet, pats the place beside her. Her voice is deliberate. "Very . . . restful."

Cowboy puts down the beer and reaches for the zip on his coveralls, and at that moment he stops, his motion frozen. Sarah turns her head and listens, hearing the distant baritone throb of the helicopter growing as it moves in from the north. "Fuck," Sarah mutters. She can see the fever rising again in Cowboy's eyes, the brightness she'd seen two days before when he'd stalked from his delta . . . the love of speed and metal, the obsession with the crystal interface and the electronic extensions of his mind hurtling at the speed of light. . . . In these moods Cowboy seems surrounded, like an atomic nucleus, by a shroud of electrons, impenetrable, free from earthly attachments, immune. . . . He uncoils his long legs and stands up.

"Sorry," he says, but he's already gone, his mind lost in some internal space, insulated behind his plastic eyes. He blows a kiss in her direction and leaves. Sarah reaches for her beer, picks it up, puts it down again. She's lost her thirst. She rolls on her stomach, feeling the fitful ventilator breeze begin to cool the sweat on her back.

Later in the day she's on communications duty. There isn't

any heavy traffic, and messages are being kept to a minimum to lessen the chance of Tempel detecting the net. She sits in the big, still room, the foam pads of her headset chafing her sunburned forehead. She hates the military atmosphere here, the guards, the duties assigned from above, all the emphasis on security and discipline that cramps her dirtgirl style. The screen before her is blank except for a white cursor. Across the room, a communications tech is doing something with cables, insulating tapes, male/female connectors. The cooling system in here doesn't seem any more efficient than in her own room. She taps the keys in frustration, a line of gibberish, then wipes it.

If she'd worked it right, Sarah knows, she wouldn't be here, sitting in an inflated target in the middle of a former nuclear testing range, helping a collection of range rats take on the Orbitals in a few homemade jets. She could be looking down on Nevada from a weightless home out of the well, living there in exemplary alloy immunity with Daud, the both of them cleansed of the mud that had clung to them all their lives. If she had just managed Andre better, if she had not let sentiment contaminate her actions . . . if she had kept her desire pure and titanium-hard, she would be safe now, wrapped in the perfect insulation of vacuum.

The cooling unit whispers of futures that will never be. She knows the one that is most likely: charred bodies wrapped in melted metal, a personal death, a figure with uncertain features but equipped with Andre's metal irises and Cunningham's whispering voice, coming with the supersonic suddenness of a bullet. This whole ridiculous homemade venture exploding like shrapnel, each survivor seeking cover, turning on one another in their search for safety.

The tech bangs on something with the butt end of a screwdriver. Sarah grins and relaxes in her chair, pushing the headset back, wiping her forehead. She closes her eyes and rolls her head, feeling her neck bones crackle.

Foolish as it sounds, there is no place she would rather be than here.

An incoming call tickles her mind as a signal begins

bleeping on her screen. She adjusts the headset over her temples and sends a mental signal. Her nerves cringe in response to the cold pulse of distant crystal madness.

"This is Roon. My people found the time and date of the shipment."

Sarah flips on the recorder. "Ready to receive," she says into the mic; no point in using the headset for chat.

"Is that you, Sarah?" The forced intimacy of the words whispering in her head is worsened, made almost unendurable, by their tonelessness, her knowledge of the man sitting in his alloy castle, stroking the shining hair of one of his victims while he purrs into his chips. "I remember you very well. Smooth olive skin, and the scars you wore with such defiance. I would have taught you the futility of such defiance, Sarah. Taught you the joys of submission."

The frozen, remote voice turns her bones to ice. She's going to have to edit this recording; she's not going to let anyone else hear this. "I'm not Sarah," she says. "If you don't have a message for me to pass on, clear this channel."

"Ah." Even through the tonelessness Sarah can sense Roon's pleasure in her anger. "As you wish. The new shipment is coming down tomorrow on the Venture-class shuttle *Argosy*, arrival time calculated as eighteen thirty-two. The shuttle will be landing at Edwards, not Vandenberg. It will be escorted by six Hyperion-class frigates."

Sarah's heart is crowding her chest. Tomorrow is much too soon. Cowboy's pilots haven't even flown together yet. And Edwards is the Orbital's military and testing field, not their commercial port—no facilities to land the frigates at Vandenberg, she figures. They're big ships, capable of maneuvering in space and atmosphere both. But on the other hand, the change might be good—Edwards is closer to the base in Nevada, and the shuttle will be within Cowboy's range for a longer period.

"Message received," Sarah says, and repeats it to make certain.

"I'm sorry, Sarah, I truly am." The cryogenic voice sounds infuriatingly superior. "I know this is too soon for you to make adequate preparations. But your failure will only delay the historic relationship for a short while. The new order will evolve regardless. The pure inevitability of the data demands it.''

Sarah snaps off the recorder. She tries to cool the anger in her voice. ''We will proceed as planned,'' she says. ''We will down the shuttle.''

There is a fractional hesitation in Roon's voice. ''Understood,'' he says. And his presence fades from the network. The white cursor begins to blink again.

Bastard, Sarah thinks. If we go down, if there's nothing left, I'm going to pay you a visit and run Weasel right into your brain. Leave the planet a little cleaner when I'm done.

Sarah pages the Dodger and calls him to the room. She uses her headset to edit Roon's comments and has the new version ready when the Dodger walks in. She plays him the recording and watches the concern build in the older man's eyes.

He cuts a plug of tobacco for a long silent moment. ''We can do her, maybe,'' he says. ''But we're still missing a pilot.''

Sarah hunches over her screen. ''I'll find you one,'' she says. Maurice has told her about some guy who, last anyone heard, lived on Catalina. He's moved and no one knows where.

She digs through records, finds his address, calls his old neighbors. One of them mentions Santa Barbara, where she has to go through the same procedure. This time a neighbor mentions Carson City. Jackpot. The man's almost next door.

He turns out to be in need of thirty K in gold. The Flash Force arranges for helicopter delivery tonight.

The Dodger beams at her and pats her on the shoulder. ''Good, Sarah. We've got our team.'' He shifts his tobacco from cheek to cheek and looks for one of the cuspidors his people have brought with him. ''Your Maurice is flying in tonight. I've got to get all the pilots together with him so they can get his lecture on Orbital tactics.''

More military stuff. Sarah's glad she won't have to deal

with it. She's got another hour left on the monitors before she can break for dinner, and even then it will be a mass meal served in a special tent, too reminiscent of her childhood meals in DP camps for her to look forward to it with any appetite.

The Dodger shuffles away. Sarah watches the white cursor blink and wishes she had something cold to drink. Then the cursor is racing across the screen with a piece of incoming data, and a new voice is tickling Sarah's temples: "I want to talk to Sarah. Tell her it's her brother."

Warmth touches her faintly. "It's me, Daud."

"Sarah, who is that guy I was talking to?"

She looks up at the tech who is still fiddling with the cables, wishes there was privacy here. "I don't really know. One of the cutouts, I guess."

"Is his name really Randolph Scott?" Daud's voice sounds a little wrong. Like he's tired, or maybe high. A warning whispers in Sarah's veins.

"I doubt it." She lowers her voice and speaks carefully into the mic. "How are you? Where are you?"

"I'm fine. Nick and I found a place. He's got a little money put by."

Where did you get it? Is he paying for the endorphins that you're putting in your veins? She wants to ask the questions but she knows what the answers will be, that she'll never know the truth as long as she's hiding in Nevada.

"Have they been bothering you? Are they watching you?"

"Not so I can tell." Then there's a noise in the background, a domestic sound like someone closing a refrigerator door, and Sarah's blood turns to fire.

"Where are you calling from? Are you calling from the apartment?"

"No." There's a fractional hesitation before Daud's answer that makes Sarah certain it's a lie. She can see him standing by the phone, a cigarette in his hands, his eyes shifting nervously at the word.

She leans forward into the monitor. Her voice is so urgent

that the tech across the room turns his head to look at her. "Daud, tell me. I won't be angry if you just tell me."

"No," Daud says. There's a definite anger in his voice. "Why don't you ever believe me? I just said no."

She knows him too well, and knows this, too, is a lie. "Daud, things have started happening here," she says quickly. "I can't talk. I'll call you when it's safe."

Daud spits out his anger. "Fucking bitch! I told you—"

"I love you." Tonelessly, her hands already slapping the stud that ends communication. She looks at the board, sees nothing out of the ordinary. She looks up at the tech. "Breach of security," she says. "Tell somebody. I'm sure someone was monitoring that call."

Chapter Twenty-two

Sarah stands with Maurice on the desert floor, the breath hammered from her lungs by the pulsing heart rising from the earth. Cowboy's delta hovers in the dark, a smooth blackness against the sky, its downward-directed jet blast raising an opaque cloud of dust that pours through the starry night. Sarah narrows her eyes against the tide of dirt and feels her neck and shoulder muscles tense, waiting for someone to fall from the sky. . . .

The schedule's too tight, they tell her. With the intercept coming the next afternoon they can't shift their base and still hope to make the mission. They don't *think*, they tell her, that any program could have traced them through the multiple cutouts tied into the net. They'll just have to increase security, fly in a few more people and defensive weapons, and hope that the Flash Force experts are right.

The delta lands, its whine diminishing. The dust storm subsides. They're three quarters of a mile from the command tent: the deltas are being dispersed to make it harder to find them. Sarah finds herself looking up at the diamond-flecked blackness above, the muscles still tense in her shoulders and neck, and then realizes she's waiting for a rock. If Tempel has their location, there is no easier way to dispose of them.

The ground crew rushes up with camouflage nets. The canopy lifts, and Cowboy stands in the cockpit, his black helmet reflecting the stars. Sarah walks up as Cowboy drops down the ladder to the radiant sand. She can hear Maurice following quietly.

"Cowboy, Daud called and—"

"I know. They told me while I was flying in. I took some extra evasive action just in case they had something looking for us."

He is weary, she can see that even in starlight. There is a red line around his nose and chin where the anesthetic mask scored the flesh. He pulls off his helmet and wipes sweat away. "Something's got to be done about that brother of yours, Sarah."

She feels herself prickle. "He's my problem." Maybe they got to him, she thinks, maybe Nick has been sitting there all along, purring suggestions in to him. Maybe he just didn't care any longer, didn't want to exercise his new legs heading for another phone.

"Your problem may have just blown this base. Your problem may get us killed." He reaches out a gloved hand to touch the fading bruises on her cheek. Sarah turns her head away. "He's responsible for this," Cowboy says.

"He's not." Crisply. "That was my mistake, not his."

"He let them ambush you. Whose mistake was that?"

Sarah doesn't answer, just shakes her head. She feels a sting behind her eyes, in her sinuses. Daud is faithless, she knows, but that doesn't change anything within her. It doesn't change her responsibility for the things in him that make him faithless, and it doesn't change her own faithlessness, her attempted betrayal that put scars on her heart as well as her face. Instead, it was her goals she betrayed, her chance to live away from this. . . . She feels a hole in her chest, a vacuum where her purpose has been torn free.

Cowboy turns from her, holds out a hand to Maurice. "I'm glad you can be here," he says.

Maurice's quiet, sad smile seems another face of the night. His eyes glitter like a pair of distant artificial moons. "I'm pleased to be given the chance." He's wearing his blue silk scarf tucked between his neck and the collar of his shirt, the faded badge of his old allegiance.

"You're the last to arrive. I have a briefing arranged. About the Hyperion frigates and the tactics they will probably use."

"Now? Let's do it, then."

Sarah follows them during the long walk to the bubble tent. They converse in a jargon-ridden aeronautical slang that seems far more opaque than necessary. The language of their secret club, she thinks, the exclusive society of those who worship speed and mechanical violence.

She avoids the briefing, meaningless to her anyway, and finds instead a sandwich and a cold lemonade, then goes to her little room, strips, and stretches out on her pallet. The air tube whispers monotonously. She's got another six hours before she's on shift again, making missiles in the oven of the assembly trench.

Her head on her pillow, staring at the gray crook of her own elbow, she gazes back over her last weeks and tries to find the point where her loyalties changed, where she surrendered her dream. . . . Somewhere things shifted, away from herself and Daud, toward something more complex. Survival was a simple enough goal, survival for herself and her brother—that and flight from the mud. The new loyalties are a lot more complicated than mere survival. Cowboy's people, the panzerboys and pilots, are not, so far as she can tell, survivors. They're not as flamboyant in their search for extinction as the Silver Apaches, but there's something about their quest for the absolute that gives her pause. . . . They chase oblivion with every ride, and they rank themselves on how far they can push into the dark eye sockets of a crumbling death's head in the sky, push and still come back. . . . They talk about Cowboy as if he is immortal, as though his life is magic, but she knows that if he keeps stretching that fragile envelope between himself and the darkness, someday it will snap, and Cowboy will spin alone into the night.

Within a few hours all six deltas could be melted epoxide on the California desert, their pilots' ultimate quest fulfilled, and what of Sarah's new loyalties then? The little tent city would have lost its purpose, its center. With luck the Flash

Force might give her a ride to the nearest town. Daud is weak and faithless, but she knows she can force him to accept life. She doesn't think that's possible with Cowboy.

He doesn't join her that night: the briefing runs late and in early morning there's some kind of problem with one of the jet engines that needs every experienced hand. Sarah lies on her back and stares at the ceiling, wondering if the rock will come, if she will see its glow through the tent fabric before the shock wave hits.

The rock falls in midafternoon. Sarah is working in a trench with the last of the two air-to-air missiles that are being set in their cradles, ready to be delivered to Maurice's delta, hidden under camouflage nets a mile and a half away. She's dressed only in a one-piece bathing suit and sneakers, her armored clothes and gun hanging from one of the bomb cradles. She's seen Cowboy only once today with some of the other pilots at the breakfast tent. Since that time she's seen only the three men helping with the missiles, and Maurice, who's sitting patiently in his delta waiting for the rockets to be fed into the slots in his wings.

And suddenly alarms are ringing. Sarah snaps upright, seeing the blank, appalled gaze on the faces of the missile assembly crew, and reaches for the submachine chopper, her armored jacket and pants. She vaults toward a small slit trench a few yards distant. She's not going to be caught near that much explosive in a fight.

She jumps into the trench, breathless already in the unbearable heat, and reaches into her jacket pocket for the inhaler of hardfire. She can hear the whooping alarm, the sound of running feet, the rising whine of panzer engines as they begin turning over. . . . Hardfire races along her nerves, her muscles and blood coming alive. She jams her feet into her trousers and fumbles with the zip. Then she's paralyzed for a second as something tears apart the air over her head, as she gazes up into the blue, expecting from the sound to see the black ablative needle of an Orbital frigate aimed straight between her eyes . . . she sees nothing. The shock throws

her against the sand wall of the trench. The air is full of grit
pouring down from above. There is more tearing of the air,
more shocks. Artillery, she realizes. Mortars or something,
big ones. Walking their rounds up and down the base.

She sits up, coughing the grit from her lungs. The sand
that coats her sweat resists the fabric of the jacket as she pulls
it on. The explosives are moving away and she chances a
look over the rim of the trench, blinking away the sweat and
dust just in time to see the armored angular shapes of four
panzers topping a ridge half a mile away, trailing dust plumes
that seem to throw half the desert into the sky. Howling
brightness splashes the ridge as Flash Force automated
defense systems fire sheaf rockets. Behind her someone is
screaming. One of the Dodger's panzers is moving, building
speed over the flat. It howls as it moves behind her, and
Sarah realizes it's putting her between two fires. She throws
herself flat on the surface of the trench.

A shrieking in the air, concussions, the scream of metal
and engines. The mortars march back and forth again, hammering the earth. The sounds seem to move away from her
and Sarah chances a look again.

In front of her, slightly to the right, one of the intruder
panzers is hit, black smoke gushing skyward from its aft
section. A dorsal minigun turret is flashing with a basso
moan. The panzer's cargo doors are down, and men are
rushing out and fanning over the surface, men in desert
camouflage and black helmets. They seem to move in synch,
their heads turning to scan the ground around them, one of
them always looking in every direction so the unit has an
ever-present 360-degree awareness, their arms and legs moving with alarming speed and efficiency. Hardwired, with
crystal for small-unit combat, way out of Sarah's league.
Sarah feels gratitude they're out of range of her machine
pistol and there will be no temptation for her to shoot and
draw their fire.

An intruder panzer races by on her left, dust rising in a
sheet. She turns as it smashes headlong into one of the
parked deltas, brushing it aside like a car ramming a tricycle.

The delta spins aside and moans as its spars give way. The panzer roars on, the delta's camouflage net flapping from its bow. Then the canopy of dust reaches Sarah's position and blots the world from view.

Panic flutters in her throat. *I don't have the crystal for this,* she thinks. She drops back into her trench and reaches for the machine pistol. If anyone gets in the trench with her, she'll kill him; otherwise, she'll stay out of it and wait for circumstances to declare the winner. Sucking enemy bullets is all a streetgirl is worth in these situations, and Sarah knows it. It's time to leave the defense to the Flash Force: that's what they're paid for. The hardfire wailing in her veins, she plants her back against the wall of the trench and points the chopper at its opposite rim. Hopes she'll be fast enough when the time comes.

Explosions shake the planet beneath her. The crackle of small-arms fire is added to the roar of missiles and the scream of jet engines. Dust falls in clouds, dropping on her arms, gathering in her lap, coating her lashes. She keeps brushing it off the Heckler & Koch with quick movements. At one point the dust clears above her and she looks straight up and sees a delta, stalled and falling wing-first right at her. She realizes it's Maurice from the distinctive configuration of his craft, and then she sees a glint of silver as a missile shoots above his high wing and careens into the sky. Sarah waits helplessly for the impact, for the laden epoxide body to crush her, but the delta's wings seem to grab just enough air to keep it aloft, and the plane twists and disappears out of her vision. She braces for the impact but there isn't one. Maurice has somehow sidestepped the missile without falling into the fatal embrace of gravity.

Mortars begin plashing around her, and she huddles deeper into her jacket. Then the mortars are gone, and Sarah realizes that the volume of fire has slackened. Most of it is small-arms fire now, with the occasional roar of a minigun or hammer of a machine gun. The dusty sky overhead is tainted with blue. She shifts, crouching on the balls of her feet, and risks a look.

Columns of smoke rise from the broken desert floor. She sees four smashed panzers within her range of vision, as well as the crumpled delta, a gutted Flash Force limo, and the fuel truck, broken and burning brightly. Bodies dot the landscape, most of them in the bright coveralls worn by the Dodger's people. She doesn't see anyone moving, but there's fire chattering from somewhere. A black peregrine falls out of the sky, and she recognizes Maurice's delta, flame shooting from its wings as it launches rockets. She hears the explosions but can't see what he was shooting at. Then the delta soars up into the sky again.

Sarah drops back to the trench floor and tries to wipe the sweat and dust from her face, feeling it smear. Weariness wars in her with the hardfire; she's exhausted herself simply with the effort of living through the attack. Daud, she thinks dully, brought this down on them with only a phone call. She can feel her fingers tightening on the butt of her machine pistol, her jaw muscles clenching. She pictures Weasel scoring Daud's soft new flesh, flickering for his false blue eyes. Hears Daud's panicked evasions as she makes her own calculated strikes. . . .

The delta whines overhead. All fire has died away. She can hear cars and trucks moving. She shakes herself free of her vision and peers out of the trench again, seeing men in camouflage armor and black helmets rising from the ground with their hands over their heads, Flash Force people moving out in vehicles to round them up. Mercenaries, she thinks angrily. When they capture one another they have agreements that allow for fair treatment and parole of prisoners. Not like the world she lives in, where no mistakes are allowed.

"Technical personnel report to their team leaders." A bullhorn brays from the direction of the command tent. "We need a head count." Sarah rises from the trench. The next half hour is an exhausted blur of motion, sweating labor performed around scenes of horror, all the while expecting to hear again the alarms, the sounds of another attack.

Maurice brings his delta in, and Sarah wrestles her pair of missiles out of the trench toward his craft. Other armorers are running up to reload the miniguns. She learns it was Maurice who saved the fight, the only pilot in his delta when the attack came. He'd flown over the ridge and blown away the mortars that were ranging on the deltas, and then helped to take care of the attacking panzers. Two of the deltas were destroyed on the ground, the rest—dispersed behind ridges or hills, protected by camouflage—survived, partly because the two defending panzers stood in the way and took most of the enemy rockets.

Maurice is standing in the cockpit when she arrives. "Maurice," she says. Her heart is hammering wildly. "Where's Cowboy? Have you heard?"

"He's okay. He and the *Express* both. Spent the fight in a slit trench."

Sarah breathes easier, tries to smile.

"It's okay, Sarah," Maurice says. "We'll bring the shuttle down." His reassurance seems weaker when Sarah sees that the two missiles she's putting in his wings are the only ones he has left. He's used the others on the panzers.

"I'm okay." Jimi Gutierrez is brought past in a stretcher improvised from a blanket. His skin is blackened, both legs are burned away at the thigh. Somehow he's still conscious. He's smiling, the braces on his teeth gleaming in the burned and shredding face. "I'm okay, I still got my sockets."

Sarah waves to Maurice and runs back to the command tent. It's down but it's being propped up, its contents hastily readied for evacuation. Things are being packed up and moved, and the wounded have to be delivered to a hospital in Vegas. As Sarah jogs over the stony desert, she passes a pair of surviving enemy panzerboys being executed by a couple of the Dodger's techs. The machine-pistol fire echoes off distant hills. The panzerboys, like Sarah, are not subject to the professional courtesies offered between mercenary groups. The rest of the surviving attackers, Japanese mercs flown in overnight by suborbital shuttle, stand in emotionless sweating lines as they're stripped of their armor and weapons. She sees a slight, blond figure standing among them and freezes.

It's one of Cunningham's two associates, the smaller one.

There are abrasions scoring half his face, blood trickling onto his white undershirt. One arm is bound up, red soaking through the improvised bandage. "Sarah," he says.

An explosion burns behind her eyes. The chips make the movement easy, economical. She walks a burst up his chest and watches him fall, sees the wary eyes of the Japanese as they shift away from the line of fire.

"Hey," one of the Flash Force men says, raising his gun.

"He's not a merc. He's Orbital personnel." Despite the fury burning in her veins her voice stays cool. "He's not covered by any agreements." The mercenary looks at her doubtfully. He's got a little mustache with flecks of dust on it. His eyes are hollow, red-rimmed. She holsters her pistol and bares her teeth at him. "You see any more round-eyes with this group, they're Orbitals. Where was this guy taken? Cunningham—Calvert—was probably with him."

She can see the cords standing out in the soldier's neck. His voice is a suppressed scream. "Who the hell *are* you? I don't have any instructions—"

Behind her, she hears the rising whine of engines. She turns her back on the babbling mercenary and sees four deltas rising from hidden folds in the desert, hovering like black insects on columns of shimmering heat. Their sound begins to change as the deltas start moving forward, their needle points rising like dark fingers toward the sky.

"Hey. Who *are* you?" The mercenary jabbers at her. She can see the dots of sweat on his face, the staring eyes, the hands shaking as they clutch his gun. All the suppressed fear bursting forth in the violence of his question.

"Hey. I wanna know—" The man is weeping. Sarah watches the deltas rise into the sky. Her breath catches in her throat. "Dammit," the man gasps, "you just can't . . . just can't *shoot* someone. . . . That's not . . . You gotta have *authority*."

The man's tears patter on his uniform, making fresh clear pathways in the dust. Sarah runs for the command tent, finds an officer, explains. It turns out the man was captured with the mortar crew, knocked out by Maurice's rockets before he got a chance to escape.

"Calvert was probably with him," Sarah says. "He's running Tempel's effort out here. You'd better find him."

The deltas have long since vanished into the sun when two all-terrain vehicles full of Flash Force mercs move off in a trail of dust for the mortar site. Sarah rides with them, next to the officer in the back of the vehicle.

The mortar lies on the desert, a black broken tube flung 200 yards from where its ammo erupted under Maurice's rockets. There're remnants of a comm rig here, too, that kept the attackers in communication with their base. The officer searches the rough hills with enhanced eyes. He points. "Pickup and rendezvous for these guys was probably back that way," he says, and gives the commands that send most of the Flash Force on foot toward their quarry. The two vehicles move off on either flank, hoping to drive Cunningham in toward the men on foot.

Sarah clutches the side of the vehicle as it lurches over the ground. Sweat bounces from her armored shell. Dust coats her skin. She stares at the desert, intent, her fingers on the butt of her machine pistol.

She misses the end. There's a burst of fire from off to the left, and a crackle on the officer's radio. He slaps the driver on the shoulder and points. The vehicle turns, accelerates in a blossoming cloud of dust.

The head shot that killed him went in through an eye and removed the back of his head, but Cunningham's face is still recognizable. Sarah looks down from the vehicle at the dusty corpse, the broken steel spring that was Cunningham. The officer looks at her for confirmation.

"He wouldn't have let himself be taken alive," she says, and the officer nods and looks down at the corpse with a measure of respect.

"Put him in the back," he says, and his troopers sling the corpse into the vehicle and then jump in themselves. Sarah watches the body as it bounces back and forth to the lurches of the vehicle.

Sarah looks at him, thinks of the last time she'd seen him, that back room in the Plastic Girl when they had said good-bye, and when Sarah had wanted more than anything else to have Cunningham's ticket, have it at any price. Here, she thinks, was the price of it, a shallow grave on the desert floor. A mudboy come back to the Earth to die.

She glances west, into the sky. Cowboy is there, probably already grappling with the Tempel jockeys. Sarah raises a hand to her throat, a gypsy woman touching iron.

Beyond her sight, she knows, the sky is stained with fire.

Chapter Twenty-three

Alcohol shrieks through Cowboy's heart. His epoxide skin burns at the touch of the air. *Pony Express* arcs over California, riding into the darkening face of a Mach three sky.

Cowboy's late for the planned intercept and knows it, and so he's hurtling as fast as he can across the roof of the world. The shuttle has only about seven minutes in the air between the ion blackout and landing at Edwards, and the deltas will have to kill it during that time. After the chase and a fight over the Mojave, Cowboy figures that he won't have enough fuel to get back; he can only hope to bring his ship to a landing on a flat piece of desert or a dry lakebed, then call for a fuel truck to top up the tanks and give him a run for Colorado.

He feels grit between his skin and his face mask, biting his skin. Little mementoes in the shape of dust particles, remembrances of a long hot afternoon in a slit trench, crouched with the Dodger as the Orbital mortars walked up and down and the deltas died in a storm of jet-powered Chobham. Not his kind of fight, not something he was chipped for.

Now it's time for revenge. Already he can feel pulsing radar energies directed downward from the dome of the sky. Seven distinct pulses, two frigates in the lead, crashing through the atmosphere with their wings drawn in, their ablative skin trailing fire. Point men, clearing their path of anything that may have survived the Orbital strike into Nevada. Then the shuttle, marked by its more powerful radars, trailing by twenty miles. Two more pairs of frigates behind, each at a twenty-mile distance.

"This is Cowboy. We've acquired the target."

While his ground people acknowledge, Cowboy snarls the contempt for the Orbitals' amateur setup. The laws never seem to learn that a fighter craft using radar gives its position away to a passive detection system long before the radar itself will ever see anything. The Orbitals will probably see Cowboy on infrared long before they pick him up on radar.

The deltas howling toward the Orbitals are also in pairs, Cowboy in the lead with his wingman, Andy, a former deltajock, two miles above and behind, trailing to port. The two ex–Space Force people, Diego and Maurice, flying second string twenty-five miles behind.

Coded Orbital transmissions rain against Cowboy's crystal. The brown rim of California drops into the sea. The frigates ahead are bright infrared bullets foreshortening toward Cowboy's brain. He pulses a signal to Andy, and *Pony Express* begins to jitter through the sky, the airframe quaking, trying to dance away from the frigate's lasers. The delta buckets up and down, yawing, correcting, yawing again. Cowboy runs through the checks and finds that his systems are surviving the atmospheric hammer. Through his skin he feels an additional pulse of microwave, then a second—orbital radar-homers on their way. He drops a decoy missile that should give out a strong radar image.

He fires an antiradiation-homer just to discourage the frigates from using their radar sets, and an instant later hears confirmation from Andy that his wingman's done the same. His sensors go wild for a second, proof that he's just jittered across a laser track, and gives a death's-head grin to the sky and the alloy intruders. Some people aren't coming back from this, and he figures it should be the Tempel men. It's time someone gave them a comeuppance.

There's a glimpse of silver over his canopy as the radar-homer slews past at a converging rate of eight times the speed of sound. Cowboy bellows inchoate defiance into his

face mask. There's a flash of infrared off his port bow, and
Andy reports, "We hit one, C'Boy!"—and then *Pony Express*
is shuddering in the frigates' slipstream, shedding thermite
flares to discourage heat-seekers. There's nothing between it
and the shuttle.

His nerves wail in triumph, taut like the strings of a steel
guitar. The dorsal minigun slams into the air and begins its
roar, spitting out a steel wall in the path of the target.
Argosy's a smaller and more maneuverable craft than the
other shuttle that *Pony Express* met in the sky, but the delta
can still fly rings around her.

Missiles are coming from behind, radar-homers whipping
in tight converging loops from the frigates. Cowboy keeps
his minigun firing while dropping radar decoys and sideslip-
ping the missiles. He's flying right-wing-down at the end of
his maneuver, the translucent Pacific blue beneath him, a
surface geometry of tinted depthless glass . . . and then the
shuttle's there, a giant black-nosed shadow with visible sonic
shock waves moving like spiderwebs over its giant wings,
gone in an instant but burning its image into Cowboy's
gunsight eyes. Cowboy's tried to stitch her with his minigun,
but it doesn't look as if there's been much damage. *Pony
Express* does flip-flops in the *Argosy*'s slipstream, the vast
sonic boom moving through its spars like an earthquake
through California soil, making a sound too deep to be heard
by anything but gut and bone. . . . Cowboy feels the crystal
in his head burning hot as he controls his ship, twisting it,
pointing the nose up, cutting in the air brakes and throttling
back. *Pony Express* slows as if it's hit a sea of honey in the
sky. Cowboy's neck muscles clamp down against the g-forces
draining blood from his brain. Then Cowboy drops the nose
and feeds more fuel to the engines as he triggers missiles that
will loop and follow the shuttle.

He's just performed what's known in the trade as a yo-yo,
which should bring him out behind the *Argosy* in the classic
kill position, but the maneuver's cost him speed and it will
take him a while to catch up. But he can feel Orbital breath
on his neck. The next pair of frigates are dropping on him

like falcons, a classic bounce, their big rockets giving them faster acceleration than any delta can hope for. Cowboy's still jinking even in his dive after *Argosy*, but a laser burn blows some of the rear sensors and he can see heat-seekers on his trail, bright needles rotating through the sky.

He and Andy have planned for this. After passing the shuttle, Cowboy yo-yoed right while Andy did another yo-yo to the left, presenting the frigates with two separate and diverging targets. The frigates opted to keep together and bounce the leader, but that's left Andy free. He sweeps out of his yo-yo with the frigates right in front of him and his crystal humming with the sound of heat-seekers asking for a target, and he drops a pair of missiles that turn one frigate into a dazzling eruption of fuel and flashing oxidant, tumbling alloy scraps and burning insulation. The other frigate breaks away, dropping thermite decoys, leaving Cowboy free.

But there are still missiles after him, distracting him from the vast target just ahead. He drops more thermite and suddenly there's a rattle on the armor, metal vaporizing on the Chobham. Someone's spent minigun rounds, falling from on high.

Suddenly Andy is gone. His delta is tumbling and breaking up into a sheet of flame, and all Cowboy knows is that for a few seconds there's a weird electronic *EEEEEEEEEEE* noise wailing distantly in one ear, the sound of a radio broadcasting the melting of its own components. . . . Cowboy thinks that Andy may have sucked a minigun round into an intake, but he'll never know. Other things are attracting his attention.

He's still getting radars pulsing from six enemy craft, so that means the frigate struck with the antiradiation missile is still in the game. The Hyperion-class is tough, Cowboy knows; the missile may just have bounced off its ablative shield. That means five frigates against three deltas, and one of the deltas has only two missiles.

Blackness fills his vision as Cowboy nears the shuttle, as his heart labors to keep his brain supplied with oxygen in the face of his acceleration. The shuttle is a big target directly ahead, but two more frigates are swooping at him from on high—their acceleration is appalling—and suddenly there are more missiles coming at him than he can deal with. Systems shriek as he sideslips, fires antiradiation homers, pops the minigun targets again, and tries to put a wall of thirty-millimeter rounds in front of the frigates. . . . He's close enough to the nearest to see the bright splashes of hits, but suddenly there are red lights flashing in his mind, the dorsal minigun signaling it's out of ammo. More red lights are layered onto his perceptions as a laser vaporizes some hydraulics and *Pony Express* begins to vent control fluids into the atmosphere, and then there's an even bigger red light, this time outside the canopy, as one of the antiradiation missiles finds a home. The target frigate simultaneously loses parts of a control surface and its aerodynamics, and runs into a solid wall of unforgiving air, coming apart in about a tenth of a second. . . . The other frigate jitters away, punctured with minigun hits, trying to get its redundant systems on line. Cowboy redlines the engines and feels his head punched back onto its rest. He's lost some of his control surface, but his computer seems to be compensating. He's only got about three minutes left before the shuttle touches the desert floor.

The leading frigates have looped and are boring back for him; the two other deltas, Maurice and Diego, have yo-yoed around, and the rear two frigates are trying to bounce them. . . . They're smarter than their friends and have split, each going after a single target. Cowboy launches radar-homers for the shuttle, a big slow target right on the horizon. He pops the belly turret and fires for the two frigates right ahead, and suddenly one of them—maybe the one weakened by a head-on encounter with an antiradiation missile—is erupting in smoke. He sees the hot flare of rockets as the pilots eject, but suddenly there's a laser lance punching through his polymerized flesh, and *Pony Express* begins to die.

Crystal systems boil and explode in the heat of coherent light and the delta becomes unstable as both the main fly-by-wire comp and its backup bubble and die. Cowboy shrieks as control systems invade his head. The delta's aerodynamics are superb, but at this speed anything that tries to maneuver is inherently unstable, and anything that doesn't is a target. Cowboy's fighting his craft, making minute adjustments, and even though he's coping with them one by one, there are more oscillations coming in than he can deal with. The air turns hard, and the delta shudders, losing more systems, and begins to corkscrew toward the ground. Agony is trying to crawl up out of Cowboy's anesthetized body. He's blind but for the news from his displays, hydraulics, and airflow, punctured systems and reluctant control surfaces. He's lost his view of the target and he howls in protest. Dimly there's a feeling of the earth coming up. . . .

And then he's bottoming out over the Sierras, the mountains' green fingers reaching up to tag him but falling short, and Cowboy is hauling back and feeding alcohol to the burners again. His crystal has built the necessary routines to keep *Pony Express* on the wire. There's not much room in his head for anything else, and he looks up into the blue sky, his vision returning to see the shuttle a vast shadow in the sky, beset by black shapes that swoop and dart like swallows. The speed of the fight has slowed down and its cubic volume decreased; Cowboy can see it all from his point of low vantage. There are only three frigates now, and one of them seems to be damaged and keeping its distance. One of the deltas is staggering away, trailing fire, the other doggedly staying in the fight, dodging Orbital missiles. There are only seconds left before the shuttle crosses the Sierras and drops to a landing at Edwards.

Pony Express arcs upward. A tone sounds in Cowboy's crystal; he fires a heat-seeker automatically, but his artificial eyes are fixed on the *Argosy*. More tones sound, and the delta jars with each missile it launches. A frigate trails flame and tumbles to an encounter with a mountain, but Cowboy's mind is full of control surfaces, blazing crystal, knowledge of engine and surface heat, eager weapons systems, the compelling flood from the electron world pouring into his mind at the speed of light. . . . He's a creature of the interface now, his brain a processor. His black wings shudder in torment.

The spars that are his ribs moan. Heat flashes through his black epoxy skin. His heart threatens to explode as it feeds alcohol to the engines. The target fills his narrowed vision. He rolls and sprays the shuttle's belly with minigun rounds, but he's out of ammunition in a few seconds and all his missiles are gone. The shuttle is battered, but it's a tough ship, still on target for landing. The mountains drop away and Cowboy sees nothing but desert rolling on to the brown horizon.

Neurotransmitters fall on crystal, electrons pour from Cowboy's sockets at the speed of light. Control surfaces bite the air, howl in anger. The interface demands a certain solution, and the decision is taken without conscious volition. But somewhere in Cowboy's mind there is a realization that this is the necessary and correct conclusion to his legend, to use himself and his matte-black body as the last missile against the Orbital shuttle and win for himself a slice of immortality, a place in the mind of every panzerboy, every jock. . . .

Cowboy accepts the decision of his crystal. A bark of triumphant laughter bursts from his lips as the shuttle grows larger and larger in his vision.

A black fragment intervenes, spiraling between Cowboy and his target. Cowboy recognizes Maurice's distinctive delta, sees the damage on wing and fuselage, Maurice's sky-blue helmet in the cockpit, its opaque face mask fixed on the juncture of his delta's course and the shuttle. . . .

Argosy explodes as Maurice drives his delta into the juncture of wing and fuselage. Cowboy's crystal is coping with the impact of alloy shuttle parts vaporizing themselves on the delta's battered skin before Cowboy realizes that his own death is no more, that it's been usurped by Maurice, and by the time that's brought home to him, the shuttle and Maurice are well in his wake, rubble spilling to an impact with the Mojave, stirred by the wind of his passing but no longer a thing that can interact with his own destiny. Anger rises in his mind at the thought of his fate being stolen.

"Target destroyed. This is Cowboy. It's done." He's crossed miles of desert during the course of his short transmission. He doesn't pay any attention to the acknowledgment. There are still two frigates behind him, both crying for vengeance. He's out of weapons and has only a few thermite decoys left. He hauls in a tight turn to the south, dodging out over the desert, the delta invading his mind again as the unstable craft vibrates, his correction of the control surfaces lagging behind as he begins his high-stress maneuver. But there's a frigate right behind, its laser blowing away more sensors, heating the delta's polymerized skin, seeking a weak place in the armor. . . . Cowboy dodges one missile, then another, tries to sideslip the frigate while triggering a thermite decoy. His crystal is humming a warning that there are only a few minutes of fuel left.

The frigate tries to follow the nimble delta but can't, overshooting; but a missile pulls harder g's, and Cowboy, with his burned rear sensors, hasn't seen it. It runs up one of his twin Rolls-Royce engines, and suddenly *Pony Express* is unstable again, venting droplets of molten alloy as it slews across the sky. Cowboy's mind adjusts control surfaces, fuel flows, balances. Fury explodes in him. He looks for the target and finds it, hauling *Pony Express* in a tight S-turn to head straight for the frigate and knock it bodily out of the sky. . . . But with one engine gone the delta has lost its acceleration, and Cowboy can't catch the Orbital frigate. Another laser lances into *Pony Express* from behind, the crippled frigate coming up for the kill.

Cowboy turns to look over his shoulder, shrieks in rage at the infrared vision of more missiles boring in. He drops thermite and dances out of the way, but it feels as if his control is eroding. The maneuvers are making the delta more difficult to handle, and the rough ride is glitching up more systems. There are red and orange lights all over his remaining engine display. An Orbital laser punches out a panel, melts a spar. *Pony Express* lurches, recovers. More missiles are on the way. Cowboy tries to haul the delta around for the ramming maneuver again, but the controls won't answer any radical course changes.

He can feel *Pony Express* moaning with the strain. He

knows the delta might be tough enough to survive the missile that will take out the remaining engine, that he might be able to land it on the desert if he doesn't lose any more control surfaces. Data swarms into his brain, the craft telling him that it's capable of surviving. The missile comes nearer. There are no more decoys to drop. A steel guitar plays sadly in his mind. Cowboy gazes up into the sky and sees only emptiness.

Rockets flame as he rides up and out of the delta. A wall of wind smashes his face mask. Sky and earth tumble. He screams with the pain that suddenly surges up from his body, no longer masked by the anesthetic and by the demanding swarm of data from his sockets. Suspended in the air, his brain swimming, he never sees the final impact as *Pony Express* slams into the desert.

His body has not fully awakened when he lands. Fortunately the desert is still; his canopy collapses and drapes itself over a Joshua tree. The hot desert air scalds his throat with every breath. Pain shrieks at him in ever-insistent tones. He knows some ribs have gone, probably when he was wrestling *Pony Express* after the laser burned his comps, and his left forearm apparently failed to clear the cockpit when he punched out, and it's now hanging ragged and bloody.

Amusement rises and he laughs, and then the laugh turns to a cough and he feels something break inside. He tastes blood in his mouth. He turns his head to spit, and something runs down his face.

Cowboy punches the quick release and frees himself from his chute, then pulls off his helmet and takes the dead studs out of his skull. He rolls carefully onto his side and tries to get to his feet. He fails, spits blood, tries again, succeeds. His left leg scraped the canopy punching out and it feels like it's lost a lot of skin, but it doesn't seem broken. He takes a pair of steps and laughs again, then bends over as coughs rack him, as blood fills his mouth. He hawks it out and then straightens his shoulders defiantly.

He's landed on a rocky ridge overlooking a two-rut desert track. A column of smoke rises a mile away, where *Pony*

Express fell after it tore itself to pieces battling the air. Another, vaster black pillar stands far to the north where the wreckage of *Argosy* lies tangled with a delta.

A pair of sonic booms throb through the air, and Cowboy can see the infrared signal of the two frigates circling back toward Edwards. Cowboy gives them the finger and grins. "You lost, you bastards." He cackles and begins to hobble down the slope.

There's a growling, whining noise coming from down the track, and Cowboy props himself against a scalding rock and waits. It's a chrome turbine tricycle coming to investigate the wreck. Cowboy reaches for the pistol in his holster and fires a pair of shots into the air. The driver's head turns and acknowledges his wave with a nod. The trike pulls off the road and the driver begins walking up the slope.

It's a dark-skinned woman with a shaved head, some kind of bodybuilder, with her muscles increased and shaped by hormones, her breasts as irrelevant on her massive expanse of chest as a pair of peas. She's wearing an alloy reflective mesh bikini top and baggy reflec trunks, with soft moccasins laced up above her ankles. Cowboy sees freckles on her shoulders, deep beneath the dark skin, and a necklace of bleached rattlesnake skulls. She looks at him with sea-green eyes.

"You look in bad shape, linefoot."

Cowboy reaches into his pocket and pulls out a half ounce of gold. "You can earn a second one of these if you get me to Boulder City," he says. "I don't want to go through any Free Zone customs checks, either."

She nods. "Fair enough. But I don't think you're gonna make it that far, not on desert roads."

"That's not your worry."

"You got a med kit someplace?"

Cowboy nods upslope. "Yeah. With my chute."

Wordlessly she moves upslope to the chute, drags it off the Joshua tree, and weighs it down with rocks. She picks up the med kit and brings it down.

Cowboy is sitting down when she gets back, the gun

hanging limp in his hand. She takes it from him and puts it
back in his holster. He almost faints with the pain as she
pulls off the top of his g-suit. She cleans up some of the
blood, disinfects the cut, tapes up his ribs, ties up his broken
arm in a sling. Then she fires some endorphin into his right
biceps and the drug whispers gracefully between his pain
receptors and his efficient hardwired nerves. He fades so fast
that she has to help him down the slope to get him on her
cycle. As he mounts behind her he notices three freshly killed
rattlesnakes draped over the handlebars.

He can hear sirens from the north, and there's a billow of
dust on the track, moving closer. She wrestles the trike off
the road and cuts across country, moving slowly so as not to
raise a dust cloud. The jouncing is easier on his ribs than he
thought it would be.

Occupied California extends east to Beacon Station. The
trike weaves down desert trails, up mountain ridges, drives
fast across a dry lakebed. Cowboy leans his head back against
the rest and drowses. The endorphin murmurs in his mind.
The trike gets onto the expressway east of Silver Lake and
the ride gets easier, the turbine screaming. Cowboy watches
the working of the driver's powerful shoulder muscles as she
dodges potholes. Dead snakes flap in the wind. Amusement
rises in him again.

"Hey, lady. You're driving right into a legend, you know
that?"

She gives him an incurious look over her shoulder. "I
figure that legend's your own business, man."

"I wish I could see the screamsheets."

"I wish I could see the other half of that gold. I don't
suppose that's gonna happen right now, either."

He laughs, coughs, laughs again. "You remind me of
somebody."

"Is that supposed to make me feel good?"

He laughs some more. Licks his dry lips. "You got any
water?"

She hands him a plastic squeeze bottle. He fills his mouth,
spits it overside, fills his mouth again and swallows. He

hands her the squeeze bottle and she clips it to the trike frame. Cowboy leans back and closes his eyes again, feeling the cycle swerving under him like a carnival ride. The setting sun licks the back of his neck.

With his eyes closed he can still feel the punch of the afterburners, the song of the missiles in his crystal, the feeling of *Pony Express* living in his nerves, his veins. Gone now, a wreck on the desert floor. The last of the working deltas, the last not cannibalized to make the graceless panzers that Cowboy dislikes. He's got more reason than ever to hate them now that, for a short while, he's been a flier again.

The endorphin patterns bright images behind his closed lids, the images of green displays glowing deep in his mind, the sight of silver missile fins rotating against the sky, *Argosy* growing larger and larger as he loops up to intercept . . . the sight of extinction filling the canopy, the nearing obliteration demanded by crystal and interface . . . the dark wedge blotting out the steel sky, the interception proof of his devotion to life at the speed of light . . . the final impact that secures his place in the sky, his last triumphant grin drawn taut like the smile of a skull. . . .

Cowboy opens his eyes and draws a breath, the shriek poised in his throat. It doesn't come. Fear dopplers along his triggered nerves. The cycle girl is weaving across night asphalt, dodging between potholes picked out by her headlight. "Fuck," Cowboy says. He tells his nerves to shut down again.

"You say something, linefoot?"

He gazes at the necklace of skulls, the ridged hollow rattler eyes staring at him. The eyes of Mistress Death, whose cool and tenebrous lips brushed against his in the sky. A tremor shakes him. "Nothing much," he says.

"That's what I thought."

"Can I have some more water?"

He drinks half the squeeze bottle this time before handing it back. His good hand is trembling so much he almost drops it. Pain is lurking deep in his chest, the endorphins wearing off.

"Are your people going to miss you?" he asks.

A massive shrug. "My sisters'll miss me when they miss me."

"They all got muscles like you?"

"That's why we live together, man."

She turns her head to look at him. Starlight glitters in her eyes. "You got anyplace in Boulder City you want to go?"

"A public phone'll do. Then maybe a hotel."

"Whatever you say, linefoot."

The lights of Boulder City splay out into the night. The cycle idles while Cowboy fights stiffness and pain, and manages to stand upright. "Right thigh pocket," he says, after a moment of struggle. "A credit needle."

"Okay." She unzips the pocket and plugs the needle into the phone for him. He puts a stud in his forehead and thinks Reno's number. "This is Cowboy. I'm in Boulder City."

"So are the Dodger and his people. Where have you been?"

"I'm hurt. Tell them to get a medic."

"Right away. I'm tracing your line now so I can tell them where you are."

Cowboy sags against the telephone. Pain pulses in his chest. "Hey, Reno," he says. "Did anything come back?"

"Diego force-landed on the desert. The Orbitals got him and his delta."

Sorrow trickles into Cowboy. "Fuck. Nothing left then. I lost the *Express*."

"Build another. We won."

The news interests him only slightly. "Yeah?"

"Tempel crashed. We didn't need the net; all we had to do was wait for it to go below five hundred and then start buying. Roon came out and announced to the screamsheets that he was mounting a slate for the board, and he got so many proxies in the first five minutes that Couceiro resigned before there could even be an election. Roon's going to shuttle up as soon as he ties up a few loose ends. He's already announced a policy of retrenchment."

"Good for him." Talking seems to hurt more and more. "You got my location yet?"

"The Flash Force is on the way. You can hang up if you want."

He reaches for the credit needle and yanks it out. He sticks it in his breast pocket, pulls out a pair of half-ounce coins. "You get extra because you have such a winning personality."

The cycle girl takes the coins with a grin. She puts them in a belt pouch and swings back aboard her saddle. "You want me to stick around?" she asks.

"I'll be okay." He looks at her dully. "Hey, you got any need for extra money? I need someone to run messages from time to time."

She nods. "Blackwater Well Bio Station. I'm a desert ecologist."

"No kidding."

Her turbine winds up, then she gives him a last grin and accelerates away. He watches her taillights recede to the vanishing point and closes his eyes. He hears rather than sees the long car pull up beside him.

"Cowboy? Just put your arm around me."

Sarah's voice. He opens his eyes and sees her tall form, feels her hands touching his clothing. He gives her a shadowy grin. "It's been a long day, huh?"

"Easy now. Just slide into the car."

"Maurice killed himself. I was planning on dying, but Maurice did it for me. Right in the arms of Mistress Death."

"Take it easy. The other foot now."

"I was always chasing her. Didn't know it till now."

"Rest your head here, on my shoulder."

He feels warmth against his cheek, mumbles, "It's a fuck of a thing, being a legend in your own time."

The car speeds away on silent wheels.

Chapter Twenty-four

"**A**re you sure you can handle this?"

"I have most of the data on Tempel we collected. And memories. Mine and his. I think I can do some good."

"Yeah," Cowboy says. "I always thought I could use friends in high places."

*   *   *

It's an old place, a one-room cabin with a cheap tile floor, old wooden furniture held together by wire, a sagging double bed with a tufted bedspread.

Cowboy is lying in the bed, humming "Face Riders in the Sky" to himself while he watches a video report on the Tempel crisis. The situation is at an end, the reporter says. Stock values are rising cautiously. The Orbital Soviet has announced its confidence in Roon's administration. The new directorate has sent Couceiro to Africa, to finally touch the planet he had seen only as a blue and white sphere contaminating his view of the monochrome airless universe. *Have fun foreclosing on Ghana*, Cowboy thinks. He reaches for his whiskey and sips it, then props the glass on his arm cast.

He turns as his door opens and sees Sarah coming in, feeling a wave of desert heat on his face as he looks past her, through the door, into a brown stony reach stretching all the way to California, vanishing into a trackless blue sky.

Sarah closes the door behind her. She's dressed in a long-billed cap, jeans, reflec long-sleeved shirt. "You're awake," she says.

"Yep." He reaches for the whiskey bottle. "Join me?"

"Too early." She pulls off the cap and tosses it on the battleship-gray kitchen table. Shakes her hair free. "The Dodger wants to see you later. Business. And his wife is flying up later this afternoon."

She sits beside him on the mattress. He turns off the vid control and moves over to make room for her. He winces at the pain in his scraped leg. Sarah puts her arm around his shoulders. He leans back against her warmth.

"They have horses here," she says. "I've never learned to ride."

"I can teach you." He looks at her profile, the turned-up nose and parabolic perfection of the lips, the dark skin outlined in a soft haze of light from a window behind her. She turns to him. "The broken arm won't . . . ?"

"Not much. No."

They're on a weathered old Nevada dude ranch that the Flash Force has designated as a backup base. Western thirdmen and panzerboys will be drifting in through the next week with the intention of arranging a peace. Cunningham's dead and Tempel has withdrawn its backing, and suddenly Tempel's thirdmen are floundering in the dark, surrounded by enemies with sharpened knives.

The thirdmen will be talking with the Dodger. The panzerboys are planning to talk with Cowboy. His plan of a panzerboy association seems to be taking shape. Maybe it can hold the peace together, if thirdmen who cause their neighbors grief suddenly find they can't get transport to the East for their action.

                    *   *   *

The voice doesn't sound right. It has a kind of tremor, an echo maybe—as if two voices were speaking, not entirely in synch.

"Reno?" Cowboy says. "You okay?"

"I'm into the big crystal here, Cowboy. My God, the plans these people have! They've got the next thousand years in their pocket . . . but there's a funny quality to it. They know the shape they want the future to take, but they don't know what they want *themselves* to be. They're up here, and they're lost. Once their obedience to Earth gave them meaning, and then their struggle against it, but now they don't know what to do. They're too distracted by their structures. They got their independence, but they don't know what it means, and they're looking for the things that will give it meaning. Some are after dominance—of the planet, each other . . . Do you know they're stockpiling nerve gas up here? In case other blocs attack? They're that crazy. Some are lost in dreams of bigger and better hardware—as if the machines they create will give them the definition they lack. The others are content to be parts of the structure, to take their form from their own corporate ecological niche. Content to be programmed by the others.

"They're vampires, Cowboy. They're sucking up Earth's blood, because that's what keeps them alive, but they don't know what *living* is for."

"My capacity for pitying those people is a bit limited," Cowboy says.

"Pity," says the voice, "is not what they need."

*   *   *

Sarah looks at Cowboy carefully. He's sunburned and battered, but after a night's sleep the tension that's been a part of him for the last few days has eased; the fevered intensity dissipated. He shifts against her and winces. "Need some painkiller?" she asks.

Cowboy raises his glass of whiskey. "This is all the painkiller I need right now."

"Maybe I'll join you after all." Sarah reaches for the bottle and drinks. "I just talked to Michael. He offered me a sort of a job."

"What sort of job?"

"Adviser, I guess you'd say. Counsellor—that's the old term. He says he trusts my connections. And my instincts."

"Glad he's noticed." Cowboy rubs his bristles. "You going to take it?"

"Probably." A taut wire of amusement vibrates through her. "It'll get me off the streets." She grins and raises the bottle again. Drinks.

She'll check into a hospital, she thinks, get herself some more crystal. The full Santistevan hardwiring, independent of hardfire. Firearms. Small-unit tactics. And not just streetgirl stuff, either; she wants chips for accounting, shipping, stock market manipulation. The stuff she'll need in her new position as the Hetman's counsellor.

"You'll travel," he says.

She cocks an eye at him. "Yes. So will you. We can see each other." Because, she thinks, what they have is a wartime thing, a fusion made under pressure. . . . With the pressure gone, things may fall apart. Because there are things she knows and can't tell him, because she's lived a life that, whatever he thinks, he doesn't really want to know about. Because he has his own ideas of the world and his place in it, and she can't understand them. They will have to ease carefully into the peace, into each other, and know it might not work in the absence of the things that brought them together. There ought to be room for that, the coming apart. Or the other. Especially the other.

She takes another drink. "You promised to show me the autumn aspens. And all I've seen is this fucking desert. You owe me."

"Daud," he says. She feels coldness touching her at the name, at the inflection he gives it. Knowing, the both of them, that Daud is responsible for yesterday's catastrophe, that there are broken hulks on the stony Nevada plain, shards of aircraft lying under the protective waves of the Pacific, men wrapped in canvas and covered by thin desert soil, all with Daud's smoking signature. Cowboy won't forget that, and his code does not treat treason lightly.

"I'm buying him a ticket." Lightly, hiding the dread in her. "Getting him away."

"What if he doesn't go?"

Reassurances freeze in her throat. Because it is Daud's nature to betray, and she has felt the sting of his betrayals all her life, hardened herself to them, told herself it was only because he was weak, that he needed to betray in order to know he was trusted, and she had always forgiven him. . . . But the forgiveness had infected her somehow, as if forgiving Daud made it easier to forgive her own treacheries. She doesn't want Daud around, not a living reminder of her own capacity to betray the things she cares for.

She can't stop loving him. She knows that. What she can stop is trying to *be* him.

"He'll go," she says. "I won't give him a choice."

Cowboy's eyes are hard as flint. "I won't, either."

Encourage Daud in one last betrayal, then. Of Nick. If Nick exists, if he hasn't already betrayed Daud by using him for Tempel's purposes. A final betrayal. To save his own life.

The phone purrs quietly in its cradle. Sarah answers it.

"This is Reno, Sarah." He's still acting as switchboard operator, coordinating the fragments of the net that are still in operation, keeping communications open with the various panzerboys and thirdmen who will be visiting the ranch in the next few days.

"I have a call from Roon," Reno says. "He wants to talk to the two of you."

"Tell him to fuck himself."

"He says it's business."

She looks at Cowboy. "It's Reno. Roon wants to talk to us."

To her surprise there is a grim light in Cowboy's eyes, as if he were expecting this.

*   *   *

The voice is smoother now, more in control of itself. The echo effect has vanished.

"The Orbital Soviet is unhappy, Cowboy. Couceiro was someone they liked, someone they could understand. They didn't like him being brought down by a bunch of mudboys."

Cowboy grins and reaches for his bottle of whiskey. "What are they going to do about it?"

"They can't change the rules on stock trading. The system's too big, and they're making too much money from the situation as it is, by their own manipulations. And they know they'll just drive the stock market underground if they try to restrict it—communication's just too uncontrolled, any face bank could run a market just by telephone.

"No, Cowboy." The voice is calm. "What they're going to do is put you out of business."

Ice touches Cowboy's flesh. "Oh?" he says. "How do they plan to do that?"

"They've decided that the existence of black markets, along with the way the Orbitals are competing to supply them, is a danger. . . . It's creating too many uncontrollable elements. So they're going to legitimize the markets. Later this session they're going to have one of their tame legislators introduce a bill in the Missouri legislature to repeal their tariff restrictions. That'll create a Missouri-Kentucky corridor across most of the Midwest. Once Missouri goes, the other states will fall like dominoes. The panzerboys just won't be needed anymore."

"What can you do to stop it?"

"Nothing. It's the Orbital Soviet's decision."

Despair trickles into Cowboy's veins. That's the end, then, all that he and the Dodger fought for. Abolished with a swipe of the Orbital pen.

"You've got warning now," the voice says. "You can make your preparations."

"I don't see myself as a long-distance trucker. I've been an outlaw too long."

"You're rich. You'll think of something. Look, the U.S. won't be balkanized anymore. You can take credit for that. Things are going to be a lot easier in the Northeast."

We weren't running the Line, Cowboy thinks, for the Northeast. Or for the money. That was what Arkady and the

thirdmen never understood, always thinking we could be
bought, that we would respond to economic pressure. And
that's what the Orbitals don't understand, what their crystal
world models can't figure. That we'd have run the Alley for
nothing. Because it was a way to be free.

"Cowboy?" The voice wavers for a moment. "You did
good, you know. We all did."

"I know." How long did he expect it to last? Cowboy
wonders. Perhaps not even this long. He had always thought it
would end in some Midwest cornfield, the government chop-
pers coming in waves, pouring rockets down, breaking through
the Chobham, the panzer coming apart piece by piece. Or in
some moonless supersonic sky where the laws waited to
pounce, their radars reaching out to touch him with radiant
fingertips. . . . He hadn't expected this, to be informed of his
obsolescence in a recovery bed on some sweaty Nevada dude
ranch. That all he had done, the legend he had built, was
only to put him out of business.

He laughs. A retired panzerboy, he thinks. An absurdity.

Amusement trickles through him. There is a lightness in
his limbs, as if gravity has eased. He thinks of the world
curving away below him, dark behind him flecked with stars,
the limb of twilight below, the land before the canopy burning green and brown in the light of the sun . . . the boundaries that encompassed the Alley gone, gone along with the
armored borders of his life, the zones with their internal
customs inspectors, their armed forces and restricted areas,
the ever-narrowing tunnel down which he was hurled at the
speed of light toward whatever violent climax awaited him at
the end. The legend that he had embraced, because he had
never been able to embrace life.

He's free, he realizes. And he's got friends in high places.

He figures another chapter in the legend's going to start
right about now.

*   *   *

Cowboy feels nerve warmth flaring in his limbs, a warning
signal. He thinks he knows what's going to happen. He

reaches across Sarah, unspools a stud from the phone, plugs it into his temple. "Reno," he says, talking into the wire-thin mic fixed on the stud. "Stay on the line. I want you to hear this bastard."

"Whatever you say, Cowboy."

"I've got a few other things I want you to do," he says. Reno listens quietly as Cowboy tells him. He can feel Sarah shift in surprise as he leans across her.

"Yeah, Cowboy," Reno says. "I see your point."

"Cowboy?" Sarah says. "What file are you talking about? Do I—"

"I'll tell you later," Cowboy says.

Roon's voice, when it comes, makes his hackles rise. Sarah grows tense beside him. He remembers cold alloy corridors, images of children floating in darkness, hologrammed ceilings glowing with Orbital settlements reflecting stellar light. A cold smile that smelled of corpses.

"Cowboy. Sarah. You are to be congratulated. The plan was a great success. It was blessed, and so are you."

"Thanks," Cowboy says. He takes a hearty drink of whiskey, grimaces as the fire goes down his throat. Feeling his heart pounding in his chest, a cold sweat rising on his forehead. A deep sickness in his gut, anticipation . . .

"Sarah," Roon says, "I want you to come into the sky with me." The voice is like a silken icicle caress. "I want someone to head my security team. I can't trust Couceiro's people."

Cowboy watches the scars whiten on Sarah's face, tautening under her cynical smile. "You want me to be your Cunningham?" she asks.

"Cunningham wasn't his real name. But yes, I want you to do the same job for me that Cunningham did for my predecessor. Your files say that you have the potential. Come to the sky, Sarah. Look down at the planet of our birth. Then help me shape its future." The lyrical words are somehow more terrifying coming from the emotionless, crystal voice, the cold rapture of the deepening, triumphant madness. "Be the means of my communion with the planet, Sarah," he says. "The instrument by which I possess it. The human extension of my crystal."

Cowboy sees Sarah's lips curl. "No, Mr. Roon," she says. "That's not my kind of action." Still, there is a trace of hesitation in her voice, as if she's bidding farewell to a cherished dream, having found its price.

"You will condemn yourself," Roon says. "History will allow freedom only to raptors, not to the creatures on which they feed. Stretch your wings, Sarah. I will give you blood for your Weasel to feed on."

"No," Sarah says. Her eyes are stone. "It's not for me."

"I regret your decision, Sarah. Cowboy, I hope you will be more sensible." Cowboy's mouth feels dry. He licks his lips.

"What are you offering?" he asks.

"A place. You have talents that extend beyond those of a pilot. You have a predator's instinct, you can spot weakness and act on that knowledge. You saw Couceiro's weakness and knew how to bring him down. I want you to give me that talent of yours, Cowboy."

"No. It's not my sort of work."

"You are dangerous." The cold judgment turns Cowboy's veins cold. "You have brought down a powerful man, and neither he nor his friends will forget. I offer you my protection."

"No," Cowboys says. "It's no secret, what I did. Other people could do it. Things will change."

"Your decision is that of a weakling. You are a fool." There is a frozen second in which Cowboy can almost hear the decision being made somewhere in Roon's crystal. "Still, you are dangerous. Perhaps too dangerous to be allowed to roam at will."

The crystal burns in Cowboy's skull. He had known this all along, that this would come. Because the Orbitals could not allow a free man to exist, once they noticed him.

"Reno, are you there?" Cowboy says.

"Yes, Cowboy."

"Hand this Texan's ass to him."

There is a scream in Cowboy's socket, a scream composed partly of the Black Mind program that's shrieking down the link at the speed of light, partly of the noise that is coming from Roon's throat as Reno climbs over the safeguards in his crystal and begins to write himself over Roon's mind. Cowboy can see the puzzlement in Sarah's eyes as she hears the noise coming from the phone she holds. Cowboy takes the stud from his temple and the screaming fades away. Sarah looks at him.

Cowboy reaches over and takes the phone from her hand. Over the whine of data he can hear far-off moans, cries, whimpers. He laughs

He puts the phone down on the bed between them and explains. There is a smile in Sarah's eyes, an answering chord struck in resonant steel.

They listen together till the sounds stop, and they can hear Reno's voice coming over the phone. Cowboy feels as if he's been on a long night flight, and now, through his skin sensors, whispering over the crystal, caressing his nerves, he feels the warm touch of the sun

Ben Bova

☐ 53200-7 AS ON A DARKLING PLAIN $2.95
  53201-5   Canada $3.50

☐ 53217-1 THE ASTRAL MIRROR $2.95
  53218-X   Canada $3.50

☐ 53212-0 ESCAPE PLUS $2.95
  53213-9   Canada $3.50

☐ 53221-X GREMLINS GO HOME $2.75
  53222-8 (with Gordon R. Dickson)   Canada $3.25

☐ 53215-5 ORION $3.50
  53216-3   Canada $3.95

☐ 53210-4 OUT OF THE SUN · $2.95
  53211-2   Canada $3.50

☐ 53223-6 PRIVATEERS $3.50
  53224-4   Canada $4.50

☐ 53208-2 TEST OF FIRE $2.95
  53209-0   Canada $3.50